THE
FORGOTTEN
SISTER

Kieran Higgins

Prologue

My mother, such as she was, will be remembered as virtuous and saintly, for that is the mask she showed the world. In truth, the Lady Igraine was, at her best, a witch, and her very worst, a whore. She desired Uther Pendragon's body, handsome and lean as he was, and, beyond that, she desired his power as High King. She snared him with her charms and very nearly tore the kingdom apart with her lust.

But, we move further into the tale than we should. The story begins not with their coupling, as many would have it, but decades before, in Cornwall, at the very edge of the world.

Looming above the craggy beach was the great castle of Tintagel. But, cast your eyes lower, away from the majestic, impenetrable fortress and towards the shale beach. There, in the shadow of the castle, in a wooden hut blasted and pitted by the salt of the sea spray, was the home of Petronella, the mother of Igraine.

Petronella's husband, and Igraine's father, was unknown to the people of Tintagel, beyond that he had died some years past and left his poor young wife with a child. That is if he had ever existed in the first place, and Petronella had not lain with some demon come in the night. Or, perhaps less fancifully, if he was not a deceitful youth, who made Petronella promises he had no intention of keeping.

How Petronella came to be in Tintagel, for she was a Roman-born, they having no place in the Cornish wilds save among the nobility, was not given much thought. The fishermen and shepherds

1

supposed she made her living from trapping shell-fish, and paid her little attention, her beauty having faded from all those hard and half-starved years beside the sea. What they did not know was that it was their own wives who were the source of Petronella's income.

Because Petronella had talents beyond that of a fishwife or shepherdess. For a price paid in provisions, or perhaps for a favour you may yet be asked for, she could save a boat full of men from drowning, or ensure they were taken by the sea. She could make you a good harvest, or bring blight upon a neighbour's field. And she could make sure a woman would get with child, or make certain that one was not conceived, if your evening companion was not your husband.

Petronella was feared and loved in equal measure and lived a simple life. But Igraine forever cast her eyes upwards, over the bluffs and towards the hulking stone that was the castle of Tintagel. When she shivered on the hut's floor next to her mother, she dreamed of great beds, and whole chambers for sleeping, with fires lit throughout. When the beach was barren, and Petronella's work unfruitful, she ignored her aching stomach and thought of great dishes of food she could gorge on, which she would not have to cook herself, nor catch or scavenge the contents of her pot.

A girl whose mother is one of the Wise has a choice to make when she reaches her thirteenth year and her courses have come upon her. She must choose whether to walk the same path as her mother before her, or else abandon whatever talents may have emerged. It is too foolish an age, I think, and one of the reasons I am grateful I never had a daughter. What girl of thirteen would not be tempted by promises of witchcraft?

Thirteen years came for Igraine, and she joined her mother in her practices. But, I think, Igraine was far more dangerous a witch than simple Petronella, with her curses and potions. Because, while Petronella had power, Igraine had ambition.

By the age of fifteen, Igraine had secured herself a position as a kitchen maid within the castle of Tintagel. Bronwyn, a woman of good repute in service to the Lady Gwyneth, the Duchess of Cornwall, had come to the hut seeking a charm so as to draw her husband's attentions back to her.

In exchange, Igraine made her whisper certain phrases in the ears of a wax figure, who the silent, smirking Petronella recognised as an image of the castle's cook. Then, the next day, when Igraine went to the castle door looking for work, the man was persuaded by her assurances of hard-work, and her coy smiles thrown into the bargain.

Igraine found the hard life of a kitchen maid, with its back-breaking work and early mornings, not to her satisfaction, though why she thought it would be any different than her life by the sea remains unknown. She contrived then to become a seamstress, who worked in the comfort of the Duchess' solar, despite that she had never learned any fine embroidery, weaving or spinning, for Petronella had not the tools to teach her.

Poor Bronwyn had no respite from her husband since the charm was cast, and was suddenly heavy with child. Then came a fierce sickness upon her and she was unable to sit upright, never mind sew. Igraine presented herself at the door of the solar, having drunk a tonic made from honey to sweeten her words, and told the Duchess her great dream, hitherto unmentioned before, of becoming a seamstress, though she had been too poor to learn.

The Lady Gwyneth was overcome with sympathy and took the girl at once into her service, teaching her to card wool, to spin, to weave, to dye and to embroider. And much else besides. Igraine lost her rough ways borne of a childhood along the shore and became a favourite of all in the Duchess' house.

Igraine was beautiful and remained so for much of her life. I will give her that, for all her failings as a mother, wife, and queen. It was only natural that she should attract the attention of the men of Tintagel, especially with the patronage of the Duchess securing her a dowry she would not else have had. But one man stood apart from all others - Lord Gorlois, the Duchess' son and Duke to be.

On warm summer's day, the ladies were at their work, gossiping as much as they sewed. There was a fierce clamour from the courtyard. "They return! They return!" cried the watchman, and the ladies' tittered with excitement. The men of Tintagel, including the Duke Gerdan and his son Gorlois, were back from battle with the Saxons.

"My son returns!" exclaimed Gwyneth, clasping her hands together with joy.

The ladies gasped and preened and adjusted their gowns, though Igraine wagered a fair few would not be glad to see the return of their husbands. She put down her needle and observed keenly. There was a clamour at the stairs to the solar and in burst a man still in his armour. Igraine had seen Duke Gerdan from her spying place above the bluff when she was a child, so she knew this was not him. From his slender features, shining eyes and jet black hair, and from the way the Lady Gwyneth hugged him tight, this could only be Gorlois.

4

He released his mother and turned to the room to greet the ladies he had grown up with. Then he drew an excited breath.

"Who is this, Lady Mother?" asked Gorlois, his voice hitching in his throat and eyes lighting up.

The Lady Gwyneth gestured imperiously with a ringed finger, and Igraine came forward from her seat at the window. The Duchess clasped the girl to her front and presented her to the young man.

"Son, this my new seamstress, Igraine."

He reached out and took Igraine's hand.

"My Lord," she said, curtseying. She glanced up demurely at Gorlois with hooded eyes.

He did not release her hand. Igraine smiled and tilted her head slightly. A strand of her coppery hair fell free from her coiffure and brushed the creamy white skin just above the low neckline of her gown. He stared.

"Come Gorlois, you must be hungry. Igraine, make sure that sewing is finished before the light goes."

The Duchess pulled her son from the room. Gorlois almost strained his neck to look back at the girl. Igraine curtseyed again and returned to her seat, smirking the entire way. Her hands may have been occupied with her sewing, but her mind was firmly fixed on a brewing idea, and her eye cast out towards the hut on the sea.

Petronella tossed the last of the rabbit into the cooking pot. She regarded her last onion and debated adding it to her stew, for they would be gone until more could grow. The sound of rocks skittering around the beach travelled into the hut. Petronella put down the onion but kept the knife close.

There had not been Irish raiders in some time, not since Gerdan had routed the last of them, but

Petronella had a long memory. Her senses twitched with familiarity and, breathing a relaxing sigh, she took up the onion again. She would need some flavour in her meal if she had to listen to Igraine.

The door flew open and Igraine rushed in, panting with excitement. "Mother, mother!"

"Saucy wench," grumbled Petronella. "You'll break that door and we'll have naught to fix it with. No respect for a poor woman's things now you've been up at the castle."

"You shall have doors of gold when I am finished my work!"

Her mother snorted. "Seamstress' pay gone up, has it?"

"No, mother," said Igraine, sidling closer to the older woman. "The Lord Gorlois has returned from battle."

Petronella shrugged, feigning ignorance as Igraine settled onto the stool. "So?"

"Imagine me as Lady of Tintagel!"

"How do you propose to become that?"

"By marrying Gorlois of course!"

Petronella looked up from her chopping, pointing her knife squarely at Igraine. "What has he said to you? What promises has he made? Mark my words, Igraine, given once and returned never."

A strange feeling overcame her, almost as if she was standing on a high cliff and had to choose whether to fling herself from the rocks or return to the safety of flat land. Petronella knew as she warned and threatened Igraine that all the girl said would come true.

She thought for a second there was black dog upon the shore, visible from the open door of the hut, but she was sure she was mistaken. Why would she be having visions of deaths to come? But Petronella did not need visions to know nothing good would come of it, save her own improved situation.

"Mother, have you had a seeing?" asked Igraine, feigning concern. "My future in the castle?"

Petronella shook her head. "No, daughter," she replied, for fear she added further fuel to Igraine's fire.

Petronella eyed the meagre table. "Are you staying for supper?"

"No, mother. I think it best I eat at the castle from now on, and sleep there too. I have work to do. You might help, if you have the time?"

"I'll see what I can do."

Igraine kissed her mother and began to talk of other things. Petronella put a hand on her stomach and tried to massage away the leaden feeling that had settled there. She resigned herself to what was going to happen. Petronella had always known which way life's winds would blow, and time had taught her that it was pointless to do anything other than be blown with them.

Warm spring nights settled across Tintagel and the courtship began in earnest. They feigned excuses to be in one another's presence and had many secret meetings. Igraine's wardrobe grew finer as he showered her with gifts. Gorlois, a battle-scarred warrior of twenty, was sure of himself and not unexperienced with women. Though, if he ever thought he could outsmart my mother, he was perhaps the fool Uther believed him to be.

One night, after a feast in the great hall, Gorlois and Igraine slipped away to the blacksmith's forge, knowing they would be alone since the blacksmith had long been in his cups that night.

Gorlois reached for her, but she drew back towards the sweltering forge.

"What is it Igraine?" he asked.

"You seek to shame me, my Lord," she replied, her voice as pitiful as any begging urchin.

"No, no, my love! I merely wish us to be together entirely."

"And ruin me in the process!"

She turned away and pretended to play with the blacksmith's tools, hanging above the fire. She was biting the inside of her cheek to keep from smiling.

"What would you have me do, Igraine?" he asked.

"Marry me, so none can say anything against me, against our love."

He placed a hand on her shoulder, but she shrugged him off. "You know that cannot be."

"You do not love me then?"

"Of course, I love you."

"Then what?"

"I am high-born...marriage is different for us..."

She gave a little cry of indignation. "Marriage is no different for anyone, farmer or king! There is another woman, isn't there?"

"No, no, you are the only one!"

"I don't believe you! Oh, Gorlois, tell me who she is, so I might look upon her before I fling myself into the ocean!"

With that, she let the heat and smoke of the forge overcome her eyes and she began to sob. He petted her and whispered all sorts of sentiments into her ear, but none would soothe her. Gorlois knew he was a man beaten.

"Oh, Igraine! I will marry you!" he relented. He shook his head. "You have bewitched me."

Igraine gave a knowing smile and began to imagine her wedding gown. In truth, though, I suspect not the hand of Igraine or even Petronella.

What man would not be captivated by a maiden such as Igraine, with her swinging hips and fiery copper hair? Especially if he had seen naught but hairy, unwashed Saxons for the past year?

Where Igraine had worked her magic was with Gerdan and Gwyneth, who did not raise an eyebrow at their son marrying a peasant girl from the shore, when he could have made a match with a princess of a neighbouring land, or even a daughter of Ambrosius Aurelianus, the High King himself.

By the time Bronwyn returned to service in Tintagel, she found herself lady-in-waiting to the Lady Igraine and her mother. But Bronwyn shrugged, and carried on. She knew she had a position for life at Tintagel, for fear she exposed Igraine and her mother as the witches they were.

Igraine bore Gorlois three children. First came Morgan, sly and wilful, followed soon by Morgause, who knew early the power she had over men. Then, there was I, Elaine, whose name you, in all likelihood, do not know.

I am the most remarkable of the three sisters, and all other names put to you here, in being the most unremarkable. Because I watched when I should have acted, and acted when I should have watched, and was thus left outside the record of history, and forgotten almost entirely. This, then, is my tale.

Chapter One

Morgan sat imperiously by the fire and dictated to Morgause and me exactly what time we were to go to bed that evening. Even though she was only eight, she considered herself the lady of Tintagel while our father and mother were away. At six and five respectively, Morgause and I had not the time for our bossy older sister. We wanted to play by the cliffs and leave her to her books. Our nurse-maid, Bronwyn, chuckled into her mending, earning her a scowl from Morgan.

Dark like our father, with a temper to match her vicious little eyes, Morgan reached over and gave us a nasty pinch.

"Someday, when I am Lady here, and a great mistress of magic like our mother, I shall turn you into a toad, Bronwyn."

"Best not let the priests hear you say that, little lady, or they will burn you," replied Bronwyn.

"Let them hear," she retorted, folding her arms. "I'll turn them into toads too!"

Bronwyn nodded, experienced in the rantings of children. "Very well. I suppose I had best tell Petronella too, just so she knows when she sees all these toads hopping about the place?"

Morgause and I shared a look, half glee, and half fear. A few months before, Morgan had hurried us out of bed on the night of the full moon and made us sit in a little circle of pebbles she had made, while she threw sand and water around her, calling down all sorts of dark curses on Bronwyn who would not give her extra sweetmeats at supper.

The door flung open, and our grandmother Petronella burst into the room as if she knew something was amiss and gave Morgan such a beating I thought she would kill her. Morgan had appealed to our mother, Igraine, but she had warned Morgan only thus - "A smack on the bottom from Petronella will be the least of your worries if you meddle with such things before you have been properly trained."

Petronella had not dampened Morgan's interest in the dark arts but served as an effective means to silence her when necessary. We never knew our other grandparents, the Duke Gerdan and Lady Gwyneth, though Morgan claimed to remember them occasionally when she was boastful. Gerdan had received a wound to the leg from the last encounter with the Saxons. It was not serious, but a fever had taken hold and he not lasted long when he returned to Tintagel.

With Igraine the new lady of Tintagel, Gwyneth had found herself at a loss for occupation and had set off on a pilgrimage of the great religious houses of Britain. A cough took her on the road to Londinium and only her body ever returned to Cornwall.

Morgause began to fidget beside me on the floor. "Why are my Lady Mother and Lord Father away?" she asked.

Bronwyn put down her mending and scooped Morgause into her arms, balancing the little red-haired girl on her knee.

"Your mother and father are in Londinium, to see the High King."

"Why?"

"Ambrosias Aurelianus is dying, and all the great lords and ladies have come to his bedside. He has no son, and the law of the land says he must choose an heir."

"But why have they gone?"

"Everyone must go. The High King has commanded it."

"And," said Morgan, putting down the papers of her book. "Father might become High King."

"Really?" asked Morgause, her voice tinged with excitement.

"No, silly girl," replied Bronwyn. She looked at Morgan. "Don't speak on things you don't know anything about. Your mother might fancy being a queen, but your father is a farmer at heart. He's happier here, away from the battles and the finery of the capital."

"Father should be king," replied Morgan, matter-of-factly. "I would be an excellent queen after him."

Bronwyn scoffed. "Girls can't be queen unless they marry a king."

Morgan looked perplexed. "But I am father's heir?"

"That's true enough," replied Bronwyn. "But your father will find you a husband when you are old enough, and he will rule Cornwall for you."

"I don't want a husband. Our grandmother doesn't have a husband and she does quite well."

"Yes, well, Petronella is a different kind of woman." Bronwyn lowered Morgause back to the floor. "Now, enough talk of matters of state. I'll see to your dinner, little ladies."

Morgan waited impatiently for news of our parents' return and was ecstatic when the outrider finally arrived at the gates. She dragged us from the solar, out into the courtyard, and made us stand there and shiver as the caravan drew into the castle.

Father was at the head of the column, mounted on his sleek, black warhorse. He slid down from his mount and made his way over. We curtseyed, the models of perfect daughterhood. He merely nodded. His mood was quite evident.

"Hello, Lord Father," said Morgan. "Is our Lady Mother with you?"

"She is," he replied. "Though she is a good deal behind us. Bloody woman insisted on being put in her carriage. Slowed us right down, could have been here yesterday. She is only doing it to annoy me, of course."

"How was Londinium?"

"Dirty," he snapped. "Crowded. Noisy. Now, do you three have somewhere to be?"

"We wanted to wait for our Lady Mother," Morgan responded.

"You will be waiting until dawn then," he grunted. With that, he walked off in the direction of the great hall, slapping his riding gloves against his wrist as he went.

"Not waiting," simpered Morgause.

Morgan glared at her. "You will wait."

Igraine returned soon after, though we had given up on standing and were sitting on the barrels outside the kitchen door. The carriage trundled into the yard, and the door popped open.

A man-at-arms came forward to help her down. The gap was evidently far too large because a glare from the Lady Igraine forced him down onto his hands and knees, whereupon she dismounted from the carriage, using the poor man as a human step.

She was not dressed in her travelling clothes, but her finest gown, draped in the expensive furs from the northern lands. Her hair had been expertly pinned under her duchess's coronet. Rubies dangled from her earlobes but no jewellery could disguise her thunderous expression.

14

"Hello girls," she said upon spying us. She batted away my reaching hands. "I will not kiss you, you are far too dirty. Morgan, take your sisters away to the solar and then tell Bronwyn I need a bath. And your grandmother is to attend me at once."

With that, she swept up her gown and took off after our father. Morgan took her mission very seriously and deposited us in the solar with the weaving women. Petronella grumbled at being summoned but went nonetheless, bidding a haggard Bronwyn to fetch the bathing tub and water jugs.

My sisters and I had realised too late what that meant for us and found ourselves later that hour being wrestled into the bathing tub after our mother had made her ablutions. Morgan made a good attempt at escape, being faster than us, and ruthless enough to leave her sisters at the mercy of Bronwyn's scrubbing brush. But, if Bronwyn had traipsed the length of the castle to fetch water and laboured to heat it, not to mention dealing with Igraine's mood, she was not allowing her efforts to go to waste.

We dined at the high table with our mother and father that night, at the feast to welcome them home. The mood was far from light. Bronwyn slapped me twice for talking out of turn, and Petronella had taken Morgause onto her knee because she had refused to sit still. Our father and mother did not talk the entire time, looking in opposite directions as best as the room allowed. Igraine even refused to send some of her platter to the vassal lords, as was the custom.

We were put to bed in our mother's room, and Bronwyn left us to attend our mother and father in the solar. As soon as she was gone, we leapt out of the bed and down the servants' corridor to hide behind the screen of the solar. Morgause and I cared little for the talk of adults, most of it beyond our understanding, but Morgan was frothing like a rabid dog to discover why our parents were in such a foul mood.

In the round room, a fire was blazing. Our parents were seated as far apart as the room allowed. Bronwyn was pouring wine into their cups while Petronella muttered to herself over a bowl of salted meat.

"Bronwyn, Petronella, leave us," commanded Gorlois.

Igraine thrust up a ringed hand. "Stay. You may as well hear what we have to say, it is common enough knowledge in the capital."

"What has you two so out of sorts?" asked Petronella.

"Your daughter is a whore, madam," replied Gorlois.

"This is supposed to be knowledge to me, my Lord?"

Igraine glared at her mother, who merely shrugged.

"I caught her, cavorting with the new King," said Gorlois.

"I did nothing of the sort," interjected Igraine. "Though Uther did offer to make me his High Queen, if I divorced you. That much is true."

"And I am to suppose this offer came unsolicited?" he snarled.

"Yes, actually."

"I ought to beat you, Igraine, as the Romans would."

Igraine smirked. "Beat me, if you choose, but I do not believe you would see another sunrise if you did."

"Anyway," she continued. "If you had done as I suggested, we would not have our present difficulty."

"You wanted me to propose myself as Ambrosias Aurelianus' successor!"

"And?"

"Uther is his brother and a proven warrior. He had the backing of all the vassal kings and lords. And I have no desire to be High King!"

"And yet Ambrosius went and croaked, and now Uther is our High King!"

Igraine looked ready to rise from her chair and turn the full force of her tongue upon her husband, but Petronella interrupted her.

"Forgive me, my Lord, for I am a simple woman, but I do not understand. If you do not wish to be High King, what matter is it that Uther has ascended? His offer was untoward, but I doubt Igraine has been unvirtuous with him."

Igraine turned to Petronella. "Gorlois' pride was wounded, so he spirited us away in the night, without Uther's leave. Now, if he does not apologise for insulting him, Uther will declare him his enemy, and the country will be plunged into war again."

"I will not apologise," said my father. "And I will not serve a king who would claim another man's wife."

"Then seize the kingship while Uther's support is fresh and untested," she replied.

"I do not wish it for myself."

"Who then?" cried Igraine in exasperation. She leapt to her feet, casting off her furs on the floor. "King Lot of Orkney? He's barely out of breech-clouts."

Gorlois too stood, and advanced towards his shrieking wife. Petronella rose too, her hand held up to stay them, and her head cocked to one side, as though listening to sounds no one else could hear.

"Children," said our grandmother. "You have until the count of three to return to bed, or I shall see to your punishments personally."

Morgan turned as white as sheet beside me and raced us back to our mother's chamber.

We did not break our fast in the great hall that morning and ate with our mother in the solar. It was a tense affair, and my mother, grandmother and Bronwyn all looked worn.

We were sent out to play while mother and Petronella retreated to the solar. Normally Bronwyn would watch us, but the laundry for the month had begun and she was elsewhere in the castle. Morgan had become quite the little spymaster, and led us up the servant's stairs, to watch and listen at the keyhole of the solar door.

Igraine would not pick up her needle or distaff all day. Instead, she sat with her head resting on her closed fist, staring forlornly at the waves crashing along the shore. Finally, she appeared to have resolved matters in her head and turned to Petronella.

"I need you to do something for me," said Igraine.

"Me? Your poor mother? Who raised you and fed you and taught you all you know?" replied Petronella. "I've done enough for you. You are the Duchess of Cornwall, you should be doing for me."

"I have not the art to do this."

Petronella scoffed. "A spell? After all these years? I thought you beyond me in such things."

"Not this," replied Igraine. "This is not silly cantrips or love charms. This is high magic, the kind only you will have learnt. From before."

"Such things are not to be toyed with. What need have you of high magic?"

"A summoning, for one who is not fully human."

"I fear I know already, but who would you summon with such a ritual?"

"The Fatherless One. The one they call Merlin."

Petronella shook her head. "That half-mad leech. I might know little of politics, but I know enough of him. What could you possibly want to summon him for?"

"We spoke when I was in Londinium."

Petronella looked horrified. "What did he say you? What lies did he pour into your ears?"

Igraine fixed her gaze upon her mother and replied "He told me I would be the wife of the High King. I thought he meant Gorlois, but I see otherwise now."

"You cannot mean it? You would throw off Gorlois and marry Uther Pendragon?"

"It is my destiny, mother."

Morgan could not bear it any longer and she burst into the room to confront our mother. "I shan't listen to any more of this. I'm going straight to father."

Petronella looked worried, but Igraine merely shrugged. "You can try if you like, but I made sure you cannot. I put cloves in your food this morning, all three of you. And why did I do that, clever little Morgan?"

"Cloves are the herb of binding, Lady Mother, used to hold tongues that wish to speak."

Igraine nodded with glee. "Exactly. You have taken to listening at doors as of late, do not think I do not know. So I made sure that if you would go to Gorlois, your little tongue would gag in your mouth. He would think you a halfwit and send you away to be a farmer's plough maid. Do you wish to be a plough maid?"

"No, Lady Mother."

"Good girl. You may go and read one of my books if you like."

Morgan sulked off towards the cabinet and sullenly pulled a book from the inside. Morgan rarely knew when she was beaten, but beaten she was.

"Anyway," said Igraine. "He told me in Londinium that he knew of my gifts and thus to summon him with the old ways, when I was ready to discuss my future."

"Are you not content? You are the Duchess of Cornwall!"

"Not for much longer. Uther will beat Gorlois in this coming conflict, strip him of his rank and neither will want me after all that. Do you want to go back to living down by the shore? Anyway, this is my destiny."

"It is not, it is your ambition and your lust. You were never content with your lot in life, not since you could speak."

"What of it mother? You can only benefit as you did before."

"Perhaps."

"You will help me?" asked Igraine.

Petronella was stern. "Only to help myself. If I do not help you, you will seek out someone to show you the spell, or worse yet, send a letter to Merlin, and Gorlois will discover you, and we will be cast out, if we do not burn."

"Thank you, mother," said Igraine.

"Do not thank me, child," responded Petronella. "Mark my words, you will not be grateful by the time this is done. Merlin will want something from you. The halfling's help always comes at a price."

We did not witness the working. We knew only it had been cast, and must have been successful, as Igraine's mood lifted, enough to even converse with Gorlois, who thought her penitent.

Merlin arrived without much ceremony. A guard entered the solar and announced that an old peddler had come with ribbons, needles, and other fairings and hoped that the ladies might wish to purchase something.

"Bronwyn," said the Lady Igraine, addressing her servant. "Take the ladies off to flirt with the vassals, or some such amusement. I wish to see his wares before you sluts get your hands on them."

The ladies chuckled good-naturedly as Bronwyn marched them from the room.

"The children too," she added, with a wary glance at Morgan.

We followed after Bronwyn, but she soon took her eyes off us to deal with the giggling ladies, who were as wicked as children sometimes and were a struggle to shepherd anywhere. In the confusion, we again made our way down the servants' corridor to hide once more behind the solar screen.

"Only a peddler man," said Morgause, confused.

Morgan shook her head. "It's Merlin, he's come at last. Can't you feel it?"

Morgan looked fit to burst, and she clapped her hands roughly over Morgause and I's mouths, to make sure not another sound was made.

"He is here!" exclaimed Igraine, clapping her hands. "Can you not sense him?"

"Sense him?" hissed Petronella. "I can smell him."

The guard returned moments later with an old man in tow. I was too young to know it then, but Merlin had a fearsome reputation. His mother was a princess out of Wales, so pious she could only become a nun. They said the devil had come in the night and impregnated her so that she might deliver the Anti-Christ upon the earth. Petronella told me, years later, that his father was not a demon, as the Christians called them, but a faery from the hills. Either way, he had magic and guile in abundance.

He was captured by the old king Vortigern, who was building a castle on uncertain ground. It fell down in ruins each time. Soothsayers said only the blood of a fatherless child, mixed in the mortar, could keep the castle whole. They knew of Merlin and brought him before the old king. He spun him a fanciful tale about two dragons fighting in a pool under the castle and the king had spared his life. He served him then on as an adviser. He then had many other such adventures with Ambrosias, who rested the crown from his treacherous uncle Vortigern, and now appeared to serve his brother Uther.

He was the oldest man I had ever seen, and would ever see. His face was lined and creased with age, and he was bent almost double beneath the tattered cloak he wore, balancing the travelling pack on his back. His hair was long, past his shoulders and almost white. His beard too was absent of any colour and almost reached to his belt. His eyes, however, were not rheumy or otherwise impaired. They darted from side to side, quick and observant, and shone with an inexplicable fire.

"Leave us," commanded Igraine. "The other ladies may have their turn with the peddler in a moment."

The guard left the room.

"Lady Igraine. I received your summons, and I attend you gratefully."

"Thank you, Mer..."

"My name, if you do not mind, would be better kept a secret."

"Of course, sir."

Petronella entered the room, shut the door behind her and drew the bolt. She regarded Merlin warily.

"My dear Petronella..." began Merlin.

"Familiar old Druid, aren't you?" she interrupted. "I wish the Romans' had got you."

"Sadly, they did not," he replied. "I was far more fortunate than my brothers in faith."

"Meaning you kissed enough arses to be safe," she replied with spite. "You saw off Vortigern well enough, and you embraced Ambrosias Aurelianus with open arms. Is Uther Pendragon your new master, kingmaker?"

"That man will save Britain from the Saxons. I raised him myself to do so."

Petronella harrumphed and took her usual seat. Merlin took it as a signal to remove his travelling pack and cloak, a fairly fine robe and slippers underneath. He unwound a leather thong from his wrist and tied up his hair. Suddenly, he did not seem so old, or so frail. He took Igraine's proffered cup of wine and sat by the fire.

"I was glad when you sent for me. That was a beautiful piece of spellwork if I might say so. Petronella, it could only have come from you."

Our grandmother cast him a disgusted look. "Enough of your flattery, half-breed. Put your terms to us and then be gone."

"Very well," he responded. "I have seen you, Lady Igraine, sat upon the throne of Britain, at the side of Uther Pendragon. Together you will beget the once and future king."

"The once and future king?" asked Igraine, leaning forward in her seat.

The old wizard nodded. "The king that Britain will remember and call out for in her darkest hours. Every king that comes after him will want to be like him."

"And I will be the High Queen, you swear it?"

"By all I hold dear, my Lady."

"Which is very little, I would wager," interrupted Petronella.

"Shh, mother. How do you propose we proceed?"

"Gorlois must die," said Merlin. "You know this, of course."

She nodded. "I thought so. His pride will never allow him to capitulate to Uther, and his Roman ways would never permit the shame of a divorce."

"It would not do for you to divorce him. You are of the nobility only by your marriage and Uther cannot marry a commoner. But a widowed lady, who controls the duchy of Cornwall after her husband's death, that would be a firm match. Gorlois is a mighty war-leader. Your husband's defeat would silence all who would challenge Uther in the future."

"And how do we kill Gorlois, if you will pardon my bluntness, sir?"

Morgan reared beside me on the floor, but her mouth would make no sound. Evidently the binding extended to the presence of Merlin.

He glanced at Petronella. "Your mother is not unfamiliar with poisons."

"No," said Petronella. "I summoned you, and that's the only part I will play."

"Very well. I will see to it that Uther declares Gorlois his enemy. Tintagel is impenetrable in a siege, so you must convince Gorlois to ride out. When he does, we will ambush him on the road. In the meantime, Uther will enter the castle and claim you as his wife. A perfect victory."

"A perfect victory," seconded Igraine.

"He has not said what he wants from all this," cautioned Petronella.

Merlin chuckled. "Petronella, surely all this suspicion does not do your health good? I have merely one request."

"Name it," said Igraine.

"The son I have foreseen. I must be his foster-father as I was Uther's. He cannot be the once and future king without proper tuition."

Before Petronella could speak, Igraine barked her answer without hesitation. "Done."

Beside me, Morgan had gone deathly pale. She led us from the room, not speaking. She did not speak the rest of the evening, and could not be brought to levity in anyway, not even in her favourite pastime of pulling my hair.

Merlin departed from Tintagel a few hours later, after he had donned his peddler's garb and allowed the ladies of the household to purchase a few items. We fed him and Igraine waved him off, as though he was really an old travelling merchant and not the man who would bring about her husband's downfall.

Later that evening, word came from Uther that Gorlois was now a sworn enemy of Britain. An angry Gorlois summoned his vassals and together they fortified Tintagel. From then on, he talked of naught but war. No doubt Igraine wheedled and nagged at him, and soon he grew bold and swore to ride out with a war-band against the usurper king if he came, rather than the more sensible option of remaining ensconced in his coastal fortress.

"Father might win against the king," said Morgause one night in bed.

"He won't," said Morgan gravely. "Father's men are good fighters, but Uther has more of them. Merlin will use his magic to make sure they win. And mother has made sure we cannot speak of this to father."

Morgan did try, several times, and each time her tongue turned to lead in her mouth. She even tried writing it, but only scribbles came from the quill, despite Morgan's perfect penmanship. Wasting paper gave Igraine an excuse to beat her viciously and Morgan did not try again.

Our Lady Mother was agitated and she did not let us out of her sight the entire time, for fear we would find some way around the binding, but it was pointless. The day came and, I know now no man or woman could have stopped it, never mind a child. Some moments are written in the stars.

"It is time," said Petronella, some weeks later.

We were stood upon the battlements, looking out over the threatening waters of the bay.

"How can you tell?" asked Igraine, her normally coiffured hair wild about her shoulders. "He said he would send a signal, he did not say how."

"Look there, daughter!"

Petronella gestured out towards the cliffs. There, swooping in circles, was a bird of prey. The merlin, from which the old enchanter took his name.

"You are certain?"

Our grandmother nodded. Igraine seemed distraught for a second, but her ambition swallowed any other thoughts and she was once again the woman we knew.

"Mother, take the children to the solar, keep them there."

"Gladly. I'll not play a part in your spectacle."

Petronella took us to the solar and summoned Bronwyn to attend us. We sat there, and the two women tried their hardest to keep us entertained. We played games, we ate sweetmeats, and Petronella and Bronwyn told us all the stories they could think of. They even let Morgan pretend I was her doll, and she dressed me up and paraded me around her pretend court. But the diversions waned, and soon no force could keep us from watching at the window.

Our father had mustered most of Cornwall to his banner. Some were simple farmers, armed by our father and promised gold, and others were his vassal lords and their sons. Cador, our cousin and Gorlois' second, patrolled the assembled men. Our father, not much of an orator, was doing his best to stir up the men.

"Uther Pendragon stands at our borders! He would take your lady and humiliate your lord! How could that man ever be king? What we do today, we do not do for my pride! Today, we fight for Britain itself!"

The men gave great cheer and Cador marched them from the courtyard, their armour and pikes shining in the sun, the horses of those who could afford to be mounted whinnying. My mother stood off to one side, clapping and blowing kisses of good luck to the men. A small contingent of men-at-arms, some of my father's best, remained behind.

"The Lady Igraine will hold Tintagel while I am away," said Gorlois. "No man has ever taken it by force, but Uther will not get that far."

With a great "yah!" he rode from the castle and the great gates of Tintagel were barred to intruders.

"Your orders, milady?" asked the sergeant, more out of formality than anything else.

"Have your men patrol the battlements, and several down here by the gate," replied Igraine. "When you change out the watch, I will have food served in the great hall."

Igraine joined us in the solar and fidgeted immensely. Bronwyn tried to soothe her lady and got a slapped hand for her troubles. Petronella had gone to lie down. None of us uttered a sound and we went to have our dinner in the great hall. Igraine sat in father's ornate carved chair and sent down the best dishes to the guardsman, every inch the dutiful lady missing her husband gone to battle.

We sat on in the great hall, and my mother played dice with some of the men. Her game was interrupted by a page boy.

"Milady, the sergeant bids you come to the gate," he said.

"Whatever for?" she asked.

"He says the Lord Gorlois has returned."

Igraine rose at once and almost ran to the gate. Morgan sped after her. Morgause and I took each other's hands and toddled after them. The sergeant and my mother were arguing.

"Am I not your lady? Did your lord not say I was to hold Tintagel while he was gone?"

"That is true, milady, but..." he protested.

"But nothing. Open the gate."

"It is hard to believe that my Lord has returned so soon," said the sergeant.

"So you would keep him out?"

The man stuttered and Igraine shoved past him to open the panel in the gate. Through the gap, a rider was visible.

"My Lord Gorlois?" she called.

"Yes, Igraine, it is I!"

"Returned so soon from battle?" asked Igraine.

"Merely a lull. I've come to seek succour from my Lady wife."

"Fool," muttered Petronella, come out from the great hall. "Gorlois would never say that."

"You must enter at once," said Igraine. "I have a fire in the hearth and there is hearty food and mead in the hall. Open the gate!"

There was a hue and cry and the gate lumbered open on its great hinges, pulled by the men-at-arms. The rider trotted through to the courtyard. Then, clear as day, we could see what mother and Petronella could, and the sergeant could not.

That was not Gorlois astride the horse. It could only be Uther Pendragon. When we looked at him, it was as if looking at our reflection in a pool of water. He shimmered and blurred, was dark haired one minute and fair the next, clean shaven and then bearded.

"A glamour!" breathed Morgan. "Not even grandmother could do one like that."

"Come, my Lord Husband," said Igraine and she led the false Gorlois by the hand, giggling much unlike herself.

They stole away to the master chamber. Petronella lifted me up in her arms, and pulled Morgause after her, Morgan following behind. As we walked, my grandmother whispered over and over again "So it is done."

And so it was done. Uther lay that with Igraine that night and changed the island of Britain forever. In the morning, there was a pounding of hoof beats as a legion of men crossed the drawbridge, bearing the banner of Pendragon. My mother walked shamelessly into the courtyard, hand in hand with Uther, the glamour faded in the strength of the morning sun.

He was tall and broader than my father. Uther kept his hair long, unlike the cropped Roman fashion. He was fair and had a short but full beard of a similar colour. His muscles were clearly evident, straining beneath my father's old red tunic. Uther Pendragon was handsome indeed.

My mother threw up her treacherous hands and the sergeant gave in to the insurmountable pressure, opening the gate.

Merlin strode into the courtyard, his robe dusty from the road. He carried a staff but did not lean on it. There he seemed a cross between the old, frail man we had seen at first and the robust politician he had proven himself to be.

"Gorlois, Duke of Cornwall is dead. Long live Uther, Duke of Cornwall! Long live Uther, High King of Britain!"

We bowed, all of us, in the dirt of the courtyard, the servants, the men-at-arms, the women. And so, Uther was the unchallenged High King of Britain, and my mother his High Queen.

Chapter Two

You must think me very harsh, or say I have inherited my mother's ambition. The truth is, I was very young. And powerless to do anything. I was the third daughter of a duke, so I had no inheritance to rely on. Nor had I Morgan's will, Morgause's beauty, or my mother's powers. So I kept silent and welcomed Uther Pendragon as my new father.

Time soon lessened my memories of Gorlois, and I came to care for Uther. Mark this, I only cared for him, I did not love him. I saw the cruelty of which he was capable, and in the first decade I spent at his castle at Camelot, I saw his ambition, which he called love for Britain.

Morgause was easily bought with trinkets and promises of a good marriage when she was older. Only Morgan rebelled. She would not eat, or would go days without speaking. She would bring up Gorlois at every turn and no matter how hard she was beaten, she would begin the cycle all over again.

Then, of course, was our half-brother Arthur, begat that very day in Tintagel. We only knew of him, we did not know him, for he was gone before we could. To me, who had never seen a pregnant woman before, it was all quite simple. Our mother grew quite round and then, suddenly, she had this little squalling babe in her arms.

I remember crying for the first few months after Arthur's birth. As soon as he was born, Petronella departed Camelot to become the stewardess of Tintagel, since most of my mother's female attendants had come with her to Uther's castle. She did not shy away from telling us why she was leaving. She could no longer bear the presence of my

31

mother, nor that of Merlin, Uther's constant companion. I missed her dearly, and even Morgan, who still feared her wrath, was inconsolable for weeks.

At first, Igraine was happy, that much was evident. Uther showered her with gifts, tributes from across the kingdoms of Britain, and she delighted in organising his grand feasts. Arthur was her darling, she would let no other nurse him. A more callous woman would say he was her protection. Under the laws of Britain, no man can put away a wife that has borne him a living son.

My mother must have forgotten her bargain with Merlin. No doubt Igraine had made many promises in her life she had no intention of keeping, and never thought that someone would call on them.

He took Arthur early one morning before the household had risen, and was far enough beyond our borders that Igraine's screaming went unheard. She beat down doors and shook the servants roughly. Soon most of the castle had gone into hiding, and Uther had to be entreated to see to his wife, who was overturning chairs in the great hall as if Merlin was cowering under them with the babe in his arms.

"Where is my son?" demanded Igraine of the High King as he entered.

"My queen, he has gone into fosterage with Merlin, as we have discussed."

"He is too young! Who will nurse him?"

Uther's response was calm. "The house he has gone to, the lady has recently had a child of her own. She will nurse him while Merlin tutors him."

"A-hah! So it is a noble house then? Whose?" she questioned.

"I cannot tell you," he replied.

"You fear I would go and get him?"

"I do not fear it, I know it. If I told you where he might be found, you would ride out at once, and Arthur would be back here by nightfall. It would undo all Merlin and I have worked for."

"You have betrayed me, Uther!" shrieked Igraine.

"Serves you right," said Morgan, watching the proceedings with great amusement. "I lost my father, so you can lose your son."

"You little bitch!" cried Igraine, and she flew at Morgan, who skittered from the room, cackling as she went.

Uther took his wife by the arm. "Leave her, I'll send Bronwyn to tan her hide later. Be calm, Igraine. I was fostered by Merlin, and it did me no harm."

Igraine seethed, then begged, and tried all her tricks, but Uther did not relent. Arthur was to remain with Merlin until the time came for him to return as Uther's heir.

Fosterage was common enough, especially for sons of kings. But Arthur was too young, and Merlin would soon become more of a father to him than Uther would ever be. And that could never be a good thing.

Igraine did not relent. She took to being seen in the great hall only by written command of the High King and had few civil words for him for the first few years. She neglected all the household work, leaving the running of Camelot entirely to Bronwyn, who was greatly unequipped for such a task.

She sat, from daybreak until dusk, at the great table in her chambers, with the obsidian mirror, a bowl of water and the casting stones, looking for a clue to Arthur's whereabouts. She could not find him, not with all her spells. Merlin was indeed a mighty magician.

Evidently, Igraine did not take Uther to her bed again, after his great betrayal, for no more sons or daughters followed. I would not be surprised if that had been part of Merlin's great plan, so the kingdom would have only one heir, and no division.

After some years of employing spies to roam the country and accosting Merlin and other visiting dignitaries at every opportunity, she gave up on finding our brother and turned her attention towards us.

We learnt all that great ladies should learn. To spin, to weave, to sew and dye. We learnt to supervise servants, to run a laundry and a kitchen, to host a great feast, to preserve food so it will last through winter and to make medicines for any ailment. Bronwyn taught us much of that, but our mother taught us to dress, to converse, to dance and to flirt.

To Morgan, she taught the darker arts, cloistered in the shadows of Igraine's chambers. It was a desperate attempt to win back her daughter's love, but Morgan would forever hate our mother, and pretended so long as she learnt her spells and potions. After her thirteenth birthday, upon the first full moon, our mother took her away and made her one of the Wise.

Morgan was insufferable thereafter and lost all subtlety. She threatened all who would oppose her with curses and soon, not even we, her beloved sisters, could stand her presence.

She went far enough with Uther, tormenting him with what he had done, stealing another man's wife, winning Tintagel by trickery, ambushing Gorlois on the road. She called him weak, a coward and Merlin's puppet. And one day she went too far, and Uther decreed she was banished from court.

"You simply cannot banish a thirteen-year-old girl," stated Igraine. "Goodness knows she's vicious, but banishment? She has nowhere to go. Your enemies will laugh at you, that you hated a little girl so much you sent her from court."

"You are right," he acknowledged. "I will put her in a nunnery. The one at Glastonbury."

Morgan's face betrayed more than she would have liked, and once Uther knew he had found her weakness, he pressed his advantage. Morgan had burned her bridges with anyone inclined to plead her case, and within the week, she was to be sent to be schooled by the nuns at Glastonbury.

As a high lady of the court, we gathered at the gate to see her off. She was in a sober dress, her dark hair bound up under a hood. Uther smiled victoriously. Morgan's face was twisted with wrath.

"Your carriage awaits, stepdaughter," he said.

Igraine gave her kiss goodbye and so did Morgause and I. Bronwyn packed her a little bag of comforts and made sure the girl's cloak was fastened tightly. When the time came, Morgan refused, however, to be stand and be penitent, nor did she accept defeat with grace.

"I swear to you Uther," she intoned before all assembled. "My father will have his justice."

She reached under her cloak and in her hand, dripping fresh blood, was a cow's heart.

"You have broken my heart, Uther Pendragon, so I shall break yours," intoned Morgan, and she began muttering under breath.

She gave the heart a great squeeze and it turned to mush in her hands, blood and tissue dripping onto the paving stone. She tossed it at his feet, and turned her back on Camelot, trundling off in her carriage.

Uther was never the same after Morgan's curse. He was only a man of forty, but he slowed considerably. He struggled to catch his breath and was plagued by pains in his chest. Igraine could not be moved to break her daughter's curse, even if she could, and my sister and I did not know how. The great king even got down on his knees and begged Petronella to help, but she said it was blood magic, and only Morgan could undo it. Merlin was nowhere to be found. And I know now, it suited the old enchanter's purposes for Uther Pendragon's time on this earth to be fixed.

Morgan, of course, could not be entreated to undo her foul work from afar, and Uther did not recall her to court for fear his enemies learnt that all he had built was threatened by a thirteen-year-old girl.

As he declined, Morgause and I grew. We did not see our sister in the seven years she spent in the convent, though she wrote when the nuns permitted it. Morgause and I were initiated into the Wise too, down in the cold cellars of Camelot where none could see. We wrote to Morgan to tell her, but she replied that she had far surpassed us in such things, having found the Abbess to teach her high magic she could not have learnt elsewhere.

In the intervening years, we buried Petronella. Her work at Tintagel tired her, and life had not been kind to her. She received a cairn of stones upon the grassy hills outside the castle, overlooking the little hut where she had lived her life in Cornwall. Igraine left her a cup of wine and a little chunk of salted meat as a grave offering. Morgan was not permitted to come for the rites, following Igraine's letter to say our grandmother had died, and the response that came had words we doubt Morgan had learned in the nunnery.

We soon knew that Uther had faced his own mortality and had been beaten when the great assembly was called. All the kings, dukes and lords of Britain were to come, Merlin also – without Arthur, who would be eleven that year – and even Morgan was to return from Glastonbury

"It can mean only one thing, Elaine," whispered Morgause, her excitement palpable. "Husbands."

At seventeen, Morgause was the image of our mother in her youth. She had her vibrant red locks and her jade green eyes. She was tall, but shapely also. Igraine kept a careful eye on her, for she was far too familiar with the guardsmen and male servants, and past the age where such things could be permitted.

I had reached sixteen and looked neither like my mother or my sisters. I suppose I took after Petronella before her hair had greyed. My hair was a golden colour, and many a noble mistook me for Uther's natural born daughter. I did not think I was pretty, with my strong jaw and low cheekbones, but mother said I would do very well indeed.

By the time we had reached the entrance hall to greet the returning Morgan, Morgause had given a lengthy discourse on the age, wealth, attractiveness and other comparisons between the powerful men who would be attending the assembly. She had made her best picks and warned me to stay as far from them as possible.

Morgause could be very naïve for someone who seemed so worldly. Just because Igraine had chosen two husbands in a row did not mean we had the same freedom. We would take who we were given, and I prayed that day for a good match.

We entered the hall and could see, quite clearly, that the girl of thirteen was gone. Stood by the great door of Camelot was Morgan, now twenty years old. She was dressed in the robes of a novice nun, a dark, harsh black that showed none of her pale skin, bar her hands and face. Her hair had grown so dark that it was impossible to distinguish it from her robe.

She held out her hands and beckoned to us. "Come, sisters, embrace me."

Her voice was deep for a woman, rich and commanding, no doubt strengthened from constant use in praying and reading the gospel. She took us both into her arms.

She looked down. "Of course, you must be Morgause, I knew at once from the hair. And Elaine, your hair, it is so very bright. I would have thought you would turn dark like our father."

From this close, I could see her face so clearly. Her eyes were like coals and set firmly within her sharp-featured face. She was very much Gorlois' daughter, what little I remembered of him and had seen in my dreams.

"Come," she said. "Lead me to my chambers, I must change into something more courtly."

The servant boy carried Morgan's saddlebag, which held the few possessions she had. We made our way to the quarters Morgause and I shared, and which was to be Morgan's also for the duration of the assembly. Morgause's second best dress was lying on the bed, with a few pieces of borrowed jewellery from Igraine.

"Bronwyn is coming later, to adjust the dress for you," I said.

Morgan smiled. "Bronwyn is still in our mother's service?"

"Yes," I replied. "Though goodness knows why, she is very difficult."

Morgan took a little mirror from her saddlebag and began to examine her reflection adorned with the jewellery. Morgause's interest was piqued.

"That is a very good mirror, it gives a very true picture," said Morgause.

"It is from the Far East," replied Morgan. "A gift from the Mother Abbess, for scrying, of course, she abhors vanity in women. But what she does not know will not hurt her."

"May I look in it?"

"Of course, Morgause," she said, handing it to her. "You may look in it anytime you like, so long as you do not break it."

Morgause took it at once and began to preen, tilting it this way and that to best catch her likeness. Morgan took me by the hand and led me to sit beside her on the bed.

"Tell me, Elaine, what of your studies? Mother, when she deigns to write, says you are very clever."

"I can read and write," I replied. "I know a bit of Latin too, and I'm not bad at the other things, the dyes and the simples, and using an account book."

"And your other studies, under mother?" she asked.

I did not normally talk about such things and feigned ignorance when a serving girl would beg some charm of me. A loose-lipped woman will always burn said mother. But Morgan seemed so impressive and I yearned to impress her in turn.

"I know all of the herbs that grow here, and most of the ones from mother's book. I can cast a circle, and I know the thirteen lesser charms, and six out of the thirteen greater charms. My healing magic is poor though and I struggle with dream-walking."

"I'm very good at that," added Morgause, who then resumed her explorations of the mirror.

"She is," I whispered. "But mostly because she is very lazy and can fall asleep in a moment." Morgan and I shared a smile.

"Are you going to become a nun?" Morgause asked absently.

"Silly sister!" exclaimed Morgan. "I could no more bow before the Christ than I could bow before Uther Pendragon."

"Then what do you intend?" I asked.

"It is the reason I have come," she responded. "I want to take up the duchy of Cornwall, as is mine by right."

"I do not think Uther will permit it," I said. "Cousin Cador has ruled there for some time and you have not been a friend to Uther these past years."

"I will marry Cador if I have to, but Uther cannot keep it from me. It is the law of Britain. And if the king does not keep the law, why should anyone follow him?"

Morgan seemed very wise, but even I knew that did not sound true.

We dined in the presence-chamber that evening, away from the bustle of the great hall. Igraine seemed enlivened slightly at having Morgan back, though they did not speak much. The greeting between Uther and Morgan was tense but courteous. Merlin also joined us, but Morgan did not even regard the old man.

She sat in her chair and was resting her elbow upon the back, more like a conquering Saxon than a great lady.

"Did the Abbess teach you to sit like that?" sneered Uther.

Morgan gave a little laugh. "Mother Abbess is no great friend of yours, Uther Pendragon, not since you ceded some of her abbey lands to King Cradelmant."

Uther sighed. "Then Mother Abbess is not unlike you, Morgan, for she knows how to hold a grudge. That was nearly ten years ago."

There was a laugh from the other end of the table and we stared. Merlin was in conversation with Morgause, who obviously thought whatever sordid story he was regaling her with very funny indeed.

"My apologies, my Lord, my ladies," said Merlin, though he did not seem very sorry at all, staring at the neckline of Morgause's gown.

"Quite alright, Merlin," said Uther. "But it has come a time that we spoke seriously, though."

Morgause leaned forward. She was getting her husband after all this time.

"You have all come of age now, some of you long past it...I will not be around forever..." Uther struggled to lay his hands upon the necessary words.

"My Lord," said Merlin. "If I may? You seem to have some difficulty?"

Uther nodded, and Merlin continued for him.

"You have come of marriageable age, and your King and I see it that it is time for you to have husbands, of whom will be of great importance in the time when Uther's reign draws to a close and your brother Arthur's begins."

Igraine pursed her lips. "You chose husbands for them? Without consulting me?"

Uther closed his eyes for a second and massaged the bridge of his nose. "What would you know of political marriages, you old harridan?"

"A damn sight more than you," she replied.

Merlin held up a hand to silence their bickering. "My King, my Queen, if it please you?" They grew quiet.

"Lady Morgause, I shall not keep you in suspense much longer, you look fit to burst," said Merlin. "You will marry King Lot of Orkney."

Morgause looked confused, then angry. "King Lot must be forty if he's a day! And he is King of the Orkneys! I do not even know where that is!"

Morgause's protests became more and more squeal-like. Soon she was unintelligible but Merlin continued.

"For you Lady Morgan..."

Morgan interrupted the advisor. "I know the best course of action here. I shall marry cousin Cador and rule Tintagel for you. Surely that is why you called me here?"

Uther shook his head. "No, it bloody well is not. I would not give you Tintagel in a thousand years, where you could take yourself off to the Cornish wilds and plot against me in that impenetrable fortress. Not after all you have done."

"After all I've done? After all you have done more likely!" she exclaimed in reply. "It is mine by law! You cannot keep it from me."

"I am the law!" he cried, thumping his fist on the table.

"It is my counsel, Lady Morgan," interjected Merlin, as Morgan's mouth formed a reply. "That Cador has ruled well enough in Cornwall and thus should be granted the dukedom in his own right. No, you shall marry Uriens of Gore."

"You old demon!" cried Morgan. "Uriens! He has buried three wives these past sixty years."

"And who does she get?" asked Morgause, pointing at me.

"The Lady Elaine will marry King Nentres of Garlot," replied Merlin.

"Nentres! Nentres! Nentres!" shrieked Morgause, getting louder. "She gets Nentres!"

"Is that supposed to be good?" I asked.

"Good? He is as handsome as bard's hero and he is only twenty! You little bitch!"

Morgause made motions to climb over the table and Igraine had to rush to hold her back. She hissed at me like a beaten cat, before sobbing into Igraine's shoulder. Our mother regarded her with distaste and tried to shrug her off.

Morgan knew as well as I that Uther could have her bundled into a sack and dragged all the way to Gore if he so chose, so she merely rose from the table, bowed mockingly to Uther and swept from the room with a flutter of her borrowed gown. Her pride would permit nothing else.

Morgause could not be consoled, so the King dismissed us. I rushed to hide, for I feared Morgause's wrath, but she was too fast for me. Exiting the chamber, she gave me a vicious shove, and I collided with the stone wall.

"You cheating little bitch!" she cried. "What charm did you cast?"

"None," I replied, truthfully.

She screwed up her face in anger and pinched the skin of my arm, twisting it wickedly. I screamed.

"Undo it! Or else cast it for me!"

"I did not!" I cried, trying to push her off, but she pinned my wrist to the wall.

"Morgause!" exclaimed our mother. "Away from her at once, you ungrateful little slattern! To think, you are to be a queen..."

Igraine marched down the hallway and bundled Morgause away.

"I hate you, and I am never speaking to you again!" Morgause called over her shoulder.

Igraine did not return to comfort me. I slid down the wall and crumpled to a heap. I rubbed at my bruised arm and began to cry, from the pain, but also from my sister's words, and from what lay in store for me.

Uther emerged from the presence-chamber, and walked to the end of the corridor, to look out the window. The night had grown cold, and the breeze blew in through the stone opening, rustling the window cover. He turned and saw me, hunched and sobbing.

"Elaine, are you alright?" he asked.

I nodded and brushed the tears from my face with the sleeve of my gown. "Quite alright, my King."

He beckoned with his hand, and I joined him at the window.

"Did Morgause hurt you?" he asked.

"Not badly, mother intervened," I replied. "But she has been greatly upset by tonight's announcement."

"Has she? I thought Morgause would have died had she not been given the husband she so craved."

"I do not think she craved Lot of Orkney. Nentres of Garlot, perhaps."

44

"It is a difficult thing to be both your step-father, and your king." He huffed out a sigh. "Perhaps I should have told you by alone, but I forgot that women can be so...difficult."

He continued. "I have had to think of what I was leaving behind for your brother to rule, and that should be a Britain strongly allied to him, by blood and honour. I gave Morgause, the prettiest of you - I hope you are not hurt by my saying this – to Lot, because he is a vain man, and only a beauty will do. I need him to hold the north for me, against the wild men, and to watch the eastern seas, because he has the largest fleet, being an island king. He nearly rose against me when I first became king, and I see his rebellious streak has not left him."

"And what of Morgan?" I asked. "Of Uriens?"

"She thinks I seek to punish her, but it is not so, when I could have married her to my lowliest cowherd if I hated her so. No, Uriens is itching to rebel, a final battle for his twilight years. A slip of a girl like you or your sister would only insult his dignity. I gave him Morgan because he needs a mother for his children and a woman who can keep house, not a woman for an evening's sport or to adorn his hall."

"A nurse for his dotage, you mean?"

He looked at me, both surprised and amused. "You have your mother's instincts, and her tongue too. Yes, Uriens will be gone in ten years or so, and Morgan fit to remarry, taking the widow's portion of her lands and joining them to another kingdom. With their kingdom lessened so, in men and supplies, Uriens' sons will not be able to rise up."

"You and Merlin have planned this well. Nentres too? He is important?"

"He is young, and become king only last year, and will be much honoured by a match with you. He is quiet and thoughtful, and I think Morgan too imperious for him, or Morgause too flirtatious for his pride."

He placed a hand on my shoulder. "He will come to treasure you, as I have. You have become like my own daughter. Why, we could be so with our looks! Your mother thinks I do not miss my son, I do, but Britain needs a learned king more than I need my son. But you have been a comfort to me, these last few years, and I know you will care for your brother when I am gone."

Uther was rarely so forthright with feelings. I was surprised.

"I have been grateful for your kindness," I replied.

In truth I was. He had every right to cast me out, his wife's daughter by the man he called a traitor. Many a year I too feared the nunnery or worse.

"Tell me, though, surely it is not just Nentres' happiness you need?"

He smiled and squeezed my shoulder in his large hand. "No, that is true. Garlot sits near to here, and all who would turn on this castle must march through it. A loyal king would rise up the moment warriors crossed his fields, but a disloyal one would stand by and ignore them, and that would never do."

Could I really keep a man loyal? Was that my duty now, to charm this Nentres and bear his children so he would ever be watchful for invaders and not seize Britain for himself? It seemed so large a task for a sixteen-year-old girl.

"Now, go to bed, Elaine," said Uther. "Your future husband comes tomorrow, and you must look your best."

I left him there, staring out across the lands of Camelot. I could see he had many other things on his mind than the pattern of the stars.

I entered the bedchamber with caution, casting about for a sign of Morgause and a surprise attack. Only Morgan was inside, brushing her hair in the front of the little silver mirror. She looked at my reflection and addressed it.

"Morgause has been sent to sleep elsewhere for her un-ladylike behaviour. Mother thinks a night on a wooden pallet with the servants will teach her not to be so ungrateful."

Her voice was tart, and her strokes of the brush vicious. Evidently she was contemplating her marriage to Uriens of Gore. I did not wish to discuss marriage further, so I passed on through the room and into the inner chamber, where the bed sat in the centre.

As I stripped to my shift, leaving my dress for Bronwyn to see to in the morning, and climbed into the bed, I was struck by its sudden barrenness. All my life, I had shared a bed with Morgause, and now she hated me. We fought like all sisters did, but this felt different. Battle lines had been drawn. Then I thought about how I would have to sleep next to a man that I did not know for the rest of my life, and the bed seemed tiny, like a burial box.

I awoke to the sound of hushed voices from the other chamber. The moon was still out in force beyond the castle window. It was late indeed. I strained to hear. It was a man, talking to Morgan! Surely she would not be so foolish? Not when her marriage to Uriens was so close at hand, and any cause to reject her would ruin her for life!

47

I slid from beneath the furs and tiptoed across the cold, bare stone floor to stand against the partition. Closer, I could hear the conversation. It was indeed a man, but I knew this voice. I had spent twelve years listening to it.

"You will not undo it?" asked Uther, the desperation evident even as he whispered.

"You will not give me Tintagel, what is mine by birth?" replied Morgan.

"A woman cannot hold Cornwall. Be its heiress yes, its figurehead, but never its queen regnant. A woman to stand against the Irish raiders, the Saxon invasion, and the rebels in the Summer Country? I never thought you so stupid."

"And what is wrong with a woman as the lady of the coast? Such things were common enough before the Romans."

"Times have changed. The men would never follow a woman now."

Morgan took a seat by the fire, which had long since been doused. "And I cannot marry Cador? It would strengthen his claim."

"Merlin feels that Cador's claim is strong enough. But Uriens could turn the moment I die and Arthur..."

"Sod Merlin! Uriens is old enough to be my grandfather."

"He would not take the others, they are mere chits of things."

Morgan laughed, low and deep. "And I am a matron I suppose, unmarried by twenty?"

"Merlin advised..."

"Do you do everything that decrepit half-breed says? Can the great High King not think for himself? Where was Merlin when the pains in your chest overtook you?"

"He had business elsewhere in the kingdom. When I was able to consult with him, he said it was too far gone for any intervention."

"It is not too far gone. He said that, you know, because he wants you gone."

"Lies!" he barked, and then remembered the silence he was keeping. "So you can undo it?"

"I have told you my price. Cornwall in exchange for your heart, old man."

Uther sunk into the opposite seat. He seemed very old and very tired. "I cannot. All I worked for this past decade, to be undone when I appoint a woman in charge of our western coast?"

"If only my father had been strong enough to seize the crown and put an end to you and your ambition!"

"Morgan, you are too harsh! I bore Gorlois no ill…"

"No ill! You seduced his wife and murdered him on the road!"

"I loved your mother, and she loved me in return."

"My mother loves no one but herself."

"What's done is done, Morgan."

"That much is true."

They sat in silence for some moments, regarding each other.

"I cannot keep Uriens loyal for Arthur, it that is what you believe," said Morgan, after some time.

"You must. Britain depends on it."

"Would Britain not depend better on Arthur's sister holding some of his most important lands?"

Uther laughed. "You have your mother's stubbornness."

Morgan was serious. "I swear, Uther Pendragon, if you cannot do what is right, for once in your pitiful life, I will see to it that all you have built with my father's blood lies in ruins."

With that, Morgan rose from her chair, and I darted back to the bed. I made it under the covers in time for Morgan to join me. She tossed and turned for some time before she was able to sleep.

Bronwyn brought us food the next morning, set upon the table in the outer chamber. "I thought it best you eat away from the presence-chamber, where Morgause is currently," she said.

Thankful, I sat down to eat. Bronwyn smiled at Morgan, who smiled in return, but her eyes were guarded. Their reunion the previous day had been affectionate, with Morgan clasping the older woman's hands tenderly and Bronwyn exclaiming "Little lady! How've you grown!"

"You're hovering Bronwyn," said Morgan.

"It's just…" Her voice cracked, and her eyes watered. "I have only sons, milady, but you are like daughters to me. I am so happy to see you married."

"I'm not," said Morgan. "I would rather see myself a hundred other things than an old man's drudge."

I had almost forgotten what was to happen that day. My stomach soured and pushed away the rabbit meat. We were to meet our future husbands and, if no objections raised, we would be married by the end of the sennight.

Bronwyn continued nonetheless and was swooping around the room, calling out the various preparations that had been made for our weddings. My heart lowered in realising that no one thought to tell us, and I questioned why these things must be done in such a hurry.

Are women really things to be bought and sold in a day's trading? I knew it could be so, I knew my marriage would always be political, but like this? I felt like a cow, sold at market and in a new barn by dusk.

"I took your gown from the last feast and I added some new embroidery on the hem and sleeves," she said, lifting up the dress for me to inspect. "And sewed cloth-of-gold along the neck. It is a gift from your mother."

I nodded and tried to continue my morning meal, but it would not go down and I gave up readily before I turned sick. Bronwyn bid us wash from the ewer because she had not the time to draw a bath for three girls and our mother.

She then proceeded to thoroughly abuse us, all in the name of beauty. She scraped our skin almost raw with a pumice and then rubbed us down in oil of lemon. Our hair she coiled tightly around our heads, and I felt like I was three years old again, for Bronwyn delivered a stinging smack to my bottom each time I tried to resist her.

My dress was laced as tightly as my hair, and I thought I would return what little food I had consumed. Bronwyn even tucked rolls of linen into my undergarments, to push up my breasts and make my hips appear fuller and rounder.

"Only places a man really looks," she said, with an air of resignation. "You'd think he was buying a dairy cow or a breeding bitch."

To finish, she applied chalk powder to my face, red stain to my lips and a little line of kohl around my eyes, a black powder from some far-off land that itched, but I feared further attack if I rubbed it off.

We regarded ourselves in the little scrying mirror. Bronwyn did good work, that much should be said. Slender Morgan looked positively voluptuous and I hardly recognised the woman who stared back at me with sultry eyes and pouting lips. They were brides, not the studious little girl I grew up with or the carefree self I thought I knew so well.

We made our way to the great hall with a slow walk, taking as not to disturb any of the preparations Bronwyn had made. Uther stood upon the dais, with my mother and Morgause beside him. She looked resplendent in a new gown and coiffured hair, and my mother too was attired in her best, as though she was the prospective bride.

Morgause glared at me, then turned her head to the door of the hall and did not look at me again, though her neck must have surely hurt from its stiffness. Igraine's hand was not far from Morgause, and her nails would silence any embarrassment she might cause on this important day.

The page alerted Uther that the convoys of kings had rendezvoused at Sorviodunum and now were sequestered in the courtyard, refreshing themselves. Uther instructed the boy to invite them to join him when it was convenient, which was double-speak for they were to join him right away.

The men-at-arms opened the great doors and in they strode, the three vassal kings. Together they approached the throne and sunk to their knees before the dais. One man stood out amongst them, and he could only have been Nentres of Garlot.

He could have passed for younger than his twenty years. His hair was a dark as raven's feathers and sat in an unruly mess. The beginnings of a beard and a moustache darkened his mouth, and a smile sat naturally upon his wide set chin. He was not very tall, but he was broad and well-muscled.

He seemed so familiar, but I knew I had never seen him before. I would have remembered. He looked across the dais and sought me with his eyes. I was quick to pull my gaze downwards, and I stared at the embroidery on my hem.

The other two were as easily identified by their ages. Uriens was old, as nearly as such as Merlin. He was tall, but stooped, as though his great grey beard dragged him downwards by the chin. He was thick too, with years of muscle gone over to wastage and fat. Still, he wore his sword close at hand, as though war might erupt within a few feet of the throne.

The remaining man was Lot. A most unremarkable man, of average height and build. He was not unattractive, but nor could he be called handsome. However, his clothing was free of any stain of the road, and he was draped in fur and heavy gold. Whatever Lot lacked in looks or martial prowess, he surely made up for in wealth and Morgause's keen eyes could not have missed this.

"My brother-kings!" called Uther in welcome, and he pulled the men from their knees into embraces. Releasing them, he took Igraine's hand and presented her to the three kings in turn.

She curtseyed low and asked after their journey, their health and of their harvest. All the while, her smile never left her face, nor did a single hair escape from its arrangement. My mother never gave one hint of her low birth. From where we stood, Igraine gave every impression she had been raised at the court of the grandest king.

"Now, you have the pleasure of meeting my dearest stepdaughters, whom you will soon call your queens."

Uther gestured to us with a great sweep, truly king of all he surveyed.

"Princess Morgan, lately returned from school at Glastonbury. Morgan, I present King Uriens of Gore."

Morgan swept down from the dais, her jade green gown of the finest wool billowing behind her. She presented her hand to Uriens, as though she was a priest bestowing a holy sacrament. She was made to be a queen, it seemed, but with her pale skin, a strange queen of the faery lands perhaps.

"Princess Morgause, come greet King Lot of the Orkneys."

Morgause's pride won out against her recalcitrance, and she greeted Lot as though he was her every desire. She smiled when he kissed her hand in greeting and fingered his great gold chain in awe of its shine and purity. I sensed Lot would part with a great many such trinkets in the course of their marriage.

"And finally, my youngest, Princess Elaine. This is King Nentres of Garlot."

Nentres locked eyes with me firmly and strode with his hand out like a soldier facing battle. He grasped my hand and I felt the power and strength of his arms coursing through his fingers. Then a curious heat followed, and I was quick to withdraw my hand.

"No objections?" whispered Uther, low so that none of the others assembled could hear. The other kings subtly shook their heads. The marriage contracts were accepted.

"But you must be hungry!" called Uther. "Bronwyn, you may tell the kitchens to serve us!"

Uther gave a loud clap, and Bronwyn darted off in perfect time to signal the cook that the first round of food was to be served. This was merely a meal to soothe any hunger pangs that had arisen, not a delight of delicacies that would be served later at the great feast, but would be a culinary spectacle nonetheless. Uther would not want them to think he kept a miserly court.

We were seated beside our perspective husbands. Uriens proceeded to bore Morgan with a discussion of his many, many children and their accomplishments in the arts martial while Morgause put to Lot a series of questions as to where such jewels and furs as he wore could be obtained, and if he had many of them.

Nentres and I looked at each other, and then away, but we found no respite in our companion's conversations, so we looked at each other again, and then decided to stare straight ahead, down to the rows of tables seating Uther's warriors and vassals. We tried to speak to one another, but only awkward noise came forth from our mouths, so we abandoned that course, and made industrious work of the platters set before us, avoiding all contact with our eyes.

"Bronwyn," said Uther, catching the passing servant by the arm. "When the lesser men have finished eating, instruct the porters to begin to rearrange the tables, so the guests may have a view of the dais. I want all the men here to see what occurs tonight."

"Yes, Sire. The Queen has also requested we begin to move the flowers into the hall."

Uther nodded. "Very well."

She curtseyed and went to carry out his orders.

"Bronwyn," I whispered as she passed, rising from my seat to speak to her. "Why are we moving things?"

"For the ceremonies, my Lady," she answered.

"The weddings are to take place tonight? Not tomorrow or the day after?"

"That is why we are so rushed, my Lady," replied Bronwyn.

"What? That is most unusual."

Bronwyn whispered conspiratorially. "Uther fears Morgan might abscond in the night, and I reckon Morgause wouldn't be far behind."

It suddenly felt very warm within the hall. I pulled down the neck of my gown as far as modesty would allow, but the heat continued to rise. I made a rush for the side door, out into the kitchen courtyard.

It was snowing lightly, more like sleet than anything. It was most unseasonable and I knew, as soon as the flakes touched my skin, Morgause had whistled a storm to interrupt her nuptials and my mother had banished it as quickly as it had come.

"Princess Elaine," he said quietly. I thought I had imagined it, so low that it could have been a whisper of Morgause's spell-wind.

I turned and there was Nentres of Garlot, making his way across the slippery stones of the kitchen courtyard.

"Are you quite well?" he asked.

I curtseyed low, remembering Igraine's lessons, and the manners that had failed me in the hall. "I am, my Lord."

"We will be husband and wife," he replied. "You may call me Nentres."

I nodded, then took to studying the stone walls. In the time we stood out there, I knew where all the moss grew and which bricks needed replacing. I would wager he did too.

I could feel him shift his gaze to me, and I turned my head towards him on instinct. He looked me squarely in the face, his eyes as brown as the bark of a young tree. Abruptly, he spoke, breaking the silence in the courtyard like a fallen dish.

"If you do not wish to marry me, I will release Uther and you from the contract."

I shook my head. "Uther will take it as an insult, and the peace will be undone."

"But...I am confused, my Lady. You seem so...disappointed."

"I learnt of my marriage only yesterday. I knew the day would come, eventually. I know I could have made a much worse match, to a much older man like Morgan or a far off island like Morgause."

He furrowed his brow in confusion, reminding me of a squirrel darting about in the woods. I stifled a laugh.

"But then, why are you so forlorn, my Lady?" he asked.

"Because," I replied, surprising myself with my honesty. "Imagine having to spend your life with someone you have never met, in a place you have never been to?"

"Forgive me, Princess Elaine, I cannot speak to unknown places, but I too have to spend my life with someone I have never met."

I drew breath. I was so surprised at myself that I had not considered he too was in such a situation. From the moment I knew I was to marry Nentres of Garlot, I pictured him as the aggressor, wheedling Uther into offering my hand in marriage as the price for his vision of Britain united.

Silence descended upon the courtyard. Nentres withdrew from me and returned to the castle door.

"I will make a bargain with you, Princess," he said from the shadow of the archway. "I am not a Roman, so if you wish, after a year and day, to be rid of me, I will send you home without any fuss.

You will be free to marry again, and I will hold to the terms of Uther's peace."

"I will hold you to that, Your Highness."

He smirked. "I would not expect any less from you."

With that, he returned to the luncheon. I followed after.

Uther kept a Christian court, like his brother before him, despite their own pagan upbringing. Most of the nobles were of Roman stock, the remnants of the conquerors mixed with the once conquered, and were mostly Christian. He had trouble enough keeping them in line, and a holy war was not the way to go about it.

Gorlois had been a Christian and as far as he had known, so was Igraine. We had grown up participating in the rites, both at Tintagel and Camelot, but now that we were older, we knew that one cannot both be one of the Wise and a Christian. Uther was lax in his own observances and welcomed Merlin, who could not hide his Druid learning.

A priest had been brought to perform the ceremony. Or was he a bishop? I confess, I did not know then the difference. I thought them all rather strange. These men who shut themselves away, denied themselves any of the rich experiences of life, to practice their confusing religion. How could there be only one God in a world so vast? And he a man? Surely, it takes both man and woman to bring forth life?

As the priest intoned the blessing, I looked down at my hand strangely, as though an extra finger had sprouted. There was now a ring there, of burnished gold. A little piece of metal that meant so much.

"You may kiss the bride," the priest said.

Before I could react, Nentres touched his lips to mine. I ground my foot down hard against the floor so I did not shame him by pulling away. I wanted to wrinkle my mouth in distaste, even as a strange flutter took place in my stomach.

In quick succession, like deals struck at a market stall, all of us were married, and all of us were queens. The men all went to congratulate one another and left us standing together, three sisters, three brides.

Morgause could not bear to stand beside me, so she strode off to join her friends, those daughters of Uther's nobles who were fostered at our court, but with whom I had little in common. My sister was my only link to their self-serving vanity.

"I do not fault you, Elaine," said Morgan. "If I too had known of Uther's plans, I would have cast some spell to ensure I emerged with the best of the spoils."

"I did not know," I replied sharply. "Uther told me nothing. I found out when you did."

She looked at me askance. "Hard to believe, that is. You are his dear favourite, little blond Elaine who has forgotten our father."

"I have not forgotten...never mind, this is not the place. There was no charm cast."

Morgan shrugged. "Perhaps. Either way, look at us, we are queens!"

She leant in close to whisper. "I am stuck with fat old Uriens, but that is Uther's mistake. I will take the kingdom of Gore and rise against him. I will kill him, and Merlin too. I shall be the High Queen of Britain, and Gorlois shall be avenged. Join me sister?"

I stared at her agape. She drew back and smiled at my shock. "You have not the stomach for this game, I think. Speak not of what I just said."

"Morgan, leave us," commanded Igraine, emerging from the crowd of people who rushed to flatter her with kind words about her beautiful daughters and their wonderful marriages. "I will come to speak to you soon, but Elaine is leaving tonight."

Morgan inclined her head, a vicious barb resting behind her tongue. She disappeared to unknown places, leaving our mother and me together in the hall.

"I am leaving tonight?" I questioned, my chest tightening.

"Yes," Igraine replied, in a tone that brooked no argument. She laced my arm into the crook of her elbow, and together we walked towards my chamber.

"Elaine," she began. "I trust I do not need to explain the duties of a wife, especially on this night?"

"No mother, you did so quite thoroughly before. Too thoroughly perhaps, to a fourteen year old girl."

"Best you were prepared, some girls are married younger than you or I were" she replied. Her voice wavered, and she swallowed the rising emotions. "Your grandmother never spared me the realities of life, and I am thankful for it."

"Mother..." She patted my hand to hush me.

"I have had much time to think about my life, these past twelve years. There is much you know, witnessed too, and much you cannot conceive of. I have done wrong in pursuit of my goals. I am not here for absolution, and no God I worship would give it. I paid my debts, first in blood and then in sorrow. Promise me, that all I have done, that it has not been for naught."

"I know not what you ask of me, mother."

"It is simple. Your brother, Arthur. We do not know him as we should. Why, if we passed him on the road, I have no doubt we would not know it was him. But he is the once and future king, and you must support him. I have foreseen it. His ascension is not long to come."

"Uther is truly dying then? From Morgan's curse?"

"Her curse, yes, or perhaps it is just his time. Some men are born with weak hearts, and others strain them with worry and exertion. I know not the truth of her spell, for it is the blackest magic. I cannot fathom where she learnt it, if it was not just simple mummery. But when Uther goes from this world, we must prepare the way for Arthur."

"What can I do? Surely you...?"

"There is naught I can do. The kingdom balances on a knife edge, and the rulers will struggle with the thought of a king we have never seen before, and him raised by Merlin. No doubt Merlin will come up with some plan, but the kings and lords will still rebel. When Uther dies, I will flee into sanctuary at Glastonbury, because the old laws still hold sway, and say that if a man can claim the queen, then the kingdom is his fairly won. And that cannot happen. Merlin may also contrive to be rid of me too, for fear I might turn Arthur against him, or lead the boy into foolishness."

"Will you stay in Glastonbury?" I asked.

"Perhaps, or your brother might welcome me back to court. I do not know what the future will hold, though I have tried to see. Whatever the outcome, you must hold sway over Nentres, and keep him loyal."

"How will I ever do that?" I asked. My head was spinning from those powerful words she threw at me, like arrows at an enemy's shield.

Igraine smirked, and she did not seem that she had aged at all. "Men are simple creatures, though they present themselves otherwise. Keep a good hall for him, make sure there is always food and wine, flatter him with your beauty and compliments, and when the time comes, bear his children. I have taught you spells to this end, but many women do this without the art to help them."

"Is that all I am to be? Like a sow in the field, shuffling around her muck and delivering litter after litter to the farmer?"

"Well, when you put it like that, it does not sound so appealing. But what more could you possibly want? Food? A bed to sleep in? New clothes when you want them? Servants to do your bidding?"

I was at a loss for a reply. She hid it well, that her formative years had been harsh, shivering and starving by the coast. To me, having lived all my life in the great castles of Tintagel and Camelot, those things were a given.

"It is all I have wanted," she continued. "These past few years, to see you married so well. I thought I would have a hand in your marriage contract, but Uther has chosen well regardless."

She reached out to me and stroked the side of my face. She looked as if she was to say more to me, or open her arms to embrace me, but neither occurred. She simply shrugged and returned to whatever occupied her mind.

Bronwyn helped me pack, Igraine barking instructions from the corner of the room. The porter carried the heaped chest to the door, full of my dresses and the little jewellery I had. There was also pewter plate inside, as well as delicately embroidered linens for my trousseau. Igraine had tucked a little pouch of gold coins in behind all these, as well as a small box of things one of the Wise might need.

I went to the door of Camelot too, changing from my wedding dress, which mother said I must keep for occasions of state in Garlot until I had a wardrobe of my own, wearing instead an old cream gown of hers that she had adjusted to fit me. I pulled on a fur-lined cloak, the air still chilly from Morgause's conjuring.

Out in the courtyard, the porter was loading my chest onto a cart. Nentres sat in the back, watching us approach.

"Nentres has no carriage apparently," said Igraine. "I must see to your sisters, they leave upon the morn."

And, with that, she was gone, with no more words to say to me, even though some girls went to be married and never saw their family again for a decade, or some never returned at all, dying in their child bed. I wanted to cry.

Morgause was there, waiting in the shadows as I approached the cart. She pointed at me, with her left hand, and I drew back. The right hand to heal, the left hand to harm. A witch should never point, especially with her left hand.

"I hope you feel the pain of my betrayal," she said.

"I never betrayed you!" I cried, looking about for our mother to rescue me as she had before.

"You did, you worked a spell and left me out!"

"I did not! But you will be happy with Lot, I can see it."

"Be that as it may. I never want to see you again. Do not dare write to me."

She turned on her heel, back inside the castle. I had only the option of moving forward, as the great door of Camelot shut behind me. I walked towards the cart, and Nentres held out his hand to help me up. I took his hand and heaved myself up into the cart beside him. He looked at me, a strange expression on his face, and then ordered the driver to take us on.

Chapter Three

The kingdom of Garlot is a strange place for those who grew up in the southern lands like me. Cornwall was wild, yes, but Garlot was wilder yet. They had submitted to the Romans in name only, and no man of Garlot lived a Roman life. There were no villas, no robes, and few Christians.

The journey was uneventful, and no further than the distance I travelled from Tintagel to Camelot. I thought we would stop, as dusk began to settle, but we pressed on. Nentres spoke little during the journey, occasionally pointing out landmarks of interest and once, strangely, patting my hand and telling me how blessed he was to have me for his queen.

It did not occur to me, as the cart trundled onto my new home, that I would be a queen: that I would have subjects to rule and princes to bear. I am glad that it did not, or I would have leapt from the cart and made off into the night.

We arrived at the fortress, Caer Mor, as night had lain firmly across the land. It was nothing like the proud Camelot or the windswept Tintagel. It sat within a ring fence of tree trunks driven into the ground and bound together with lengths of leather. There were several wooden outbuildings scattered about, like the type the Saxon settlers had built along our eastern coast.

The central hall was the bastard child of wood and stone. Which building material had come first was unknown, but either a wooden fortress had been shored up with stone, or it was a stone building whose holes were patched with wood. It was a few levels high, and a strange angular shape, so that none could approach without being seen. It looked more like one of Uther's war camps than my future home.

Nentres helped me from the cart. He tried to manoeuvre me onto the paved stone path that led to the hall, but the hem of my cream gown swept across the muck nonetheless. I tried to keep the look of disgust from my face. He led me inside. The place was deserted, only the men that had accompanied us milling about.

We entered the hall. Nentres' hall was nothing like the grandeur of Camelot, designed to hold and home at least a hundred men in one sitting, draped from eave to corner in Uther's pennants, banners, and standards.

The ceiling was low, low enough that I might swing myself up into the rafters if I so chose. A young Morgan would have had a field day hiding and spying up there. There was only a lonely, much repaired standard bearing the fruitful tree of Garlot propped up in a corner. A fire burned in the stone pit in the centre, the smoke wafting up through the chimney above. Furs lay strewn about the hall, and their bulk and rustles led me to believe that some warriors were bedded down in the sides of the room, as is custom. They did not stir, or come to greet me.

"Come," said Nentres, beckoning me. "Warm yourself by the fire."

I step forward and held out my hands to its crackle. From the shadows emerged an old woman, withered and with long grey hair to her shoulders, fringing the rough homespun dress she wore. She picked up a wolf pelt and draped it over my shoulders. I took it gratefully and pulled it over my narrow shoulders, ignoring the fusty smell that emanated from it.

"Are you hungry?" he asked, gesturing to the communal pot, swinging gently in its trivet.

I shook my head. He looked to the old woman.

"Take your new queen to her chamber."

She nodded. He twisted his mouth, as though he had more to say, but thought better of it and bid me goodnight. I followed the old woman up a twisting stone staircase to my chambers, a tallow candle lit before her to guide our way in the dark. I could think of nothing to say, and this woman was much unlike Bronwyn, who thought nothing of addressing her betters without leave.

"Forgive me, but what is your name?" I asked.

"Mila," she replied

"Where does the king sleep?"

"Normally in the room we have given for your chambers, my queen, but he will sleep down in the hall tonight until you have settled in."

I was relieved. There would be no bedding ceremony as some kings would have it. Mother's instruction and Morgause's stories, courtesy of the older girls, did not make it sound at all enjoyable.

She opened a stout wooden door, leading into a chamber. A chill wind blew in from the stone window, which had not the rough greenish glass of my window at home, or even a fabric drape. There was a bed, a stout construct built for two people and well made up, my chest at its foot. A table sat in the corner, writing materials strewn about it, and in the corner an ewer and bowl for washing. There was no fire lit.

"Have you need of anything, my queen?" she asked.

I shook my head dumbly. My wedding chest and travelling bag had been brought up and sat neatly at the end of the bed.

"I will take my leave of you, then." She bowed and left, shutting the door behind her.

I thought she would offer to undress me, and ask if I wanted her to sleep in the bed with me, to warm it, like a proper lady in waiting. But at this small castle, she was probably stewardess, house-keeper, and chatelaine all in one, and had not the time to tend to a sixteen-year-old queen. I should have ordered her to do so, to light a fire, but I remembered not ever having to ask a servant for anything. Bronwyn was well-trained, a lady-in-waiting her whole life.

I went to the door and drew the bolt. I cast off my dress, cloak, and pelt to the floor. Mila could pick it up in the morning. I battled with the stays of my corset, and let all of Bronwyn's trickery fall too, though I kicked it beneath the bed so no one could see.

There was something that had been bothering me from the moment I saw Nentres. He looked so familiar to me, yet I had never seen his face before. I had need of guidance, and could not look to my mother for it.

In my travelling box, there was a little oil and a few herbs. Mother said it was all she could spare, and that I ought to make my own store. I sprinkled the herbs in a loose circle around the bed, careful to ration what little I had. With the oil, I drew the sacred symbol upon my brow. I lay down on the bed and closed my eyes, chanting the sounds that would bring about dream-walking. My body gave a jolt and spirit roamed free.

The Temple is unlike any building that still stands in Britain, for they were all sacked when the Romans drew back. It stands atop a hill, and the path is surrounded on all sides by dense forest. In-comprehensibly tall, it gleams in white marble.

Torches burn on each side of the great bronze door which should always be open if your intentions are pure. Inside, statues of long-forgotten personages adorn the recesses of the walls. In the centre, lit by great hanging censers is the altar, is an altar, built of the same white marble as the temple, as though it all had been carved from a single giant block. Mother could never explain why it looks as it does. It just does.

Upon the altar lies the Great Book, a giant scroll that one could never unwind if they spent a lifetime in that place. It is ancient but has never faded after time immemorial. The Great Book holds many secrets, and often we are not permitted to look, or see what we do not wish to, but the images were clear upon the paper that time.

Hundreds upon of hundreds of drawings of a man and woman, dark haired and light-haired respectively, hand in hand throughout history. In Roman times, and in times far further, with strange creatures, bizarre clothes and in fantastic places no storyteller could conceive of. The names were different every time, but I recognised these two nonetheless. It was I and each time I was with Nentres.

"Soul-mates," I said aloud, breaking the deathly silence of the Temple. My vision blurred, the Temple moving past me with great speed and a strange sensation like I was rising very high and falling very fast at the same time. To speak is to break the spell because the greatest of magic is done in silence.

I awoke in the bed with a jump, as though I had fallen from a great height. My stomach twisted. How could we be soul-mates? I barely knew him, yet he was one-half of my soul? I should have been comforted, but instead, I felt like a cornered fox. The story of my life had been written long ago. I tried to fend off the hopelessness this thought offered and tried to find some comfort in sleep.

I was awoken the next morning by a great noise like thunder, though the skies were clear. Getting up, I looked out of the stone framed window, casting about for the source of the noise. There, in the yard, were at least thirty men, marching up and down in tight lines. I watched them, fascinated. Sometimes they formed the shape of an arrow or a trident, or lined up side-by-side, their shields interlocking, before breaking and then regrouping, starting the drill all over again.

There was a knock at the door.

"Enter," I called, thinking it was Mila come to rouse and dress me.

It was not. Instead, Nentres entered the room, looking more unruly than the previous day. Our wedding day. How strange it seemed, to think I had myself a husband. I was quite aware that I wore only a plain white shift, quite threadbare from a year's wearing. My embroidered linen garments remained folded inside my travelling chest, unneeded on my wedding night.

"Did you sleep well?" he asked.

I nodded, inching towards the end of the bed where I could reach for the fur throw to cover myself.

"Good...um...we do not keep regular hours as such here in Caer Mor, you are free to wake and break your fast when you please, just let Mila know."

"Thank you. I am sorry you spent the night in the hall, I know this is your room."

"It is fine." He gave me a gentle smile. "It reminds me of the days when I was still a prince."

The room grew silent.

"What were you watching?" he asked. "At the window?"

"Oh, your men. The battle drills. They do this every morning?"

"Yes, every morning and evening," he said with pride. "Those are the landless warriors, second and third sons who hope to win my favour through their prowess in battle so that I might grant them land or make them a good match."

"And they need all this training?"

"They have little other occupation. More so now, my treaty with Uther means I must supply him with a standing troop of fifty to patrol our border with Camelot and be prepared to raise a further levy of three hundred."

It seems such a large amount of men, though I knew Uther commanded a standing army of least a thousand of solely his own troops. I do not think I knew even fifty people.

"Normally I would be with them, but I thought you might like to ride with me to the market town, purchase anything you need."

"Very well...Nentres," I replied, forcing my tongue into silence as it reached for the etiquette of titles.

"Excellent," he said, clapping his hands and rubbing them together, almost disguising the red tinge of his cheeks. "Let me know when you are ready to leave. I will fetch Mila for you, she should dress you, should she not? We have not had a lady here in some time, you see, so we are a little un-prepared."

After Mila dressed me with unpracticed hands, I went down to the hall and broke my fast with a dish of milky oats. Some warriors came and bowed before me, and I had to race to remember Igraine's lessons on the taking of oaths. I hoped I had sent them away proud of their new queen, not somehow offended.

Some time later, Nentres brought me a woollen cloak. In a bold red, and cut so, it could only have been a lady's cloak. I wondered where it had come from.

"Dug this out for you," he said, by way of explanation. "You will need it for the ride. It is cold on the road this time of year. Oh, you can ride, can you not?"

"Yes, if you do not mind me riding astride. I cannot ride side-saddle, I never had much practice at it."

He smiled. "I am glad you said that because it occurred to me that I have never seen a side-saddle in all of Garlot. It is the Londinium fashion I think."

I took the arm he proffered, and we went out into the courtyard, where a saddled bay mare was waiting for a rider. He helped me to swing myself up onto her, and I clung on for dear life. Riding was a skill that was considered a necessary instruction in Camelot, but one with minimum attention given to it.

Morgause would have suggested she ride pillion, pressed close behind him. She had learnt well from my mother. I could not be so bold, no matter how handsome he looked that morning. To think of Morgause, many miles from me and unlikely to see one another for many years, parting with angry words, pained me. I clutched at my stomach absently, the hurt so real it could have been a canker in my gut.

"Are you unwell?" he asked, bringing his own warhorse, a stout black creature, to a halt.

I shook my head. He told the horse to walk on and I followed. Behind us, two silent guards rode behind us. We made our way out of the fortress gates and onto the road which had been obscured by the sides of the cart and the darkness last night. I could see the flagstones laid by the Romans, and how some had crumbled.

"This road is very poorly maintained," I said, and then winced as I realised how it sounded. "I am sorry, I..."

He shook his head, and I could see a smile warm his face. "I know what you meant. There is only one of these roads in Garlot, from Caer Mor to Merriwyn, the town we will visit. It was all the Romans needed to build. The knowledge of building roads is somewhat forgotten to us here."

He pointed to a trail poking its head from a forested area. "That," he said, "is one of the paths we normally use in Garlot. They criss-cross the forests. I think they came from deer trails originally and we widened them over time. Until the Romans cut down much of our forests."

"My sister, Morgan, she might know something of the Roman roads from her schooling, or know of someone we could ask."

"Good, and we could have them brought to repair it. You may write to the Queen of Gore any time you wish, you need only inform Mila, or our castle scribe Portimus, and they will see to it."

"Who is Portimus?" I asked.

Nentres gave a slight chuckle. "Clearly you have not met him then, because you could never forget him. He is quite a fat man and fond of food in excess. I found him through a friend in town, who said he was looking for work as a clerk. Few of my men can read and write, you see, and kingdoms run on paper these days. I think he might have been a Christian monk, on the run from his holy house."

73

"What makes you say that?"

"His Roman name for starters, and his ignorance of our Gods. He talks very little about his life before here, and it is never the same story twice. And his hair sits quite unusually, I think he once had the top shaved and it has never grown back quite right."

"He sounds strangely amusing," I said.

"Yes," he agreed. "He is indeed." He smiled at me and I smiled back.

We reached Merriwyn in less in an hour. We came upon open gates built in a sturdy wooden wall, and a sentry, upon catching sight of us, ran off to spread the word the king had arrived. We dismounted outside the gates, and the guardsmen took ownership of our horses.

Merriwyn hummed with life, loud and busy, unlike what I had seen so far of Garlot. There were round buildings of wattle and daub, and then there were great two-storey buildings, square and made of sturdy wood like the kind found in Londinium. People rushed about, herding livestock, fetching water, working at the tasks of their lives while their children played. I could smell the roasting of meat and hear the cranking of the water pump. This vibrancy passed to me, and I grew excited to see the place.

Along the main dirt road, which cleaved the town in two, stalls had been erected on both sides, and people hovered around to look at the wares piled upon them. There were foodstuffs, household goods, and fabrics, and I became curious.

As I made to go to a stall, I noticed we had been discovered. A well-dressed man came running towards us, before almost flinging himself to the ground. This man babbled his welcome, offering food and refreshment, and other unintelligible mutterings. Nentres pulled him to his feet and asked after the state of the town and how the market was performing that day. I gathered he was the headman of the town.

People began to emerge and come towards us. The guardsmen placed their hands upon the hilt of their swords but did not become threatening. Some stood and stared at us while the braver few began to approach and bow. When Nentres announced that I was his queen, people took even more interest, especially the women. They observed my dress, my hair, my manner, and I hoped they found me satisfactory. It was somewhat overwhelming, so I was grateful when Nentres took my arm and led me to the first of the stalls.

Uther was fond of public appearances and often brought Morgause and me to some of the nearby towns for the people to see us, bribed with sweetmeats and trinkets from the stalls. He relished it, the people throwing themselves down into the muck before him, refusing to take the coins he offered for their wares. They thanked him for making them safe, or repairing a well, or suchlike, and he lapped it up like a cat before a bowl of milk.

Nentres was Uther's opposite. As anyone would move to bow, he would rush to them and beg them not to, and anyone who complimented him was met with a face blushing redder than any maiden.

He followed me from stall to stall, and anything I wanted, he said I could have it, gesturing for our guards to pay the vendor and take up our burdens. I confess, I went a little mad, this being the first time I had truly been free at a market, and went home that day with many things I did not need.

There was a stall outside a blacksmith's forge, selling tools. From a peg hung a great seax knife,

75

like the Saxons wielded. I had seen many presented to Uther as trophies over the years, and Igraine once hit me a slap when asked if I might hold one. It was a thick blade with a dangerous point. I wondered what it would be like to be the owner of such a thing, to wield it in battle. I wondered if it made you strong or brave, and if it was as heavy as it looked.

Nentres caught my glance. "Do you want to visit that stall? Do you need pins or…"

His voice trailed off as I imagined he struggled to think of sufficiently feminine items one could obtain from a blacksmith. I shook my head, debating whether or not to tell him about my interest in the knife. I decided against it after the voice of Igraine reminded me how improper a lady with a knife would be.

"Just looking around." I unrolled some of the bolt of fabric before me, feeling its softness. Its blue colour was rich, and would make a pretty dress, but still sober enough for daywear. "I like this fabric," I added.

He smiled. "Then you shall have it."

I told the merchant how much I needed and he cut it with ease. Nentres gestured to the guardsman to pay the man and add it to my bundle.

"You will look very pretty in that colour," my new husband said, as we walked back to the horses. I tried not to blush and worked to quash the nervous twist of my stomach.

We returned from the market town, and Mila and I went upstairs to put away my fairings. Caer Mor had no presence-chamber or solar like Camelot, but Nentres arranged for us to dine in a small room off the hall, which appeared to serve many purposes. Taking a look at it, I contrived that I should make it into a not-quite-solar, for how many kings and queens spent all of their time in the hall in the company of their vassals? Then again, I thought, who am I to change the way things have been done here? I abandoned my plan almost as soon as I had thought of it.

The dinner was very fine and served on the pewter plate which was a gift from Uther. But soon, our conversation faded, and I grew more and more unsettled by the silence. All of Igraine's teachings failed me one by one. I could think of no compliments to pay him, no interesting tales with which to regale him. Pushing my breasts forwards elicited no reaction from him, merely making me feel uncomfortable. I had questions for him, but not the confidence to ask them.

Still, it seemed not to dampen his spirit, as he smiled down the table at me. He looked at me in the fading candlelight.

"Might I visit you?" he asked.

"Anytime you like. This is your castle after all."

"No," he said, turning his head away. "I mean, might I visit your chamber?"

I nodded, slow, deep and deliberate, so that I did not shake my head. Igraine would not want me to refuse, and my marriage depended upon it. I must please him, and get with child, and seal Uther's peace.

So I opened the door, as willing as I could, sixteen and nervous when the knock came. I had dressed in my embroidered shift, a delicate fabric woven by a true master of thread. My hair was loose about my shoulders and shone in the candlelight.

"You look beautiful," he said, as he took my hand and led me to the bed.

The act itself was not unenjoyable, despite Nentres' surprising bulk exerting its weight upon my slender form and the uncomfortable creak of the old wooden bed. There was only a little pain to begin with and no great deluge of blood as I feared. No, it was within me, afterwards, that was most strange. I should have felt warm, but instead, I was cold. I had never been so physically close to someone and yet never so alone.

I rolled away from Nentres and pulled the sheets tighter around me. He had enjoyed himself, that was clear, but I was simply confused. Was this the price of Uther's peace? My body? Had an evening with me bought Camelot a standing troop of fifty and a levy of three hundred?

Nentres did not feel like my soulmate. He felt like my owner. Did he buy me with a trip to the market and a tasty feast? I felt weighty too. Was I now with child? Had we conceived the prince of Garlot, or must we try again and again until I was pregnant like we were breeding horses in a stable?

Camelot was counting on me, Uther was counting on me. Somewhere, in some faraway hall, at Merlin's side, little Arthur was counting on me to preserve his future kingdom. It all felt like too much, so much so that I should scream like a madwoman. Wife, queen, mother, sister, and the living paper of a peace treaty. I would surely fail.

Nentres rose at dawn to lead the training. I waited endlessly for Mila to come, for no page slept outside my door, like in Camelot, to summon her to me. She finally arrived late into the morning, bearing a trencher of leftovers to break my fast. She dressed me a little quicker, practice improving her hand.

"I suppose, Mila," I began, "that you and I must have a discussion about the running of the castle. You must show me the stores, the kitchen, the laundry and the account book."

"Begging your pardon, my queen, but Queen Gertrude, the king's late mother, never busied herself with such things. Best left to me, Your Highness."

"Where is the Queen Mother?" I asked.

It was unusual for her not to have come to greet me, and I knew the answer as soon as I posed the question. I felt like a fool.

"Died of that sickness we had, two years back. Nasty business that was, killed the old King Bruden too."

"And Nentres has no brothers or sisters?"

"Not for want of trying, my queen. The sickness killed his sister Adel too, and his mother lost many children still in the womb."

"Oh. Well, if I am not to help in the running of the castle, or have the companionship of the royal family, I must meet my ladies."

"Your ladies, Highness? I know it is true for most places, but we have no ladies here, apart from the servants. All the families of note live in their own steadings, quite far from here, and do not send their daughters here. There was no need before, having no queen. But I suppose you could command them to do so?"

I shook my head, a little bewildered. "No, not now at least. I could embroider?"

"Little need for it, Highness, we dress plainly here, but I'll fetch you some mending if you want busy work."

I nodded and sat in the chair by the window. How was I to occupy myself from then on? There were few books to be had by the looks of things, no ladies to make my friends, no household to command. What was I to do for diversion? Muck out the horses? Or was I to begin my tasks of bearing heirs right away, devote myself to it without distraction? I felt as though I should fling myself from the window.

I ate, I slept, I walked the courtyard and occasionally I visited Merriwyn with Mila, though she did not allow me too much say in the purchase of household goods, so I had to content myself with obtaining items with the few coins Nentres gave to me with each visit. I still had my bolt of blue fabric and had been slowly making it into a dress.

With all the free time I had, it should have been done in a week or two, but I drew it out for fear of losing all occupation. When it was done, I decided to add delicate embroidery to the wrists, the neckline, the waist and the hem. Perversely, when I made a mistake or did shoddy work, I experienced a little thrill, as it meant the making would last a little longer.

When it was done, I was resolved to purchase another bolt, perhaps in green, and do such fine work again. I would be the best-dressed queen in Britain, but with nowhere to wear such things to. When I was deep in work, my mind would wander and I would imagine a life as a seamstress. I thought I could make a decent living from my work, and fantasised often about running away to open a dressmaker's.

Nentres and I spoke very little those weeks. I rebuked much of his effort to make conversation and made none of my own. He, in turn, increased his drills to three times a day, and would patrol areas of Garlot that had never needed patrolling, putting an end to imaginary bandits and poachers.

Sometimes he would be gone for days at a time, on business for the crown. Once, he went to a feast

held by Uther and did not invite me. When I had
heard he had visited Camelot without me, I panted
with anger, like a heifer in labour, but he merely
shrugged and pointed out that he did not know
whether I should like to visit my mother and step-
father since I never had much to say to him.

I threw down my spoon at dinner, splashing the
red sauce covering our venison over the table. I do
not like venison, but Nentres had it served anyway
against my orders. I, in turn, had a pie made of
pears, which I knew he hated. He looked up at me.

"Yes?" he asked.

I turned over my thoughts, choosing my words.
I could tell him again how angry I was he did not
take me. I could tell him I was bored beyond belief. I could tell him that waking each day was a
challenge in willpower. But instead, I chose to lash
out and shame him.

"Your Highness," I addressed him, my tone
cold. "Your queen would be much obliged if you
were to consider her indisposed and find yourself
other accommodation for the evening."

"Fine," he barked.

We had not repeated the act of bedding since I
had given him my maidenhead. Each night, when
he reached for me, I feigned a headache, or said
my womanly parts were troubled, and he had given
up asking. Still, I had not denied him his bed to
sleep upon, it was his castle after all. But the insult
of leaving me behind rankled me far too much to
be so accommodating.

A darkness descended over me the following
day. Sunlight came through the window and as
soon as I caught sight of it, I turned away from it
and wished I had no cause to see another sunrise.
I wished to fall into a deep sleep, like a maiden in

a story, to wake only when Garlot and Camelot had crumbled into dust.

I did not get up to break my fast. I sent Mila away each time she came to dress me. The only time I stood that whole day was to use the privy. Igraine would have accused me of sulking, and would have had Bronwyn slap my legs until I rose, but she was not here to do so. She was in Camelot, where she had let Uther sell me into marriage.

And when Mila came again the next morning, I refused to get up again, and told her to bring me some bread and set it upon the table, and leave me be until I called for her. She did come, though, multiple times, asking if I was unwell, and did not leave until I threatened to throw the candle holder at her. The next day, she came only once, to leave a new bit of bread, and take the old one away.

I was content, laying there on my back, staring at the ceiling and counting the stones in the walls. I could count and count to my heart's content. While I was counting, I did not have to speak to Nentres, I did not have to cry and I did not have to think.

It did not please Nentres when I had behaved thus for nearly a month. I heard the shouting from the corridor, nothing distinct, but the harsh barking of a man in anger. Still, it was not enough to rouse me. There was a clamour in the corridor, and Nentres could be heard shouting "Where is she? Is she abed yet?" Then, with an almighty bang, the door flung open and struck the wall. Nentres stood in the doorway, heaving with exertion and rage.

"Get up!" he bellowed, red-faced and panting. "Do you know how you shame me? Lying in bed from dawn to dusk? You are a queen! Get up and rule!"

In a sudden surge, I sprung up from the bed and met him head on. I stood barely an inch from him and screamed into his face. "I am a golden cup, sold by Camelot and bought by Garlot!"

He drew back, stung. He twisted his lips, breathing heavily like a great snorting bull.

"I think I have done well, to be so kind, when I am denied my right to visit you."

"You have no right to anything of mine!" I spat. "Least of all that."

He bit down on the words that must have been fighting to come forth.

"Fine, Your Highness," he replied, as if by rote. "Do as thou wilt."

Many a month went by, cold and alone in the tower of Caer Mor. Nentres did not return to the chamber, and the whole castle knew that we were married thus only in name. Mila's fierce tongue quickly put paid to the gossip of the serving girls, but still the warriors sniggered. A king unmanned by his queen. Had he not been prince and king their whole life, they would have seized the throne from him. How could they believe he would protect their lands and families when he could not even sleep in his own bed?

I hated myself. Far from home, without a child, a husband who despised me. My letters to Morgause went unanswered. I did not write to Igraine. She would merely write back to chastise me, accuse me of being a spoiled brat and ask me why had not worked the magic she had taught me to bring forth a child and seal Uther's peace. All I could think of was that my year and a day were elapsing fast, and I could return under Nentres' promise. But would he still allow it? And would Uther take me back into Camelot, the stepdaughter who could not fulfil the one task he had set her?

Morgan wrote to me, though, in the hand of the people who lived here when Britain was still young and from whom the Wise are descended. She was compelled to conceal her writings from the world because they were treacherous indeed, and kings like Uriens beheaded their wives for less.

It is not pleasant, she wrote. *He is a randy bastard, and will not be kept from me. Quick with his fists too, but only when he has an audience. He would not dare beat me in private, he knows I would nail his cock to the wall. I have tried to be rid of him repeatedly. Short of poisoning his food, there is nothing yet that can get him. But it suits me for him to be king, for I am queen only while he is alive. When he dies, he will have a whole host of sons and their wives squabbling for the throne, not to mention his illegitimate children.*

Bring Garlot to heel. Do what I am powerless to do. Bring Nentres under your thrall, silence dissension among the warriors, and when the time is right, march upon Gore. Unite the kingdoms, and then turn to Cornwall and Northgales. Imagine it, the whole west coast under the rule of us sister-queens? Surely even Uther Pendragon would fear such an alliance?

I burnt that letter, for fear one among us in Garlot could read it, and wrote no more of such things to Morgan. Her letters continued in a similar tone until she sensed that I had no desire to do such a thing, and more banal things became her topic of choice. For every three letters she sent, I replied with only one. I grew tired of relating to her the trifling activities of my day and went back to counting bricks.

Mila entered my chamber one day. She had already brought my morning bread, so I ignored her. She stood by the wall, her head down. After some time of studiously staring at the wall, I sat up in the bed and looked at her.

"What is it Mila?"

"The King commands your presence downstairs."

"Tell him I am indisposed."

"He said you would say that and that I am to ignore you, and help you dress, or else he would send a warrior to drag you down in your shift."

I debated whether the satisfaction of provoking him to such ends would outweigh the humiliation it would subject me to, and pride won out in the end. I stood up and allowed Mila to remove my shift and then lace me into a gown after I had washed cursorily from the ewer.

I made my way down to the hall, avoiding the eyes of the warriors, and Mila gestured to me to enter the anteroom. Nentres was there, sat in a chair. He nodded to me, and I curtsied. That was the most interaction we had had in months.

"We will be going on progress soon," he announced. "I wish to visit the steadings of my warriors, and see if Garlot has changed any this past year."

I wanted to be surly and roll my eyes, but the idea of a progress intrigued me. Uther had several during my years at court but we were never allowed to accompany him. Only my mother had that honour, casting him resentful glances as they departed from Camelot. I had seen very little of Britain in my life, and even Garlot would make for an interesting experience. So I merely nodded in assent.

He looked at me warily. "On progress, certain things will be expected of you."

"Like what?"

"To greet the nobles, to converse with them, ask about their farming and so on. And the women

85

of the house, if you can make friends with them and impress them, it will be of much use. I would like you to show honour to some of the warriors by sharing your dish and pouring their wine. And..."

I stared at him expectantly. "Do continue."

"You might have to sing in the hall, or recite a poem. Igraine taught you something?"

I nodded. "You shall have your spectacle."

I could sing, not that I would ever make for any sort of entertainer. The harp too, I could make some pretence of melody.

"And...there will be... That is to say... We will be expected to share a bed, and show some affection."

"I will not embarrass you any further than I already have."

"Thank you. We depart in three days."

He looked as though he had more to say, but he simply gestured that I could go. I bowed my leave and withdrew.

The third day came and I dragged myself from my bed with all my might. Mila had instructions from the king to arrange my hair, braiding it carefully to support a golden coronet atop my head. After she had laced me into my fine blue dress, pinned carefully underneath for riding, she helped me fix elegant sapphire earrings in place. I had not known I had access to such jewels.

When I went out into the courtyard, there was no horse and groom waiting for me, only a mounted Nentres staring at me impatiently.

"Am I not to go?" I asked. "There is no horse."

"You will ride with me," he replied, reaching down to help me onto the horse behind him. I did not move. He tucked his bottom lip beneath his teeth and scrunched his eyebrows. The face of an exasperated man who had clearly been expecting that discussion.

"I cannot spare the horse for you alone. And I do not yet have a carriage suitable for such a journey. As you have seen, there are no Roman roads in Garlot. We must take the forest paths, and horseback is quickest."

His men had begun to stare. My cheeks started to flush. Before I could change my mind, I took his gloved hand. He removed his foot from the stirrup and I placed mine in, then taking his hand, I swung myself up behind him.

"Hold on," he said and gave the horse a tap with his boot. I took a hold of the saddle, but the leather was rough without gloves and the angle of my grip was difficult to maintain. We moved on and I cursed myself when I lost my grip and was forced to grab his shoulders.

"My waist, Elaine. You will fall if you hold onto my shoulders."

"Your shoulders will be fine."

"You will most certainly fall."

"Then I will fall."

"Suit yourself," he declared, and we continued on our ride.

He was right. Many times I did wobble on the horse, but I staunchly refused to take hold of any part of him bar his shoulders.

We passed through Merriwyn, but Nentres' only contribution to progress there were waves and nods. After an hour, we stopped to water the horses and rest our tired legs. There was a little waterfall, hidden here in the forest, a babbling jet of water cascading down dark black stones and over little green pockets of moss. It splashed against the shallow gully from which the horses drank before it continued its journey onward and underground.

"To where do we travel first?" I asked him, as he passed me the skin of water. I was surprised how freely they drank of it in Garlot. They either did not get sick that often or knew where clean water could be easily got.

"To the steading of Meron. He is a powerful...lord."

"Why do you hesitate?"

"He was not born so, only a lowly villein, but he slew his master and married the dead man's wife, and has been a little king in his own right."

"Do you fear treason from him?"

"You are very direct for a woman."

I did not answer. He continued. "No, I do not fear him, as such. But he has many warriors at his disposal. He is a warlord, truly more so than anyone who has ever held that title. If there were no battles to be fought, and I did not need his men, he would have no use and no power. It has been like that under my father, and will be like that for however long I may live."

"Thank you," I said, as he finished.

"For what?" he asked.

"Being honest with me," was my reply.

He pulled himself up onto the horse and then reached down for me. I swung myself up again, but this time, I took hold of his waist. I told myself it was because I did not want to fall, but even that did not ring true with me.

Within our second hour, we had reached the steading. The main residences were bounded by a high wooden wall, and the wall was so wide I could not see where the walls joined one another. It had no large central building like Caer Mor, but had many, many smaller buildings, and could safely be called a hamlet. It was so strange for me to see a man who was not a king or a high-ranking lord have such a large steading.

As we approached, we could see some commotion in the yard. People were standing in a circle, watching whatever was occurring. We drew closer, and I could see a woman, running towards us. A man so huge he could have easily have been a bear was lumbering after her, shaking his fist, his face getting redder and redder. The girl was crying and tearing at her gown in desperation.

"I won't go!" she screamed. "You can't make me, and I won't!"

The man advanced on her. "By the Gods, girl! The king approaches! Get in that bloody hall, and make yourself presentable! And you will leave tomorrow!"

Nentres geed the horse further into the courtyard and we slowed to a halt before the man.

"What is going on here?" he called.

The man, who I took to be Meron, bowed as low as his great bulk allowed. "Good King Nentres! Welcome!"

Nentres' voice brooked no argument. "I asked you a question, Meron."

"A family matter. My daughter, Nalia." He gestured for the girl to bow. "She turned sixteen this morning, and a good marriage has been arranged for her. I had been hoping to ask your approval this evening, and the girl could be married tomorrow after Your Highness leaves us."

"And to whom have you promised her."

"A son of Wythn, my Lord."

Nentres nodded. "A good match. His lands are near to here, are they not?"

"That is correct, Sire. It has put an end to our squabbles over the drainage of our adjoining lands."

"Good, good. One less thing for us to discuss this afternoon. But, forgive me, Nalia looks most distressed."

"She is reluctant, Sire. She fancies herself in love with my second, Forwin."

"I am, Sire! We are soul-mates," cried Nalia. Meron advanced on her, his club-like fist raised high to strike her, but she did not stop crying out to my husband. "Please, Highness, I do not want to marry Wythn's son, please do not permit it."

I could feel Nentres shoulders tense under my hands.

"Stop this," I whispered. "Before he hits her."

He reached around his waist, passing me the reins of the horse. I took them and moved back as far as the saddle allowed so that he might drop from the horse. He walked towards Meron, and the other man abandoned his attempts to strike his daughter, who had darted out of reach.

"Come, Nalia," said Nentres. "Your father has made you a good match, and I would a poor king to you if I denied it so that you can marry Forwin."

"But I do not love my betrothed. I love Forwin," she replied. "Please, do not make me go."

I lowered myself from the horse, seeking to comfort the poor girl. A guard appeared to take the reins from me. I wondered if, as queen, I had the power to interfere in such matters.

"Who might this beauty be?" asked Meron, turning his attention to me as I approached.

"This is my new queen," replied Nentres. "Elaine ferch Gorlois, Princess of Camelot."

He bowed to me and snatched a sleeve of Nalia's dress to pull her into a curtsey. She did not avert her eyes from me as she should from a lady of my rank, instead locking her gaze on me, watery tears imploring me to do something.

"You see, Nalia," said Meron. "The Queen must be the same age as you. I bet she did not cry to Uther Pendragon when she went to marry our King."

She did not reply. She only stared at me once more. My stomach turned with a sympathy I had never felt before.

"What if," offered Nentres. "You went only to Wythn's son for a year and a day, and if the marriage was not suitable, you could return to your father."

Though he spoke to Nalia, I could feel his eyes on me.

"Ha!" laughed Meron. "There will be no divorce, Sire. You and I both know Wythn is a sly fox. No marriage, no accord between us, and he will go right back to ignoring the lower fields as they flood."

"I will enforce it."

Meron raised an eyebrow. "Will you make camp then, outside his steading in the rainy season, to remind him to do as you bid?"

Nentres did not reply, though I could see a red flush of anger creeping up above the collar of his tunic.

"If you agree to the match, Sire," said Meron. "I will take her forth tonight, so she does not disturb the rest of your visit."

Nentres gave only the tiniest nod of his head. Nalia started screaming as though she had been speared, and tried to take off in a run, but Meron grabbed her around the waist and hoisted her from the ground. She cried out and kicked out with her feet, but he did not let go.

"Stop fighting, girl! You're going to Wythn's steading and that's final!"

"I won't go! Forwin! Forwin! Forwin!"

A tall man, with thick, red, curly hair, emerged from the hall, and started towards them, but he stopped in his tracks as Meron bellowed to him "Don't even think about it, boy!"

Nalia slid from between Meron's arms as though she were a freshly caught fish, and lay down upon the ground, pulling her cloak over her head and burrowing against the dirt. Meron tried to pull her by the cloak, but she held fast.

I moved in front of Nentres.

"Do something!" I begged.

"What do you propose I do?" he asked, his voice quiet and resigned.

"Forbid the marriage."

He leant in close. "And anger Meron?" he whispered. "I cannot."

Behind me, I could still hear the girl's screams, and the dull thuds of Meron's fists as he reigned blows upon her. My body took action before I could bid it not to. Reaching around his waist, I slid Nentres' dagger from its scabbard. Clutching it firmly in my hand, I spun away from his hand and marched on Meron.

He seemed even larger as I drew closer. Though at least two heads taller than me, I reached out my hand and pressed the blade to his throat. He stopped beating her, and I could hear his breath tightening.

"What is the meaning of this!" he hissed and turned his head as far as the blade would allow. It had already made a small nick against the flesh of his neck, but he ignored the rising red blood and its accompanying pain. Then he let forth a snort of laughter, as soon as he saw it was me from the corner of his eye, and not Forwin.

"Queen Elaine! Ha! Nentres, call off your bitch!"

The whole time Nentres had been calling to me to stop, but I ignored him. The knife was almost thrumming in my hand, I fought both the urge to drop it in the dirt and the urge to press it deeper into his neck.

"What do you hope to do here?" he asked.

I steeled myself. "I want you to stop beating your daughter. And then I want you to send a messenger to Wythn, to tell him she will be marrying Forwin."

"No." His voice was strangled, but there was no hint of fear.

My plan did not seem so effective, and I cursed my anger, my action without thought. Nalia pulled the cloak away from her face and was watching in shocked silence.

"You will do as I say, you brute!"

My voice had reached such a high pitch, I sounded like I was whistling for a hunting dog. Meron's voice, however, was still forceful, despite the blade inching deeper into his flesh.

"Trial by combat," he said. "That is how we resolve such things in these parts. Are you willing to fight me for it, my Queen?"

I looked him as keenly in the eye as our positions would allow. "I will. If that is what it takes, I will you fight you for her right to marry who she chooses."

"Stop this!" cried Nentres. He locked eyes with me, and I could see the fire of my eyes reflected in his. "Elaine, release him! Nalia will marry Forwin before the sun has set and I will make sure Wythn abides the terms of our agreement."

"You swear?" I asked Meron, pressing down slightly on the blade.

"I swear," he replied. "Summon someone to perform the ceremony."

Nalia stood up, and Forwin came to take her hand. I withdrew the blade, stepping back from Meron. He grumbled, and put up a hand to rub his neck. I handed the dagger back to Nentres, and he took it, scabbarding it with a strange look on his face. He was angry, that much was obvious, but there was something else unknown in his eyes. He looked away from me to Meron.

"There will be no retribution for this," said Meron. "Rest assured. Shall we go inside?"

Nentres strode past me, ignoring me. Meron reached out to take my arm. He tucked my hand into the crook of his elbow. To an onlooker, he looked like a dutiful host, but the force with which he grasped me could have been enough to crack my bones. I resisted the urge to scream. He leaned in close.

"I don't appreciate your interference, my Queen, not in family matters, in local business. But your ferocity becomes you. You will make a fine queen. Be careful, though. Your actions have won my respect, but such behaviour could easily cost you support elsewhere."

He patted my hand in a fatherly manner, but I could barely breathe, and did not relax until I sat in the women's part of the hall with his wife, Aleyna, and Nalia. The girl was effused with joy, and could not stop thanking me. "Thank you, my Queen!" she would exclaim.

"Forwin was going to challenge him," she explained. "But surely he would have been killed. But neither do I think I could have forgiven him if he had killed my father."

94

Whatever Meron's failings as father and vassal, he was a good host. My cup was never empty, my plate never bare. If it grew cold, a servant would bring me a fur to wear. After the quick ceremony, more a formality than anything, Nentres and Meron had begun some sort of drinking contest, downing cup after cup of ale while their warriors chanted and banged the tables.

"I think it best we retire," suggested Aleyna. "They will be at that for some time."

She cast me a knowing glance as if to say all husbands were the same, but I could not return it. I realised I knew very little about Nentres. I do not think I had ever seen him in his cups at Garlot. But then, how would I, when I rarely frequented the hall and did not share a bed with him?

We were housed in the second best bedroom in Meron's home, a snug, stout room with a bed piled high in furs. Aleyna was kind enough to help me undress, and I climbed into bed. I realised it was the first time I had been alone, bar using the privy, all day. I breathed a sigh of ease and set about falling asleep.

Some time later there was a clatter, and Nentres stumbled into the chamber. His scabbarded sword lay on the floor, clumsily kicked from its rest. "Shh!" he hushed it, a finger to his lips, as though it was a barking dog or unruly child, not an inanimate object. He giggled and divested himself of his tunic, crawling beneath the furs.

"You're drunk" I spat.

He lay back and stared at the ceiling.

"I have been long in my cups madam, it is true," he replied, lacing his hands together and smirking like his retort had been of the greatest wit and worthy of history's notation.

I rolled my eyes and turned over, huffing out a sigh. The chamber was silent, save his tossing in the bed. Then he spoke, some time later, his words just shy of slurred.

"All I ever think about is you."

"What did you say?" I turned back on my other side, fixing my gaze upon him.

"Do you not think, ever, of me? Of this marriage, of all we could be, of all we could do together? I was so proud when Merlin came bearing Uther's treaty. A marriage to a princess of Camelot, of similar age. A great beauty Merlin said, and smart too. A true queen. My Garlot was to get a queen like no other. I dreamed that night on the road to Camelot of all we could achieve. Garlot would have roads and schools, like the Romans. Maybe a...whatchamacallit...hospital? For the sick? Instead, you cried and sulked. Why?"

"I..." I was at a loss for words. I feared many things in that moment. I feared my own truths, the devastation I felt these past months. I feared that I would perhaps expose some of my own failings. I feared his fists, in case drink drove him to be a man that beats his wife. And, strangely, I feared I would hurt his feelings.

"I miss my home, my sisters, even my mother. I had no time to adjust to the thought of being married but suddenly this man was kneeling in Uther's hall. You took me away and bedded me, and I had no house to run, no companions and no occupation but to set about bearing children."

"Sorry," he replied, like a scolded child. Silence came once more until he spoke again.

"When you threatened Meron, I was so angry but so proud at the same time. Here was a woman standing up to a man that even I fear. So proud. What a queen you could be."

He turned to look at me. "I just want someone to fight for. And someone to enjoy peace with. So alone. When they all died. And a school. Learn letters instead of swordplay."

"You are not making sense."

"You're...not...making..."

With a snore, he was fast asleep. I felt the heat of his body beside me, having drawn closer to hear his ramblings. It was so different from the cold bed in Garlot, where not even Mila slept beside her mistress. And even though he stank of sweat and ale, I laid my head carefully upon his chest and pulled myself tight against him. Perhaps, for one night, we could pretend we did not hate one another, and that we were not alone.

If Nentres recalled what he spoke of that night, or was shocked to find me embracing him the next morning, he did not speak of it to me in the fresh sunshine. After breaking our fast on the remains of last night's feast, he and Meron went to discuss business, so I helped Aleyna with the carding of wool.

"You have quick hands," she said.

"They are well practised with things like this," I replied, dragging the dried thistle through the strands. "I have little other occupation in Caer Mor."

"Nalia is still abed with Forwin," she remarked. "My daughter is married. How strange. I did not think when she was first born I would see this day. She will be very happy with Forwin, I think. Thank you, Highness."

"It is good she has a choice," I said, somewhat sourly.

She quirked an eyebrow at me. "We always have a choice. Even when we think we do not. Even doing nothing is a choice. You made your choice yesterday, and saved my daughter from a terrible situation."

Excusing myself, I got up from the table and went out into the yard. Nentres was there, adjusting the saddle of his horse.

"I am sorry," I said to him. He tightened the strap and then looked at me.

"For what?"

"For threatening Meron, and for other things I do not wish to discuss."

He nodded. "I accept your apology, and offer you mine if it helps."

"It does," I said. "Does your offer still stand?"

"My offer?" he asked.

"To permit a divorce, after a year and day?"

"Yes," he said. "But you would still go? I thought you would calm your doubts after such time."

"You would have me stay? After all we have said, after all we have done."

He turned his head away and fiddled with the strap again. He released it once more with a sigh and turned to face me.

"I love you and that is all I truly know," he said.

"You cannot love me, you do not know me!" I exclaimed, incredulous.

"But I want to. If you would let me."

"Show me Nentres, then," I offered. "Do not show me the King of Garlot, the lord of Caer Mor, the ally of my step-father. Just show me Nentres."

"I will," he replied. "If you will show me Elaine, not the Princess of Camelot."

The Nentres that travelled with me from Meron's steading and beyond was different, attentive and kind. He joked with me and teased me, without cruelty. He made sure I wanted for no food or drink, and I was never bored with all the stories he told, of summers spent at these steadings dotted around his country, making mischief with the sons of his father's warriors, or the faery tales of Garlot's forests that he learnt at Mila's knee.

I grew less and less recalcitrant about my time upon the horse with Nentres, and soon looked forward to it as the best part of my day, the pretence to hold him and listen to his deep, rich voice retell those stories that delighted him as a child. He swelled with happiness and nearly lost his hold upon the reins as he raised his hands to tell about a long-forgotten ancestor.

When we reached a steading, we slept together side by side quite happily and, though the men who accompanied us remembered a time we did otherwise, we spent our nights on the road together in a tent among the trees. Let them think what they would, it did Nentres no harm to be seen as master of me once again.

We did not lay with each other, I could not yet bring myself to that, but the possibility that we might be friends delighted me. I remembered only the end of Igraine's marriage to Gorlois, the sniping at one another and her eventual betrayal, and then her long, unhappy marriage to Uther. They would have been happier apart. Merlin could have surely found cause among the old laws to dissolve the marriage, but they all knew they could not separate, or else all would see that Uther had turned a respected war-duke against him for naught.

On the road home, he told me about his sister, Adel. About her soft brown hair, and the way she laughed as she teased him, and the love she held for all people in Garlot, how she would be the first at the birth of a new baby, or the passing of an old friend, offering comfort and help.

"She sounds wonderful," I said. "I should try to be more like her. I do not think she would have pulled a knife on Meron."

"No, perhaps not," he agreed. "But you need only be yourself. You stood up for what was right. If a king, or a queen, in this case, did that even only half of the time, they would still be a good ruler."

He reddened. "Come, we must hurry if we want to make the most of the light."

Chapter Four

We returned from our progress two different people than those who had left. Yet, despite my new found respect for him, I could not bring myself from the foul humour that settled across me and confined me to my bed. We fell back into our old lives, our old separation from one another, yet we could not go back to spending our nights separated, so I permitted him to share my bed each night and silence the warriors' dissension. Still, I could not stir within myself the feelings needed to lie with him, even if part of me was no longer repulsed by the idea.

Every morning since the one I arrived in Caer Mor I had been awoken by the sound of men practicing in the yard. One morning, driven by some unknown force, I dressed and went out to watch them. Nentres stood in the centre, surrounded by a ring of his men. One by one they would advance and try to strike him with their dull practice blades, and he would fend them off.

I was captivated by this. It was like a dance, spinning and turning, ducking and weaving, swinging out and in, the clang of blade on blade like the drums, the squelch of boot in mud like the strings of a harp.

A warrior caught sight of me. He signalled the others to stop and then he bowed to me. Nentres turned, surprised, and then bid the others repeat the exercise somewhere else. He walked over to me, still holding the practice sword.

"How are you?" he asked.

"I am well," I replied. "And you?"

"Well."

We stared at each other for some time, and I could not think of anything to say. Nentres spun the handle of the practice sword in his hand, twisting it so the dull blade caught what little of the sun its used length could reflect.

"Elaine..." he too seemed at a loss for words. Finally, he said, in a resigned air, "Elaine, what can I do to make you happy?"

"Teach me," I said, surprising us both.

He looked down at the blade in his hand. "You want to learn to fight? Why?"

"Forget I spoke, my Lord," I said, turning towards the castle.

He caught me gently by the arm, smiling. "Of course, I will teach you. It is just unusual for a southern lady, for the Roman-born. But, Elaine, do you feel in some danger?"

"No, my Lord...Nentres. I have always been interested, and Uther indulged me slightly when I was younger. He missed his son sent into fosterage and I think it helped him a little. But then Igraine said such things were not proper for a lady to learn and I was barred from the practice yard."

"You are welcome in my practice yard anytime." He smiled boyishly. "You will need exercises, to strengthen your arms and legs. And you should learn to use a bow also. I know, I will have a suit of practice armour made, one that would be suitable for a woman."

I furrowed my brow in confusion. "Why, what difference would that make?"

"Well, you would need one that is lighter for your frame, and that...makes certain accommodation." He gestured, red-faced, at my bosom.

"Oh!" I laughed, and he joined me. There, in the afternoon sun shining on us, I started to come alive again.

"You could teach me also?" he asked hesitantly.

At first, I did not understand, but his meaning became clear. I lowered my voice to a whisper. "Magic, you mean?"

He laughed. "Elaine, you need not lower your voice. In Garlot, we do not sneer down our noses at witchcraft and then turn to it in desperation when things do not go our way. We see it as it is — a gift from the Gods. And Uther made no secret he was giving me a witch, as well as a queen."

"Did he now?" I wanted to frown at the thought of my step-father listing my qualities like a stallholder bellowing his wares on market day, but I could not. It was a perfect moment, and it could not be ruined. Nentres stared at me expectantly.

"Oh! I cannot, I do not know how, for it is different for men. Warlocks exist, but I think all I have learnt would be useless to you. The higher magic was not taught to me. Perhaps you are too old also? Druid boys started young, far younger than those boys who go into the Christian monasteries."

He shrugged his shoulders. "That is disappointing. Perhaps if we had met earlier?"

I smiled in return. "Perhaps."

He taught me as he promised, and strived to teach me as well as any of his warriors. He told me I must present myself in the practice yard the following day at dawn. I hardly slept at all in anticipation, and stood there, bleary-eyed and blinking in the cold morning sun of Garlot.

"You are wearing the leathers I sent?" he asked as I trudged across the muck towards him.

"Yes," I replied. "How did you get them to fit me?"

"They are my old ones from when I was younger and slighter," was his response. He hefted something from the ground and I could see it was armour.

"I had this made for you, though," It was a breastplate of iron, polished and glinting in the light. "Our blacksmith relished the challenge. He had to use two bowls for the...the...um...necessary changes," he said, losing some of the easy authority he wielded here in the yard.

"You can say breasts if you want. I shall not be offended."

He balked and I resisted the urge to laugh at him. Changing the subject, he asked me to turn around and lifted the breastplate over my head. He helped me into the armour, pulling the stays fast so I was stuck fast between two iron plates.

"It is so heavy," I complained. "How do you walk in this?"

"You keeping walking, no matter how it hurts, until it feels like feathers. That is how. There is no point in learning to fight without armour and then finding you are like sack weighed down with stones when you have to fight in it."

Giving the straps another tug, he reached down and lifted up two iron bracers, gesturing for me to hold out my wrists.

"Surely not? I can barely lift my arms as it is."

"Oh yes, especially in the practice yard. Sometimes swords slip, even dull ones, and I do not wish my queen to be one-handed. And on the battlefield, a clout from a bracer can be as good as any sword."

He strapped them on, and I was glad I was prepared for their weight or my arms would surely have fallen off altogether.

"Now," he said, "take this."

He passed me his sword, a common spatha. I took it, expected to be able to swing it with the easiness he did, and yelped when I nearly dropped it. Between its weight, and the heavy press of my armour and bracers, I could not raise it beyond waist height, even with both of my hands.

"I see," he said. He reached out and took back the sword, scabbarding it and passing it to one of his men.

"Try this instead."

From the rack of weaponry, he took the shaft of a spear which was missing its head, waiting for repair, and broke it swiftly over his knee into two pieces. He passed me one of the sticks.

"Hold this in your right hand, at the base. Make a tight fist around it. You must learn to fight one-handed, and then two-handed will come much easier. Come at me!"

I stood and stared at him instead.

He shook his head. "You must be prepared to strike me, or there is no point in learning."

So I pretended he was Morgause, turned his dark hair to red, and took a swing at him, intent on revenge for her attack in the corridor of Camelot. He blocked it easily, a hard tap from his stick at the base of mine causing me to drop it.

"Careful," he warned. "It is better to cut an opponent twice than decapitate them in one swing. When your attacks are wide, it opens you to an opponent's thrust."

We continued, me striking and him blocking, correcting my stance, my grip, reminding me to stay tight, keep my swings constrained. More often than not, I would be disarmed, or be stuck lightly on the arm or chest, or end up in a heap in the dirt of the yard. I scored a hit once, a gentle tap against his knee. He chuckled.

"I like the way you think," he said. "But I think that is us done for the day. If you wish to continue, I will expect you here every morning, and at evening practice if you can stomach it."

"What do I do with these?" I asked, swinging my bracer-clad arms.

"A warrior always keeps his – I mean her - armour and sword close at hand. So, for the time being, bring it to our chamber with you. It will be your job to clean it and maintain it, I do not want to see a servant do it. You should also be able to get in and out of it alone. There will be no ladies in waiting to help you don armour in the case of an invasion."

"You expect me to fight invaders?" I asked.

"Why else learn? I would not ask you to teach me to sew, and never make something to wear?"

"Fair point. Do you wish to learn to sew?" I teased.

Before I could stop myself, I reached out to touch his elbow. He covered my hand with his own.

"Maybe when we are old, and I am too stooped to fight. We can sit by the fire and sew together. Our children..."

He took a sharp inhale of breath and stopped. I looked down at the ground, withdrawing my hand, and tried to swallow my anger, and my shame. I had enjoyed that day and wanted to hold onto those feelings.

"I will return to our chamber," I said.

He inclined his head in agreement. When I looked back, he was standing lonesome in the practice yard, swinging his aimless sword at imaginary enemies. He looked like a boy at play, and it was both endearing and the saddest thing I had ever seen. Later, he joined me in the chamber, and as a silent apology to one another, we help each other remove one another's armour.

Near a sennight later, he woke me gently. I sat up in the bed.

"I have a present for you," he said, pointing to the table in our chamber. Upon it lay a red cloth, covering whatever he had brought me.

"You have made many presents to me as of late," I said. "The armour, for one. Feeling guilty?"

He laughed. "Open it, and see if I am guilty, or if I am by far the best husband in the land."

I approached the table and removed the red cloth. Upon it was a sword, but not a spatha like the one we practiced with. It was short, no longer than the length from the tip of my middle finger to my elbow. It had a short guard too, and the pommel was large and rounded. The handle was wrapped in smooth leather.

"I have never seen a sword like that," I remarked.

"Neither had I," he replied. "Until the quartermaster pointed out one like it to me. That one was too old to be serviceable, so I had this one made for you, in its image. It is shorter, so it will be easier for you to wield. Its short blade will let you use your smaller size and speed to your advantage, and get in close for a stabbing motion."

I picked it up, testing its weight. It was light and I could wield it easily, spinning it in my fingers.

"I am most impressed, Nentres."

"I am glad you like it," he replied, a blush spreading across his cheeks.

We looked to one another, and I smiled.

With the daily exercise in the practice yard, I began to lift myself from my despair. There were still moments where it overtook me, but I was better equipped to deal with them and did not take so often to bed. My mind too needed some pastime, so I set about learning all I could about this place in which I lived. Mila told me all her stories and then sent for reinforcements in the form of bards and washerwomen when she exhausted her supply. From Portimus, I learnt geography and history and Nentres permitted me to sit in council, provided I spoke only when invited. Soon, I took over the hearing of petitions of the common people, when Nentres was too engaged elsewhere and I felt I acquitted myself wisely and fairly.

We practiced often with the knives. Well, not as such. The theory was on the use of the knife, but the practice was done with two dull wooden spoons from the kitchen, whereupon a misstep cost only a splinter at its worst.

I struck forward, with the spoon-knife, stabbing downwards. He caught my wrist and twisted ever so slightly, just enough for me to feel the threat of what the full force of his movement could do. One of the first lessons I had learned under him was to submit at such times, lest an injury be inflicted. Save your struggle for the battle, he had said.

I dropped the spoon-knife to the ground. Now was the time to twist my arm around his, like winding wool around a distaff, and lean into his body. The right placement of my feet and waist would topple him into the dirt. He would clap his hands at me and tell me how proud he was, how he could see how much I had learned. Then he would pick himself up and we would carry on.

Instead, I stood and did nothing. He loosened his grip, barely holding on. I leant in close. He tensed, preparing for me to throw him, but still I did nothing. He was so close to me that the rise and fall of his chest touched my elbow. There was a strange heat rolling off him, and my heart was beating so fast I thought it would start to thud against the inside of my armour.

I felt the urge to kiss him. I knew I should submit to his hold, or make a move to throw him, and we could restart the bout, but I was captivated by these new feelings. Or old feelings. Feelings that predated the names Elaine and Nentres. Feelings I did not know I had, or might always have had. Feelings I could not have understood until I understood myself.

Feelings that I could not resist. I pushed myself up onto my toes and kissed him. His lips, to my surprise, were soft against mine. He leaned in closer and I slid my hand up into his hair.

Flushed and panting, I pulled back. He tried to speak, but no sound came forth, only gasps. I could see the desire in his eyes and, for the first time, I felt it reflected in myself.

I reached out and tickled him, poking my fingers into the gap between his breeches and tunic. He laughed like a child and tried to bat away my fingers.

"If I had a second knife," I teased. "Then you would be dead."

"It would be worth it," he replied, with a grin as bright as the midday sun. "But I shall keep a close eye out for any enemy warriors who try to kiss me."

It could only have been love. I could not sleep unless he lay beside me. I could not eat unless he sat across from me. I would have fought the Saxons single handed if it gave me one more moment with him. One look from him could cause my chest to rise and my stomach to turn on itself. How I ever thought I hated him, I did not know.

I grew to love Garlot, as much as I loved my husband. Tintagel was a distant memory, the faintest scent of salty water and the echo of crashing waves. Camelot was almost a life lived by another. But Garlot, with its untamed forests and wild people, was my home.

I cannot recall how or why the fog lifted, only that it did. I believed in myself again. I did not feel the pressure that had nearly crushed me in my early days. There was only me and Nentres. Where it had been hopeless before, I had hope.

Our marriage became full again. I did not shy from his touch and often reached for him of my own accord. There were no feigned headaches, and no nights spent in the hall. I made my own choice and it became not a duty or a task, but a pleasure. I felt strong and powerful, more so even than when I wore armour and held a sword. I was owned by no man, no country, only our love.

"Elaine, do you know what day it is?" he asked, as we reclined in bed, eschewing the morning practice for another few moments together.

"No," I said, shaking my head.

He smirked. "I am glad to hear it. It has been exactly a year and a day since we married."

I nodded. "I will go and pack then. Ready a horse for me, I am for Camelot before dusk."

His face fell, and he swallowed a lump in his throat, as though his heart had floated into his mouth. I laughed.

"Of course, I am not leaving. Do not be so stupid, it does not become a king! I could not think of anywhere else I would rather be."

And thus, I stayed beyond the year and the day. Knowing that I had a choice to go, I could not fathom ever leaving Garlot, leaving Nentres. Knowing that I had it in me to be strong, I did not feel weak. Knowing that I had it in me to be happy once more, I could not feel sad.

We returned once to Camelot, to another feast held by Uther. Nentres brought me that time. Uther had failed terribly in the passing year. His blonde hair had turned grey, and his muscular frame had wasted. He gasped with stolen breath as he came to meet us. As I reached out my face to kiss him, I could feel his leathery skin against my lips. Even merciless Igraine seemed moved to help him as he walked.

Alone with my mother, she had very little to say. She asked me if I was with child. When I said no, she asked if Nentres and I did our duty by one another. I said yes, and she chastised me for failing to employ my magics to such an end. Following her scolding, Igraine asked if Arthur was in Garlot, and I told her I knew nothing of my brother's whereabouts. Then she admired the embroidery on my blue dress and asked if I could do a panel for hers.

The rest of the feast proceeded as feasts do, and Igraine said little else to me that was not in earshot of Uther's guests. I resolved then to never see her again unless there was great need, and not to waste paper in writing to her. I would make a new life in Garlot, one of my own choosing, and of my own design.

Chapter Five

Four years came and went and Garlot was truly then my home. It was during this time I became not just a true queen, but a mother too. That cold winter's eve, Nentres lay beside me, almost purring in sleep. I lowered myself from the bed with great care, making sure not to jostle him. I pulled on my boots and draped myself in a woollen cloak, but stayed in my simple shift. Moving through the corridors of Caer Mor, all was silent. I tiptoed past the chambers of the married warriors and weaved my way through the sleeping men on the floor of our hall, out into the night air.

It was cold and crisp, but the brush of the wind against my skin thrilled me. I whispered to the wind, and an eerie whistle carried itself across the courtyard, into the ears of the sentries. As I passed, they did not turn their heads, their attention mysteriously captivated by the mist creeping over the hills.

I made my way out into the woods, into the clearing. As soon as I saw it, I knew it was for me. My place, carved out for me in the great hulk of the woods, as though prepared for me by the ones gone before. There was no holly or mistletoe, but it was perfect nonetheless, with the ancient oak towering above me, enclosing me in its sacred space.

Casting off the cloak, I tossed aside the cloak and raised my hands in the ancient gesture to greet the moon, supreme among the stars in the blackened sky. Once in a month, when the moon is full, some secret place shall ye gather, and be one with the powers high and low, of this world and the next. That is the way of the Wise, what we must mark in exchange for our power.

I let the silence of the night settle over me, and opened my mind to the world unseen. Then it occurred to me. This was the third month I had come to the clearing and had been without my courses. I looked down at my stomach. Was it possible it was more rounded? Surely not?

I looked up at the moon, like a mother's smiling face, and I knew it was true. I bore no physical signs yet, but I was with child.

"Thank you," I said to the moon. "Thank you."

I grew, far quicker than I expected. My stomach became round, full and surprisingly hard to the touch. Once I told him, Nentres grew more and more attentive until Mila had to chase him from our room. He would rub my back and help me when I was unsteady on my feet. Those moments, together, were some of the happiest in our life.

I did not write to Igraine to tell her, nor Morgause. The latter probably would not have cared, while the former would crow with victory, as though she was one who had conceived. Morgan gave her cursory congratulations, and relayed that she grateful she was not in the same position, having employed all her cunning to ensure Uriens lost interest in her.

I soon entered my ninth month and was, by that time, eager to be rid of the child who made moving so difficult, made me hungry all the time, and confined me within hobbling distance of the privy. Nentres and I spent much of that time sequestered in our chamber, his hand upon my expanded stomach.

"It is bad luck, I know, to name a child before it is born, but have you given any thoughts to a name?" he asked.

"I thought Adel, if it is a girl."

He gave me a warm smile. "Perfect. Just perfect."

"Bruden, perhaps, if it is a boy," I added.

He shook his head. "No, to name an heir after a predecessor, it is...overwhelming...for a child. I was named after my grandfather, and all my life I have struggled to be even half as good as the people remember him. Or the stories they think to be true. No, no, Elaine, let him be the first of his name, and figure out what sort man he wants to be by himself. I like Hoel. What do you think?"

"Sounds like a Saxon to me." I wrapped the name around my tongue. "But I could get used to it."

I was brought to bed that evening, and by next morning I had given birth to a baby boy, calling him Hoel has we had previously discussed. Holding him in my arms, I felt as though I was cradling the world's most precious jewel, that I could never let him out of my sight. I was filled with wonder. I was a witch, and a none too shabby one at that, and yet this was my most mysterious conjuring. I had made a person and fallen in love with it at once.

We continued on, the three of us, in utter and abject happiness. I had a babe to suckle, to bathe and to keep from innocent things that were suddenly very dangerous, like cold winds and ill-attended fires. Nentres doted on his son, and he continued to train me in the ways of battle, and welcomed my opinion on matters of state. We were busy, and fulfilled.

I was sat in our bed when the news came. Hoel was fond of playing there with me, the sheets becoming great mountains and low valleys for him to explore. He was fast, and needed watching, or else he would topple over the edge.

Nentres entered the chamber, Mila not far behind him. Kissing the top of his head, I passed Hoel to Mila, who he loved more than if she was his natural grandmother. I had heard heavy hoof beats not long previous, and knew Nentres would have news to share.

"Was that a messenger come a-riding?" I asked. Despatches from Uther or the other vassal kings were not uncommon. There was always some matter of diplomacy or war that needed my husband's attention.

He was downcast, working his upper lip between his teeth. "Word from Camelot. Uther Pendragon died earlier today."

I nodded. What could I say? We had been preparing for this day since Morgan's curse took effect. The sole reason for my marriage was to secure Uther's legacy.

"Do you wish to go to Camelot? To be with your mother?"

"There is little point. Igraine will have departed for Glastonbury at once, before Uther is even cold."

Nentres nodded. "Sensible, your mother. There are a few of the more ambitious kings who would not hesitate to seize the throne by marrying your mother."

"Will we attend the funeral rites?" I asked.

"Perhaps not. If Igraine does not see fit to do so, and she his queen, there is little point in us. These things become little more than an evening spent in your cups, being courted by the contenders for the throne."

Getting up from the bed, I moved to the window and looked out over the forest, to my sacred place. I would go there later to offer some prayers to ease Uther's passage to the underworld. I felt a tinge of sadness. I had lived twelve years at Uther's court and he had tried his best towards me, with gifts and games, if not kind words.

Feeling guilty, I tried to remember Gorlois, and failed. My clearest images were of him in his final few days. Regret, anger, sorrow; I wished myself to feel these but I could not. Gorlois had died before I had a chance to know him, and clinging to his legacy with bitterness, like Morgan, did us no good. He had been killed by Uther long ago and now his killer was dead too. The wheel of life turns on.

"Who rules us now?" I asked. I had been too young to truly remember the death of Ambrosius Aurelianus.

"No one. Each king and lord are now sovereign entirely in their own lands. A pact was made, when the Romans left, that we should set one above us all, so that there would be no fighting amongst us for land, and that we could stand together against invaders. Britain will always be ruled by the Britons because of this. But with the high throne vacant, they all may decide to return to the way things were before."

"And you, what will you do?"

He shrugged. "Whatever is best for Garlot. I would not lie to you, sovereign rule appeals to me greatly. We would not have to raise a levy against the Saxons or the Irish if we did not want to, or send our grain if there is famine. But then, if another king, say Cradelmant for example, set his eye on our forests, none other would have to help us. Perhaps we gain more together than apart."

"And what of Arthur?"

"He is Uther's heir and nominated successor. That counts for much. But still, an assembly would need to be called and it put to a vote. What age is your brother now?"

I thought on it, recalling the age I had been when he was born. "Sixteen, I think?"

Nentres winced. "That is young. I was nineteen when I became king so unexpectedly, and I struggled. Had I not your stepfather's favour, my warriors would have put me out of my own castle."

I wondered what Arthur looked like, and what sort of man he was. Uther did for me what he could. I thought I had repaid him with my marriage, but perhaps the balance would be paid in full if I at least tried to love my unknown brother. I would try, but I could not force my husband to do so. He would make his own judgement.

We passed the next few days in relative silence, as though Caer Mor mourned for the fallen High King. In truth, we had much to think on. Merlin will have fetched Arthur from his hiding place, and would soon present him as Uther's nominated successor. Nentres would thus be called to elect a High King, either in Uther's castle of Camelot, or in Londinium where Ambrosius Aurelianus had held his court, and he might bid me come too.

If no king was elected, we would have to look to the nature of Garlot, so that it may sustain itself where no other king could be commanded to help us when we had need of something. Trading would be particularly difficult, if the southern lords decided to enforce a toll on the routes to the ports.

Nentres and I were occupied with debating these issues many a night, as weeks passed from Uther's death, and these discussions spilled over from the hall to our bedchamber. One night, before I could begin an impassioned defence of our

118

policy on crop rotation, a crow appeared with a caw, landing with a flap of its wings upon the window sill. Nentres rose to shoo it, but I stopped him upon seeing the note tied to its leg.

"It is a messenger, for me."

"How do you know?" he asked.

"I just do."

I slid out from under the covers and approached the bird softly. With a gentle touch, I reached out and stroked its plumage. It tapped its beak against the stone and then proffered its leg for me to remove the note. Having done so, it leaped out into the night. I unrolled the paper and began to read.

"What does it say?" asked Nentres.

"It is a note from my mother," I replied. "She has taken ill in Glastonbury, and wishes me to visit her."

Her silence in the weeks since Uther's death was unsurprising, but not unexpected. She would be seeing to herself first, and then to her plans for the future.

"Let me organise riders for you," he said. "You can leave whenever you like, Glastonbury is not far. I would go too, I should like to see the queen again, but I have so much to do tomorrow."

He caught sight of my face and asked "Elaine, what is wrong?"

"She is dying. She has to be. My mother is not one for sympathy, nor filial duty. If she wants to see me now, she knows she does not have long."

I lay down on the bed, worrying the paper between my fingers.

"You cannot be certain, Elaine," he reassured me. "You will not know until you go. Try to sleep, please."

I nodded, and relaxed into his welcoming arms. Yet what little sleep came that night was fitful. I was certain my mother was not long for this world, and that would come with demands. I was for Glastonbury upon the morrow.

Laying on the low bed, wrapped in furs, in her plain linen shift and undressed hair, a phrase of Igraine's was brought to mind. Common as muck, she would say to me, when I had been rolling about in the forest, or caught fighting with the kitchen boy. Stop behaving as though you are as common as muck. I learnt then that death makes all men equal. Lying there, the High Queen looked as common as muck.

Her eyes were sunken, her face deathly thin. She was always pale but, this time, her skin had a sickly pallor. She stretched out a bony hand and beckoned me.

"Come, daughter."

"My Lady Mother," I said, greeting her as I took a seat on the small wooden stool. I grasped her hand. It seemed so cold.

"You are dying?" I asked, unable to be delicate.

She nodded, breath wheezing in her throat.

"What is wrong?"

"A cough, and a fever," she replied. "They come and go, but I know I do not have much longer."

"Merlin, did he...?"

"Poison me? Curse me? Quite possibly. Or it is just the great wheel of life, turning so I am bore against the ground."

I nodded, searching for a reply. "I have a son. Hoel. I would have brought him, but he is too easily unsettled for such a journey."

120

"Excellent," she replied. "Now Nentres cannot put you away. When the boy is old enough, you must send him to Arthur for fosterage. Arthur must see him as his own son, and thus, forge Garlot and Camelot as one kingdom."

I dropped her hand as I struggled to hold back my anger. "Will you not ask if he has spoken yet? Taken his first steps? If he takes after his father or his mother? Instead you plot to elevate him to a station he cannot yet even conceive of."

She shrugged. "I have not the time to be subtle. My son needs his allies if he is to become king without question."

"Is that all you care about? Arthur being king?"

"He has to. He must."

"Why? What does it matter when you are for the Underworld soon?"

"If Arthur does not become king, then I am but a schemer, a harridan, a whore. But, mother of the once and future king? I am redeemed thus. I have delivered Britain her saviour and I can die a free woman."

"Free?" I asked. "Because you are in slavery somehow?"

"Yes, impudent girl, I am. I am a slave to the things I have done in pursuit of my ambition. I see him in my dreams. Gorlois, your father..."

"Yes, I know who that is. I am not entirely ignorant of my own upbringing."

"Then you know what I did?"

I fixed her clearly in my gaze. "You conspired with Merlin to lie with Uther, cede Tintagel to his forces and murder my father on the road. I remember a little and Morgan made sure we knew the rest."

She did not shrink from my gaze. "I thought I would be happy when I had Tintagel. Then I thought I would be happy as High Queen. And when I found I was not, I told myself all I had done was destiny. My destiny because I birthed a king, a king who would put an end to wild men in the north, Irish raiders, Saxons and the injustice that is wreaked on ordinary men and women."

"And you must make that come true? At the expense of your other children, who you never loved? You shut yourself away, gave little comfort when we were sick or upset, emerging only to teach us how to bat our eyelids and cook up spells?"

"I have loved you in my own way, Elaine. I raised you the best way I knew how. I brought you into a world where you would not be hungry, or cold, where you could find a man to protect you from the cruelties of this life, and taught you the art should he fail you. I will not shy from the truth. You were born only because Morgan and Morgause were not sons. But I did right by you, as Petronella would say. I did right by you."

"There is more to motherhood than feeding and clothing the child."

"Correct my mistakes then, with...Hoel. Yes, correct them with him, as I corrected Petronella's mistakes with you. I gave you two fathers, and you wanted for nothing, a princess and now a queen."

I adjusted the folds of my dress and huffed out a sigh. "What do you want? It is not to hold my hand in your last hours."

She shook her head. "I could not write to the others. Morgause is too far away, and Morgan would not come, no matter how I would plead. You are my only hope, Elaine."

She stretched out her hand and I took it again, holding tight despite the chill of her bones. I do not know about daughterly affection, but my pride would not have it ortherwise.

"Has your brother come forth from his hiding place?" she asked, and the hope on her face could not be disguised.

I shook my head. "No, not yet. There has been no word of him, and Nentres has not been called to any assembly yet."

The light died in her face.

"I shall not see my son then," she said. "For I will certainly die before he is crowned."

She looked up from the bed, into the corner of the room. There was nothing there, save a dark shadow cast by the curving arch of the door. Yet the horror with which she stared at that nook sent a chill down my spine. Had she glimpsed a vision of the Underworld for which she was destined?

"It is best that Gorlois did not die in vain," she said, never taking her eyes from that spot on the wall. "Arthur shall be the king Britain needs."

She squeezed my hand tight. "Please, please, Elaine. Promise me. Help your brother. Do it for me. Do it for Uther. Do it for Britain."

"I will," I promised, even if, in that moment, it was just to get her to release her death grip upon my fingers.

I sat with Igraine most of the day, helping her sit up, or spoon broth into her mouth with a patience I did not know I had. Throughout the day, she would bring the topic of conversation back around to my brother, and what I must do to assure his throne. Finally I tired of it, and asked one of the nuns if they had a bed for the night, and they showed me to a small room with a bed for travellers. I wondered how much of my gold they would expect in a donation.

I awoke before the morn, shaken awake by a novice nun.

"Please, my Lady, come with me," she pleaded.

"Who said you could wake me?" I said, irritated. "What do you want?"

"Come, my Lady, please."

"What is it?" I asked. "Tell me!"

She looked down at the floor. "The queen...she is dead."

I rose, silent and followed her into the chamber. The silence in that room was deafening. There were two novices there, obviously the ones who had found her so. They were crying, but no sound came from their mouth. I waved my hand, dismissing them.

I approached my mother. Indeed, Igraine was dead. I realised, looking down at her, I had never seen a dead body before, except those already wrapped in shrouds and ready for burial. She was strangely flat as if the air had been sucked out of her. Even her hair, which had thinned with age but still remained long and vibrant, seemed lesser and greyer.

I sat down on the stool and looked at her, wondering why I felt nothing. No sadness, no grief, nor even impish delight that she was gone. I do not know how long I sat there simply watching her.

A woman entered the room, garbed in the black robe and white headdress of a nun. She waited until I had acknowledged her before she spoke to me. She gave her condolences, and I asked if she was the Abbess.

"Mother Abbess is absent on abbey business," she replied. "But I am the Prioress here. I am sorry to have to ask you, but have you given thought to the funeral arrangements?"

I did not know what to do. By all accounts, she was the Dowager Queen and entitled to a great funeral of state, but we had not even a King. I had no command of Camelot, not being Uther's natural daughter, so she could not be brought there. Was I to bring her to Garlot?

The Prioress sensed my confusion.

"We could arrange something here. But...?"

"What is the matter?" I asked.

"Forgive my ignorance, but I know that Uther Pendragon was not a Christian. We open our doors to anyone in need of charity here, but the Lady Igraine? Was she a follower of the Christ?"

"Oh yes," I said, resisting the urge to smirk. "The Lady Igraine was a very devout Christian. She would like nothing more than a proper Christian burial."

"Very well. I will send for a priest from the brothers' house, and some of the sisters will prepare the body. We can have the ceremony tomorrow if it pleases you, my Lady."

I nodded, and continued to stare at Igraine's body. The Prioress placed her hand on my shoulder.

"My Lady, I think you should return to your bed. I will bid the sisters come now. You can see your mother tomorrow, when she lies in state."

"I...I do not know what to do," I murmured. "Should...should I tell somebody?"

She looked at me with kind eyes. "I will go across to the Abbot and speak with him. He is a very worldly man, and will know the protocol for such a situation."

I gave my assent and left to go lie down in my bed again. But I did not sleep. My only thought was of Igraine, and how puzzled I was that my feelings were as cold as she now was. I offered the customary prayers and then tried to close my eyes. I would rest, even if I could not sleep.

On the solemn walk to the burial grounds, the next day, I struck up a conversation with the Prioress again.

"Did you know my sister, the Princess Morgan, now Queen of Gore?" I asked.

"I did, my Lady," she replied. "We were friends, as such as an abbey permits a novice and a lay sister to be friends. She was a great favourite of Mother Abbess. I think she wished for her to take the habit, and remain here to be her successor. But your step-father had other plans."

"That he did. What did you think of my sister?"

She could not meet my eye. "She was very learned, even before she came here."

She led me on, followed by the mourners. Some novice monks bore the High Queen in a litter ahead of us. Of the crowd that walked the well-trod path behind us, some were monks and nuns, and some were professional mourners brought from nearby towns, and the rest were those who had come to gawp at the burial of a High Queen, an event where they would not ever have been welcome.

They laid her down into the earth and intoned a sober prayer in Latin. This was to be my last revenge on Igraine. It would not bar her from the Underworld, or the next life. The Gods of the Wise care little for what is done with the mortal shell once the soul has departed, but Igraine would have fumed at the man telling her that her only hope to be saved from the fires of Hades was the Christ. It was almost enough to make me laugh when I knew I should not.

I stood and watched until the last shovel of dirt had been filled in the grave. They sprinkled grass seed over the bare patch of earth, and blank stone had been laid flat by the grave.

"We will place it when the earth has settled," said the Prioress by way of explanation. "But we will send someone to carve it tonight. You may visit the grave any time you like, you need not ask our permission."

I nodded, and thanked her. I could see in the clouds that I would return to Glastonbury, but it would not be to visit Igraine's grave. Her soul had left her body, and gone on to a new life, or to the fields of rest, or perhaps even to somewhere she might be punished for all she had done. I knew my next visit to Glastonbury would be many, many years from that day, and I hoped I would not be coming back to die as my mother had done.

After the ceremony, I begged off the Prioress invitation to return to the abbey, knowing that it would be endless mourning and prayers, preferring to take a bowl of thin, weak soup and be on my way home.

I made a donation to the abbey, quite a sizeable portion of my travelling purse, but I thought it fair for arranging a funeral. As I made the sombre ride back to Garlot, I wondered if I would yet shed a tear for Igraine. But even when Nentres greeted me with a deep embrace and I told him the news, I still did not cry.

Back at Caer Mor, I tried to write to Morgause. But each word I wrote seemed wrong. Still, near four years later, I had no words of apology for the great wrong she thought I had done her, and I none from her regarding her violence. How could I convey the death of our mother to her when I could not even convey one ounce of my feelings?

I wrote to Morgan but she did not reply to me herself. Instead, a letter came in a round, quivering hand. It was her scribe, informing me that the

Queen of Gore was sad to hear of the death of her mother and would write to me soon.

So, when a messenger came with a letter, I thought it for me, but it was a great scroll addressed to Nentres, sealed with a royal crest I could not make out in the wax. I hovered over my husband's shoulder as he set about reading it, my curiosity unbridled.

"Who writes to you, Nentres?" I asked, when he had finally finished reading and re-reading it.

He looked up from the letter, crumpling the parchment in his nervous hand. "Lot of Orkney."

"And what does our dear brother-in-law, who never busies himself with such things normally, have to say?"

"Arthur Pendragon has been proclaimed High King."

"But no assembly has been called?"

"Only one of the southern lords, led by Sir Ector. Arthur pulled a sword from a stone and Merlin holds this as a sign that he should be confirmed. Lot writes to me that Garlot should reject this, and meet him in a sennight for a council of kings."

My mind was spinning. A sword from a stone? Why did that sound so familiar? And why did I feel like Merlin had done something altogether quite duplicitous?

I took the letter from my husband's hand and studied Lot's careful flourishes upon the page. He wrote that, not long after the death of Uther, Merlin had brought Arthur forth from the house of Sir Ector and revealed him as Uther's heir before the southern lords. Together they travelled to a Christian holy place not far from Sorviodunum, and there Merlin showed them a stone with a sword embedded within it. Whoever could pull forth that sword would be High King of Britain, the old enchanter said. They all tried, heaving and panting, but my sixteen-year-old brother pulled it free as though it was a table knife set in butter. And thus, he was our High King.

I chuckled. Nentres stared.

"What is so funny, wife?" he asked.

"Merlin truly bested Igraine, it seems. He hid Arthur in fosterage with Sir Ector, Uther's dearest friend, a house my mother visited many times, and yet she could not find him."

This did not amuse Nentres as it did me. He merely frowned in distaste.

"Merlin is wicked indeed."

He sat down, and beckoned for Mila to fill his cup.

"You look like a man who has made a decision, dear husband."

"I have," he said, almost weary. "I will attend this council of kings and hear what Lot has to say."

He left the next morning and I had little sleep the three days he was gone. I knew whatever my husband decided, it would have consequences for me and my brother, not to mention the people of Garlot, our subjects who I came to love, and to the peoples all across Britain. What of my promises to Uther and Igraine?

I listened eagerly for the sound of hoof beats, and was rewarded on the third day, when an outrider announced Nentres' return, and his orders to stoke the fire in the hall and have food prepared. As he and escort returned, I played the dutiful wife, spooning stew into bowls for the hungry men.

"Do not," he bid as I approached him, my open mouth ready to burst into questioning. He kissed me on the cheek. "Let me eat first, and then you may ask me."

He shovelled stew into his mouth, and I fidgeted beside him. He shook his head to quiet me, lest I speak again. He rose and the men bowed.

"We shall repair to our chamber," he said. "This is not a conversation for all to hear."

We made our way to our bedroom, and I helped him divest himself of his armour and riding gear.

"So?" I asked, sitting on the edge of the bed.

Nentres folded his arms across his chest, taking the measure of me before he spoke. "There is to be a rebellion."

I leapt to my feet. "A rebellion?"

"Keep your voice down!" he hissed.

"Sorry," I apologised. "But a rebellion? They mean to rise against Arthur's ascension?"

He nodded. "We reached a decision. It has not been done right. A sword, pulled from a stone? Strange yes, a portent, possibly, but a right of kingship? Never. Why did Merlin not call an assembly, for all the kings to vote? Why has Arthur not written to us, asking for our support?"

I shook my head. "I do not know my brother as I should."

I looked at him keenly. "Will you join this rebellion?"

"Yes. Do not try to sway me, Elaine, I have given my word, and I agree."

"You will lose many men, the southern lords are strong in forces and in gold."

"It is the price we pay for a better Britain."

"Who will be king then, when this rebellion be over?"

"There will be an assembly. We will do this in accordance with our history, our traditions, and

130

our laws. And we will see that Merlin has no hand in it."

"And from these rebels we will choose our leader? What is to stop another rebellion if the choice is not well liked?"

"I have no answer for you. If I could give you a reason for that, I would be a wise man indeed." He smiled at me. "Maybe I will be chosen?"

"You would seek the high throne for yourself?" I asked, shocked.

He shook his head, his attempt at levity lost upon me. "No, I do not. It is a sorry place to sit, forever threatened. But only a liar would say he had never imagined himself there. Or would turn away from such a seat once offered."

I did not know whether it was a premonition or a mere daydream. But I saw it, clear as day. Myself, sat upon the throne of beaten bronze in Camelot, wearing the finest gown of imperial purple, trimmed with russet fur. My head was heavy with a crown and before me kneeled all manner of men and women, farmers, warriors, priests and maidens.

It could be wonderful. Britain would shine like never before under my hand. Roads would span the length of the country, irrigation ditches would feed our crops even when drought loomed, and we would grow rich, trading with the east. No manner of people would threaten us, for our army would be most fearsome. My justice would be swift. I gritted my teeth and banished the vision from my mind, as reluctant as it went.

"Who then? If not us?" I asked. "Lot of Orkney? He will undoubtedly be a strong contender, as he was before Uther's ascension. Or Uriens may well propose himself, and none of us will want Morgan for a queen."

He shrugged. "Leodegranz? He has the wealth. Surely among all these kings and nobles, there is one man fit to rule us?"

"And Arthur is not this man?"

"No," he replied, shaking his head. "He is not. He is only sixteen and was raised by Merlin. Goodness knows what nonsense he filled the boy's head with. Is he man enough to make his own decisions, or is he the demon Druid's mouthpiece? Arthur has a birthright, that much is true, but that does not make him the High King. The High King has always been the choice of an assembly, and we choose the best man for the job. And we do not choose Arthur."

"Then it is settled, or at least you have settled it. You are to plunge the kingdom into war, set the people of Britain at one another's throats, when we should be looking to the Saxon threat, or wild men in the North, or even those rumours we have heard, of a new Roman Empire? Shall I go to the nursery and put a sword in Hoel's hand now? Save us the bother in a few years?

"Do not be difficult Elaine, I know he is your brother. I know you promised your mother, promised Uther, that you would help him. But he is not the right man to be High King. Perhaps in a few years, when he has seen more of the world, beyond Sir Ector's walls and Merlin's lies."

"Is Merlin so dangerous?"

Nentres shrugged. "My father never trusted him."

"You are not a Christian, so surely it is not because his father was a faery?"

He shook his head. "No, not as such. But he is devious, and sets the kings and lords against one another, for no obvious reason. I mean, do you even know what he plots and schemes for?"

"No," I replied, honestly. "I thought, perhaps, it was the restoration of the Druidic faith, the end of the Romans and their Christ, but he never tried to, not under the three kings he served previously. I know now he would not want such a thing, a class of men and women who could rival him for power? Peace and prosperity for Britain perhaps?"

"Whatever his end," shrugged Nentres. "Only Merlin will benefit, I can tell you that."

We lay that night in silence. There was no time for speech. Nentres mind worked with plans, how many men he could levy, how he would arm and feed them and which terrain he would challenge Arthur upon.

My mind was equally occupied that eve, plotting too. How would I keep Nentres from joining this rebellion? What if he lost? What if my brother was not a forgiving man?

Equally, what if Nentres was the victor? Would he have to slay Arthur? I could forgive myself for failing to prevent Gorlois' death, I was so young, but to stand by and allow my husband to kill my brother? And then, the possibility of ascending to the throne? I did not know if I had the strength to deny myself such power.

I could not sleep, so I rose and took myself into the nursery. Hoel, approaching his second year, was sound asleep, careless of the problems of this land. I pulled the blanket tighter around him, and rested my hand gently on his little stomach, feeling the rise of fall of his breath.

I never conceived another child after Hoel. The birth was not difficult, not as some woman have them, but my body was never the same after. I lost the weight of pregnancy quick enough, but my courses were heavy each month, and could not be relied upon to be regular. I knew I would not become pregnant again, no matter how hard we tried.

I resolved then that Hoel must not only live, but live in a world of peace. But who would give us this peace? Uther had tried his best. Would it be Arthur? Or would it be one of these rebel kings?

Chapter Six

Nentres rode out, at last, to join the rebellion, taking with him nearly five thousand men in total. Hoel cried when he went, though at two years old, tottering about and still struggling to speak understandably, I do not know if he truly understood the gravity of the situation.

Morgan wrote to me, exulting my husband as an example of kingship, and was more complementary of Uriens than ever before. Had she pressed Uriens into this? A final revenge on Uther, who had married me and my sisters to prevent this very thing from happening?

I did not respond to her letter. A second letter came days later, and I thought it was Morgan writing again when I had failed to respond. No, I would have been grateful for such a letter. Instead, it was Merlin, in quite vulgar language, threatening forceful retribution against Garlot and my husband if we did not capitulate to Arthur soon. It sent shivers down my spine, and I cast many spells of protection upon my husband and my kingdom, though, I knew deep down, if Merlin himself chose to come against me, we stood little chance.

Nentres had left me regent in his absence, and my days became quickly overwhelmed. He made it seem effortless. Yet there disputes to settle, trades to tax, and endless people to see. I collapsed into bed each night, exhausted. Not only was the actual business of governing taxing, but my mouth almost hurt from being so careful with my choice of words. I could not afford to offend an important man in my husband's absence, nor could I be seen to too often command men who would chafe at a woman's orders.

On one such day of courtly business, I chose to repair to my chamber before midday, to take a few moments rest before Portimus brought more petitioners before me. I had no sooner lay down upon the bed than I was awoken by a strange sound.

Bells were ringing. I wondered how I could hear them, when we had no churches close to Caer Mor. Why had I never heard them before?

I rose from my bed and went down the stairs again. The few men-at-arms that remained were shuffling about the hall, talking in low whispers. They could not meet my eye.

"What is it?" I asked.

They looked at each other, and were silent.

"Oh, for goodness sake!" exclaimed Mila. "That's the alarm bell, in Merriwyn!"

"An alarm bell?" I gaped. "They are attacked?"

Is it Merlin, I wondered? Had he finally come upon Garlot? One of Nentres' men, Lomar, was finally brave enough to speak.

"Saxons have raided it, my Lady," he stated.

My head was spinning. Speaking was a challenge as I struggled to put words to my racing thoughts. Already my stomach was twisting with fear.

"Why are you still here?" I asked. "Surely the men must go at once and rout them?"

He stumbled over his words, stuttering until he finally said "We are too few, Highness. Most of the men are on campaign with your husband. And the King ordered that we stay here in case of attack."

I looked to Mila, but she had no answers for me. Instead, those in the hall stared at me. I thought I would sink under the weight of their eyes. Then I realised. They were waiting for an order, and I must give one, or chaos would break loose.

"Don your armour," I commanded. "And fetch thy sword. We will ride out at once, and send the Saxons scurrying."

My words belied my true feelings. I wanted to return to my bed and pull the covers over my head. Could word be sent to Nentres? He was gone near a month, and he had not sent word of where he was camped, for fear it was intercepted. I very nearly sent for aid from Merlin, though Nentres would never have forgiven me, nor could I be sure that Merlin had not inflicted this invasion upon us.

"Has anyone seen Portimus?" I asked. "He must ride for the nearest steadings and summon men. Garlot must not fall."

"That fat fool will be cowering in the forest somewhere, at the first sign of trouble," said Mila sourly. She approached me and placed her hand on my arm.

"My Lady, you do not mean to ride out yourself? We must fortify the gates."

I shook her off, angry that such a thing had not occurred to me. "Yes, we must fortify the gates."

The men-at-arms had not moved. I challenged Lomar.

"Why have you not done as I asked?"

"Which is it, my Lady? Should I assemble a party, or fortify the castle?"

"Surely there are enough men to do both?"

He shook his head. "No, my Lady, there is not. If we send men to Merriwyn, then Caer Mor will be defenceless."

"But we cannot leave Merriwyn to invaders!" exclaimed Mila.

137

"We must, or the whole of Garlot would fall," replied Lomar.

I was silent. They were still staring at me. I wished I had the sort of power of Morgan, or Merlin. If I did, perhaps I could make Nentres appear in a puff of smoke, and lead where I could not.

The bells stopped ringing.

"Your decision has been made for you, my Lady," he said.

"Whatever do you mean?" I replied, but I knew the answer as soon as I spoke.

"The bell has stopped. Merriwyn has fallen."

"Perhaps the threat is defeated?"

He struggled to meet my eye. "No. The bells are to ring in a different pattern if it is passed."

"We waste time with this discussion," said Mila, shaking me with a gentle hand.

"Fortify the gates," I ordered Lomar.

He gave a small bow and went to do as I ordered. I stood at the door of the hall and watched as they closed and barred the gates, archers assembling on the parapets. There was a cold sensation creeping up my lower back.

"I have fortified the gates, my Lady," said Lomar, returning. "But it will do us little good."

I knew. I could hear the raucous shouting, the steady beat of boots marching along the Roman road. Whoever had sacked Merriwyn had finished and turned their attention to us.

"Who comes against us?" I asked.

Lomar looked very pale. "Saxons, Highness. I recognise their war chants."

There was heavy thump and the hall door flew open. Men began to stream inside, the sounds of screams, and the clang of metal on metal outside. The door was bolted.

"What is going on?" I demanded.

"The Saxons have breached the gate!" cried a guard.

"Why have you abandoned your post?" I asked.

"Forgive me, my Queen, but there are too many."

Mila had turned white beside me, and I am sure I was equally as pale. A heated discussion was going on in the corner of the room between Lomar and the guard.

"What is going on?" I demanded. "I am the Lady of Caer Mor, and nobody will talk to me!"

Lomar looked to the guard. "Anwyl believes we should flee."

"Absolutely not!" I responded. "We cannot let Garlot fall to the Saxons. Whatever would Nentres say?"

"We must decide soon," said Anwyl. "Or the Saxons will burn us out of here."

It was too much for a queen alone. I had only been playing at war in the practice yard. This was reality come knocking.

"Then we make a stand," I said, and I looked to Lomar. "Send the men out to fight."

His nostrils flared, and I could see he would have liked to have been anywhere else in the world at that present moment. He had thought himself the lucky one, remaining at home while Nentres took the others on campaign. Even so, he steeled himself, drew his sword and gestured for the others to follow him out into the courtyard.

"I will close the door behind me. Make sure you bar it, Highness."

They went forth, out into the sounds of death and destruction, shutting the door. Mila and I heaved together and managed to draw the large wooden bar.

139

"We cannot linger here," said Mila. "We will not be safe for long. We must flee. What of the prince?"

I ignored the stab of horror that raced through me as I realised I had left my son unattended, and almost forgotten him.

"Come Mila!" I barked, and we went at once upstairs.

"Fetch Hoel from his room," I ordered her. "Quickly now."

She did as I bid, while I set to work, tossing the papers of state into the fire, throwing treasury gold under the bed, except for a small purse I shoved into Mila's hand when she returned with my son. I had no time to don my armour, so I snatched up my short sword, holding the blade tucked against my forearm.

I pulled Hoel by the arm, dragging him roughly behind me. The poor boy, white-faced, wide-eyed and trembling, did not argue or protest. Down the stairs, we raced, into to the hall. I could hear the cries from the courtyard, feel the stomps of boots as the floor vibrated underneath me.

I threw open the door to the kitchens.

"You must go," I ordered her. "The Saxons are upon us. I will see you have time to escape."

The old servant shook her head. "No, mistress, I cannot leave you."

I turned her towards the kitchen, tucking Hoel's hand into hers.

"Take him, Mila! As far as you can into the country. And...and if you cannot get him to Nentres, then find someone to raise him as a farmer. Keep him from this wretched life we live. Now, go!"

I turned my back on them because surely, if I looked at my son, my nerve would falter and all three of us would be cut down like grain as we tried to flee. I heard Hoel cry out for me, so I hardened my heart and prepared to face this threat against my home. Why else had I learnt to fight, I thought, if not for this?

There was a thundering against the door of the hall, and I could see the great bar begin to splinter with the weight of the body throwing itself against it. Time slowed. An immense calm had settled over me. I knew I was afraid, I knew I was angry, but I felt nothing. There was only me, my sword and my hall.

I reached for the fire pit and withdrew the poker, its end red with the heat of the flames. Poker in one hand, and sword in the other, I withdrew into the shadows of the hall.

The door finally gave way, showering the room with splinters. There was only one Saxon who entered. He ran in, a bloodcurdling cry emanating from his throat. He stopped and looked around. To him, the hall was abandoned.

He walked to the centre of the room and cast confused looks about the place. He called over his shoulder, in his strange language. His attention elsewhere, I sprung.

I struck with the poker first. I brought it down hard against the side of his face, taking care to press it deep into his flesh. He squealed like a butchered pig, and sunk to his knees, grasping for the floor like a starved man for a piece of bread. I let the poker clatter to the floor and, grabbing his unkempt hair, cut the Saxon's throat in one, swift, flawless motion.

I clamped my mouth shut, biting down on the sudden urge to vomit. I had not been expecting that. Blood was seeping onto the hem of my dress, escaping from his clutching fingers as he squeezed at his neck in vain. He rolled onto his front, twitching soundlessly.

I pressed the back of my free hand to my mouth, trying to cover the stench of blood, a salty iron tang, and goodness knows what else. My stomach was cramping, my throat only just resisting the compulsion to heave.

There was a creak of a loose floorboard behind me. Another Saxon.

Turning, I caught the strike of his blade with the edge of my own. He was unprepared for the force of my counter and wobbled on his feet. I slashed at him again, from left shoulder to right hip, and he fell with a heavy thud. Quickly, I stabbed down with my sword, piercing his back, in and out, like I was embroidering and my sword was my needle.

He tried to crawl away, but he was dead before he had travelled even an inch. There was a low moan, and his companion had expired too. Again I gagged and gripped the sword hilt tighter.

My nerve was faltering. I looked to the door and saw another approaching. He looked at me. Letting out a cry I did not know I was capable of, I took a run at him, swinging my sword. He jumped back to avoid the blade, and I pressed my advantage, trying to remember what Nentres had taught me.

Our swords clanged upon one another, with a great ring of steel upon steel, he disarmed the sword from my hand. It slid across the floor with a disheartening scrape. I will die here, I thought, but I will stave off my death long enough for Hoel to get to safety.

I kicked out with my boot, flat against his knee-cap. He grunted, but it appeared to cause him little injury. It should have broken, or at least cracked at little under the force of my kick. I jumped at him and tried to force his sword arm down. We scrambled a little, but then he managed to loop one of his great arms around me, and with an almighty shove, threw me face first against the wooden wall of the hall.

Reeling, I struggled to keep my eyes open. My ears were ringing, my head swimming. The last thing I saw was his huge fist surging towards me, and the world went black in a cacophony of pain.

When I woke, I could feel hard wood beneath my back. I looked around, my vision still a little blurred. I winced. My face was tender, and probably quite badly bruised. Looking down, I could see my hands were bound in rope.

I was in a cart, but one designed for the transport of prisoners, the sides high, and barred with iron and wood. We were passing fields, places I did not recognise. I wondered how long I had been unconscious for, and I had previously awoken at all.

The sun was much lower in the sky. It was a new day. But how many new days had passed? Where were we going? I lay many hours in that cart, feeling sick to my stomach from fear and confusion, unable to lift my aching head for most of the time, catching rare glimpses of passing fields and forests.

Finally, the cart drew to a halt outside stone walls. We were at the gate of a large town, perhaps even a city. But I had been to Sorviodunum and Londinium. This was a place I did not recognise.

The door to the cart opened, and a man beckoned to me. I drew back into the corner of the cart, tucking my knees against my chest. He grunted and reached for me, so I twisted my legs away, trying to make my body even smaller. He grunted again, catching hold of my dress and pulling.

I sucked in a deep breath and began to scream with all my might, kicking at him as best as I could. He tightened his grip on me and dragged me by the legs from the cart. The more noise I made drew more Saxons, gathering round me in a circle to stare with their unkempt hair and strange clothing.

He motioned that he would strike me, so I stopped screaming. I realised that I had made an error. The best time would be to escape when there was only one guard, now I had many.

"Where are we?" I asked the man. He looked at me as if I was mad, and then I realised he did not understand what I was saying. I pointed at the walls of the town.

"Where are we?" I asked again.

Another Saxon raised his hand to silence me, but a companion of his stopped him.

"Jorvik," he said, pointing at the walls too. "Jorvik."

The place was called Jorvik? Had they dragged me all the way to Saxon lands and I had not woken? I felt ill, but in staring wildly around me, I caught sight of a sign, daubed in red paint. It was graffiti making light of the exploits of an evidently well-known figure in the town. It was in Latin, and I recognised the name of the place. We were in Eboracum, a city in the north of Britain, in the kingdom ruled by Pellam. To my relief, I had not crossed the sea, but I was still very far from home.

Another Saxon grunted at me, and I realised they were not grunting, but speaking in their own language, which my ear was only beginning to identify. He reached for me, and I ducked away. He reached out again, and caught my wrists, untying the knots that kept them bound. He took the rope away while another pointed towards the city gate.

Their intention was clear. I started moving. We walked through the city, along the main street. There were people, Britons by the manner of their dress, going about their daily business, but with their eyes averted as best they could. I wondered when the Saxons had captured the city, and how long they had been occupied. Why had no news reached me in Garlot?

We walked until we reached a large square, a common area in the city. There was a man there, with long dark hair. It was glossy and been arranged with bones and other decorations with a care reserved for the finest of lady's maids. It belied his great height, his broad shoulders and the huge seax knife hanging from the belt around his fur tunic.

I recognised him. It was the Saxon who had bested me. The group brought me before him and then withdrew. He looked me up and down, with a vicious smirk, no doubt recalling our last encounter.

He pointed to his chest. "Uthred."

That must have been his name. I did not respond or offer mine in return.

"Come, witch," he said. I recognised those words. I knew he was not speaking the language of Britain, so they must be the same in Saxon. I thought he was talking to me, but then a woman emerged from an open door.

She was old, as old as Mila. To a first glance, she was a Saxon, dressed in her rough spun woollen tunic and leggings, and fur pelted cloak

"You speak Latin, girl?" she asked.

. Her Latin was perfect and bore the accent of one priest-taught. This woman, whoever she was, was from Britain, and Roman-born too.

"Very well," I answered, hoping that my translation was perfect. I had learnt Latin from a young age but had no need of it in Garlot. "And I am a queen, you will address me as such."

"Spirited. We'll soon put an end to that."

"She killed two of my men," said Uthred, in broken, accented Latin. "She'd better be worth the trouble."

"Oh, she is. She's good ransom and, if I'm not mistaken, she'll be of particular use to me. Bring her to my tower."

The two Saxons seized me by the shoulders once more and began to haul me after her. They were dragging me into the tower of a sizeable house, the home of a wealthy merchant, or a leading man of the city. Up the stairs we went. I could have kicked and screamed, goodness knows I wanted to, but I had not the energy.

We went to her room. It looked like an apothecary, but I knew better. I could smell the smells that had lingered through my childhood, of baneful herbs and other things known only to the Wise.

"My name is Olwyn. I want to test you," she began, but I interrupted her.

"I will do nothing for you, there will be no tests..."

She slapped me, hard enough for my ears to ring and my bruised face to sting once more. I gritted my teeth, clenched my fists and made to seize her, but she held up a hand, and suddenly my body became very sluggish.

"Don't argue with me, my girl," she warned. "I have powers you can't even conceive of. And even if you can get around me, those two boys out there will make sure you'll have nowhere to go."

She reached down into a wooden box and returned with a sleeping dove in her hands. In one swift motion, she threw the dove onto the table, breaking its neck with a twist of her wrist and took up a knife, slicing it from neck to hind.

"Read it," she barked.

"Read what?" I asked in reply.

"The entrails." She poked the creature with the knife, and some of its guts poured out onto the table. "Quickly, before they lose their shape."

I stared at the blue-grey masses, the red colour fading as the blood drained into the cup Olwyn held close by. I turned away, the acrid stench of the blood threatening to return the contents of my own stomach.

She sighed, almost barking in anger. "Stupid girl! Wasted a portent you have."

"I do not know what I am looking at, or for!"

"Your mother never taught you to look for the signs?"

"She did," I spat. "In the clouds, and the rivers, in the fire, the ink, and the black mirror. Not in dead birds."

"She should have. Nothing gives a better picture than flesh and blood. Right at that moment, twixt life and death, the future is never clearer."

She tossed down her knife. "We'll try again tomorrow. In the meantime, pluck the feathers, clean ones only mind you, and take out its eyes and beak. Good for charms of concealment those are."

I turned from the carcass in disgust. I could see what she was doing here. She was working vile magic for Saxons ends. Had she been the one to counter my charms? The ones that should have kept a threat from Garlot?

147

"Did you choose to be their sorceress?" I asked her.

She looked up at me sharply, and I wondered if she would threaten me, or hit me again.

"I did not choose to go with them, but I chose to stay," she replied, her beak-like nose flaring with irritation.

"Why?" I asked. "From what part of Britain do you hail?"

She did not answer. I tried another tack.

"What is your name?"

"Olwyn. I told you, don't you listen, girl?"

"No, you have another name, from before you were a Saxon."

She looked me up and down, fathoming how I knew that was not her true name.

"Oenone. Saxons can't pronounce it, so I gave them the name of a girl I knew once."

She became stern. "Ask me any more questions and I will cut out your tongue and add it to my brew."

Four weeks I slaved for Olwyn, fetching water to boil and wood for the fires. I cooked her food, well-watched so I did not poison her, and made up her bed for her each night. I laboured too at spell-craft, cooking up noxious charms, ones to strip the will from enemy fighters, to pull secrets from the lips of prisoners and potions to give the Saxons strength.

It sickened me, not only that her ingredients seemed only to be blood, entrails, and human misery, but the thought of the warriors these spells were designed to harm, men like my husband. I tried to resist her with all my might, but I was weak. She seemed to know where I was at all times and carried a switch of hazel to strike me with if I dallied. Once, when no amount of slaps could make me help her, she starved me. I ached with hunger for near a week, almost delirious, before I gave in and told her I would make any spell she wanted if she would only give me a piece of bread.

My thought to bargain with her, to learn more about her, bond with her and beg her mercy was soon abandoned. She had no mercy, and I did not doubt her continued threats to cut out my tongue if I spoke out of turn. I quivered in silence and went many days without speaking.

Escape was at the forefront of my mind always, but never did any chance present itself. Olwyn did not sleep until I was sound asleep and she always woke before I did. Outside the door, there were always at least two burly Saxons, too many and too big to fight. The only time I was not watched was when I used the privy, but always under guard.

Until, out of the blue, I was delivered into safety. One day, working alongside Olwyn in her foul endeavours, there was a great hue and cry from outside the door. The sounds of battle and the rough cries of men struck and beaten.

Olwyn's eyes twitched back and forth from me to the door. I could see it in her eyes. She was scared. Whatever was happening outside our foul workroom, it unsettled her greatly and made her suspicious of me again. This then was my chance to escape, and I resolved to take it.

The door flung open, and in burst a man over six foot tall. He had a mop of dark, unruly hair and handsome features, which were not unfamiliar. This newcomer was dressed in Roman-style armour, and my heart swelled with hope.

"You are British?" I asked. This man could well have been an enemy of my husband, but I was desperate to escape, grateful even for a change of captors.

He nodded. "I am Gawain, son of your brother-in-law Lot," he said.

I breathed an audible sigh of relief. "By his first wife, Mirelle of Lothian?"

"Yes, my Lady, I have been sent by King Arthur to liberate you."

That confused me, but I had not the time to think about it. Olwyn, who had remained silent throughout, was inching slowly towards the door, a work knife in her hand. I leapt for her, intent on having my revenge.

I shoved her hard against the work table. It jostled, and a few clay pots tumbled to the ground, spilling their vile contents onto the stones. She threw up her gnarled hands, the knife discarded, and cowered behind them. In that moment, she was so old and frail, the second clout I wanted to give her seemed excessive.

"If I ever see you again," I warned, holding my clenched fist close to her face, "I will make you wish I had killed you."

She shook her head fearfully and retreated into a corner. Without Uthred or his cronies to bolster her, no switch in her hand and a knight looming over her, she was not so brave.

"We need to run, my Lady," said Gawain. "Are you prepared?"

I nodded and took off, racing from the room, through the stone corridors until we reached the staircase and descended.

"May I call you aunt?" he asked, taking two steps at a time. "You are, after all, the sister of my stepmother."

"You may, though I think, perhaps, we are the same age?"

He chuckled. "Yes, that is true I think...Look out!"

A burly Saxon rounded the corner of the staircase, rushing toward us. I struck out at the Saxon, driving the heel of my hand into his throat, as Nentres taught me, and following with a swift elbow to his face, hearing a satisfying crunch as his nose broke. A kick sent him tumbling to the foot of the staircase. Gawain stared at me with his mouth open.

"Close your mouth, nephew."

We ran on, bursting through the front door and into the courtyard. Gawain drew his sword, but the Saxons were more concerned with fleeing the fortress as the advancing knights closed in on them. The sounds of battle overwhelmed me - screams, hoof beats and the clash of blade on blade. There was a whizz and a crack, and an arrow splintered into the wall behind me.

"The Saxons are shooting at us!" I cried.

"Oh," replied Gawain. "I think that might be our men, missing. We must push on, towards the encampment outside the walls."

We encountered no resistance as we made our way onwards. Gawain commandeered a horse as it wandered aimless and riderless past us. He hoisted himself onto its back, grasping its mane and reaching out a hand to me.

"One thing, Sir Gawain," I said, looking down at my dusty dress I had been wearing for weeks, my tangled hair and my dirty hands. "Do not ever tell Morgause you saw me like this."

He laughed and pulled me onto the horse behind him. He brought the horse to a fast run and rode towards the city walls. The city of Eboracum blurred past me, dirt flying up from beneath our horse's hooves, arrows flying, swords clashing, fallen men both Saxon and British lying in the streets. Yet none of this impressed upon me. I felt that the air was sweet again. I cared now only to see my husband and son again.

We passed through the gate, and into a camp outside the city walls. It was desolate, apart from some painted followers sat grumbling around a cooking pot. All the men must have been in the charge. He drew up the steed and helped me descend.

"My tent is over there." He smirked. "It is the biggest one, with all the banners of Lothian. My squire will be cowering in there, tell him I said he must feed you and find you new clothes."

"Why is that so funny?"

"He is not much of a cook, and definitely not a seamstress. He will have to ask the whores, and I think they terrify him more than the thought of battle. Speaking of which, I must return to the battle. What is mine, is yours, aunt. Take succour where you can."

He turned to remount the horse, but I reached out and tapped the shoulder of my rescuing knight. He turned to face me once again.

"I am tired, Sir Gawain, but tell me, what is the state of Britain, the Saxons have told me nothing in captivity."

"The rebellion was losing against Arthur because there was dissent among the kings and lords," he replied. "They could not unite, and soon many abandoned the cause, leaving only my father, your husband and King Uriens. But then the Saxons' took advantage of our confusion and invaded the entire east coast. Morgause heard somehow that you had been taken and convinced my father to abandon the rebellion to fight against the Saxons. He sent me to lead his troops among Arthur's men. Rescuing you, retaking this city, those are our top priorities."

"My husband, is there news of him?"

"He is commanding forces in the city of Wyndesan. They are entrenched, or else he would have come himself."

"Can you spare some men to escort me to Garlot?" I asked. "Once there, I can raise another levy to assist my husband in Wyndesan. Then we could march on other Saxon strongholds."

"I am sorry, aunt," he replied. "But Arthur has commanded you be brought to Camelot. He has questions for you."

Chapter Seven

The squire fed me as Gawain promised. He returned, flustered, from the camp followers with a rather suspect dress, not intended for a lady of my rank or modesty, so I kindly brought it back to the ladies, and instead borrowed from them some soap and scent. Threatening the squire with a horrible execution if he spied upon me, I bathed from a bucket and, donning a spare surcoat of Gawain's, washed and mended my gown as best I could. I resolved I would burn it when I had something else to wear. It reminded me too much of captivity, and that fiend Olwyn.

The battle in Eboracum raged another day or so, putting an end to the Saxon occupation. Faced with sitting alone in the camp, with naught but Gawain's quivering squire for company, I began to assist with the tending of the wounded and the feeding of the men.

Finally, when Gawain said it was safe, I walked the streets of Eboracum. I looked for Uthred and Olwyn, spurred by a quiet vengeance. I wanted to face them, and show them they had not beaten me. Uthred I found in no time, his decapitated head mounted upon a pike in the centre square, happy maggots munching upon his eyelids. Olwyn evaded me. I knew the extent of her powers, unsurprised if she had turned herself into a hawk and flew from the city. Or, more than likely, she had been the one to cut the throat of the poor butcher's boy and steal their delivery pony from the yard.

There were many stricken by the Saxons in the city of Eboracum. Houses had been raised to the ground, food and gold stolen, women raped and men killed for looking at the wrong warrior, hunted in the alleys for drunken sport. I joined the effort of Gawain's troops to bring relief, distributing food and necessities. Helping those people who had been so afflicted, I began to feel like myself again. I knew I would never have my revenge on those who had killed my men and kidnapped me, so I vowed from that day that no one should ever have to feel as I did, powerless and threatened, even if I had to don armour and sword myself to see it come true.

In truth though, I had merely traded one form of captivity for another. Gawain was a pleasant enough jailer. He kept me well fed, and treated me with all the respect due to his aunt and the Queen of Garlot. We laughed often enough, as I told him tales of Morgause's childhood and he regaled me of many incidents she had incited in the Orkneys and in Lothian. But we both knew I was not free to leave the war-camp at Eboracum.

"I have news, aunt," he said, some weeks after my rescue. "Your husband was relieved by Arthur's forces, and together they routed the Saxons back to the east coast. They are contained within the lands given to their settlers in the last treaty."

"I can go forth from here then?" I asked, trying to keep the hopeful edge from my voice.

He could not meet my eye. "No, my Lady, I am afraid not. Arthur has commanded we set out for Camelot, now that Eboracum is under our control again, and the roads are safe once more."

At least ten days we were on the road to Camelot, and I saw more of Britain than I ever had cause to. Mounted on a grey mare, I rode alongside Gawain and he pointed out the lands we passed. As we moved along the great road to Camelot, there were many blackened shapes along the sides, and a closer inspection proved them to be the burnt remains of dwellings and farm buildings.

"Did the Saxons do this?" I asked as we passed yet another.

Gawain gave a solemn nod. "Yes, or some of the rebel lords as they passed, if the people here were for Arthur."

"My husband would never do such a thing!" I responded, indignant.

"No," he said, holding out a placating hand, and offering me his winsome smile once again. "I am sure he would not."

Time and time again, there would be people upon the road, marching along in tattered clothes with their hands out to us. I struggled to avoid their eyes as Gawain bid his squire distribute gold coins to them.

"Who are these people?" I questioned.

"They are people who once lived in those burnt-out shells."

"Have they no lord to look to them?"

"Few lords care for their people so deeply aunt."

I looked down, surprised at my own naivety, and asked no more questions, even as we passed people hoeing at hard dry earth, or scrabbling in the muck.

We came upon the castle of Camelot, jutting thick and proud from behind the hill. It was exactly as I had left it, before the death of Igraine. Four, thick square towers bounded the stone walls, guarded arches bearing entrance as we crossed the wooden drawbridge, over the murky moat. There was more to Camelot though than what could be seen with human eyes. It had once been a hill fort of the people who stood against the Romans, and had many tunnels going deep into the hillside.

Across all the empty land around Camelot there were tents and encampments, and some people were even building wooden structures. Little fires gave off grey smoke, wisping above the peaks of the brightly coloured tents. And such noise! The screaming of the battle of Eboracum was nothing compared to the rumble of that crowd.

"What are all these people doing here?" I asked.

"They are the kings and lords," Gawain replied. "With their families, and their men, and all their attendants. Arthur will have summoned them, to swear fealty to him, now the feast of Pentecost is upon us."

There were many banners, and I struggled to recall the lessons in heraldry Uther had given me. I could not identify many of them, but there were kings and lords from across the country.

"Pentecost?" I wrapped my tongue around the familiar name, reminding me of days in Tintagel. "A Greek word, meaning the fifth day?"

He shook his head. "The fiftieth day, madam. It is a Christian holiday. I keep forgetting that you and Morgause are pagans."

I looked at him in surprise. "You are a Christian, Gawain?"

"Like my mother," he replied, nodding. "Most of Arthur's court are Christians, or have converted."

"So, what is Pentecost? I do not remember my lessons as a child. We have had the spring solstice, so I know the day is passed, the one in memory of the Christ when he rose from the cave."

Gawain was nodding in the saddle. "Easter, aunt. Pentecost marks fifty days after this, where the Christ sent his Holy Spirit to his followers and they formed the church."

158

"A day of beginning, and of loyalty. Auspicious for the taking of oaths. Arthur is wise indeed."

"No," replied Gawain. "Merlin is wise indeed."

We entered through the great door, as Gawain's squire saw to our horses. There were many people lining the entrance hall, and all the way up the length of the great hall.

"Come aunt," said Gawain. "I will take you straight to Arthur. He will want a break from hearing all these petitions."

"These people mean to petition him? There are so many."

"Such is the burden of a High King."

As we came upon the stairs to the presence-chamber, our way was blocked by a familiar face. Lined with age, but still standing as tall as his great staff, was Merlin.

"Where do you both go?" asked Merlin.

"I have rescued the Lady Elaine..."

"As I foresaw. I mean, where do you both go right this minute?"

"I am bringing her to Arthur. He said he wanted to see her, as soon as we had secured the city."

"I do not know if I can permit her in his presence," said Merlin. "She might endanger him."

"I am no fool, Merlin," I interjected. "Even if I did bear my brother ill will, I would not be so silly as to attack him in a castle full of guards."

"I know you have been playing at swords in Garlot." He scowled at me. "And you were fool enough to disobey me and allow Nentres to challenge Arthur's rule."

I had no response to this. Gawain sought to save me from Merlin's glare.

"Arthur will be furious if he knows you kept his sister from him, not when he has longed..."

Merlin held up a hand. "Fine. I will bring him from the great hall. Do not take her to the presence-chamber, it is too confined for guards to enter easily. Bring her to his chamber."

He left us with another glare in my direction.

"Quickly," urged Gawain. "Before the old demon makes his return."

The High King's chamber was unchanged from my time in Camelot. I stood, pacing before the empty fireplace. Above the hearth, a huge sword hung. I longed to examine it, but it stank of magic, and I was loathe to bring a curse of Merlin's upon me.

Gawain had left me some time ago. "I have men to see to," he said, excusing himself. "Do not worry," he continued, with a wink at me. "Arthur is a pussycat really."

"The High King!" announced a guard, breaking the silence of the room in two.

I sunk to my knees at once.

"Rise," was the command from his strong voice, though I could hear the youthful tones there too.

I stood up, and could see him standing there in the doorway. He entered, and Merlin and the guard meant to follow.

"Leave us," he directed them, banishing them with a wave of his hand. The guard went at once but Merlin lingered until a second glance sent him on his way, tapping his staff along the stone floors. The High King shut the door behind them.

He was much unlike any man I have met, save his father Uther. And his father's son he was. He was strongly built for a boy just become a man, and imposing. His prowess as a warrior could not be denied, for he was well-muscled, and his legs looked both thick and capable of great speed. His

160

golden hair shone in the light of the fire, but his eyes were jade green, and brimmed with secret mirth. Some part of our mother had made itself known then.

In the face of his beauty, I had to remind myself that this man was my half-brother, and my husband's enemy. But, perhaps I misjudged Igraine too harshly, if he was truly made in his father's image.

"They tell me you are my sister, Queen Elaine of Garlot," he began.

"I am, Your Highness," I replied. "By our mother's first husband, Gorlois of Cornwall."

Silence hung in the room. He gestured to the table and I sat. He reached to pour wine from the jug, and I held out my hand.

"I will do that, my King, as is proper."

I took it from him, and poured too hearty cups.

He blushed. "You must call me Arthur, or brother at least."

I smiled, trying to put him at ease, though I knew well the awkwardness he felt. "If it pleases you. And you must call me Elaine, or sister."

"I will," he said and sat beside me with a bounce like a dog come to play. He was not so grown then. "You are not my prisoner, if that is your presumption. You are free to return to your lands any time you like, now we have met one another at last."

"I am grateful brother. That is very chivalrous of you."

"I could never keep my sister hostage!"

"Though I suppose Merlin advised you otherwise?"

He looked down for a minute, then fixed me in his gaze and I could have sworn I was conversing with my mother.

"Yes, but I would never do something so shameful, though your husband hates me so," he said.

I laughed unexpectedly, then raised my hand to cover my mouth, but it escaped nonetheless. "He does not hate you! Why, he does not know you! He bears you no ill, but he struggles with the thought of a sixteen-year-old king, especially one who was raised away from the court, by Merlin of all people!"

"I cannot help my age, nor my foster-father. But I am the once and future king."

"Perhaps, but would you not appoint a council of people to advise you? Other than Merlin? If you asked some of the less ambitious rebel kings, it would quickly put paid to the uprising."

His face lit up. "And the table could be round, so that no man can sit at its head, and put himself above the others. Perhaps we could even look to the Romans, they had other systems of government before the Emperor, where much of the people were equal."

"Forgive me for interrupting you, but perhaps you excite yourself? Form the council first, and a table will follow. And your Roman government, if you so wish it."

He smiled and nodded, his golden hair bouncing upon his head. "Wise counsel sister!" He leapt up from the table and I reached out to settle the wine jug, for fear it toppled over. "Why! You must sit upon it!"

I laughed. "I do not think the vassals will look kindly upon a woman advisor. Few men are like my husband, who allows me to be seen to give him advice."

I summoned forth the deepest voice I could muster, in perfect imitation of a hardened king. "Women are to wed, bed and breed."

He blushed, but laughed nonetheless. Then he grew serious. "I cannot be at war with my sister. Will Nentres not relent?"

I knew Nentres treasured me dearly, and would forever be in the debt of a man who saved his wife from the Saxons, and returned her without harm, though he had cause to do other otherwise. But husbands are wont to be contrary, just because they can.

"Nentres will have much to think on when I return. I will do my utmost to convince him otherwise. Now I have seen battle for myself, Britain must have peace."

"Britain must have peace," he echoed.

"Come," he said, beckoning with his hand. "See this!"

I rose, and he showed me to the mantle, where the great sword in its leather scabbard lay in pride of place.

"This is Excalibur." He held it aloft, still scabbarded.

"The sword you pulled from the stone?"

"No sister, Merlin keeps that. This was given to me by the Lady of the Lake."

"Of whom do you speak?"

"Niniane, Merlin calls her, or Vivian in Latin. She rules the Isle of Avalon."

"I do not know much of Avalon."

It was never talked of at Tintagel or Camelot. Morgan asked Petronella about it once, having seen it mentioned in a story, but our grandmother told us that we had no need to know anything about it.

"It is a wondrous place. Though," he conceded "I have never been there, save upon the shore to receive Excalibur. It is an island, in the Summer Country. It looks tiny, and you cannot see it at all, because there is a thick grove of holly trees all the way around the island. It looks too small to live on, but Merlin says there are vast caves and tunnels beneath the island, and its people mostly live there.

"He has been?"

"Often. I think he spent much time there, during the Druidic purges. He said that it was home to nine Druidesses, the most powerful of all and they cast spells upon the island, so it could not be entered by those who would do them harm. Niniane is the last of their daughters and rules there now."

"And why did she give you Excalibur?"

"It was forged long ago, by a man come from the east, where the Christ lived. It was foretold his sword would save Britain, so the Druidesses imbued the sword with their power, so no man can lose a battle with it. And the scabbard, it is enchanted so that no man who carries it will bleed from a cut. It is the sword of the once and future king."

He passed it to me. Its weight was incomparable to my short sword. It took both hands to hold lengthwise, reminding me of my early days in the practice yard. I returned it gratefully to his outstretched hands. He clasped it tightly, before returning it to its place on the mantle. He looked at me with keen eyes.

"Can you sense its power?" he asked. I hesitated.

"Easy sister, I bear the Wise no hatred, so long as they use their gifts for good, not ill."

164

I sighed in relief. "That is good to hear. Yes, I can, very much so."

He looked downcast. "I cannot. I wish I could. I hear our mother was very powerful."

"Yes, and our grandmother more so. We come from a lineage of powerful witches."

"But no warlocks?"

"Not that I know of. Merlin did not teach you any of the art?"

"He said I had no aptitude. And that I must be a Christian regardless, and no follower of the Christ can be a warlock."

"That much is true, they have commands from their God to burn any who would make a spell," I replied, restricting my other words as they formed in my throat.

How I yearned to correct the poor boy, so mislead by his foster-father. To wield such a sword, one must have even a little of the art, even if they do not know it. But Merlin was crafty. If his charge learned to use magic, what need would he have of his Druid advisor? And the other lords would mistrust a warlock king, but would respect a Christian king. Merlin had this whole country in his thrall, like flies in a spider's web.

"You look disturbed, sister?"

"I am worried for my son," I replied. "I have not seen him since I was taken by the Saxons. My servant will care for him well, I know, but still, I know not even if they escaped the assault on my castle."

But he was safe. I could sense it. I would know if he was dead, surely a mother would sense if something befell their child. I had tried to dreamwalk and scry, but without the proper tools in Eboracum and now here in Camelot, my art had failed me.

"Are you hungry?" he asked, as we resumed our seats. "I have kept you from your supper, in my excitement to meet you."

I laughed. "You were excited to meet me?"

"Oh, yes! My sister, who grew up with my mother and father, here in Camelot. You must be able to tell me so much about them."

"You never met them? The whole time you were at the house of Sir Ector?"

He shook his head. "No. Anytime they came, Merlin would take me to the forest. I did not know then I was their son. He told me it was because I was a pauper in the home of Sir Ector, and not fit to meet a king."

"You did not know you were to be our king?" I asked, surprised.

He shook his head. "I knew only that Sir Ector was my guardian, and Merlin my foster-father and tutor. I only found out when Merlin came to us on the eve of Uther's – my father's, I mean – death and told me. Then I pulled the sword from the stone before the lords."

"You were never suspicious, not even as Merlin taught you kingship?"

He shrugged. "I thought, perhaps, I was Sir Ector's illegitimate son or the son of a disgraced lady who had given me up. I did not know they were lessons in kingship then. Merlin told me I must be learned, for how else was I to make my way in the world, with no family, no property and no rank?"

My heart almost broke in my chest. I had known only of Igraine's loss and her neglect of me as its result. But poor Arthur, all alone in that house, fed and watered, but none to love him. Thinking himself an outsider, unwanted, abandoned. Fearing his future, with none to stand behind him. If Nentres ever agreed to such a plan for my child, I would kill him.

"I will tell you anything you wish to hear," I offered, my voice as tender as when I sang to Hoel.

He jumped up from the table, and I had to lean all my weight forward to keep the bench from tumbling over.

"I will have food sent up here at once! And a chess board, so we can play as you tell me."

He clicked his fingers, and a page ran into the room to answer his summons. He ordered more food than we could possibly eat between us, enough sweetmeats to put a cook's hand raw in their making, and then sat on the table, drumming his hands upon the wood like an errant child as we waited for the servants to come.

As trenchers and bowls were put before us, he stared at me with expectation. I took a deep breath, and began at the beginning, with Petronella and her little hut on the Cornish shore.

He beamed at me. Never, I thought, could someone be so happy, as I told him about the happier things I remembered, Uther's jousts or the tricks Morgause and I played on one another. When Arthur said I was free to go, it had been my resolve to depart at once. But I could stay at least one night, if only to keep that smile upon his face.

Arthur let me sleep late the next day, having kept me up begging for stories and memories. When the maid came the next day to rouse and dress me, bearing a tray to break my fast, I asked after Bronwyn. She told me our old servant had returned to her sons in Cornwall.

The maid instructed me that I was to join Arthur in the presence-chamber as soon as I was ready, but the tone of her voice suggested I make my eating and dressing very quick. I still only had the old dress I wore in captivity, so we tried our best to make it presentable, despite the fact I had made much mending of it in Eboracum.

I made my way to join Arthur with all the composure and comportment befitting a queen such as myself, but if I had known, I would have run the length of Camelot to get there.

Standing there, in the presence-chamber, was Nentres. I ran into his arms and thought I would never be able to let go unless it was to fold Hoel into our embrace.

"I am so sorry," he breathed into my ear, his voice almost cracking and tears threatening to spill. "I am so sorry I left you unguarded."

"Hush, I am safe now. All is well."

"I am sorry I did not come for you. If I had known, I would come for you at once."

"And let Wyndesan fall to the Saxons? I would never forgive you."

"I promise Elaine, I will never lose you again. I will find you, I will always find you."

"Hoel, is he safe?" I asked.

"He is in the care of Mila at her brother's steading," he replied, as my heart stopped thudding in my chest. "Her son rode through the battlefield to get me news of him."

"Brave man. He must be rewarded."

"He will, my love," said Nentres, stroking my hair.

There was a cough from beside the throne. Merlin was staring at us expectantly.

"Have you seen the error of your ways then, King Nentres?" he asked.

Nentres jaw clenched with anger, and I rubbed a gentle hand beneath the cuff of his leathers. He squeezed my hand in return and then let go of me, getting down on his knees.

"I capitulate, Arthur Pendragon, and recognise you as our High King," he began, and then he unbuckled his scabbard sword, laying it at Arthur's feet. "I recognise you as my liege lord. Garlot is your vassal, and I pledge my men and their swords."

Arthur jumped up from the throne, as happy as he had been playing chess and eating sweetmeats.

"Excellent! You must call me brother, Nentres, now we are at peace. You are the husband of my sister, and my sworn brother-in-arms. Why, I will make you a general of my troops! For only such a skilled warrior could have held out so long against me!"

He went to embrace Nentres, and I had a strange feeling in my stomach. It was a sense of happiness I felt only in Garlot, when I was with Nentres, or when Hoel was born. I realised that, despite our short time together, I had come to care for Arthur. Despite Merlin's scowl at Arthur's easy forgiveness, it felt good to have peace between my husband and brother.

Arthur permitted us to repair to our chamber so that we might have some time alone and allowed us to eat there too. How I wished I did not have to leave that room, save to travel back to Garlot and see my son.

"Are you well?" Nentres asked, for the hundredth time that evening. As we laid together in bed, he placed a comforting hand on my stomach.

"Quite well, husband, if you must ask again?"

He looked at me with sad eyes. "Mila told me what happened."

"That I fought a Saxon horde so that she could get our son to safety? Why, I thought you would be proud?"

He nodded. "Quite proud. But you killed two men. Their bodies were still in the hall when I returned."

"I am sure you have killed far more."

"I am a man, a warrior, and a king."

I shrugged. "I had much time to think about what I did. It sickened me, at first, but I would have done it again, for Hoel, and for you."

"You are my warrior queen." He leant down and kissed my bare shoulder. "And all was well as it could have been, in captivity? The Saxons are not known for their kind treatment of prisoners."

"Nothing untoward happened, if that is what you are asking. A few slaps here and there. No more than I received from my sisters growing up."

He pulled me close, but his eyes did not lighten. What a thing to be a man and feel such pride, and be so distraught when it is wounded.

"I am sorry that you had to capitulate to Arthur," I offered.

"Do not blame yourself," he replied. "Our defeat was coming. So many had turned from the cause and that left only Uriens and Lot beside me at the Battle of Bedegraine. Uriens would have fought to the bitter end, but Lot was for turning at any moment, whatever would serve his ends first. I think he realised that he may not have become High King if we were indeed victorious. Even if you had not been taken, we still would have had to call a truce to fight the Saxons."

"And the threat is defeated? We are safe?"

"Yes, my love. Garlot is free of any Saxons. There may yet be another battle against the Saxons, but we are sure now of victory, being united.

I have thought long on this, on the road to Camelot. It is not fair to judge Arthur by age or by whom he was raised. I was in his position once, and had I not Uther's support...But if we are here to guide him, perhaps..."

"Yes," I agreed. "If he can keep to those ideas he has. He seems to inspire Gawain, and I have come to know my nephew well. I cannot shake this feeling, Nentres. That we are meant to be here, at his side."

I met many people during our stay at Camelot. There was Sir Kay, Arthur's foster brother who I gather had not been the kindest of childhood playmates, but all seemed to have been made well between them, and Kay was made seneschal of Arthur's lands. And many other knights, lords, and kings besides, all of whom had distinguished themselves in battle or had glorious deeds to their names.

Always there was someone else I had to be introduced to. When Arthur and I were walking together among the crowd in the hall of Camelot, he pulled me by the arm, saying his greatest friend had returned at last.

At the end of Arthur's rush, there was a man. He was fine featured, with olive skin, and dark eyes. His beard was close slipped, but his hair was long, falling in neat curtains either side of his face, obsidian ends brushing the collar of his robe.

"Sir Lancelot du Lac, a faery prince of Avalon," said Arthur.

The knight laughed. "Sire, you make much of my time there, but it was only a few years."

"You are of Avalon, sir?" I asked, intrigued.

He smiled, and I could see he was handsome indeed. Alongside himself, and with Gawain and this Lancelot fellow, Arthur was building himself a very pretty court indeed.

"In a manner of speaking, my Lady. Do you know of the kingdom of Benwick?"

"Yes, across the sea?"

He nodded. "My father was king there, but we were driven from it when I was a boy. We arrived here in Britain, and my mother, she was of the old religion and knew Niniane well. She was kind enough to take me in, and fostered me until Uther pledged troops to restore my father."

"I remember the campaign well, Uther said it was most difficult."

"Yes, there are parts of the land-across-the-sea who still consider themselves under Roman rule, though they have heard naught from the empire in decades. One these kingdoms, Gaul, is governed by a man named Frollo. He lent his aid to the battle. He is...he is most cruel."

"I am sure my sister need not hear such things," said Arthur. "Though I know it is a matter of great importance to you. Tell her more of Avalon."

He turned his bright, white, straight teeth on Arthur, and looked at him with indulgent affection, like he was a child asking for another minute of play before bed. Lancelot, despite his fatherly attention, was not much older than Arthur, and younger perhaps than me.

"He loves stories of my old home," said Lancelot. "Though I have told them until the river ran dry. It is an island, surrounded by trees, great groves of holly and mistletoe which were holy to the Druids who made their home there. But we lived underground, in tunnels carved into the island itself. No man has ever traversed them all, and even my foster mother did not know where they all led, or what was in every room. She said there may even have been a tunnel to the Underworld or to the realm of the Sidhe."

Arthur sighed. "If I were not King, I should like to be an explorer, and learn the mysteries of Avalon. There must be many forgotten places across Britain that want remembering. We focus too much on the pain of the past, and not what we can learn from it."

I wondered if he meant those pretty words he kept offering, or if they were just Merlin's phrases. I turned back to Lancelot. "Do you see your foster mother still?"

"Alas, no," he replied. "None can set foot upon the island without her permission, lest they face a terrible curse. I cannot reach her, for I know not how to send her a message."

"That is a shame."

"Well, I am a Christian now, and the priests would not like it. Forgive me, Sire, but I would like to rest, and there are many more I must greet before I retire."

He bowed his leave and went. Arthur smiled after him, then took my arm and threaded it through the crook of his.

"What do you think of Lancelot, sister?" he asked.

"It is not for me to say," I replied. "But I like him well enough."

"He is my dearest friend and a brave warrior. I might have been slain in this rebellion a hundred times were it not for him."

We took a turn about the hall.

"I have been thinking," he began. "Many of the kings who fought against me, I have taken land from them, as punishment. There is some in the north quite close together and I thought to join them as one, together, as a new kingdom, and set Lancelot at its head."

"Is his kingdom of Benwick not sufficient for him?" I asked.

"It is a small kingdom and ravaged by its time under Frollo. It cannot support any growth, and I wonder how long it will be before it is annexed by another kingdom, or Gaul comes for it again. But Lancelot lent many men to my cause, dispossessed from their own home by the conflict, and as king of this new land, he could make grants to them."

"Lancelot has not asked this of you?"

"This is of my own making. I have not even consulted Merlin yet."

"Well, beware the man who would ask such honours of you. But Lancelot seems well bound to you and your cause, and it would do you not harm to have a man in the north under your banner."

"Again, more wise counsel," he said. "If only I had you with me from the start."

I grew inclined to walking about in Camelot, with a freedom I did not have when I was there previously. One of my favourite places was the battlements, where I could see for miles around. However, that day, Merlin was standing there, his staff in hand. He leant upon it, staring out into the hills. Spying him, I tried to turn back before he caught sight of me, but he turned and beckoned me.

"Come, Lady Elaine, and see the view. It is spectacular."

I approached him with caution. The idea of being alone with Merlin at such a great height was most unnerving. His power thrummed from him, like great waves rolling across the shore. I took meagre steps towards him until I was close enough for my liking.

"Your sisters come," he said.

"How do you know?" I asked.

"Uriens sent word he and his queen were for Camelot by the end of the sennight, and Lot pledged Morgause as his ambassador, for he is trapped by a sudden raid from the Picts. But, mostly, I can sense their approach. The daughters of Igraine are powerful, they do Petronella proud."

I wanted to ask how he knew Petronella, and why she would not speak of him unless pressed, but I was not sure I wanted to. Merlin heard my unspoken thoughts, by his craft or by his skill in reading people, I did not know.

"Let Petronella's secrets die with her," he said. "As my mine will one day, and yours too."

"Can you really see the future?" I asked. "I sometimes have feelings or seeings of portents, but it is never clear."

"Oh yes," he replied. "I can never see what I wish to, but my visions are as clear as that hilltop over there."

"What did you see then? For my mother, I mean. What did you see that made her betray my father?"

"I saw a sow lie with a dragon and give birth to a great boar. It speared many men, and their blood ran out into a field that bloomed fertile."

"Ah, the boar and sow for Cornwall, the dragon for Uther, the field for Britain. I see, almost. I have not your skill for interpretation, nor your flair for bringing it to pass."

He smirked at that, and then grew serious. "Do you hate me for what I have done? Did you hate Uther?"

"I tried. I tried to have vengeance for Gorlois, but to carry that weight in my heart, like Morgan does? It is heavy, and I chose not to."

"If Morgan resumes her path to revenge, she will one day live with ghosts, as I do."

"Sound advice."

"Hmm. What then, of Arthur?"

"He is my brother, and I owe oath to Uther and Igraine to be his faithful champion. But I too can see his goodness. And such designs he has for Britain! Is it wrong of me to hope he will deliver us from Saxons and other invaders, that he will finally unite us?"

"No, not wrong of you at all. That is why your father died, why your mother bore him, why I raised him."

"You raised him well, I concede that point." I tried to look him in his eyes of fire and found I could not. I looked away. "What do you want from all this, Merlin? Are you truly a servant of the Gods, or do you have an ulterior motive?"

"My life has been long, and hard, Lady Elaine. I have learnt many things, but this was the most difficult lesson. If you know what you desire most, guard it well. Once spoken, people will try to take it from you."

Silence rolled over Camelot, such was the power of honesty from Merlin. I had no response, and he had nothing to add. We stood in silence, almost companionable, until he decided to ruin my newfound respect for him.

"Do you think Morgause is still as busty as she was?"

I harrumphed and left him to his depraved imaginings.

Morgause was the first to arrive. At the head of a whole column of warriors, she looked both beautiful and fearsome. She wore a dress, the shade of which just touched purple. It was a crime to wear purple in the court of the High King, but Morgause's teasing of the law only added to her aweing appearance. She strode into Camelot, not the ambassador of a vassal kingdom, but the returning conqueror.

She greeted Arthur first, as was appropriate. He bowed to her, lower than he should have. There was something indeed quite odd about their greeting. He kissed her proffered hand and held onto it far too long. Morgause did not give the formal words of capitulation as she was supposed to, instead a red flush rising up her neck, and was drawn into wild laughter at some joke of Arthur's beyond my hearing.

Moving on, she curtseyed to the rest of the assembly. Rising up, her eyes locked with mine. There was hurt there, but relief too. I broke the silence, fearing that, if I did not, we might never speak again.

"Thank you, Morgause. For saving me."

She nodded. "Whatever has passed between us, I could never allow my sister to be kidnapped by Saxons. I saw it in my scrying pool, and I knew I had to do something. I saw that hag you were with too. I hope you killed that old bitch."

I shook my head. "She got away. I cared more about getting free, but I went back to look for her."

"You leave her to me. Women in the Orkneys know how to work a curse, and I have learnt much from them."

She held out her arms to me. "Come, sister, embrace me."

I went forward gratefully, and she folded me against her breast.

"I worked no charm," I said against her dress. "I swear it, on the life of my child and my husband, on the honour of Garlot."

I felt her nod, her copper locks brushing against my forehead. "I know the truth now, Elaine, and my ill will has long gone. I regret now our harsh parting, and should have written to you, but my pride would not allow it. Besides, Lot has been a husband to me beyond measure."

I pulled back. "Is he good to you?"

"Oh, yes," she answered, holding out her hand. "Look at this ring. There are no gems like that in the earth of Britain. Men died to bring this to me."

So, then, it was not marriage as I knew it. But Morgause was happy, and that was enough for me.

"You say you have a child?" she asked.

"Yes, a son, his name is Hoel. But first, I must ask, you know our mother has died?"

"I know. I may not be able to come and go easy from the Orkneys, but news of a queen's death will still reach us."

"I was there. She bid me come."

"How awful for you. I am glad I was so far away. It would have been so terrible to see her near the end of her life."

She took my hand. "Let us speak of her no more, only to say that we hope she is happy where she is, and that none of us are too sad to see her gone. Now, come help me settle in, and we can tell each other all about the past four years."

Morgan was next to arrive, on the arm of Uriens. He was stooped and haggard, more so than the day of my wedding, and I wondered if his health was failing. After Uriens had made his formal capitulation, Arthur welcomed Morgan to court, gathering us three sisters to him in the presence-chamber.

Morgan and I embraced each other, as did Morgan and Morgause. The four of us stood, holding hands in a circle.

"It is so good to have our family reunited," said Arthur. "I do not know how I ever felt alone in this world when my family was so near to me. It is a shame that our mother and my father could not be here to see this."

"Yes," said Morgan, though her tone implied sarcasm. "They were sad days for us, and for Britain, when we lost Igraine and Uther."

"I must go," said Arthur, releasing my hand. "There are many more to see, but all of you must sit at my table this evening."

We bowed as he left.

"That is going to take some getting used to," said Morgan. "Bowing to a sixteen-year-old boy. Come, sisters, join me in my chamber."

Morgan went on ahead while Morgause and I came later. Morgan had changed from her black riding habit to a blue gown in the Roman style. It was so fine that I had to compliment her on it.

She shrugged. "Uriens has his uses sometimes."

She gestured to the chairs, and Morgause and I sat.

"Have some wine sister?" proffered Morgan, a clay jar in her hand. I nodded happily, pleased to have the three of us together and alone at last. I settled down beside the cup she filled and took up my embroidery, stitching a little green forest. Those lengthy days alone in Caer Mor had practised my hand into that of an artist.

"When do you return with Uriens?" asked Morgause.

"Too soon," she replied. "Perhaps before the end of the sennight, or sooner, if Uriens tires of the kitchen wenches. He has pledged his fealty, and that is all he came to do. It is a question of whether his anger wins over his pride. He did not enjoy Arthur rescuing him from the Saxons, I can tell you."

"Is he so very bad to you?" asked Morgause.

"He is. But one day, he will push me too far."

Morgan glanced around the room, and then said in hushed tones "Sisters, a spell of silence, if you please?"

She held up her hand to cast the charm, and Morgause and I lent her our power. Now none would be able to listen to our conversations unless they were hidden behind the tapestry.

"What is the need for such privacy?" I asked her.

"I have a matter of great importance to discuss," she replied. "It is about our brother."

"What about our brother?" asked Morgause.

"I do not know if we can support him. In my eyes, his claim is weak."

Morgause's hair was tucked up under a burnished gold crown, far grander than my own that I wore on few occasions and grander still than Igraine's had been. She plucked at a tray of fruits brought at great expense from the east, discarding the ones she felt not to her satisfaction.

"Lucky it's not up to you then," replied Morgause.

"Sisters, do you remember Petronella's story of the Fisher King?" asked Morgan.

I nodded. "The High King who grew sick and weak from a wound to his groin, and so did his kingdom. The land died, the river dried up and the people lived in misery. All the king could do was fish in the dry river beds until a brave warrior brought mercy to him."

"It was not a story. It was our history."

"And from whom do you know this?" I asked.

"Mother Abbess, of course," she replied.

"And what does this have to do with Arthur?"

"The Fisher King failed in his duty to his people, to protect them, to feed them and to maintain his line. High Kings are sacred, Elaine. They are the embodiment of Britain, appointed by the Gods themselves. They, the land and the people are one. When the Fisher King died without issue, the Druids intervened. They had to bind the land to another man, or Britain would die. For this spell, they used a sword and a stone – symbols of Britain and the power by which a king rules."

"Are you saying Merlin performed such a spell and passed it off as a miracle of the Christ?"

"That is precisely what I am saying. Arthur is an imposter, and Merlin's magic has set him there."

"To what ends?" asked Morgause

"Arthur was conceived outside of Uther's marriage, with a woman who was the wife of his enemy unjustly killed. The Gods would not look favourably on Uther, or Arthur, unless Merlin intervened."

"But what harm could it do?" I asked. "Arthur appears to be a good man, and well supported, even by our own husbands."

"Arthur is no more a true king than Uther was," she replied. "Druid magic can make any man king, or any woman queen, for that matter."

181

"I know what you mean." I threw up my hands in exasperation. "This again, Morgan? You, queen regnant of Britain?"

"Have you no ambition, Elaine? Look at us. Standing here, in this room, are the three most powerful women in Britain. Between us, we hold our country's destiny in our hands. Our castles in strategic positions of great importance, our rich farmland, and forests...why, Morgause, your husband almost rules the sea because of his fleet! One move from us and the country will be ours."

"Morgan, you misunderstand," I said. "It is our husbands who rule so greatly."

"No, Elaine, you misunderstand," she retorted. "We could easily take power from these men, our so-called husbands, and rule in our own right."

"Taking power is easy done, but keeping it is another matter entirely."

"And could we not, with all our magic and cunning? How about it then, we the three sister-queens of Britain?"

"Ha!" spat Morgause. "And I suppose you the leader of us?"

"As is the way of things. I am the eldest. But even the Wise do not live forever, and each of you would have your turn at Britain's head."

I gathered up my embroidery. "I cannot listen to this. This is treason, against our king and our own brother."

"But have you no ears for my plan?" asked Morgan, smirking.

I stayed. All the better to thwart her, I reasoned. In truth, though, I could feel a curiosity quickening in me, one that would surely bloom to ambition if left unchecked.

"Arthur must be removed, of course," she continued, knowing she had my full attention. "While he lives, the magic of the Druids stays strong within him. We must unbind the spell, and the quickest way to do that is his death."

"How?" asked Morgause, her eyes bright as her mind worked. "Arthur has lived too long under Merlin to be got with poison, and he will be protected from sorcery. Merlin and our mother will both have seen to that."

"And no man can defeat him in battle," I added. "Not with the magic of Excalibur and its scabbard. Will you be hiding under his bed with a dagger then?"

Morgan shook her head. "No, in the arts martial, Arthur remains supreme, and assassination by mundane methods leaves too much to chance. But all men are vulnerable to blood magic. Igraine cannot protect him from something she knew nothing of."

"The curse you placed on Uther took eight years to fell him in the end," said Morgause. "That is far too long."

"But representational magic?" suggested Morgan. "Take one thing that is like the other, and stricken it, and both shall fall."

"I have never heard of such a thing," Morgause declared. "What would you even use? No poppet would work, unless you had some of Arthur's blood as you say, and if you were able to draw blood, why not kill him by your own hand?"

Morgause smirked hard, aglow with the vicious ingenuity of her plan. "Arthur's son. Properly done, you could curse the boy to death and kill the father. All he needs is a son, and kings are obsessed with sons. We will not have to wait long, especially not if we quicken things with our magic."

"No!" I exclaimed. "No more. You are talking about harming a child. I will go straight to Arthur."

"And tell him he cannot have a son because his wicked sister will put a spell on it? He will laugh you out of court, if he does not think it a hairbrained scheme to put your own son on the throne."

"What has this got to do with Hoel?"

Morgause turned to me, her face awash with incredulity. "Surely you know? Surely it has not escaped you?"

I shook my head dumbly. She continued.

"Hoel is Arthur's nephew, and the son of Nentres of Garlot, a powerful king. He is, until Arthur decrees otherwise, the heir with the strongest claim."

I gritted my teeth. "Abandon this course, or I will tell Arthur, my own position be damned!"

"Oh, be silent sister," said Morgause. "Morgan will have charmed that wine you have been gulping. Cloves to bind you, or another of mother's tricks."

Morgan eyed me, like a hungry cat about to seize a bird. I reddened under her gaze, feeling like an utter fool that I did not suspect such a thing.

"What about Merlin?" I asked, desperation entirely evident. "You think the half-breed will allow this to go unchecked?"

"You leave Merlin to me," said Morgan. "I have plans enough for him."

"Then I shall hear no more!" I cried, snatching up my embroidery once more, the needle sticking into my closed fist. "This talk stains my very soul."

I swept from the room, blood flowing freely into the little thread forest.

I tried to tell Nentres that night in our bedroom, but my tongue gagged in my mouth. He thought I was choking and hammered upon my back so hard I thought he might break it. I abandoned my attempts to tell him. I was young at the time, but I had seen the effect of mother's binding upon Morgan. It would take many years before I could devise a way around it, and the cause could be lost by then.

So I watched her, and Morgause too, because I did not know what role she would play in Morgan's plot. I could see Morgan watching me too in return

Morgan had learnt a hard lesson when she had taunted Uther, and played a more subtle game with Arthur. When I would contrive to be alone with him, show him that he should be wary of her, she would be there, telling him about how Uther was a great warrior, and discussing all those Greek writings Merlin had taught him. He would ask me to join in their discussion, and Morgan would smirk. She knew I had never read any of them, and would be forced to go from the room lest I seemed ignorant. Morgause too fought for Arthur's attention, and I wondered what sort of game my sisters were playing. Morgause would not speak with me about her intentions. She was still considering her loyalties, she said.

The next day, Arthur requested I join him in the presence-chamber. Merlin was there too, and both were wearing smiles.

"Have you heard the news, sister?" asked Arthur. "I am to be married."

"That is wonderful," I said, grasping his shoulder in congratulations. "To whom?"

He smiled his bright smile again. "To Guinevere, the daughter of King Leodegranz. She is the prettiest girl in all the land, so they say."

I looked at Merlin, and he nodded at me, acknowledging his victory. Leodegranz, King of Cameliard, was wealthy and had many men. If he was loyal to Arthur, so too would be any king who had need of Leodegranz' gold. As far as I knew, Leodegranz had only one child, which would make Guinevere his heir. Merlin had much to teach if you were prepared to learn his wicked ways.

"I will need you, sister," said Arthur. "I have no lady here to be my hostess, so I am asking if you will be chatelaine until Guinevere comes, and organise the wedding festivities."

"The Lady Elaine?" interjected Merlin, incredulous. "What would she know of such things? Garlot holds no great events such as this. Perhaps the Lady Morgause might be better suited?"

Arthur looked at me, and though he had known me only for weeks, I could see he was serious.

"Apart from you Merlin, and perhaps Lancelot," he said. "There is no one I trust more than the Lady Elaine."

"I would be honoured, Sire," I responded, curtseying, and feeling the warmth of Arthur's words in my chest.

We held a great feast that night, to celebrate the engagement. I drank much that night, nerves getting the better of me. I worried that the food would not be well received, and a riot would break out. When I began to slur my words and be unsteady on my feet, Nentres decided it was time for us to retire. I was very upset, for the dancing was about to start.

I could not keep my vision straight, and seemed as though everything was very funny, even when it should not have been. It was as though I was staring at the image in a cracked mirror.

I kept stopping, unable to support my own weight and threating to spew the contents of my stomach onto the floor, much to Nentres' disapproval. At one such delay, the sounds of giggling and whispering could be heard. I looked down a corridor to spy a red-haired woman lead a muscled man into her chamber.

"Was that Arthur and Morgause?" I asked

"No," huffed Nentres. "Now get a move on!"

A few days passed and we assembled, some of us still with sore heads, in the great hall of Camelot to meet our soon-to-be High Queen, and I confessed to Nentres I was a little nervous. I wanted my brother to be happy, and never before I had arranged such festivities, or managed a castle this size. I could see why women such as Bronwyn and Mila were in high demand.

There were many gathered here, and a great number of the vassals who had come to pledge allegiance at Pentecost decided to remain behind. There were many strangers as there were familiar faces.

"Who is that man?" I asked Merlin, pointing discretely at the man in the embroidered mantle.

"That is the Lady Guinevere's bishop, come to do the ceremony," he replied. "Arthur will be most honoured by his presence."

"You raised a Christian, Merlin?" I asked him, it being something I had always found most strange.

"My Lady, I mean no offence, but it would be proper to address me as Lord Merlin." He smiled smugly. "The King has been gracious enough to restore my ancestral lands."

Merlin's lands are part of Uriens' kingdom. Morgan must have frothed like a stricken horse when she heard the news.

I shrugged. "I repeat my question, Lord Merlin."

"It is the religion of the land, whatever we staunch pagans may think. The people, they will forget the old Gods soon enough."

"Our Gods punish disloyalty," I replied.

"And the Christ rewards his followers with eternal life. If you were the simple folk, who live and die in their hundreds, from famine, from wars, plagues and corrupt lords, which faith would you choose?"

"But we ourselves know that life is eternal, but from one body to the next, one life to another. The circle, with no end and no beginning."

He smiled his devious little smirk, and I quickly remembered from where he was spawned. "The Christ is a God of peace. What better religion for this new, unified, tranquil Britain?"

"Now you employ your Druidic rhetoric and forget I am too am so learned. Did you raise Arthur a Christian because rich and pious Leodegranz with all his land and troops would only allow his treasured daughter Guinevere to marry another Christian?"

He fixed me with a cold stare, and a lesser woman would have fled his presence at once. "Little Elaine has become quite the statesman."

"It would be proper to address me as my Queen. But since I am at my brother's court, Princess Elaine will suffice." And, with that, I abandoned Merlin among the throng and returned to my husband's side. I folded my hand inside Nentres' to hide its quivering.

He looked down at me. "Careful Elaine, or you will make an enemy of him. And Merlin always bests his enemies." He tightened his grip around my hand. "Arthur's coronation is proof of that indeed."

"The Lady Guinevere of Cameliard," announced Sir Kay to the assembly, and we all sunk to our knees before her, like a great wave rippling around the room.

Guinevere's beauty was not an exaggeration of a bard's tale. She had hair the colour of honey, and a smile as sweet. Her dark blue eyes were bright beneath her fanned lashes, proud above her rosy cheeks and slender mouth. Guinevere had the sort of beauty that turned heads, and that kings would kill for.

Followed by a man of middle age I assumed to be her father, she went straight to greet Arthur. I could see he was taken with her at once, and she with him. He took her by the hand and led her from person to person to introduce her. When she got to me, we exchanged curtseys.

"I am very pleased to meet you, sister," she said.

"And I you, sister," I replied.

She greeted Nentres and passed on.

I did not get to converse much with Guinevere after her arrival, bar a few moments' pleasantries. My time was almost entirely taken up in organising her wedding, ordering her and Arthur's favourite foods from the kitchen, ensuring we had place enough for all the visiting nobles to stay.

When the day came, I felt like crying. Not from happiness, but from exhaustion. As they proceeded together towards the bishop in Camelot's chapel, I was swaying on my feet from tiredness. I was also irked by my sisters, who stood at the back of the chapel, gossiping in hushed tones.

"Do you think Arthur and Guinevere will be happy together?" I asked Nentres.

He smirked a little. "Clearly you have an opinion, dearest, or else you would not have asked for mine."

I rolled my eyes. "They seem much taken with one another, but they are only sixteen. That may fade, and an unhappy marriage makes for an unhappy kingdom, as we ourselves have seen."

We turned back to watch the ceremony. My vision began to swim, and I thought I was going to faint. I reached out to grasp Nentres' arm, stop myself from falling, but I had touched nothing but air on either side. The chapel appeared to be empty, save for Arthur and Guinevere standing at the altar. I looked at her and saw flames, a striking sword, and a gaping wound. I drew back in horror.

"Elaine! Elaine! Are you alright?" called Nentres, as though he was leagues away.

I closed my eyes and opened them again. I was back in the chapel, thronged with people. The ceremony was drawing to a close, and Arthur was lifting Guinevere's veil, drawing in close for a kiss.

"What is the matter with you?" my husband asked. "I thought you had died, you grew so white and cold."

"I have had I seeing," I whispered, my words still unsteady in my mouth. "At least I think it was."

"Of what?"

"Of her," I replied, nodding towards the bride. "Of death and destruction and her."

I shrugged. "It could easily be a vision or my wild imaginings. These things are never certain,

190

not even to one such as me. I have not Merlin's gift."

"Put if from your mind," suggested Nentres. "And focus on today. The future is never certain, you say that often enough yourself."

In the following days, Guinevere had not yet taken over her duties as mistress of Camelot, preferring to spend her time sequestered with Arthur or praying beside her father in the chapel. I went one day to do rounds of the castle and found men rearranging the furniture in one of the antechambers off the great hall. Curious, I went inside and found Merlin staring with a sour eye at a huge round table made of wood.

"Have you seen this monstrosity?" asked Merlin, gesturing to the table.

"It fills the entire chamber," I replied, marvelling at the size. "Wherever did he get such a thing?"

"Leodegranz had it made for him, as part of Guinevere's dowry. Only he could afford so much wood."

"What is its purpose? We have tables enough in Camelot?"

"He is going to form a council of knights and kings to sit at it," said Merlin, distrustful eyes watching me from under his grey brow. "I wonder where he got such an idea from."

"Uther had a council, I remember."

"Made up only of myself and Sir Ector. This table seats fifteen comfortably."

"More even," I teased. "At least thirty sitting close."

He scowled at me, and I knew I had best leave before I provoked him further.

Deciding that it was time Guinevere got used to the running of her own castle, I went to her rooms. She was reading by the window, some sort of ladies' prayer book, I gathered.

"My Queen," I said, bowing. "Might I have a moment?"

"Sister Elaine," she greeted me. "I have to thank you for helping with the running of Camelot. I wonder if you might now have the time to instruct me upon it."

"Certainly," I replied. I took a seat beside her and began to explain about the laundry, the kitchens and the like. I did not insult her intelligence by explaining the generalities of running a house, of which I was not an authority, but the specifics of Camelot.

"And what of the household budget?" she asked. "From where does the gold come from to make purchases?"

"From the royal treasury, Highness. You need only ask if you require funds."

"And who looks after that? Sir Kay?"

"Oh, Merlin manages that for Arthur, you need not worry."

I saw her frown. "You do not like Merlin?" I asked her.

"He is the son of the Devil, so my father says," she said. "But regardless, I like not how Merlin stares. I know not if he thinks unclean thoughts, or just to swallow me whole. Do demons eat the flesh of humans, surely they must?"

"I do not know," I replied. "But Merlin is a lech, not a cannibal."

"I would move easier in my own castle if he were not here."

"Rest easy, Highness, Merlin oft has business about the country and will not always be at court."

But Guinevere was right. He always seemed to be nearby, watching, observing, and scheming. But as much as I feared him and his reputation, knew the role he had played in the making of Britain, I was intrigued by him and his power.

That night after dinner, he was there, in the solar. Merlin was sat by the fire, a pewter goblet in hand.

"Will you be at court often Merlin?" I asked, settling a safe distance from him.

It was still cold that night, and I had relished the opportunity to sit near a fire, but Merlin had scuppered that plan.

He smirked. "Keen to have me gone?"

"No, my Lord, merely a question. Not everything is double speak with me."

"Like with me, you mean?" he asked. "Oh, my Lady, how you wound me."

He took a long sip of his goblet and was silent. I shrugged and looked about the solar for some recreation, embroidery or reading or knuckle-bones.

He put down his goblet. "Go on, no one ever got anything by not asking."

I stopped searching. "Whatever do you mean?"

But he was right. Something had been on my mind, an idea.

"Could you teach me? High magic?"

He shook his head gravely. "No. It is not for women."

My eyes turned sharp. "Ha! Morgan knows as much of high magic as you do, I bet."

"True, she is well learned under Mother Abbess. Oh, the power that girl has. If I had foreseen her, matters might have been different. Petronella did well for herself indeed."

"See, there are three women who have mastered the art."

"And this is why I refuse. You do not master the art, it masters you, and you become a slave to its power, and to the will of the Gods you serve in exchange."

"I think you lie, to keep women from it, like much on this island."

"No, I mean that women rarely have the discipline. You must devote yourself entirely. No time for children, or husbands."

"Petronella..."

"Petronella was Petronella," he interrupted. "And did she cast great rituals by the sea? I think not."

"You have baited me here, only to cast me down. Do you fear the power of women, Lord Merlin?"

"Only their power to excite me in certain parts," he replied with a vulgar gesture.

I turned away and did not speak to him again. When Arthur joined us, I quickly made my leave of the solar. The Gods may not have been kind in robbing me of my choice of man, but at least they were kind in giving me Nentres.

When the festivities were over truly, we returned to Garlot. Forced to play-act by her binding, I bid Morgan goodbye with a kiss and a smirk from her. Morgause I hugged tightly, and we promised to write often, though it could be a month before a letter reached the Orkneys and a response made. And so often Morgause was at Lothian that letters would be undeliverable.

"You have other means of speaking with one another," suggested Morgan, her superiority dripping from each word.

"Remember mother's warning," I retorted. "A frivolous witch burns fastest."

She scowled, and joined her husband by their horses. Morgause and I shared one last look and then I left.

I settled quickly back into my old life at Caer Mor. I was afraid that Hoel would not know me, but he immediately clasped himself to me when I returned and stayed there all evening. I indulged him because I was glad to see him. With his small body in my arms, I felt as if a lost limb had been returned to me. Mila and her son were richly rewarded with gold and gifts.

The bodies of the Saxons had been cleared away, the damage to our walls fixed. The physical signs would fade, but my people carried other signs. Many had lost their menfolk, men I had ordered to fight the invaders, and my soul was heavy with this for some time. The markets at Merriwyn were subdued, and people were suspicious of strangers. I vowed then Garlot would never yield again, and neither would I.

Chapter Eight

Nentres entered our bedroom, a worried look on his face. I knew at once something was amiss. I tried to rise, but he gestured for me to remain in my bed. I had retired earlier and had been expecting him to join me soon. But not to bring bad tidings.

"I have some news Elaine, and I do not wish you to worry yourself," he said, "But four riders have been spotted entering our borders, armed and pulling something behind them. A chariot; that was how the farmer described it."

"Saxons?" I asked, my hand reaching of its own accord for a sword I was not wearing.

Nentres shook his head. "Unlikely, not in such a small number. And to be pulling a cart or suchlike? No, but some mischief may yet be afoot."

"Scouts or even fore-riders?"

"Possibly. I am just letting you know, in case we must prepare ourselves for battle."

"Is this the life we lead from now on? In constant preparation? Worrying about enemies at our borders?"

He sighed. "That is the life of a warrior, and a king, and perhaps it is his wife who feels it most keenly. But Arthur has promised us peace, and I am foolish enough to hope that in later years we will not have to live as such."

We climbed to the battlements the next morning, and stood and stared, waiting to catch a glimpse of the riders and their strange burden. They approached, first a speck of black against a far-off hill, then four clear man-shapes making their way down the old Roman road. They were indeed pulling a chariot, an old war-chariot by the

197

looks of it. In the back, on the chariot floor, was a misshapen heap of material.

"Do they come against us with some new weapon?" I asked, struggling to keep the edge from my voice.

"I do not know. But they are close enough now we must prepare."

"I will send Hoel to Mila, after she has dressed me."

I descended the ladder and went to my chamber where I put on my leathers, breastplate, and bracers, and scabbarded my short sword, a newly made one, my original having been lost as some Saxon's trophy. I would not be caught unprepared again. By the time I was ready, Nentres had assembled a band of men in the courtyard, armed with swords and spears. I joined them.

The riders were close enough now to be seen from the spy hole in the gate. They stopped at a safe distance, as the laws of hospitality dictated, and made no move.

"Open!" called one of the men.

The doorkeeper looked to Nentres.

"Make no move unless I say," he warned him.

I peered out of the opening. The lump of material began to rise up, taking the shape of a hooded figure. In its gloved hand was a white banner, daubed with a red symbol. It held it up and waved it from side to side.

"I do not recognise that heraldry," said Nentres.

"It is not heraldry," I replied, as I took a second look. "It is a symbol, an old one. It is a symbol of truce and a request for help. From one witch to another."

"This better not be some trick, Elaine."

"We must open the door," I said. "Too many stories have begun with a terrible curse enacted when one of the Wise was turned away from a door. All these stories have some heart of truth."

"Lay down your arms!" called Nentres. "And we will open the gate!"

The men did so, and Nentres signalled to the doorkeeper that the gate could be pulled open. They approached slowly, palms open and flat to show they carried no weapon. The figure put down its banner and made its way into our courtyard, careful to keep its hood about its face.

It curtseyed to Nentres. It was a woman then.

"Take me to your queen," she rasped, a dry voice like a parched bird.

"I am the Queen of Garlot," I stated.

She raised her head to look at me.

"What in the name of the Gods are you wearing?" she exclaimed, her voice becoming familiar at once.

She drew back her hood, revealing copper locks tumbling loose, and a slender chin with rouged lips. Morgause had come to Garlot!

"Sister! What are you doing here?" I asked.

She raised a finger to her lips, for my voice had reached a loud tone in my surprise.

"I come on urgent business," she said. "None must know I am here, save only those who can be trusted."

Nentres saw to the feeding of her men while I led her by the hand into the hall. I offered her food and wine, a blanket to warm her, but she shook her head. I took her into our little solar, for privacy, and hoped she would not find anything amiss. Lot probably had a far grander hall than ours.

"You still have not explained why you are dressed like a man," she said. She raised a lascivious eyebrow. "Does Nentres ask you to dress like that?"

"It is armour. We thought you were invading."

"Perhaps I should, and ban you from wearing that."

"Morgause!" I chided. "You are welcome, but why have you come? Alone? What is this urgent business?"

She looked around the room as if spies lurked in every shadow, and I could see her dry humour was only to buy her time. She drew back the folds of her cloak. Her stomach was swollen and rounded. She was in the early stages of pregnancy.

"I am with child," she stated.

"I can see that. Why would you put you and the child at risk by coming so far?"

"Because it cannot be Lot's," she said.

"Why ever not?"

"I know of only one woman who has conceived without lying with a man, and she is a Christian story."

"You mean to say you and your husband do not do your duty by each other?" I asked.

I wondered why I had such a tone of derision, when I too had been in such a situation. But Morgause had reported her marriage to be happy when we were together at Camelot.

"Apart from the bedding ceremony," she replied. "Which I endeavour to forget with the utmost of my ability, I have never lain with Lot. He much prefers the company of the stable hands, and I too, if I am being honest."

"It is the child of another? And you fear Lot will punish you for shaming him?"

"No, do not be silly. Lot and I have an agreement. Since I am so often not in the king's bed, apart from arranged appearances, he has said any child I may carry he will take for his own, and thus bring forth the child he is unlikely to beget."

"What then made you flee across Britain?"

"He will never accept this child."

"Why not?" I asked.

"Because it is born of incest," she replied.

I looked up in horror, knowing at once the meaning of her words, recalling that hazy night in Camelot. "You lay with Arthur?"

She fixed her eyes upon me, her gaze both steely and desperate. "Elaine, you judge me, but I could hardly contain myself. It was as though I was drunk on the strongest wine. To be near him was excruciating. I knew what we did was wrong, but my judgement was clouded. And I did not think I would get with child...unless..."

"Unless what?" I prompted.

"Unless I was under a dark spell?"

"You think Morgan had a hand in this?"

"She wanted to get her hands on Arthur's son. What if this was her way of bringing it about?"

"There is only one way to be certain," I said. "A spell of seeing, to reveal the truth of the charm."

I fetched some herbs from the kitchen, candles from the store and a bowl of water from the laundry. I bolted the door, and together we laid out the items in their proper place upon the table. Settling down in our chairs, we held our hands over the bowl of water, moving them in clockwise circles, chanting low under our breaths the words to turn the water from mere liquid to a window to the spirit world.

201

The water bubbled in the bowl, grew cloudy, and then cleared to reveal some indistinct shapes. We worked to hold the vision together, like pulling a strong and stubborn ox. If a spell had been cast, we should have seen a vision of its caster, and portents of their methods and reasons. But something was holding us back, preventing us from seeing.

We saw only what she wanted us to see. The bowl bubbled once more, and when the cloudiness cleared again, we saw Morgan lying upon a Roman sofa, reclining in robes of purple.

"What have you come questing for sisters?" she asked, her voice filling our minds.

Morgause spoke aloud through gritted teeth, straining against the force of Morgan's wards. "The spell you cast. The spell upon Arthur and me."

"I cast no spell to make you lie with Arthur. You did that all by yourself. I just wanted to make sure you would conceive. I knew that the royal nursery would be impregnable, but not my sister's womb, when she is complicit in my plan."

"And you think I would carry a child and then hand it over to you?"

"You would keep the spawn of your unnatural liaison, even when it would keep you from the throne of Britain? We cast the spell and hand the child off to some fishwife to raise until it croaks. You will have more, Morgause, true heirs to our lands."

Morgause was close to tears. "I cannot carry this child much longer."

"Then deliver the child in Garlot. Elaine will know the potion to quicken the pregnancy, and I am sure you have enough magic between you to keep it alive. Then bring it to me, at the border of

Uriens' kingdom, and we shall be elevated beyond all men."

"No!" cried Morgause, and she tossed the bowl aside. It hit the far wall, water sloshing down onto the floor.

"I will clean that up," she said, before sobbing into her hands.

I guided her upstairs to my bedroom. Nentres agreed to sleep down in the hall, so I put her to bed, where she cried heartily until she had fallen asleep in my arms.

I permitted her to break her fast in my room that next morning and brought in Hoel to meet her. He was excited to know his aunt, and it lifted her mood to tickle him and play with his little wooden knights that Nentres had carved for him. But I knew time was short, and serious matters needed to be discussed, so I sent him back to Mila.

"This cannot be all that uncommon," said Morgause, voice far calmer than her wringing hands and bloodshot eyes suggested. "The stories from the Greeks, of the man who did not know his mother and fell in love with her. Or the kings and queens of Egypt? Were they not always brother and sister?"

I snorted. "And they fell to the Romans, after centuries of madness plagued them. You speak of the Greek, Oedipus, whose mother hung herself and he gouged out his own eyes when they learnt the truth. No good will come of this, Morgause."

We sat in silence for some time, words tumbling away from our mouths like trying to catch raindrops.

"Elaine," she said finally. "Brew me a tonic of pennyroyal."

"You mean to be rid of the child?"

She nodded. "You are right, as always. And Morgan cannot have this child, I will cast it from me before she can work any evil with it."

"You shall have the tonic tomorrow afternoon. I need time to find the leaves and brew it."

She stood, silent, and left the room.

Morgause was fidgeting near the solar table, as I chopped and ground the herbs that next day.

"You should come to the Orkneys, sister," suggested Morgause. "In the summer, of course, it's very beautiful. Not the winter, those are terrible. We spend most of the winter time in Lothian, where Lot has been regent for Gawain these past years."

Her nervousness showed, babbling to me about things I knew well enough. I let her ramble on. I had a little cast iron pot of boiling water in which I was adding the pennyroyal to stew into a tea. She would have to drink it, all of it, and it would bring on her courses when there should be none. It had been four months since we left Camelot, so it would be painful for her, but I swore I would see her through it.

There was a knock on the door, and Nentres came in. We had seen little of each other since Morgause arrived, and I had no time to tell him all of what was going on. He knew only that Morgause was pregnant and Lot was not the father. He had asked no questions either, not once he caught sight of Morgause's belly.

"King Lot is here, demanding that he be given entry."

I paled. We were so busy, searching for herbs and cloistered in there brewing them, we had not heard the sounds of arrival. "How many men does he have? Can we get word to the steadings for troops, or are the walls surrounded? Why are you not wearing your armour?"

Nentres stared at me. "My armour? His men are watering their horses in the yard and Mila is seeing what we can spare from the stores to feed them. I meant that Lot is outside the door to this room. He does not want to be rude and barge in, it is not his castle after all."

"But he has come for Morgause! By the Gods, what will he do if he sees her condition?"

"Chastise her, I suppose," he replied. "But are you proposing war with Orkney? Because as far as the laws of Britain go, she is his property and if we do not let him see her, there will be trouble to be solved only on the battlefield."

Lot emerged from the corridor, popping his head around the door. "Come, Nentres, old boy, none of that talk, you are scaring your wife. Greetings, Queen Elaine...sister, I should say...are you well?"

I curtseyed. "Quite well, King Lot, brother," I replied, cursing my politeness.

Lot was as unremarkable as the day I first saw him, only a little older, perhaps nearly fifty now. But still his clothes were grand, and he carried himself with an air of entitlement, despite how he was my unwelcome guest. He nodded in his wife's direction as he entered the room.

"You finally went mad then, I take it?" He asked her. "Absconding in the middle of the night, I thought you had taken flight on a broom. Whatever could possibly be the matter?"

"How did you find me?"

"You were spotted by a trader I do business with, when you made the crossing. And by a friend of mine with a tavern in Powys. A fool could have worked out where you were heading."

"Seen by your spies, you mean."

Lot shrugged. "Let's not blather on. Why do you have me chasing you across the country?"

Morgause strode out from behind the table, her rounded figure clear to see. "I could not hide it any longer."

Lot regarded her stomach, rolling his eyes. "Is that it? I thought we talked about this?"

He looked at us. "Everything here stays between us, yes?"

We nodded, silent, Nentres already finding his face tinged red. It was clear he wanted to leave them to it, but I still feared for my sister when the truth would out.

"I don't mind whose the bastard is..."

"It's Arthur's," she interrupted.

Nentres immediately turned to look at me. I shrugged. I would have told him eventually.

Lot's eyebrow shot up. "As in the High King? Your brother?"

"Half-brother."

"It is still incest," he snapped. "Did he force himself on you? I wouldn't be surprised if he wasn't right in the head, hidden away in the forest with Merlin for sixteen years, boy's bound to be a little..."

"He didn't force himself on me...I wanted to," she interjected, her hands on her swollen hips.

He was quiet for a few moments, then he spoke. "Are you stupid? Pregnancy got your wits addled? Why would you even open your mouth? If you didn't want to be rid of it, why didn't you just keep quiet, instead of bolting? Nobody would have been any the wiser, unless it had two heads or something...oh, I see."

He chuckled quietly to himself. "You weren't trying to avoid me by taking the back roads

206

through Powys, you were taking the quickest route to Camelot. I knew it was strange. You were going to him, weren't you? Garlot was a last minute decision. Nerves get the better of you?"

She did not answer. Lot huffed out a sigh and sat down. He reached down to unfasten the light armour he wore for riding, but the angle of the buckle did not lend itself easily to this. Morgause walked over and undid it, remaining silent. He eased off the vest and draped it over the back of the chair.

"What did you think would happen? He'd toss Guinevere aside to marry his half-sister? You are the prettiest idiot I ever clapped eyes on."

"I love him," she said, defiant. Lot clasped her hand.

"I'm sure you do, and I'm sure he loves you. But an incestuous love child? All those pious Christian twats, the southern lords who make up his court? If they didn't all die on the spot they'd soon have him removed from his throne. Leodegranz would kick up a terrible fuss, shaming his precious Guinevere like that. He'd spend all his gold on Gaulish mercenaries and punish Arthur mightily. The two of you would have to go and be sheep farmers in Ireland by the end of it all, could you imagine?"

"But Arthur..."

"But Arthur nothing!" He guided Morgause to the chair beside him and clasped her hand tighter. "I'm sure it's illegal you know, under Roman law. You could be put to death, the both of you. You think Arthur would risk that for you? Men do desperate things to hold on to power. Oh, Merlin! He would see no harm come to his little protégé. You'd be floating in a Londinium sewer if he knew."

Morgause looked on the verge of tears. "It doesn't matter anymore. I am going to take a potion and rid myself of this burden."

Lot folded his hands, elbows resting on the arms of the chair, looking Morgause up and down like he was choosing a horse at the market. "There's no need to do that. Why, this child is a symbol of the great love between you and Arthur, however forbidden it may be. You should keep it."

"I should?"

"Oh yes! You just need to be smart about the whole thing. We will tell Arthur, quietly, and keep the child away from Merlin. To the world, it'll be a child of Lot, but Arthur will know the truth. What if it's a boy? All men love their sons, the ones they shouldn't have even more so. Arthur might even make him his heir, and you'd be his mother, the High King's mother is almost as good as the High Queen. Arthur will have to have him as a knight, or as a great lady if it's a girl. That means a good marriage, lots of gifts for us and the High King's ear whenever we need it. How wonderful!"

Morgause began to think on Lot's words and I could see her mind catch fire with ideas.

"He'd be scared we'd talk, that we would tell everyone, wouldn't he?"

"I'd imagine so," he said.

"And that would mean he would do whatever we want, wouldn't he?"

Lot smiled deviously and all the pieces fell into place. "Yes, I rather think he would."

He stood up and helped Morgause to her feet, the ideal caring husband.

"Now Nentres, old boy, I am absolutely starving, could do with a cup of wine too."

"Um," stuttered Nentres. "My servants are preparing supper in the hall."

"Excellent, excellent. Now," he said, leading Morgause from the room, "we must get you fed, eating for two now, so you are. And where is that stable hand I met in the yard, we were having a most delightful conversation about Roman saddles?"

His voice trailed off into the corridor, leaving Nentres and me to stare at one another.

"What did we just witness?" I asked.

"I do not know," he replied. "But it was more than slightly treasonous."

Supper was a jovial affair, with Lot toasting to his wife's pregnancy. No more talk was made of the unborn child's parentage and, that night, Morgause slept in Lot's room. I spoke only briefly with her the next morning. They were keen to make a return to their own kingdom, preferring the relative nearness and comfort of Lothian until Morgause was out of her child bed.

"Are you sure this is what you want?" I asked her.

"Oh yes," she replied. "Very much so."

"And what will you say? How will you explain your flight from the Orkneys?"

"Lot has already thought of that, he is so clever. He has told the men that I was confused about my pregnancy, and was so worried that I came straight to my dear sister because she has already had a child and would be able to console me. Soldiers are like fishwives, that story will be around the islands in no time."

"And his plan? To manipulate Arthur? You think that is a wise course of action? What if Merlin finds out?"

"We're not manipulating Arthur. He has a right to know about his child, and a duty to take care of it, and its mother. That's all."

"Sister, you also have Morgan to fear. She created that child for her own nefarious purposes, and she will want it handed over to her."

"I can protect myself from Morgan well enough. Anyway, from her letters, she would have a terrible time getting out of Gore, away from Uriens."

They set out that morning, hoping to reach an inn before the light went. A letter came some months later to say that the pregnancy had held, along with a request for some remedy to ease her sore breasts. Nearly a year later, she sent word to say that she had indeed given birth to a son, whom she called Mordred, likely with the same messenger that she was sending to Camelot to notify Arthur. I prayed that she had chosen wisely.

Chapter Nine

My return to Arthur's court was precipitated by a summons from my brother, saying that Britain and he were in need once again. We departed at once, summoning whatever men we could lay hands upon.

I strode into the great hall at Camelot, clad in my armour and my face painted with woad. The assembly stared agape. I would not be Igraine's daughter if I did not delight in a little spectacle from time to time.

"It is good of you to come, sister," said Arthur, reaching out to embrace me, and then Nentres.

"Your letter said you were in need," I replied. "We left at once."

"Yes, it is true. We have Saxon invaders once again. And I have heard rumblings that the treaty settlers may turn on me, for this new Saxon king has much favour among them. I will need your husband as my general once again, and his troops too."

Nentres bowed low. "It will be my honour, Sire. The men of Garlot are at your disposal. Elaine and I have brought only forty with us, our best riders, but we can muster at least three hundred more."

"We will talk business tomorrow. At the council of war. Dear sister, you are welcome as always to sit upon it."

"Thank you brother," I replied.

I spied Guinevere approaching.

"My Queen," I said, bowing at the knees.

"Sister Elaine," she acknowledged with a wary glance at my armour. Reaching out, she patted the leather of my arm quickly and awkwardly, then retreated behind her embroidered handkerchief, bringing it up to cover her mouth.

"Now," said Arthur. "You must be hungry! We must feast!"

The plans were set, the men mustered and the gold set aside from the treasury. Arthur and Nentres rode out with sundry other knights, ready to put paid to the Saxons on our shores. Guinevere took to her bed upon Arthur's departure and I was forced to stay behind, in Camelot, to see to the running of the castle. She recovered from her ill humour, but it returned when word came that Arthur had chased our Saxon invaders back across the sea, and now they set out for their homeland to remind them never to stray into Britain, lest it was on the lands on the east coast that Uther had given their forefathers in peace treaty.

I had joined Nentres in battle before, in little routs of bandits or beside him when Arthur called him, but often staying well behind the lines. However, Nentres would never permit me to be abroad with him, when he relied upon me to be regent in Garlot.

So I stayed behind too, splitting my time between Camelot and Garlot. They returned four months later, victorious. I was sore relieved to see Nentres and made him swore he would say no if Arthur asked him to battle once again. I knew that was probably a half-truth, but I extracted a promise that we would depart at once for Garlot, lest we be caught up in Arthur's victory celebrations which, knowing my brother, could last for weeks.

Though, as I was packing, a page requested I attend upon the queen at once. Wondering what had got Guinevere demanding to see me, I went at once.

"You requested my presence, Highness?" I asked, entering her chamber.

She was sitting by the window, her embroidery abandoned by her side.

"Yes," she replied. "I heard you were leaving for Garlot."

"True, now Nentres has returned from battle, he and I depart this afternoon."

She looked in my eyes and I saw her nervousness. "Guinevere, whatever is the matter?"

"Arthur does not know yet," she replied. "But I am pregnant. Not more than a few weeks, my ladies gather, but yes, I am with child."

"Congratulations, but..."

"I need you to stay," she stated, interrupting me. "In fact, I command you to stay."

If Guinevere ever thought she could command me, High Queen or no, she was in for a sorry awakening.

"Whatever for?" I asked.

"I need you here, with me. None of my ladies have ever been with child before. I need an experienced mother."

"You need a midwife or a healer. My sister, Morgan, knows much of the healing arts, you could send for her. Queen Sebile of Sorestan, she is not without skill in healing and has two sons, if I am not mistaken."

"No, I shall have no one but you. Besides, when I tell Arthur, he will insist Merlin take over my care, and I cannot have that old demon anywhere near me. He gives me a terrible fright and leers so awfully at us ladies. Why, it is a mystery why any lady should allow him beneath her skirts, with child or no."

"Ah, I see," I said. "When Arthur calls for Merlin to examine you, you can offer me as an alternative and he will be sure to accept his older sister as your nurse."

"Do not make me seem so callous, but yes, that is true. You are much preferable to the half-breed Druid."

"Can you bear to have a pagan touch you?" I asked, struggling to keep the tone of mockery from my voice.

"You are not the worst, provided you keep your spells from me and use only herbs and simples an average matron would know. And I shall have a bishop visit me every day just to be sure."

"I would wager the bishop knows more about what goes on beneath ladies' skirts than I do."

"Elaine!" she exclaimed, scandalised. "You should not say such things. We must pray for forgiveness."

"Ha! The day I ask the Christ for anything is a desperate day indeed. You may pray on my behalf while I tell Nentres I am staying to help with the birth of my little niece or nephew."

Guinevere was immensely pleased with my decision to stay, while Nentres was not. He thought my place better suited at his side in Garlot, which was surely somewhat neglected while we were both in Camelot. Nentres could not leave his second to rule all the time, lest the second decide to become first. He also thought it was time we turned our attention to bringing forth a brother or sister for Hoel. He did not share my belief I would never become pregnant again. Perhaps it was that belief that led me to stay on with Guinevere's caregiver.

Always slight, Guinevere did not grow too big as the months passed, and I feared that the baby would be born underweight; if Guinevere's narrow hips would allow it to pass. Arthur, once informed, fretted immensely, and demanded that I give a report on her progress twice daily. Guinevere yet resisted his attempts to place Merlin in charge of her care.

We finally delivered her in the spring. A fleet of midwives was brought from the town. I would not have the responsibility of the birthing upon me, having only my own and that of Mila's granddaughter as experience. She laboured from nearly sunrise to sunset and there were complications. There was a great deal of blood, so much so I was forced to look away, and much else happened beyond my understanding. Finally, we had a girl-child in our arms, but pregnancy had defeated Guinevere, and she was lucky to escape with her life. The midwife told me she would never conceive again.

Arthur was disappointed when I handed him his daughter, I could see he had been hoping for a son, but that was never going to be true with Guinevere's high, wide stomach. Still, he lit up when she turned her little head and smiled so wide I thought his face would crack.

"Will you name her, Arthur?" I asked. "It is the right of the King to name his Princess."

"Anna," he whispered. "It means graceful, and it is a Christian name, Guinevere will like it."

"A beautiful choice, Sire. Now, she needs to be with her mother."

"A few minutes longer," he replied, drawing the babe closer to his chest.

Finally, I wrested the child from his arms and brought her into the birthing room. The sheets had been changed, Guinevere washed and dressed, and the straw that lay on the floor burnt, along the cord and the afterbirth. Guinevere was lightly dozing on the bed. It would be some days yet before she could stand and walk unaided. I woke her gently and passed her the child.

Is it a girl?" she asked. "It looks like a girl."

"It is, my Queen."

"Oh," she said, disappointment evident. "I had been hoping for a son."

"Guinevere," I said, my tone grave. "I have spoken with the midwife. You nearly lost your life yesterday, and at great cost. You will not have another child."

"I will," she said, defiant. "I will give Arthur his son. Even if it costs me my life."

What a fool I thought. I took my leave before I hit her a slap. I did not work so hard alongside those midwives, toiling with no sleep, fighting the urge to use my craft to save her, to have her throw away her life again. I left her with her babe and went to seek some rest.

The next day Guinevere was more thankful for my efforts, no doubt due to Arthur's careful prodding, and the three of us had a pleasant day nursing the babe between us. Guinevere asked me to stay on as her chief lady and see that Anna was well-cared for. I accepted, on the condition that Hoel too could be brought to the royal nursery. I would not have him think of me as I did of Igraine, and have him grow up to think I cared more for his cousin than him.

As Guinevere and I laboured at the business of being mothers, she remarked "Your sister, Morgan of Gore, is to join us here soon. Arthur has invited her to enjoy our hospitality."

"Why?" I asked.

Morgause had told me in her letters Morgan had relented from her plan of blood magic when Morgause would not send the child to her. Had Morgan some new plan?

216

"I do not know," replied Guinevere. "But I find it quite strange too, considering that Uriens does not come with her. I put it to Arthur, but he said he had found her unhappy, and thought the diversion might cheer her."

Morgan was with us soon, riding at the head of a contingent of men from Gore. They had strange heraldry, appearing to be a mix of Uriens arms, and of Gorlois. It must be Morgan's own, and I wondered if Arthur had approved her having her own banner to ride under.

"Morgan!" called Arthur, welcoming her into the hall. "You are our honoured guest, sister."

"I thank you brother," she said. "And have brought gifts from Gore for you and your queen."

Arthur always lit up at the idea of gifts. It surprised me until I remembered that he was not always king, but a poor relation in the house of Sir Ector. He cooed over the treasures she had brought him, and even Guinevere was swayed, despite her dislike of Morgan.

Arthur looked at me, standing apart from the gift giving. "Elaine, will you take our sister to her chamber?"

I curtseyed to our brother. "If you will it."

He looked at me, eyebrow crooked at my curt reply. "I do."

I gestured for Morgan to proceed me out into the corridor. I did not speak to her as we walked to the bedchambers, but I could feel her keen eyes upon me.

"So quiet, sister?" teased Morgan.

I scowled at her. "Are you not keen to have me silent, else you would not have bound my tongue?"

She shrugged. "I was taking precautions. You cannot fault me for that sister."

"Arthur is a fool to have such a viper in his nest. Do not think I will not be watching you."

She scoffed at me. "I have abandoned my plan, since Morgause took the child so far beyond my reach, being that a woman of my rank cannot travel to the Orkneys unnoticed. No, I have seen the way you cater to that overgrown child we call King. Flattery will win me back Tintagel. I shall become his dearest friend, and he will be dying to name me the Duchess of Cornwall."

I huffed out a sigh of frustration.

"I have forgotten Tintagel, and Cornwall too," I said, "I do not see why you continue this."

"Ha, that is easy for you to say, the third daughter who was never going to amount to much. Had father lived, you would have been the wife of one of his warriors, not the Queen of Garlot. But I was to be his heir, with my own castle and lands, and marry a decent Cornishman, not that oaf Uriens."

"So, you will kiss Arthur's ring, and then what? He will strip our cousin Cador of his rank and hand over the keys of Tintagel to you? And what of Uriens?"

"Arthur will grant me a divorce, surely, or he would be merging Gore with Cornwall unwittingly."

"Arthur will do nothing you have described. Sometimes, for all your learning, I think you are the stupidest person I know."

Morgan sighed in exasperation. "Let us cease this conversation, for it is clear you and I will never agree. Anyway, I am grateful to be far from Uriens and his squabbling, backward little family. And to spend time with my little sister? Now, a game of chess perhaps?"

But Morgan would always be Morgan. By virtue of her rank, she was made part of Guinevere's household, and by right of her age, I should have deferred to her and allowed her to be chief among the High Queen's ladies-in-waiting. But if I did, nothing would be done in the Queen's household. Morgan refused to help Guinevere dress in the mornings, see to her wardrobe or sundry other duties. Nor would she be Guinevere's companion on walks, or help ease her moods.

They quarrelled so often that Morgan was regularly banished from her presence. Guinevere called her a know-it-all and argued that Morgan was bawdy and superior. Morgan countered, saying that Guinevere was as stupid as she was pretty and that the evening talk in the solar, of marriages and the best type of stitches, was enough to bring tears to a stone statue. These squabbles were often so strong they did not speak for days, and Arthur would have to intervene.

Morgan and I had taken to sharing a room. All the better to watch her, I thought. But even to have her near was a comfort when Nentres could not be there. Though, the more she complained about our High Queen, the more I regretted our sleeping arrangements.

"You did not come to the nunnery, but you are well educated," she said. "You speak Latin and are very knowledgeable on many topics. I am not sure Guinevere can even read."

"Ah, Morgan, do not be so cruel," I replied. "It is very unusual to find a woman that can, beyond what is needed to keep house. Anyway, I know Guinevere can read, the Christian holy book at least."

"I have had my fill of the gospel, Elaine. Seven years I was at Glastonbury, and every day they tried to make a nun of me. If she keeps prattling on about my immortal soul, I will take a sword to her."

She laughed at the thought, and then grew quiet.

"What is the matter, Morgan?"

She shrugged. "Nothing. I am just bored here. I seek a diversion. And talking about embroidery is not helping."

"I happen to be quite fond of embroidery," I replied. "It requires patience, and deftness of finger, and a keen eye."

"But you slink off to Arthur's council meetings, or to practice with your sword when she tires you. I am stuck beside her all day. She is such an idiot."

"You should not offend her so, Morgan," I warned. "Serve her as she commands, or she will make trouble for you. I have seen her prevent marriages or do other harm to an enemy. She can be as capricious as she is kind."

"Ha? Kind? Where did she get that reputation from?

"The people like her. She gives alms to the poor regularly, and you will find no greater ally for female petitioners."

Morgan rolled her eyes. "They fawn over her, simply because she is beautiful, and her father is wealthy. Is she always so...pious?"

"No," I replied. "She prays often and extols virtue, but sometimes she is jealous, moody or just downright rude. She expects beauty in most things, excellence in all things, and may the Gods protect you if it is neither. She is human, Morgan, and one raised to quite a high standard. Annoying as she is, you must take her as you find her."

But from Morgan's sour face, I could see we would never agree on the subject of Guinevere.

Nentres returned to court for a visit, and Morgan was forced to lodge elsewhere. It was quite selfish of me, but I did not see her quite as much as before, and she had stopped coming to the solar. She was, however, present at the feast of Arthur's birth.

I saw her, talking to Merlin, and my veins turned to ice. Merlin and Morgan's mutual dislike was evident, and she wasted no time in baiting him into arguments when she could. I knew she would say something horrible, and perhaps go too far. I got up from the table and made my way to them as they whispered in the alcove, far from the gaiety of the others there. I strained my ears to listen.

"There is much Mother Abbess taught me, but you could teach me even more," she said.

"If I will not teach Elaine, what makes you think I would teach you?" replied Merlin.

"Because she has not my mind or my skill. We could be great together, Merlin. Forget Arthur. Let me be the queen. I have the rank, and the lineage, you have the power. I can bring men and gold to topple Arthur."

"You have made overtures?" hissed Merlin.

"I have support among the lords of Gore, and the men of Cornwall," she replied. "Morgause can deliver us Lot, which brings us Lothian and Orkney. But most of all, if we band together, we can bring the Wise together. They are nationless, but care only for the end of the Christ, and will unite under us."

"I have no ill will for the Christians. The Wise are fading from the world, and perhaps it is best we are forgotten."

"You traitor! Your power comes from the old people, and the old ways."

"I grew up without a father, hunted and despised because of the old people and their old ways."

Morgan scoffed. "I grew up without a father because of you!"

"You hold so much hate in your heart for me, and for Uther because of that. But I understand you better than you think, Morgan," he said. "You desire only power, and power that you can wield. You would have grown tired of Gorlois and his limited ambition."

"Well, we will never know, will we?" Morgan cocked her head to one side. "We have an unwelcome guest. Perhaps we will talk some other time?"

Merlin shook his head. "You will not speak of this again, Morgan of Gore. You do not fear your brother, but I would soon show you why you should fear me."

I passed them, and paid no heed to Morgan's storming exit, or Merlin's glare. It seems she had indeed made an enemy of him as I feared.

After dinner the next night, we retired to the solar as usual. Nentres told us that he was going to going to check the horses and see that all was prepared for his journey, for he was to return to Garlot the following day, but if I knew my husband, he would be enjoying a cup of mead with his men, and then I would find him snoring happily in our bed that night.

Arthur and Guinevere were side by side at the window seat, while Lancelot stared into the fire, giving it the occasional poke with a stick. He was now so often with us, we considered him part of the family, and Arthur honoured him by allowing him to join us in seclusion in the solar after dinner. Morgan was nowhere to be seen, so Guinevere was discussing her as usual.

Her absences had begun to become more conspicuous and gave Guinevere an excuse to disparage her. This was, of course, in addition to all the other petty crimes she had committed against our High Queen, such as talking out of turn or making lewd jokes, and her staunch refusal to convert to Christianity in the face of all of Guinevere's proselytising.

Rumours were beginning to reach me, of Morgan being spotted in the strangest places, not far from the company of an unidentified man. And if I had heard them, so had Guinevere.

I suspected Morgan had chosen herself a lover from among Arthur's men, or perhaps even one of the townspeople. For her sake, it was better it ended soon, or Guinevere would be scandalised by her adultery, and send her from the court, just as she was itching to do.

"It is not right, husband," she said, beginning her nightly refrain. "A woman's place is by her husband, so our God teaches us."

"Uriens does not do right by my sister, and abuses her wickedly," replied Arthur. "He will not divorce her, and I cannot demand it, for fear he will rise up against me. Having her here keeps the peace and my sister happy. We all win."

"But why must she be one of my ladies? She refuses to do the work assigned to her, claims ignorance from her schooling at the nunnery, but I know no nun would permit such idleness. And she thinks herself so high because she is so learned."

Arthur rubbed his wife's shoulders. "Is your pride so wounded? Are you not secure in your position as the highest lady in the land? And where else should she be? She is not a servant or one of my warriors. And she cannot stay in her chamber all day."

"And see!" cried Guinevere, gesturing with her handkerchief to the room. "She spurns us yet again! The warmest room in the castle, the best wine and company, and she is off God-knows-where!"

Arthur looked to me and I looked elsewhere. Neither Guinevere nor Morgan could be swayed from their behaviour, and this conflict would continue, or come to a horrible end.

Camelot was much changed from its days under Uther. Once just an old Roman fortress castle with a few nearby steadings, it had grown under Arthur to become a thriving town, with trade to rival even that of Londinium. But, in other ways, it was still so small. Morgan had been spotted once more, and her mystery swain too.

Gossip spread like wildfire, and soon everyone knew that Morgan, Queen of Gore and lady-in-waiting to Guinevere, was having an affair with Guiomar, cousin to the High Queen and one of her dear favourites. And it was again this topic that we discussed in the solar, Guinevere, Arthur and I.

Guinevere pouted. "She has corrupted him. He was such a good boy before he met her."

I resisted the urge to laugh in her face. "My Queen, I doubt that Morgan is entirely the one to blame in this situation. Guiomar is a man, after all."

"Be that as it may, they continue to sin within my court, and I will not have it!"

"Putting that aside," said Arthur. "This affair could anger Uriens, and that will do us no favours."

"See," added Guinevere. "Now you must send her back, it is best for all concerned."

"I do not think we can do that," he replied.

"Husband, is she or is she not one of my ladies, over whom I have total jurisdiction? I defer to you in everything, in matters of state most particularly, but for once we have a subject in which I am greater informed. And yet, you refuse to send her back to Gore."

"I have not been entirely truthful," said Arthur, avoiding Guinevere's gaze. "About Morgan being at court. Uriens did not send her to be your lady, as such. Rather, it was my suggestion. She…uh…she tried to smite him, with his own sword, while he was sleeping."

Guinevere's mouth dropped open in shock. I too was surprised, but only for a moment. I was unsettled that it was kept from me, but Morgan attempting an assassination came as no shock.

"So," continued Arthur. "Uriens did not want it to be known what she had tried to do, to save face, but also, he did not want to put her to death for treason and risk my ire, so I said that she might come here until her hysterics had faded."

"Why?" exclaimed Guinevere. "She is a madwoman, she is dangerous! We could have been murdered in our beds!"

Arthur scoffed. "She bears us no ill."

You are a fool, Arthur Pendragon, I thought. If you believe that about Morgan, you are a fool. Yet, I remained silent.

"I will summon her before me," said Guinevere. "And Guiomar too. If they do not repent of their wickedness, I shall banish Morgan. And she must go, or I shall let it be known what she tried to do, and she will be punished as not just an adulteress, but an attempted murderess."

I thought Arthur would rebuke her for overstepping her authority. But he did not. "That is just," he said. "But be lenient upon her. As few have happy marriages as we do."

"Be that as it may," she replied. "But I will see no immorality before my throne."

I tried to intercede with Guinevere, but she would not hear of it. Her court was one of absolute moral character, she said. Arthur too, would not be implored to rein in his wife's behaviour. I knew Arthur's harried look, and for him, to let Guinevere have her way was worth the peace in their chamber. Merlin, perhaps, might have had some sway, but I knew he would jump for joy as high as his old bones would let him if Morgan was to be sent away from Camelot.

She was called into the presence-chamber, before Guinevere and Arthur, with Lancelot and me standing as witnesses. Guiomar was excused, and I had heard that Guinevere had asked to see him. He knew immediately what he was being accused of and had repented at once, accusing Morgan of tempting him.

Morgan was late to her summons, and I wondered why she always made things difficult for herself.

"I decree that you are banished from court," said Guinevere shortly, as Morgan bowed to her. "Guiomar says you have led him into wickedness, and I will not have it in Camelot."

Morgan looked from her to Arthur, to me and back to the High Queen, but our faces did not give her the solace she sought. I could see her proud shoulders start to slump, and the wave of desperation washed across her face.

"Please, Arthur, do not send me back to Gore," she asked. Her voice was still deep and rich, but I could hear it crack.

Guinevere narrowed her eyes. "The High King may not intercede on your behalf. You have disgraced his court and the family of his Queen. My honour, and that of Camelot, demands you return to Gore upon the morrow."

"Guinevere," began Morgan, far more respectful than she would ever have normally addressed her. "My Lady, my Queen. Uriens and I have quarrelled beyond repair. Neither us can bear each other anymore. It will cost me my life if I return to him."

"I know what you tried to do," said Guinevere. "You must do as our Lord commands, and repent of your wickedness. Remember that you must be his greatest servant. And that there is no greater affront to our Lord than adultery."

"Arthur, please do not let her do this," she begged.

Arthur looked very uncomfortable. "The High Queen has made her decision."

Morgan was struck by an idea. "Brother, please. Give me back my lands in Cornwall. I can retire there, away from Uriens, and all will be well."

"What do you mean?" asked Arthur.

"Restore me as Duchess of Cornwall," she said. "Or give me the second castle of Terrabil at least. It is my right as the daughter of Gorlois."

Arthur shook his head. "I cannot remove Cador. He has been a faithful friend to my father and to me. Who else would stand against the Irish?"

"I would!" she exclaimed. She looked up and saw the incredulity on Arthur's face. "I would too! Anyway, it is mine. Your father stole it from me!"

Arthur looked on the verge of an angry outburst. "You need to watch what you say to me, Morgan. I have humoured your discussions on the ownership of Tintagel while we are friends, but remember that my father beat yours fair and square."

Morgan looked ready to launch into another tirade, one that could perhaps have her arrested for treason, so I placed my hand on her elbow to warn her. She shrugged me off.

"Please do not send me back to Gore! Please!" she pleaded. "What about the convent? Let me go to Glastonbury!"

Arthur was clearly angered by her discussion of Uther. He called for a knight, ignoring her pleas. "Sir Accolon, take the Lady Morgan to her chamber and see she packs her belongings. You will escort her to Gore upon the morn."

"Sister!" cried Morgan, turning to me. "Speak for me, please."

Her voice was low and desperate. "I cannot go back there."

So I spoke on her behalf and regretted it deeply ever since. "Arthur, please. Can you not see how it distresses her? And what will Uriens do to her if she returns, his would-be assassin and now an adulterer? Please, Arthur, this is not your Britain, where a woman is property, to be beaten like a miscreant dog!"

"And what do you propose, Elaine?" he asked.

"Send her to back to Gore, certainly," I replied. "But Uriens must have other castles, steadings that belong to the crown. Morgan could reside at one of these. Close enough to be Uriens' wife still, but far enough from him she could be safe."

I looked to Morgan. She nodded. "Caer Tau-roc," she said. "It is right on the border, and I know there will be a small retinue of servants there."

"Sir Accolon," said Arthur, turning his attention to the knight. He was not as young as some of Arthur's knights, closer in age to Morgan's thirty. He was fair, and had most pleasing features, if he was not inclined to stare so. Nentres remarked to me often that the man had a temper, and did not deal well with authority.

"See that the Lady Morgan has all she needs for her journey tomorrow. You will take a brother knight or two and see her as far as Caer Tauroc. I will give you some gold to make it ready; if it is not in the condition my sister expects to find it."

He bowed and gestured for Morgan to proceed him from the room. She did not move, but fixed her dark gaze upon Arthur, and pointed at him.

"Mark my words, brother, you have made an enemy today. Your father sent me away once, when he feared me, when I was inconvenient for him too, and you have proved yourself his son."

Arthur stood up from the throne. "Are you threatening me, Morgan?"

"Clearly," she retorted.

"How dare you!" shrieked Guinevere, but before she could say more, Morgan had words for her too.

"For your interference, Guinevere, I curse your marriage, so you might know the pain rendered unto me by Uriens. Let it be unhappy and unfruitful, from this day on!"

I could feel the thrum of magic as she spoke those words. Guinevere blessed herself as the Christians do. I stepped forward to stay Morgan's pointing finger, but she held up her other hand in a gesture of warding towards me. Her charm was so powerful, my legs felt like lead, and I could not move.

"Easy sister," she warned. "Or make an enemy of me too."

Arthur glowered at her. "I am too inclined to forgiveness, to softness, say my council. It is not often I admit they are right. I will not wait until the morning, Sir Accolon will take you forth at once, whether you have all your belongings or not! Do not darken my door again, Morgan ferch Gorlois, or face death as a traitor to Camelot!"

Accolon took her by the arm and began to drag her. Morgan tried to stand her ground, but he was far stronger than her, and the magic she worked must have tired her. He dragged her from the room, her accusatory, pointing finger still held high and pointing at the throne.

Chapter Ten

Arthur commanded me not to follow her, and no one was permitted to leave until a page confirmed Accolon's party had taken horse, a reluctant Morgan riding pillion. I lay in bed that evening beside Nentres, unable to sleep, worrying about her. When Accolon's horse was spied returning through Camelot's arches at the end of the sennight, I was the first to speak to him, accosting him as he dismounted.

"How is my sister, Sir Accolon?" I asked.

"Distraught," he replied, struggling to keep an irked frown from his face. "She did not speak for most of the journey."

"And you took her to Gore? All the way, every step guarded?"

"Of course, I took her straight to Castle Tauroc, and gave her steward there the orders from the King."

"Did Morgan try to mislead you? Bribe you?"

Enchant you was left unsaid. With Morgan's skill, I doubted, he would ever have noticed he was under a spell.

"Never," he said. "She was silent the entire way."

"Really?" I asked, surprised. "She did not even attempt escape once?"

"No. She cooperated entirely with us, and I delivered her safely into Gore."

He could give me no more information about her, so I left him be so he could seek some rest, and report back to Arthur. What he had said did not sit well with me, it being so unlike Morgan, that I wondered if she had escaped and he was misleading me, or he had clubbed her over the head to ensure her compliance, and now she was badly injured.

I grew anxious to see if my sister was safe and well. What was to be her future now in Gore? Would Uriens now renege on his promise to spare her life, since she had been sent back to her kingdom in disgrace? Or would she spend her life in exile at Caer Tauroc, cold and neglected? I knew Arthur would not like it so, in secret, I sent a messenger boy to bring her a letter from me. I could have contacted her through the old ways, but I was as afraid of her mood as I was afraid for her.

The boy returned at the end of a sennight, Morgan banished from court over a fortnight. He was empty handed.

"Are you sure you went to the right castle?" I asked him. "There cannot be that many. Are you sure you did not take the coins I gave you and spend them in a tavern, or on sweetmeats? And then come back to me to say you could not deliver the letter?"

"No, my Lady," he replied. He could not have been more than fifteen. "I went all the way to Gore, followed the Roman road like you told me, mistress. I asked a farmer man to tell me where the castle was, being on important business for the Queen of Garlot, like you said to. He pointed the way and so I went. And the steward there, he told me that the Lady Morgan had never come to that place since her wedding and that he wasn't expecting her."

"Did you explain what had happened?"

"I did, my Lady, begging your pardon for gossiping, but I did. I told him Lady Morgan had been banished from court by the High King and was expected at that place some time ago. But he swore blind he'd never clapped eyes on her."

"You did well. It was not your fault the Lady Morgan was not there. Here, take this penny for your trouble. And speak of this to no one."

He bowed and took the coin from my outstretched hand, before scurrying away, for fear I changed my mind. My thoughts twisted in my head, like yarn for weaving. Accolon assured me he had escorted her safely. Yet, the messenger never encountered her, and supposedly neither had her steward. I wanted to believe an innocent explanation. I thought somehow the tale had been confused, but I knew, deep down, some of Morgan's trickery was afoot.

I made my way from our chamber and encountered Nentres in the castle yard. The place had been set for a great tourney, with covered stands erected for the spectators and a fearsome wooden ring in which the competitors were to fight. My husband was watching the preparations with eager eyes.

"You know I forbid you to fight," I said as I approached. We chuckled at the idea of us forbidding the other do anything that they truly wanted to do.

"I have no stomach for competition anymore," he replied. "Not when I know how often your life can depend on such skills. They are to be practiced, yes, but not exhibited."

"I am worried, Nentres," I said.

"How so, wife?"

"Morgan never reached Caer Tauroc, or if she did, she has escaped. My messenger could not deliver the letter."

"Accolon told you otherwise, so he is lying?"

"Morgan could have bribed him, or bewitched him. I do not know."

"You cannot tell Arthur, not now at least. He is preparing to fight in the tourney."

"Damn the tourney!" I exclaimed. "His sister is Gods-knows-where doing Gods-knows-what. Morgan will be spoiling for revenge. She has been banished from court once before and she cursed Uther with a weak heart, and only thirteen then. Now a grown woman, what could else could she do?"

"Very little, I imagine. She would need an army if she wanted to bring ruin to Arthur. Gore will not give it to her, perhaps the Irish or Gaulish mercenaries. She will need gold. No, Camelot is safe enough, at least until the end of the tourney."

"Morgan does not need men, she has her magic. And her cleverness. But you are right, the tourney must proceed."

Arthur had been preparing for this tourney for weeks. All his knights would be fighting, and Arthur must emerge as the victor, else he lose face before the assembly and perhaps even his crown in the process.

"I need more evidence before I can proceed," I said. "I must question Accolon more thoroughly."

"If he is complicit, he will hardly tell you."

"There must be someone who would betray him. Do you know who went forth with him?"

"Two of his men-at–arms, I think. They would never talk to you. Unless..." pondered Nentres. "I think he was accompanied by a squire. Yes, if you can get to him. Squires see much of what their masters do and are oft ignored, as well as mistreated. He may very well tell you what you want to know, given the right incentive. You go and speak to him. I will say you are delayed if your absence at the tourney is remarked upon."

"You trust me with this?" I asked.

"Yes, no one more so. Besides, it is your theory."

I found my way to Accolon's dressing tent. He was not inside, but practicing his sword swing upon a practice sack. As he looked away, I slipped past the hide covered entrance. Inside was a teenager, fifteen or sixteen by the looks of him, though his slight frame would have placed him younger still. He did not look well fed, and there was a purplish mark around his eye, hastily covered by his forelocks. He looked up from where he sat on the floor, polishing a helmet, and caught sight of me. He hastily threw himself prostrate upon the floor.

"Queen Elaine!" he squeaked.

He jumped up to bow, and then flung himself back onto his knees. I smiled at him and tried to put him at ease.

"You may rise. And my Lady will suffice."

"Sir Accolon is not here, my Lady," he said, rising again. He went to practice before the tourney."

"I do not need to speak to your master, I came to speak to you."

"Me?" he asked, surprised. "What can I...?"

"Were you with him on the journey to Gore?" I asked.

"I was, my Lady," he replied.

"And he delivered my sister, the Lady Morgan safely into the care of the steward at Castle Tauroc?"

"Yes!" he exclaimed, far too quick for my liking.

"You would not lie to the Queen of Garlot, sister to the High King?"

"Eh...no, my Lady."

He could not look at me. I knew the boy was lying. Even well behaved Hoel was fond of a few mistruths. I had experience with lying boys.

"Tell me what happened," I urged, my voice gentle. "Whatever it is, no harm will come to you. I can protect you from your master."

"I am not scared," he said, indignant. "I am afraid of losing my place."

"If you lose your place," I offered. "I will find you a place among any of Arthur's knights."

"You promise?"

"I promise."

He took a deep, comforting breath, and began. "We reached an inn, and we had to stop. Gore is so far away. So we went to the inn, and stayed there for a night and..."

"You never made it to Gore," I said.

"No," he replied, hanging his head. "We turned back two days after we set out, after..."

"After what?"

"Sir Accolon thinks I'm too young to know, but I knew."

"Knew what?" I pressed.

"That the Lady Morgan took him as her lover."

"She did?"

The boy nodded. "I heard them. Sir Accolon usually makes me sleep on the floor beside him, in case he needs something during the night. But that night, he told me to sleep outside the room. I felt someone go past me, and I opened my eyes, and it was a woman. I thought it was just a maid, but then I heard her speak. It was the Lady Morgan, I am certain of it."

"What happened next?"

"The next day, we turned back to Camelot."

I thought on it. "Two days to the inn, two days back, but Accolon was gone at least six days. What happened after you got back to Camelot?"

"We took rooms in town," he replied.

"Was Morgan there?"

"She was. But we were not allowed upstairs with them. I could not hear what she said to him. I did not know why we came back to Camelot, but I thought we were going to run away. But…"

"But?" I prompted.

"Then Accolon said he was going back to court, and we went, leaving the Lady Morgan in town."

"And do you know what she has been doing since?"

"No, my Lady," he replied. "But I can show you the house."

"Good man," I said. "Now, I must go to Arthur. If the High King summons you, will you tell him exactly what you told me? Your story will not change?"

"No, my Lady, not if you can promise me another situation."

"Good," I replied. "I want you to leave this place, never mind your work, and go to the keep. There is a servant there called Melissa. Tell her I sent you, and she is to feed you, and put you in my rooms."

I took off a ring I was wearing, a gift Arthur had bestowed on me.

"Take this," I said. "And show it to her. She will know it."

I pressed it into his hand, then I peeked my head out from the flap of the tent, and saw that Accolon was gone.

"Now is our chance," I said, and I pulled the boy by the arm out of the tent.

"Go, run, now," I urged, and he took off from the yard towards the castle.

I began to walk towards the castle too, to seek out Arthur, when I realised he had probably already made his way to his dressing tent, so I turned in that direction. Then I heard the sound of trumpets, marking the beginning of the tourney. I took off in a run towards the arena and saw that two helmed knights were already upon the field.

I looked up to the stands and saw Nentres sitting there. Pressing past the assembled nobles, I took a seat beside him and leaned in to whisper.

"I spoke to the squire, Morgan is still here in Camelot. They turned back."

He turned to look at me. "Why would she come back here?"

"Whatever her reason, it cannot be good. We must get Arthur and go at once into the town. The squire will show us."

"We cannot," he said, his voice grave. "That is Arthur upon the field, and he fights Sir Accolon."

I looked at the combatants with a new, horrified eye and saw that it was indeed my brother, wearing his red surcoat with the dragon upon it, and the heraldry of the other fighter was indeed that of Sir Accolon.

A fierce battle was raging on the field. Accolon was driving hard against Arthur, meeting blow after blow. Were it not for Arthur's speed, the bout would have been over in moments. I could see that Accolon had the advantage and was now pressing it.

What role was Accolon to play in Morgan's plot? They had returned to Camelot for a reason, and she had not seduced him for the love of him, I was certain.

Nentres drew in a harsh breath beside me.

"What is it, husband?" I asked.

"I am wrong, we must stop the tourney," he replied. "Accolon is fighting to kill."

"How can you be sure?"

"His sword strokes. They are too fierce for friendly combat and look, Elaine, see how he presses on when he should be drawing back, for fear of hurting his opponent?"

"Why ever would he do that?"

Nentres gave a hollow chuckle. "An accident is the only way to murder a king and never face the consequences."

"He means to murder him? But how, if Arthur has the magic of Excalibur, and is twice Accolon's swordsman without."

"Does Accolon's pommel, the way it glints, not look familiar to you? In fact, identical to one wielded by your brother?"

"It cannot be!" I hissed, but I knew it to be true. I could feel the power of Excalibur upon the field, but yes, it was in Accolon's hands. The sword Arthur used had its own taint of magic, a foul reek which threatened to bring bile into my mouth when dwelt on too long. Someone had used magic to give the illusion that it was Excalibur.

"You are right, Arthur has a copy in his hands."

"How was such a thing done?"

"If Morgan is in league with Accolon, then quite easily. She has a particular skill with illusion, and a little grave dirt sprinkled under a bed can bind a man in sleep. That must have been how she took it from him, while he and Guinevere slept. She will have made sure they did not wake, not after that incident with Uriens."

Still they fought on, and the battle was no closer to a finale, yet Arthur shone with sweat. His guard was low, struggling to keep up with Accolon's vicious, heavy strokes.

"We have to do something," said Nentres, his hand circling the hilt of his dagger, as though he was intent to take to the field himself. "I wish I we had known this earlier."

"We cannot stop the tourney," I said. "Without firm evidence. It will humiliate Arthur, everyone will think we stopped it because we did not want to see him beaten. And if we have accused Accolon falsely? Our own honour would be shorn."

"What then Elaine?" he asked.

"Arthur will simply have to win."

"But if Accolon does have Excalibur, and its scabbard?"

"Then I must place them on an equal footing," I said.

I brought my hands to my mouth, as though rendered in abject permanent horror by the day's events. But, instead, I was whispering, calling forth charms half-remembered. An invocation, to bring forth Arthur's strength, a spell of weakness, to slow Accolon's reflexes and a binding, to hold back the power of the sword so that Arthur may bring an end to the fight. To cast one spell can be tiring, but three against such powerful objects? My breath grew shallower as I expended more of my energy. The world slowed around me and my heart thundered in my chest. I struggled on, pushing forth my magic, my will and my intent into the world and towards the fighting men.

Arthur pulled off his helmet and tossed it at Accolon, who twisted his head roughly to avoid it. He surged forward, swinging his sword. Accolon raised his sword to meet it and then spun, ploughing a knee into Arthur's back. Arthur stumbled forward but did not fall, darting to one side to avoid a stab from Accolon. Accolon swung out again, and the sword slashed the side of Arthur's face. The crowd gasped in horror, but no one made a move to intervene. Accolon sliced at him again, and that time it made contact with Arthur's shoulder, blood along the tip of the stolen Excalibur.

I pushed more power into my spell, though I was sure I would fall down dead from the effort. With a great cry, Arthur ran at Accolon, dodging another swing, and aimed for Accolon's leg. As the knight lowered his guard to block it, Arthur feinted and drove his sword through Accolon's heart. He pulled it free, and Accolon toppled over.

Then Arthur fell to the ground in a swoon, and with the heavy clang of his armour against the ground. Nentres and I leapt up at once, and ran towards the wooden ring, ducking under the barrier. Seeing that we had done so, the other nobles also began to gather around our brother.

I reached him first, Nentres not far behind me. Arthur was weeping blood from a slash above his left eye, and a tear in his surcoat was also tinged with fresh blood.

"Arthur," I called, but he did not stir.

I knelt to shake him, but he did not make any sound, nor wake under my touch.

"Merlin!" I cried, and the old enchanter pushed his way through the crowd.

He knelt down beside Arthur and placed his hands upon his temple.

"He is breathing yet, but he is unconscious. We must wait until he wakes," he said, and then looked at me with sad eyes. "If he ever does."

"What of Sir Accolon?" I asked Nentres.

"He is dead," he spat.

Lancelot forced his way through the throng, Guinevere not far behind him.

"Husband!" she cried, and made to go to him, but Lancelot held her back.

"Careful, or you may do him more harm," he said to her.

"You saw that fight as well as I did," said Nentres. "Accolon was fighting to kill."

"Indeed, but how did he nearly manage to best Arthur, not with the power of Excalibur?" asked Lancelot.

"There is foul magic afoot," grumbled Merlin.

Accolon's corpse was loaded onto a stretcher.

"Take him to the chapel," ordered Lancelot. "And get the traitor out of my sight!"

I could see a sword lying in the dirt where Arthur had dropped it. I bent down to pick it up. When I touched it, the charm faded at once, revealing only a plain sword that any guardsman would wield. I tossed it aside and then signalled Nentres to lift the real Excalibur from where Accolon had fallen and he returned it to Arthur's side. In the confusion of the wounded king, no one paid any attention to what we did. Before I breathed an overdue sigh of relief, I caught a horrible tang in the back of my throat.

"The scabbard!" I realised, coming close to Nentres to whisper in his ear. "Arthur is wearing a copy of that too, or else he would not bleed! Nentres, stay here and keep the attention on the King. I will go and get it before any of them have the same thought to steal it."

I walked away from the tourney yard towards the chapel. Making my way through the wooden door, I spied the body of Accolon laying upon a trestle table in the centre of the chapel.

There was an attendant there already, who had straightened his clothing and brushed his hair away from his face. She was currently moistening a cloth in a bowl of water. She wore a black robe; hooded and veiled befitting one delivering the last offices.

"My Lady," I said. "Would you leave us? I have orders from the king to search his body."

She nodded and turned from the body to leave the chapel. I rushed over and cast my eye over the body, searching for the scabbard. It was not attached to his belt, nor did it lie near the table, nor on the floor. I surmised that it had come loose on the tourney yard, or along the way as he was carried to the chapel.

I turned to leave, and my eyes narrowed on one particular sight. There, in the attendant's hand, was the scabbard.

"Stop!" I cried, and I ran at her. Gloved hands tucked the scabbard away within the folds of her robe, then shot out to stop me. She grasped me by the shoulders and gave me a rough shove. I collided with the stone wall, and my breath shuddered out in a great exhale of pain.

I leapt to my feet and ran at her again as she made her way to the door. I caught her around the middle and we tumbled to the floor. In the tussle, her hood fell down, revealing stark white skin and black locks.

"Morgan!" I cried.

She wrested her hand free from beneath me and pushed her hand into my face. I could not resist, and she pushed me from her. She jumped to her feet and fled to the other side of the room. She drew a tiny knife from her gown, not particularly menacing, but the blade was still sharp and glinting.

"Back, sister! Or I will use this!"

"I cannot let you take that scabbard," I said, bringing myself to my feet.

I reached for my own knife, and I realised to my horror that I wore none, not even the little one that I cut my meat at table with.

"Why not?" asked Morgan. "He has no right to it. You think the Lady of the Lake would have given it to him, a Christian and no true king of Britain?"

"Cease this!" I cried. "Arthur is a good a king as any, even you!"

"Do you love him more than me?" she asked. "Is that it?"

"It is not about love, Morgan. It is about doing what is right."

"Oh, this is right, is it?" she snarled. "That Uther killed our father, stole his castle and his wife. Stole what should be mine. Sold me to Uriens. Then Merlin set the bastard...yes, that is right, Elaine, a bastard for Igraine was not married to Uther when they begat Arthur...set a bastard on the throne of Britain, unelected by assembly?"

"Morgan..."

"And then, when I make my peace with all this, he lets his stupid little bitch of a wife send me from court because she is jealous. Because she thinks it improper. What right does Arthur have to the magic of Avalon? How can he be the once and future king?"

"Do not make this about Avalon, about destiny. This is about you, and your desire for revenge. Morgause and I do not devote our time to revenge."

She snorted. "Morgause is less innocent than you think. And you, your head is easily turned by his kind words. You always wanted to be Uther's real daughter, and playing big sister to Arthur gives you that chance."

"How dare you!"

I flew at her, and she scraped the air with her knife. I was but a second faster and gripped her wrist. I forced her towards the wall, and turning my back against her, I bashed her hand against the stone until she was forced to drop it.

She kicked out and I jumped back to avoid it. I could see her eyes locked on the door. I would not let her escape. I swung out my fist, making contact with her face, and followed with a solid blow to her chest. She fell back against Accolon's bier, the weak wood collapsing under her weight.

She flew at me again, and I raised my arm over my head to block her blows. I swung for her again, with all that Nentres had taught me. But wherever I struck, Morgan seemed to be faster, blocking my blows like she had been practicing this her whole life. In a way, she had. She grew up hitting me, and now she fought for something she truly believed in.

She kicked my knee, and I could feel it bend in reflex. I felt a stab of pain and realised she had me by the hair. She forced me into a crouch.

"Ah! Know this Morgan, wherever you go with that, I will follow."

She gave my hair a vicious tug. I screamed.

"I will cast it into the first body of water I pass," she hissed into my ear. "But I cannot have you follow me."

With that, she drew back her fist, and drove it so hard into my gut, I was sure I would vomit. Reeling from the pain, I collapsed to the floor, holding my stomach. I watched as the door opened and a pair of boots ran outside.

By the time I got to the door of the chapel she was gone. I ran as fast as I could to Nentres but, preoccupied with the woken Arthur, he had not seen her. Back in his tent, Guinevere had wiped all the blood from Arthur's face, and now my brother was gritting his teeth as Merlin sewed the gash in his shoulder with a rough bone needle and a length of catgut.

In my fluster, I was nearly dragged from the king's presence as a madwoman, and I knew, by the time I related all, that the cause was lost. Morgan was long gone.

"So that is how Accolon got Excalibur!" seethed Arthur, when I finished my tale through heavy, excited pants, and Accolon's squire was dragged before us, nearly soiling himself in fear to recount his portion of the tale.

"Easy," warned Merlin, lowering Arthur back onto the couch. "If you tear those stitches, I will let you bleed to death. It has been some time since you were last wounded, thanks to the scabbard."

Arthur looked on the verge of tears. "Ah! The scabbard! I am undone!"

"Will she have departed for Gore?" asked Nentres.

"She cannot have gone far," said Merlin. "She will have to take the Roman roads, of which go only four ways from here. Very simple, send four groups of men on each road, and have them ride their hardest."

"Make it so," said Arthur, and Nentres and Lancelot went to see about knights to accompany them.

Nentres returned first, followed by the troupe lead by Lancelot, and finally the one led by Gawain, all with no sign of my sister. At last, the party led by Sir Ontzlake returned too, and we could see from the window he did not have Morgan as his prisoner. I think the poor man wanted to hide from Arthur, but he was summoned to the presence-chamber so that he could be taken to task nonetheless.

"We found a cowherd on the road," he began. "And he said a lady had ridden at full speed past him. We caught sight of her over the ridge, and rode at full tilt," said the knight, his head hung in shame. "We caught up to her, but...we could not catch her."

"Why not?" asked Arthur. "It is one woman on horseback."

"No, she had men...armed guards...mercernaries...with her."

"And? More than six trained knights of Camelot?"

"No, Sire. But..."

"Spit it out man," barked Arthur. "Whatever has got your tongue?"

"She turned her men into stone," replied Sir Ontzlake.

"She what?" Arthur's eyebrows had disappeared beyond his fringe, such was his incredulity. Merlin did not seem to know whether to smirk or scowl.

"She turned her men into stone. We reached them, and there was a great flash of light, and they were gone, leaving only a handful of boulders in the ground."

"Can she do such a thing?" Arthur asked of me.

I shook my head. "No, but she can create illusions or addle minds, enough for your knights to think she had done so. It is called glamour, and Morgan had some skill at it when we were younger. She used to make herself invisible. I would wager, however, that if your men had taken their swords to those stones, they would bleed as well as any human."

247

Arthur twisted his face in anger, and then finally bellowed "Get out! All of you, get out!"

Sir Ontzlake went gratefully from the room, and so did Nentres and the other failed knights. Guinevere, stung, retreated with tears in her eyes. Arthur stuck out a hand to stop me. Merlin stayed put. He never obeyed a command he did not like the tone of. We were alone in the presence-chamber, Arthur, Merlin and I.

"You are certain she will have destroyed the scabbard?" he asked me.

I nodded. "It is powerful, but it is more use to her gone than anything she could do with it."

He turned to Merlin. "You can replace it?"

Merlin shook his wizened head. "No, Sire, I cannot. I do not know the charm that was used. I could go unto Avalon to seek the magic, but Viviane will be angered you did not protect it, and she may not let me have the charm."

Arthur looked to me in desperation. I also had to shake my head.

"I am sorry, brother. Such a charm would be high magic, and if it is unknown to Merlin, it is beyond me."

"What am I supposed to do?" asked Arthur. "I am a mere mortal now, without its power."

I looked at him in confusion. "You were a mere mortal before, and now you still have the power of Excalibur. And you are the greatest swordsman in the land."

"I am the greatest swordsman in the land," he repeated, more to himself than to me.

"I urge caution in battle from now on," said Merlin. "But if Morgan has not destroyed the scabbard, we may yet recover it, and punish her for her crimes."

248

We poured more platitudes into Arthur's ears to keep him from rash action, and Merlin set about finding Morgan and employed all the magic he could muster, but she must have cloaked herself well, for he could not find her. He set spies after her, and interrogated anyone from Gore he could lay hands upon, but it was as if she had vanished into the hills, into the realm of Faery.

Not long after she had robbed Arthur of his scabbard, a knight rode into Camelot. He said his name was Manassen, and that he was a cousin of Sir Accolon, and a dear friend of his. We thought he came to challenge Arthur to a duel in revenge for slaying Accolon, but he came only to deliver a message. He said he had been captured by another knight, who accused him of laying with his wife, and that this knight was planning to drown him in a lake. Morgan and her mercenary band came upon them, and freed Manassen, and together they drowned the other knight.

Morgan would accept no gift in thanks, only his solemn promise that he would deliver a message to Camelot. "She fears you not," said Manassen. "And that she will be Duchess of Cornwall, or you will see what Morgan ferch Gorlois can truly do."

Merlin was so angry at such a threat that he demanded Manassen be cut into enough pieces that a little bit of him could be sent to every kingdom in Britain in warning not to shelter Morgan. But Arthur could permit no such thing under his code of chivalry, and Manassen walked free, back to Morgan's side.

And thus, the terrors she wreaked upon Britain began in earnest, the use of foul magic and hired men to inflict too many tales of woe to recount here. But every threat would come with a letter. Relent, she warned Arthur. Give unto her Tintagel, and all would be well again. Do not, and she would continue to bite at Camelot until not a piece was left.

Morgan formed an obsession with Lancelot and made him the target of her plans, subjecting him to plot and kidnap as often as she could. Perhaps she really thought herself in love with him, or perhaps she hated Arthur and Guinevere so greatly that she wished to wound them by destroying their dearest friend. It was indeed a mystery.

At Christmas, the great celebration of the Christ's birth, Morgan sent an assassin against the king. Was she really so desperate? The bards sang a great ballad of what occurred, a fanciful tale of giants, beheadings, and magic. But it was little the case, and perhaps Arthur liked the story better than the truth.

A giant berserker, close to seven foot tall, and nearly as wide, painted with green woad and wielding a great axe, overpowered the guards and stormed the hall. He fought with such rage that the entire hall became a great melee, and it took all of us to subdue him, fighting for our lives with naught but the tableware for weapons. Finally, Gawain wrested the axe from him, felling him with a hefty swing, decapitating him and staining the hall with a deluge of spurting blood.

And so, when Morgan's taunting letter came the following day, Nentres and I departed Camelot. I could not bear the betrayal in Arthur's eyes, and the twist of guilt. I had allowed her to plot against him, I had allowed her to go with Accolon and, for all my training, she had bested me in combat. I would carry the mark of that shame all my days.

Chapter Eleven

We were not free from Morgan's plots, in those
two years after she declared open war on Arthur,
nor were we free from threat elsewhere. We had
battle after battle on our own soil, facing Irish
raiders and less overt threats. A rumour reached
me that Guinevere had been seen kissing Lancelot
in the rose garden.

I knew it was nonsense. Guinevere would never
do such a thing, and nor would Lancelot. It was
merely the gossip of an errant maid, but it was the
sort of propaganda that lent itself to the quarrels
between kings that Arthur's knights were fond of
inciting. I knew I must work to silence it.

"It is time, I think, that a wife for Lancelot was
found Sire," I suggested to Arthur, on my latest
visit to Camelot.

"Not a bad idea, Elaine, not bad at all," he
agreed.

His marriage was a source of great happiness
to Arthur, so he enjoyed playing matchmaker when
he could.

Guinevere looked up from the castle's account
book. "A wife? For Lancelot? What for?"

"All men need wives eventually," I responded.
"Lancelot has land but no heirs."

"There is time yet," she replied.

Arthur looked at her curiously. "You object?"

"No, husband. Merely that a wife for Lancelot
will take him from here and may make a farmer of
him when we need a warrior."

She put down the quill she had been scratching
entries with and got up, depositing herself in Arthur's lap. "You would miss your dear friend. With

whom would you hunt when Nentres returns to Garlot?"

Arthur nodded. "Right, as always, dear wife."

But I had my mind set on the idea, the only way I could be certain to put an end to the rumours. So I put it to Merlin, who was intrigued.

"I do not think it will silence the gossip," he said.

"It will," I replied. "When Lancelot is married and far from here."

"Unlikely. The common people have little occupation and look to the castles for entertainment when there are no mummers or hangings. They like to make up stories about us, and it excites them to think we do naught but rut like stags in all combinations and numbers."

I resisted the urge to scowl at him. My manner must remain pleasant, I thought.

"But to serve Britain, I must say the possibility of a good match has its rewards."

"How so?" I asked. "If not to control the rumours?"

"Lancelot is Arthur's favourite, and wields a surprising amount of power over him, thanks to that stupid table," replied Merlin. "When Arthur granted him the land of Joyous Gard, he made him very rich indeed. He is a good catch."

"So you think he makes an attractive prospect?"

"Indeed. Now we need only find a maiden who is worthy of such wealth and power, and can bring advantage to us."

Merlin came to a quick decision and selected Elayne of Corbenic, the daughter of King Pellam. They had much land in the north, and we knew the value of the city of Eboracum. It was why the Saxons had taken it, after all. The overtures were made, and Pellam responded in the affirmative. Once Merlin and I had put the idea before Arthur, he liked it so much he commanded Lancelot be brought at once.

"What took you so long?" asked Merlin, as Lancelot arrived in the presence-chamber.

"Forgive me," replied Lancelot. "I was with the queen."

"You are forgiven", said Arthur. "Now, we have some news for you."

Lancelot was quiet and thoughtful, listening as Merlin explained the proposed marriage, and then looked at Arthur. "Is this your wish, Sire?"

Arthur smiled. "I wish only for you to be happy."

"Can I ask something of you? As an engagement gift?"

"Anything," replied Arthur.

"I want to march on Gaul. You have promised me since we were fresh warriors, you an untested king, that you would help me put an end to the havoc that nation wreaks upon the continent."

"So I have," agreed Arthur. "And now the time may be right."

"Absolutely not!" exclaimed Merlin. "Now is not the time for a campaign across the sea, when we have threats to look to here. What of Morgan, Arthur?"

"No," said Arthur. "I always keep my promises. We will march upon Gaul when the sea is good for a crossing."

"It is a condition of my acceptance of this marriage treaty, my Lord Merlin," replied Lancelot. "I want my revenge upon Gaul."

"Arthur freed Benwick, for what good it did him and your father," replied Merlin. "Still you remain here, at Joyous Gard, when you should be

253

across the sea. If you are so worried about Benwick and Gaul, find yourself a boat and some men. Go forth and make your ridiculous demands over there."

"No, Merlin," said Arthur. "I must do what is right. But it will benefit us in the future. Gaul will not stay from our door for long."

"As thou wilt," replied Merlin. "But no good will come of this, and I shall lend no aid."

Arthur summoned his Round Table together to discuss plans for war. Guinevere was for some reason inconsolable, taking to her bed and refusing to see anyone. I thought it was because of Arthur going on another campaign, so I went to see her, knowing too her pain, because Nentres would surely have to go with Arthur. She would not see me, so I took Anna, now a sprightly child of three, out to the fields nearby to play. When we returned, the council had finished.

"Well, husband?" I asked Nentres. "Do you go to battle once more?"

He nodded, resigned. "Arthur has commanded I pledge four hundred to the cause."

"And for what?" I asked. "So that Lancelot can have his revenge? His father was restored to the throne long ago."

"But," he replied. "Lancelot still carries the pain of his father's defeat in his heart, and the sorrow of his kingdom when Frollo, the governor of Gaul, wreaked havoc upon his kingdom."

"What is this to us?" I asked. "What concern is this man to us when Morgan roams loose?"

"Frollo must be stopped. He calls himself governor, but there is no Roman Emperor to give him authority to rule in Gaul."

"I do not like it, Nentres. I have a bad feeling about this."

"Settle yourself, Elaine. Countless times I have fought beside Arthur, and still I am here. No battle shall separate us, I swear."

And so Nentres went unto Gaul that spring, following Lancelot's hasty wedding. Elayne was a beauty and had most pleasant conversation. Hostess duties fell towards me, as Guinevere refused to have anything to do with Lancelot's wedding. The priest married them, though the reek of magic from Dame Brusen, Elayne's waiting woman, suggested her faith lay elsewhere. After a few days at Camelot, Elayne was sent to Joyous Gard to be its lady, alone. I wanted to go with her, but Nentres forbade it, knowing that I was required in Garlot.

I returned to Caer Mor, Hoel in tow, and we set about trying the return to the rhythm of our lives there. The problems of a ruling queen are tenfold, and more so it seemed when her husband was far from that place. Men who were Nentres' placid friends had much to argue with me about when he was not there. In truth, I looked upon my time in Camelot as a welcome respite.

Four months passed, and spring became summer. Hoel and I were breakfasting in the little solar in the hall when we were interrupted by the steward bearing a letter. I thought it was Elayne writing again to say how thankful she was for organising her wedding and to ask for more instruction on running a household. But no, the seal was one I knew well, the dragon of the house of Pendragon. Knowing Arthur would only write from the battlefield with urgency, I tore open the wax and the outer paper.

The note inside was spattered with rain, written on the rough paper reserved for the battlefield tents. Written upon it was two sentences. *Nentres has been captured by Frollo. Send more men.*

I stood on instinct. My mind raced, my heart quickened. I could not think, only imagine Nentres lying dead in some Gaulish jail, or tortured at Frollo's hands. I forced myself to breathe, though I could not stop the pounding of my heart. I knew I must silence my wild imagination and listen only to my instincts. I would know if Nentres was dead. I had the art, and now I must use it. I would cast a great charm of protection, but first, I must be a queen, not a witch.

"Bring me a horse, and tell the men-at-arms I will need an escort," I commanded the steward. "I will be back by tonight and by that time, you must have assembled every headman, every warlord, and every vassal, from the nearest steadings."

The steward bowed and despatched himself to do as I bid.

"Where do you go, Lady Mother? What was in the letter?" asked a frantic Hoel.

I took a seat, bringing our eyes level.

"Please do not worry yourself, but your father has been taken prisoner while commanding Arthur's forces in Gaul. The High King has asked me to raise more troops so that they may liberate him."

My words poured out before I could truly understand what I was saying. "I intend to go with them to Gaul and rescue your father."

He puffed himself up, though I could see the tears that threatened to spill forth. "Let me go too. I should be leading father's rescue, not you."

"You are seven years old," I replied, taking grasp of his shoulders. "And your father fills your head with nonsense. You are not fit to lead a war-band, having never been to battle before."

He looked indignant. "Neither have you! Except that time you got kidnapped by Saxons!"

"Thank you for reminding me of that. The men are used to my leadership and will obey me. Besides, I need you here. You must be regent while I am away."

He nodded, and I wanted to smirk at the pride that filled his face. "I must. There is no one else."

"I will ask the High King to send someone to help you. What about Gawain? You like your cousin, do you not? Or maybe Merlin might come."

"Really? I could show Gawain my new sword. Is it true about Merlin? Is he really a demon?"

"Oh, yes," I replied. "He is the son of a most wicked creature from the hills." I clapped him on the back like his father would have. "Go and see Portimus, and tell him that you are to be regent. He will have much to tell you."

He took off. I reached for the quill and paper on the table and began to scratch out my reply to Arthur, particularly my request for one of his most trusted knights to come and support Hoel or, failing that, even Merlin would do. I hoped that the old enchanter's interests were aligned with mine, at least this once. A kingdom commanded by a seven-year-old, with its army over the sea? If I was an enemy of Garlot, it is now that I should strike. But those were problems for another day, and I turned my attention to the task at hand.

The men will obey me? Why had I ever thought such a thing, never mind said it? They might humour their queen when she joins them in the practice yard or accompanies them on patrol, but to be at their head in battle? But I had an idea. Only one man need obey me, and the others would follow.

257

Lomar, now my husband's sergeant and one of my men I trusted most, entered the hall. "We are ready to depart, Highness, upon your orders. Where are we for?"

"For the steading of Meron."

It was a hard ride to Meron's steading, and I put both men and horses through their paces. I wore my velvet riding habit, a gift from Guinevere, beneath my breastplate and bracers. I had no sword, only two small daggers, one hidden beneath my skirt and another in my boot. I had hastily pinned my hair up beneath my coronet. To ride into Meron's steading, armed and armoured, would present the wrong impression. I must be both proud and weak, both a woman and a warrior. I must throw myself on his mercy and command him at the same time. We must both walk away from this exchange as powerful as ever. But, as I patted the faint outline of the dagger tucked into a leather pouch below my thigh, I thought only a fool would have ridden here unarmed.

"Make way for the Queen of Garlot!" bellowed Lomar, as our horses cleaved their way through the muck. The high wooden gate was still open when we arrived, the night-bell not yet sounded in the orange summer dusk.

I threw myself from the horse, landing in one swift motion and held out my reins in an impatient hand. A boy rushed forward and took them, a kitchen servant by the looks of him.

"Where is your lord?" I demanded.

"In the ale-house, mistress."

I snapped my gloved fingers in his face, Igraine resurrected. "Your Highness, or my Lady, if you forget yourself. Where is the alehouse?"

He pointed towards a squat little brown building by the main hall. It was a new addition from my previous visits, just like the beginnings of a stone wall that framed the outside of his steading. Meron was expanding. News to be shared with Nentres if we ever got him back.

I made my way into the ale-house, where a group of men sat at a table, a bustling ale-wife tending to the fire yonder. It was no city tavern, with food and strumpets. Just a brewery, making ale for a community that probably saw little clean water, and providing a welcome respite for husband and wife.

His men scrambled to throw themselves to their knees before me, but Meron rose slow and deliberate, bowing at the waist. Now at least sixty, Meron was old and haggard, what little hair surrounding his bald pate now grey-white. He was still bulky and seemed to fill the room when he stood. If I had the time, I would have laughed at the thought of my untrained sixteen-year-old self challenging him to single combat.

"Queen Elaine. You do me much honour with your visit. Care for a drink?"

He slid his tankard whittled from horn towards me, down the table. I pulled out the seat in front of me and sat down, careful to arrange my gown like Guinevere would. I slid the tankard away from me, leaving a clear line of sight from me to him.

"Leave us," I commanded of the men. They waited for a nod from Meron before leaving.

"You have come late in the evening, my Lady, so you seek not our society. What is it?"

I steeled myself. "Nentres, as you know, has been leading Arthur's campaign in Gaul. He has been taken prisoner by the governor, Frollo. Our High King bids us send men to free him."

He smirked. "But your husband already raised a levy of four hundred, so you have come begging for troops from me, because I have men to spare. So why should I?"

"Why should you what?"

"Spare them. Why should I give you more men, when four hundred must be dead or captured?"

"Because Nentres is your king. Because I am your queen and I command you."

He snorted a little. "Not good enough reasons. I do not like to throw good warriors after bad."

He looked me up and down, from coronet to folded skirts. "You must be desperate if you have come to me. Can your mighty brother not raise troops elsewhere?"

"He is doing so, but I need well-trained men, and lots of them, very quickly."

"Which I have in abundance. I have nearly a hundred here in the hall, and can get two hundred more with a word."

"I have summoned the others to Caer Mor, they will match what you give me."

"But I doubt they have as many or as good."

He rose from his chair and made his way towards me, drumming ringed fingers on the table as he went. He stopped and perched his weight down on the table beside me, which gave a mighty creak. I hoped he had not imbibed much. If he fell, he would surely crush me.

"Some might say you are foolish."

"And why is that?" I asked.

"To come here, with only a few men-at-arms, and tell me your husband is captured, likely killed I might add, and his best warriors with him. One dead queen and even my kitchen boy could be king. It has all the makings of a Roman coup, worthy of an emperor."

The fire flickered, casting shadows along the walls, making the vats of ale seem like hulking beasts ready to pounce. I could hear his men outside. The ale-wife was long gone. Meron held out his hand to examine a large gold ring on his finger. I moved my hand lower in my lap. If he tried anything, as his demeanour would suggest, I would have only seconds to draw my dagger before his great hands would be around my throat. Killing Meron would be a mistake, but walking out of there anything less than the Queen of Garlot would be a greater mistake.

"You desire to be king?" I asked, my voice breathy.

"Who doesn't?" he asked, revealing his teeth in a smile like a hissing cat. "You were a princess out of Camelot. I am common. You don't know what it is like for us, searching for food and water, scraping together coin to pay our way through winter, attaching ourselves to a warlord to die in our hundreds just so our families will not starve. Some men got to where I am now by farming or trading. I made my mark by killing. What's one more life to be king and never be hungry again?"

Nentres told me once that a fight is already won or lost in the minds of men before they ever cross swords. Those who are determined to live, those who have something to fight for, they will always be triumphant. A prepared opponent, who knows every move they will make before they make it, they will fight another day.

I was determined to live, determined to rescue Nentres and keep the crown he had trusted me with for so long. I would use Meron's great weight against him, let him bring himself to the ground. Then I would draw my daggers and fight like a scratching, cornered cat, screaming for my men all the while. I would be wife, queen and mother yet.

"Or, I could get a son on you. Claim your enemy's wife and all his chattels are yours, I've done it before. Claim a queen and a kingdom is yours, so the old laws say."

I gritted my teeth. "If you could manage it at your age."

He burst out in laughter, a great neigh like a horse in labour. The table gave another weighty groan and Meron raised himself up and onto the floor, returning to his seat. I bit down on my sigh of relief, determined not to show my fear. I willed my hand to release its tension, where it lay ready to spring for my daggers.

"Your beauty has faded over the years, Elaine," he said. "There is only your steel core left."

"How fairs Nalia?" I asked in reply.

"Nalia fairs well. Forwin has given her three sons, little fighters through and through. I've named the eldest my heir. You did well with that match, I don't mind admitting. Got more out of that than better drainage in my lower fields."

"Will you pledge your troops then? Since I cannot command you to lend them, will you offer?"

He nodded. "You have my word. Three hundred men, by this time tomorrow."

"I will be forever grateful."

"I want something in return."

"What?"

"I want freedom from taxes for the next year. And I want Nentres to lift the ban on cattle breeding with nearby steadings."

I knew I must be strong. I could not give away a kingdom to rescue a king. "Six months. And I will allow near breeding only this season."

"Done."

"Please arrive promptly at Caer Mor tomorrow. We are for Camelot as soon as possible and then on to Dubris to seek boats."

"Very well."

He thought for a moment. "Would you like some food?"

Garlot lived by the old ways. Kill your guest, fair enough, but leave them hungry and you will be cursed by the Gods. He directed me to a hall and a woman, who he called his wife but was certainly not Aleyna served me lamb stew and thick rye bread. I ate, hoping to calm the churning in my stomach. We set off again into the night after I solicited yet another promise from Meron to see him the next day.

The servants had done well in my absence. From all over Garlot came the elite, and on bended knee, they pledged their troops to my service. Six hundred men I had at my disposal and we made a fearsome sight marching forth from Caer Mor. Were the wrong person to spy us on the way to Camelot, they could mistake us for an invading force.

The day was spent organising food and weapons for the men who brought none, and making sure to leave a troop to guard Hoel. But they were forewarned, if Garlot was threatened while I was away, there were to be no glorious battles, they were to take my son straight to Camelot and the protection of Arthur's court, even if they had to club him over the head and drag him.

I rode at the head of the column, in full warrior attire, leathers, and armour, my hair braided to keep it from my face and delicate scrolls of blue woad painted on my face. My short sword was strapped to my waist. A shield in the colours of

Garlot hung from my saddle with a spare spatha like Nentres' would wield. I hoped I did not lose my short sword, for I feared I would not be able to lift that sword as easily as my own.

We made our way into Dubris and procured ourselves boats and men to crew them. Word had been sent to Lot to make use of his fleet, but it was more courtesy than anything, not knowing how long it would before a reply reached us, or if he would even try to lend aid.

I enjoyed my time on the boat, the sea wind blowing across my face. I had been on a boat before, just for trips along our river ways, but never on the open sea. Igraine would have had a fit to see her daughter playing at sailor. She had always hated it, and never allowed us to go near it, never mind engage in so common an occupation.

The march through Gaul took three agonising days. If it had been me alone, I would have ridden through the night, but I had to take care not to founder our horses, nor tire the men beyond use. Arthur had already cleared the way for us, for we found men wearing his colours along the way who helped point us towards the fortress where Britain lay siege to Frollo.

By the third day, when we reached the war tents, my sigh of relief was audible. I ordered the men to report to the sergeants and find themselves some food, while I raced into the High King's tent, interrupting Arthur, Sir Lancelot, and Sir Bedevere pouring over a map.

"My sister," said a surprised Arthur, embracing me. "I am glad your men are here, though I did not expect you to come too."

"I must," I replied. "You said Nentres has been taken. How long has he been Frollo's prisoner?"

"Two weeks," he replied, refusing to meet my eye.

"Two weeks!" I was incredulous. "Why have you not attempted to free him before?"

"The fortress is nigh impenetrable. Come, sister."

He led me outside the tent and pointed to the squat stone building near the horizon. We were encamped at the top of a hill, a good distance from Frollo's fortress.

"Do you see now?" he asked. "We have the higher ground, and potentially the numbers, and Frollo knows this. This is why he has not attacked us, and retreated inside his fortress after the first skirmish, with the prisoners. He knows we will not attack, we will waste more resources in a siege."

"Then we must ransom our men," I said. "Surely he has made demands?"

Arthur shook his head. "He has, but it is too much. He wants us to retreat from Gaul, a prospect I can truthfully consider, but also gold. And if I gave him what he demands, our treasury would be bankrupt."

"Then what are we to do?" I asked. I could feel desperation creeping into my soul. I was preparing myself to lose Nentres.

"I may have a plan," said Bedevere, emerging from the tent.

"We would be grateful for anything you can suggest," replied Arthur.

"Our spies tell us that the fortress has sent for food supplies from a nearby town. The delivery will be in the next few days."

"So we cut off their supplies, and starve them out?" I asked.

Bedevere shook his head. "No, Lady Elaine. That would take too long, so we do the opposite.

We let them deliver the food. They will have to open a gate to let them in, so we attack then."

"But surely Frollo would expect such a thing?" I questioned.

Arthur nodded. "More than likely. But if we strike hard and fast, we will have the advantage, and be inside in no time. The question is - how do we disrupt the delivery?" asked Arthur.

I caught sight of the motionless carts in the encampment. "I have an idea. We will need straw too and oil."

Four of Arthur's carts were given to us. Two we filled with oil-soaked straw, and the others we packed twenty of our best fighters into, ten to a cart, including myself.

"There is to be no argument," I warned Arthur, as he tried to protest. "If you prevent me going to rescue Nentres, you will have a bigger battle on your hands than any campaign you have fought before."

Sitting in the carts at the prow of the hill, we watched as the Gauls inched the side door open, ready to receive the supply of goods trundling towards them. As it drew closer, armed guards began to come forth and form a line between the direction of our camp and the exchange taking place behind them.

"Now," I said, gesturing to the men with the torches.

They touched the torch to the straw in the carts and it began to smoke. Arthur nodded to me. I nodded back. "Make sure you are not far behind us," I said.

"Loose!" I called, and I could feel the men behind me give the cart a shove.

With a creak, the wheels trundled forward and we began to move down the hill. We began to pick up speed, dislodging rocks and soil. In a blur of green, browns and the blue sky, we raced towards Frollo's fortress.

The flaming carts had found their mark. Being lighter, they had reached their destination before us. They smashed against the stone wall and splintered, casting flames around the base of the fortress. The men dived out of the way, lest they be caught in the inferno. In hurried gestures, the Gauls urged the men to bring the supplies inside. More began to come forth from inside.

"Now," urged Lomar, as we too approached the stone walls. One by one, we flung ourselves from the cart

The two remaining carts collided with one another in a flurry of splinters. Locked by the wheels, they sped towards the men, and they scattered to avoid them. One Gaul, slower than his peers, was caught in their paths and disappeared under with a twisted cry and splash of blood. With the Gauls scattered, the two carts disappeared into the treeline with a crash. The Gauls raced back to the door while the armed warriors made their way towards us.

"For Garlot!" I cried, and, leapt forward. I slashed down, catching a Gaul by surprise. The blow glanced across his face, opening a deep well of blood. He fell to the ground and tried to crawl away. I kicked out at him, and his head came into contact with the wheel of the cart, knocking him unconscious.

Another ran at me, and I brought up my shield to deflect the blow of his sword. I thrust it out, unbalancing him. He took a wild swing with his sword, but I slashed with the tip of my own, cutting his wrist. He dropped the sword and I jerked my elbow, the boss smashing into his face.

I could see the door, ahead of us. They were closing it, leaving their men outside the walls to our mercy. Our opportunity to get inside the castle was dwindling.

"Forward!" I cried, and hacked another warrior from my path with a firm stroke.

"We cannot break the line!" yelled Lomar, felling a Gaul with a vicious stab. "If we break the line, we will be surrounded! Wait until Arthur gets here!"

I looked up at the hill, and Arthur's men were only just approaching. If the door closed before they reached us, it would all be for naught.

"We are losing our chance!" I called back, and resolved to press on. I sprinted towards the door and, with a frustrated groan, Lomar followed me. I reached the door, and the last Gaul folded himself inside the closing gap.

"Yah!" I cried, and took hold of the iron ring on the outside of the door, heaving with all my might. I did not know whether it was magic or just sheer might, but I could feel the resistance on the other side dwindle. Lomar appeared at my side and began to thrust his sword through the cap, wounding the unfortunates who were closing the door.

"We have it!" I exclaimed as the last door puller died with a groan, and it came freely towards me. "Inside, now!"

"We do not know how many are on the other side," warned Lomar.

I shook my head, ignoring him.

"To me!" I cried, waving to our warriors with my sword. Lomar shrugged and helped me pull the door wide open. The dark corridor inside appeared to be empty. Then I looked up and saw the murder holes in the roof.

"Shields!" I ordered, and we raised them above our head, interlocking them. I felt the crush of bodies behind me, the sour smell of sweaty, bloodied men, as we formed the shield wall above us.

"Forward!" yelled Lomar, and we walked down the corridor, feeling with our hands were the others were so that we could stay together and leave no gaps in the shield wall. Thump after thump sounded against our shields, rocks and other heavy objects being dropped on us. But our shield wall was flawless

We reached the end of the corridor unscathed and found the inner door. Those of us in front brought our shields down before us and braced our shoulders against them. With "heave" and "ho", we flung ourselves against the door. Being a simple wooden thing, designed to keep out the cold, not invaders, it crumpled under our huge weight.

Pouring through it, we found ourselves in the kitchen of Frollo's fortress. It was deserted, but the fires were still lit, so it was not long abandoned.

"They will be held in the dungeons," said Lomar. "Down in the cellars, surely. This way!"

He pointed with his sword, and I had no choice but to follow. I had never stormed a castle before. We raced out into the corridor and found a staircase sloping downwards. The men and I ran down into the dark of Frollo's cellars and found another door to force open.

At the end of that room was an iron lattice, and I could see men behind it. I ran towards it, and in my haste, clanged against it. This sound drew the attention of the men inside and I could see, on the other side of the iron bars, was Nentres. Upon seeing me, he jumped to his feet.

"Quickly," I ordered. "Get this cage open."

The men found the key hanging on the wall, and with a heave, opened the door to the prison. Nentres bundled past them, straight towards me. He pulled me into his arms, and I clasped him close, though he smelled atrocious. He saw my wrinkled nose.

"I have been here some time, with few opportunities to wash." He kissed the top of my head. "Oh, you are my warrior queen. I knew you would find me."

I drew back and counted the men behind him. They waved and cheered when they saw their queen, and some were moved to tears.

"On your feet!" I called. "We leave at once!"

"How many have been taken?" I asked Nentres.

"More than this," he replied.

"Where are they being held?"

"There are many dungeons and rooms in this place. We have not a hope of finding them all before you are discovered."

"Then what can we do?" I asked. "I did not come all this way to leave them."

"We must take the castle," he replied, as though it was the easiest thing in the world.

"How? Even if all of us were armed...?"

"We must kill Frollo," he said. "We must find him, and kill him. Cut off the head of the bull, and the body will fall."

He gestured down to his unarmoured body, and I realised he would have no weapons. I reached down to my thigh and slid the knife free from the scabbard, passing it to Nentres. He took it, nodding his thanks. I drew my sword, passing my shield to one of the free prisoners. He could use it as bludgeon if need be.

"Clear our way back to that door," I ordered Lomar. He nodded and gestured for some of the men to follow him. Nentres and I went out into the corridor.

"It is this way," said Nentres.

"How do you know?"

"I have spent nearly every night I have been captured in Frollo's rooms."

"He has tortured you for information?"

He shrugged. "Mostly we just talked. He speaks our language, you know. It was more effective than any torture. If I was forced to speak to him again, I would have told him all of Arthur's battle plans."

He led me down the corridor and up a set of servants' stairs, before turning into a richly decorated antechamber. We travelled around the painted screen and found ourselves in what appeared to be Frollo's study.

Frollo was standing in the centre of the room, a servant holding out armour for him to choose, while the governor sipped from a golden goblet. The poor man grew frightened and dropped the armour. Frollo waved him away and he took off, knocking the screen over as ran from the room.

Frollo was older than I expected him to be, though he must have been quite aged by the time I encountered him, if he had been governor in Gaul my whole life. He wore Roman garb, a rich red mantle, and had his hair clipped quite close, no beard.

"Ah," said Frollo, as though we were late to a feast. "This must be the famous Elaine of Garlot."

"Surrender," said Nentres. "And you will be allowed to escape with your life."

271

Frollo put down his goblet on his ornate desk. "Go back to your cell, and take your bellatrix with you. And you will be allowed to escape with your life."

Nentres let out a roar and raced at him. I stood ready, waiting for my chance. I did not want to get in Nentres' way and end up hurting him by accident. Nentres swung out at him with the knife, again and again, keeping his other hand high to guard against a punch to the head.

But Frollo was well matched against Nentres, and blocked his blows, leaving no opening for his knife. A well-placed punch jarred his wrist and forced Nentres to drop the knife. Then, with a firm kick to his chest, Frollo sent my husband tumbling to the corner of the room.

Seeing my opening, I flew at Frollo, intending to slice his back, but he turned. His hands moved faster than I expected. They snaked around my arm, and with a tug, forced me to drop my sword, lest my arm be broken. He kicked it away and then pulled again, sending me careening across the room. As I tumbled, I saw him turn, pick up his goblet and toss it in Nentres' direction.

I collided with the wall and felt a stab of pain in my neck and back. Through spotty vision, I watched Nentres jerk his head out of the way of the flying goblet and launch himself at Frollo. He caught the governor by the midriff, and the two went down to the floor. The struggled and scrambled for dominance on the floor, but Frollo won out, levering himself on top of Nentres.

Frollo pressed down on Nentres throat, and I heard him start to choke. Letting out a cry, I jumped to my feet and aimed a solid kick to Frollo's ribs. He bellowed in pain, and rolled away, clutching his side. But it did not keep him down

272

for long, and he sprung to his feet to meet me once more.

I swung punch after punch, not allowing Frollo to have a moment's peace from my attack. He blocked them almost carelessly, but I could see him start to tire. As he over-reached with one of his own blows, I spun, and kicked as I turned, crashing my heel into his exposed back. As he grunted, and swayed on his feet, I kicked at his knee and felt it bend under my boot. He sunk to the floor.

I looked about wildly for my sword but could not see it. My eyes settled on a wooden stool. I picked it up and then brought it crashing down on the back of his head. Nentres, now on his feet, picked up the knife and drove it into his back. Frollo gave a wheezing cough, spraying the floor with blood, before falling down dead. Nentres and I looked at him carefully, to make sure he was dead. When we were certain, Nentres held out his hand to me.

"Come, my queen," said Nentres, tossing the bloody knife to the ground. "There must be a bed somewhere in this castle."

"Let us hope there is a bath too," I replied.

We laughed and laughed. Still we laughed as we secured Frollo's castle, and installed men there to help the Gauls choose a new leader, subservient to Arthur. And still we laughed as we sailed home, happy to be reunited once more.

Chapter Twelve

Nearly thirteen years had passed since Arthur's ascension to the throne. At thirty-three, I was no more a girl of twenty, but nearly a matron of forty, and parent to a boy nearly a man. Throughout this time, we were plagued by Morgan's plots.

Always, she had a man willing to fight and die for her, and always she had dark magic to aid her. Castles too seemed easy to come by, so many that people thought she magicked them from the earth, or commanded sprites to build them for her. Instead, I think, it meant she had gold to spare, and I dared not fathom how she obtained it, for it would have been wicked work indeed.

She had allies too, witches and warlocks from across the land, who worked their spells upon Arthur's knights. Every time some mischief would occur and the instigator caught or killed, there were would be some evidence Morgan had been involved.

A most particular friend she had was Queen Sebile of Sorestan, though it was said they quarrelled often and most violently. Once, together, they kidnapped Lancelot, putting him under a spell of sleep, and tried to make him choose one as his lover. He would not, and escaped with the help of their maid. They made a similar plot against Sir Ector de Maris, Lancelot's half-brother from Benwick who was evidently less able to resist their charms. He had his sport with them and escaped smiling into Camelot.

I had not known Queen Sebile to be a witch, but evidently they had been schooled together at Glastonbury. It seemed Mother Abbess' grudge against Uther was great indeed, because her pupils worked towards nothing else. I thought often of confronting this woman, who openly ran a house of learning and charity but was so wicked otherwise.

Merlin advised against it, fearing it would provoke a war against the Christians, who were growing in numbers as our kingdom became more prosperous and boat after boat of people seeking news lives in a new land sailed into Londinium. He had spies, he said, who could get close to her and inform of her actions. Besides, he argued, even if her magic was great, she would not live forever.

He dealt too with Queen Sebile, paying her a visit which must have terrified her beyond belief, as we heard no more of an association with Morgan. We kept as much of this as we could from Arthur, being as he could not afford either a war with the Christians or with Sorestan, not when peace reigned and, other than the occasional Scoti or Pict raid, Morgan was the only thorn in Britain's side.

So we turned our attention elsewhere. There was a kingdom to rule. Arthur relied greatly upon his Round Table for counsel, which had expanded so much that not all who had a seat could sit there at once. Merlin chafed at being only one voice among many, so he wheedled Arthur into creating the small council, which dealt with the most important matters of state or, more truthfully, the matters in which Merlin wished to have total say.

I sat upon his small council, along with Sir Lancelot and Sir Bedevere, and occasionally Sir Kay, much to Merlin's ire. We met in the presence-chamber, a room barely used in Arthur's Camelot. He liked being elbow to elbow with the people in the hall and needed only the comfort of the solar when he wished for intimacy. Uther, I recalled, had many meetings there. How Camelot had changed.

When I entered the presence-chamber for our latest meeting, I noticed that Merlin was absent. Sometimes he would be late for meetings, and one unfortunate page would have to go pull him away from his wine jug or a comely maiden.

"Is Merlin abed yet?" I asked.

'He took horse this morning, without so much as a by-your-leave," was Arthur's sour reply. "Did not even leave me a note. So we shall proceed without him."

We delved into matters of coin and of law, and considered the most important petitions, written directly to Arthur, considered too sensitive for an open hearing. But the matter of most concern was Merlin's disappearance. We all knew that it did not herald anything of good tidings and that there would be some matter to deal with when he returned.

When he was spied in the courtyard with a slight, brown-haired girl riding behind him on his mount, we raced to the presence-chamber to hear what he would say. When I got there, he was introducing the girl to Arthur.

She could not have been more than seventeen. She was very pretty, though quite tall for a woman. She was slender, but still her breasts were full and round, and her dress cut quite too severely to be considered proper. I wondered if she was some new plaything Merlin had found, but surely he would not be introducing her to the High King if that was true.

"This is Nimueh," he said, gesturing to the girl. "She is of Avalon, the daughter of Viviane."

I knew there was something strange about her, even as she stared demurely at the floor. It was the whiff of magic, drowned out by the power emanating from Merlin. That was why I had not sensed it.

"How did you come upon her?" I asked Merlin.

"She summoned me," he replied.

I was confused. "That is high magic, to summon something that is not truly human."

Merlin held up his hands in a gesture of ambivalence. "I was summoned and went unto Avalon. Nimueh was there, and she told me she had need of me. The girl is obviously well trained by her mother."

"You are most welcome, Nimueh," said Arthur. "But I am not sure what Camelot can do for you."

"We must offer her a home here," said Merlin. "The Lady of the Lake has passed into the Underworld, and now leaves her daughter alone in Avalon. The island has been abandoned by the Wise. Remember, I owed her mother a great debt, for her and her fellow Druidesses sheltered me during the Roman purges. You owe her too, for she bestowed Excalibur upon you."

"As I have not forgotten," replied Arthur. "And I need its power more than ever, especially with the scabbard gone."

"Sire, I could make another scabbard," proffered Nimueh.

Arthur's full attention was immediately devoted to her. "This is true?"

"In a manner of speaking," answered Merlin. "She knows of it in theory, but she has so little training in the Druidic ways. She needs some tuition before she can begin."

"But you could give her this training?"

"I could," he replied, nodding.

Arthur raised himself from his throne, leaning forward to engage Nimueh in conversation. He was engrossed in her. One mention of his missing scabbard was all it took. I knew that any counsel I had to give would be lost to deaf ears, but I could not do my duty as an adviser if I did not try.

Arthur bid Merlin take Nimueh to the kitchens for something to eat, and Lancelot wanted to ask her questions about the death of his foster-mother. I did not follow the others from the room. Instead, I took a seat beside my brother, on Guinevere's slightly smaller throne.

"I am suspicious, Arthur," I said.

"Of Nimueh?" he asked, affronted by such a suggestion.

"It is just a feeling." I shrugged. "Perhaps I am more suspicious of Merlin. Here is a pretty young girl, claiming to be the daughter of Viviane, summoning him to render aid. And Merlin takes her in? Surely, you are not ignorant of his reputation? Even the gossip of servant girls reaches the king's ear. Your own wife cannot abide him."

"Merlin raised me, Elaine," he responded. "You are quick to forget that. My lords are quick to forget that. Guinevere is harsh, and she forgets he is my foster father. It is within his nature to take in a young girl, especially when he owed her mother his life."

Arthur would have his way, and so would Merlin, and no two people were more powerful in the castle of Camelot. Arthur declared her a ward of the court, and Merlin her protector. The old lecher wanted her moved into his apartments, to better aid her tuition he said, but even Arthur had some sense of propriety and had her installed within the queen's apartments.

"I do not like her," complained Guinevere.

"Nimueh?" I asked, looking up from my embroidery.

She nodded.

"Is it because she is a pagan?" I asked, suspecting Guinevere's old refrain about our immortal souls.

"Yes, but also her immodest dress. She is a temptress."

"She has been raised improperly. And I am sure the island of Avalon has little wool merchants from which to purchase the makings of a modest dress."

I looked the High Queen in the eyes. They were not as bright as they once were, and were red-rimmed.

"You have been crying, Highness," I said, reaching for a caring tone to address her.

She turned her face from me and pressed her handkerchief to her mouth. I prompted her again, and she shrugged at me.

"Tell me. Please, Guinevere."

"It is Lancelot. He sent news from Joyous Gard this morning. Your namesake has delivered a baby boy. Galahad, he will be named."

"This has upset you?" I asked.

"Everyone from the old days, from when Arthur and I were first married, all of them have sons. I have given him a daughter, but no other children have followed. I have put his kingdom at risk."

"You cannot blame yourself."

"I do not. I blame Morgan."

"She says she cursed you, but I do not know if it is true."

"I can feel it," she said. "Like a knot in my womb. Especially when I see Nimueh, for some reason. I do not know why, but she reminds me of Morgan."

I knew that Guinevere could not be swayed from her rant against Morgan, so I let her continue, glad when the dinner bell rang.

The court grew fascinated with Nimueh. Not in the least because of her home in Avalon, and her mysterious mother who came to court only once in her life, demanding the head of Sir Balin for his role in the death of her brother, a man who could also claim kinship to Arthur through Uther, but because she was fond of less than proper dress. Many men in Camelot had eyes for her, even the level-headed Sir Pelleas.

My suspicion of her coloured most of my interaction with her. It did not help that she refused to give a straight answer to my questions about her time on Avalon, or how she had summoned Merlin. After she had been particularly evasive, I went into her room and found something that I hoped would be enough to validate my fears.

"What are you doing here?" she demanded. "These are my quarters."

"I am the queen's chief lady," I replied. "I may inspect the rooms of the ladies at court without cause. And look what I have found."

I gestured to the table, and her tools of power. Her eyes refused to meet mine.

"This, the oil, the herbs?" I asked. "These are to free the spirit from the body. What need would you have of such a charm?"

She looked down at the ground. "I…I met a man, on the way here to Camelot. And…I wished to speak to him, to see him once more."

She turned her gaze towards me, begging with her eyes. Her voice was high, like a little girl pleading not to be sent to bed. "Please do not tell Merlin, he will be hurt by this."

281

"Then why do you lead him on so?" I asked. "Surely you know his intentions toward you?"

"He has been good to me. He has given me a home and teaches me to be a great Druidess. I feel I must be kind to him."

"Kindness is not what he intends, and you will not find yourself so kind either when he gets bored of you playing coy. Tell him the truth, and do it soon. Merlin has a vicious temper. If you scorn him, I doubt even Avalon will protect you from his revenge."

She nodded, and I swept from the room, hoping she would heed my advice.

But, like even myself at that age, she did not heed the advice of older women. I caught her speaking with Merlin in the corridor to the solar. I hung back, hoping to catch the end of their conversation.

"Tonight then, milord," she said, her voice breathy with desire. "By the great hawthorn tree. We will not be disturbed there."

"Yes," he replied. "By the hawthorn tree, when the stars have risen."

She smiled and departed the corridor. Merlin turned and stared at the blank space where I had previously stood. I flung myself quickly behind the wall.

"Little Elaine, still listening at keyholes. You can come out now."

I smoothed out my dress and stepped out into the corridor.

"Merlin," I began, but he swiftly interrupted me.

"What right have you to listen to my private business? And not even to do it properly? A little rowan and I would never have sensed you."

I held up my hands in placation. "I apologise, but...Nimueh...I do not trust her. Merlin, I fear that she is not all she claims she is."

He scoffed. "She is hardly an assassin or a spy. She is a mere girl."

"You are besotted with her."

"What would you know of it?" He sneered. "Little Elaine, as virginal as a novice nun."

"Come now Merlin, I have a child, I am not ignorant of such things. But I am mistrustful of her."

"Because she shows an interest in me? Because I will teach her what I will not teach you? You are jealous."

"Of her? Never."

"You are. You know that if she restores the scabbard to Arthur, she will take your position as his female advisor. With her will not need his boring older sister at court, to scold and chide at every opportunity, and do nothing in return. Her lineage as a Druidess pales in comparison to your amateur witchery."

"You seek to wound me, Merlin. Do you know then, that I am right, deep down in your heart?

"It was an unfortunate side effect of my plans for Britain that I had ever cause to meet you or your wretched sister."

He stalked away, and I had not the stomach to do further battle with him. Let him pay the price of his lust, I thought. I went and sat in the hall with Nentres, and told my husband, who was a tad more interested in a dice game than in what I had to say about Merlin, and asked me what it mattered if she lay with him, that was her choice. He said that I was woman who did not like women, and while it was often true I had no time for silly maids batting their eyelashes at unsuitable men, his words stung.

So I retired early, and lay down on the bed, chewing on the words I would have for him later. While pondering on this, I fell fast asleep and was set for a pleasant night, until I awoke with a start.

The world had turned on its edge. I could feel it. It was like trying on a robe, and finding it too small. It was so familiar yet so strange. Nothing was as it should be. I could not sense the power of Merlin anywhere in the castle, and I knew at once that, somehow, Nimueh had betrayed us.

The bed was cold and empty beside me. Nentres has not returned from the games in the hall. I leapt up and rushed to don my leather breeches and tunic, and strapping on my short sword. Summoning forth as much breath as I could from the air, I ran from my bedroom, down the back stairs and out into the courtyard. I followed the sickening feeling in my stomach, out into the night. I flew at the gate, forcing open the sally-port with unfounded strength.

"Elaine!" called the guard, so shocked at my speed and appearance he forgot my title. "Come back, it is not safe!"

I ran, feeling my chest tighten and struggle to capture air. I ran as fast as I could. I passed hillsides, the grass appearing inky purple in the darkness of the night. The stars were out in full, and I could almost feel them urging me on. Nature was rebelling against whatever was happening. Some great crime was being committed.

I leapt over a stray log, sensing it before I saw it. I knew that Merlin would be at the great hawthorn tree with Nimueh, and though I did not quite know where it was, I followed my heart and the sick worry in my stomach.

284

I arrived at the tree far too late. Nimueh was there, clad only in a white shift. Morgan too, astride a white steed, her black robes draped over its pale flank. She wore a silver breastplate, like my own back at the castle, and a viciously curved knife hung from her saddle. Merlin was nowhere to be seen.

"Sister? Come to join us?"

"It must be undone at once! Whatever you have done, undo it!"

Morgan smirked, echoing the words we had learned at our mother's knee. "Seal the spell and it is done. As we will, so mote it be."

She cackled, breaking the harsh silence of the night with her laugh. I ran towards my sister. Nimueh flew at me, but I was not to be tested. I flung out my arm, and my elbow caught her square in the face. She grunted in pain and fell to the ground amongst the crisping leaves. I pressed on.

Morgan kicked out at me but I dodged to one side. My hands fell upon her saddle but she stretched out her hand and suddenly the metal buckle was white hot. I released it for fear I would burn my hand. I drew back and slid my sword from its scabbard.

"I will kill you, Morgan, I swear I will this time! I know not what you've done, but I will kill you!"

She rolled her eyes. "I am on horseback. I will be gone before you can reach me."

She turned her steed. "Nimueh, come!"

Nimueh stirred on the ground. I moved between her and my sister. "I will not let you both escape."

"Suit yourself, sister," she replied. With that, she kicked her horse and rode off into the night. My legs were far too tired from my run to pursue her. I was no fool. That horse could ride for days and at a pace I could not match. I let her go, cursing myself for not stopping Nimueh when I had the chance.

Nimueh raised her head to watch my sister go. "Morgan!" She cried, like a dying dog. Her hands were outstretched to the figure receding against the rising sun. "Mother! Mother!"

Her cries went unheeded as the hoof beats slowly faded from our hearing. Nimueh did not know what sort of woman my sister was. She looked so pitiful, lying in her ground stained shift, shivering from the cold and her blood weeping from her nose to mingle with her tears in ugly red blotches upon her garments. But my sympathy withered and died in my heart. I pulled her roughly to her feet.

"Get up!" I commanded. "Get up, you stupid little bitch!"

I shook her. "Where is Merlin? You wish me to strike you again?"

She pointed, one slender arm outstretched toward the hawthorn tree.

"Do not test me, you painted little harlot! What have you done with him? Is he dead?"

"He is spelled."

I raised my hand. She cried out again. "Stop, please! He is spelled, a sleeping curse. Morgan bound him into the tree."

"What?"

I released her. She hit the ground with a cry and I made my way over to the hawthorn. The tree was old and wide, nearly as thick as ten men. There was a hollow in the tree. I peered inside but could not see anything for the blackness.

Steeling myself, I reached into the hollow. At first, I felt just the wood of the tree. Then to my horror, something else. Human skin, still warm to

286

the touch. I reached up and felt a bearded face. I bit down on a scream and withdrew my hand.

I was confused and my blood was still pumping like silent thunder around my body. I could not think for rage. All I could think of was having my revenge upon Nimueh and then upon Morgan. Perhaps killing them would end their spell. I was eager to find out.

As I returned from the tree, she made her move. But I was faster still and caught the escaping woman by the hair.

I leaned in close. "I have killed Saxons and Gauls aplenty, little girl. I will cut your treacherous little throat and leave your body for the ravens."

I dragged her all the way to Camelot. She fought against me once or twice, but I quickly put paid to that with a sound blow or two. Her elbow had purpled hideously from my grip, and blood had encrusted on her face. I took great pleasure in tossing her to the floor, at the foot of the throne.

"What is the meaning of this?" demanded Arthur, still in his nightshirt, roused by the chamberlain.

"Nimueh has betrayed us," I explained. "And worked some charm on Merlin, at Morgan's behest. Our sister has taken off into the night, and now Merlin is imprisoned."

"She lies," retorted Nimueh. "She has taken leave of her mind, and stole into my chamber, where she beat me!"

I clenched my fist. Nentres, who had followed the other lords into the great hall, seeking the origin of the clamour within the castle, had to grasp me by the waist, or I would have launched at her once more, and I would have been sure to kill her that time.

Arthur shook his head. "Nimueh, I doubt my sister did such a thing."

"She did! She is jealous of Merlin's desire for me."

"Lies!" I cried, twisting to be free from Nentres' hold. "She tempted Merlin and when he went to lie with her, Morgan was waiting. They put a spell on him, and now he is trapped within the hawthorn tree."

Arthur looked bewildered. "A hawthorn tree?"

"You see!" called Nimueh. "She has gone mad."

"Rack her!" I called. "She will tell the truth then!"

"Sister, we have not such a thing."

"Rouse the carpenters then, and build it! I will turn the wheel myself if need be."

Nentres placed his hands on my shoulders and rubbed soothingly, leaning in to whisper. "Peace, wife. You are angry we are betrayed by your sister once more. Relent from this path."

I leaned back into his bulk and warmth and tried to calm myself. Yet still my blood boiled and I vowed to myself that I would scour the country for Morgan. All I needed was a few moments alone with Nimueh and I would be sure she would tell me where Morgan was.

Arthur joined us. "I believe you, sister, though I know not how it can be true."

"Nor I," I admitted. "But Morgan has had much time to learn things in her time away from court, secret things, dark things best forgotten. If anyone could find a way to imprison a man within a tree, it is Morgan."

"And Nimueh is in league with her?" he asked.

"Most certainly. I heard it with my own ears, seen it with my own eyes. I regret not telling you sooner, but I found a charm in her room for communicating over long distances. She said it was for her and her lover, but it must be how Morgan kept an eye on her."

At the mention of colluding with Morgan, Arthur cast a disgusted eye down to Nimueh. "Throw her in the dungeon," he ordered, and two burly guardsmen took her away, kicking and screaming.

"Give her a moment or two in the dungeon," said Arthur. "Then we shall go to her, and make her tell us what she has done, and the extent of her association with our foul sister."

"If she will tell us the truth," I said bitterly.

"She is terrified of you," said Nentres. "You can see it in her eyes. If we put her in a room with you, you would not even need to touch her, she will tell at once."

After Arthur had deemed she had stewed sufficiently, the three of us went to the dungeon. She was bound to a chair, leather straps about her wrist, still in her stained shift. Her hair was tangled and her blood had crusted over her face. I entered first and shut the door behind me.

"I will tell you nothing!" she shrieked, as soon as I entered.

"Oh, you will," I replied.

I began to pace the room.

"Do you know...?" I asked. "That Arthur has no torturer? Uther had one, for extracting confessions from criminals, and details of enemy encampments from captured spies. But Arthur dismissed him when he became King and made torture a crime. Too cruel he said."

I stepped closer to her, and leaned in so close my breath blew wisps of her hair about her face. "The Romans had whole legions instructed in those arts. The Romans are gone, but they have left their books behind. And I am inclined to read as of late."

I could see her begin to quiver.

"I am going to bring in the High King, and the King of Garlot, and then you will answer our questions. Truthfully. Understood?"

She nodded, or I presumed she did, for I could see only the crown of her head as she looked down at the floor. I walked to the door and opened it for my brother and husband. They entered, and took up positions around her.

"What happened to the Lady of the Lake?" asked Arthur. "Your mother, Niniane?"

"My mother, she took sick," replied Nimueh, "A cough of some sort. She was not old, but life on Avalon is hard now. Little grows there, and animals cannot come and go as they once did. We went hungry often."

"She died?"

The girl nodded, silent.

"How did you come to know Morgan?" I asked.

"She came to the island after my mother died. She said she sensed it, the death of the Lady of the Lake, and she knew at once how to find it."

"And you allowed her onto the island?"

"She was of the Wise, and she was so kind to me. I had been alone on the island for so long, I had almost forgotten how to speak. It was nice to see another living soul."

A younger Elaine would have felt sympathy for her, a girl stranded on an island with no one but her mother's corpse. Even cold, calculating Morgan would be a welcome sight for one so grieved. But I could not muster even the slightest spark of kindness. All I could feel was my thirst for vengeance.

"And she..." began Nimueh.

290

"And she what?" I asked.

"She took me off the island. Mother would never let me leave, and I had to content myself with her stories, and the occasional visitor. But fewer and fewer people came, and more left until there was no one but me and her. When my mother died, I thought I would never see the outside world."

"But Morgan showed it to you?"

"Yes," she replied.

"You should know now, my sister's kindness has always come at a price. She asked you to help her defeat Merlin?"

She bowed her head. "I did so willingly. He was an evil creature, who cost Morgan all her happiness. My mother was infatuated with him, and he used her for his own ends. To shelter him from the purges, and then to make Excalibur. He did not tell her Arthur was a Christian king. She thought she was supporting a pagan, who would put paid to last of the Romans and their Christ."

Nimueh stared intently at Arthur. "She would never have given it to you if she knew how tirelessly you work in the Christ's name."

Arthur looked away and studied the moss growing on the wall.

"Why did you come here?" I pressed her.

"To do as I have done. Learn all Merlin had to teach, in magic and statecraft, and then bring him to Morgan to face death. She knew he was proud and lecherous, and could not resist a poor girl throwing herself on his mercy."

"Can Merlin even be killed?" I asked. "Is that why you imprisoned him?"

"Merlin can die as well as any man. But we knew he would fight us, and that we could not be sure we would win. Morgan knew he cannot over-come his nature, that of the faery inside him, so she created the hawthorn tree spell."

"Ah, I see. Merlin is half faery, and faeries are believed to live in hawthorn trees. Thus, properly enchanted, he could be forced to return to his 'home'."

"It makes sense," I said, to a mystified Arthur and Nentres. "To a witch at least."

"So then," asked Nentres. "How do we reverse it?"

"You cannot," replied Nimueh. "The spell is bound in perpetuity."

"What does she mean?" asked Arthur.

"A spell lasts as long as the witch has the power to sustain it, like a fire with kindling. Usually, a witch's spells will end upon her death, but Morgan knows that would only give you further cause to kill her. So, she will have chosen another well from which to draw the power for her spell."

I turned back to Nimueh. "From where is she drawing this power?"

"The moon," she replied.

"A classic. And we cannot hope to pull the moon from the sky. What is her stricture?"

"Her stricture?" interjected Arthur, utterly confused.

"Yes, yes, something built into a spell so that it may be broken. Magic permits no spell that can-not be undone, it is unbalanced, and magic is all about balance. So, Nimueh, what is it?"

"The spell will be broken when wine grapes can be grown in the Orkneys."

I rolled my eyes. "Morgan is too clever for her own good. She always was."

"So, you see, the spell cannot be broken or un-done, not in your lifetimes at least. But at least we know we will one day have Orkney wine," she said, smirking.

My hand flew up to strike her, and she recoiled, but I did not follow through. There had been enough violence that night. And as my anger slowly bled from my body, I could see how she too had been wronged, by Morgan, and even by Merlin. The man who used her mother, abused her only friend, and then set his decrepit sights upon her the second she arrived in Camelot. How could she not then believe she was right in what she had done?

"I want to see this tree," said Arthur. I nodded and we departed, leaving Nimueh strapped to the chair in the cold dungeon.

Arthur sobbed like a little boy when we reached the hawthorn. All he could do was place his hand inside to feel the sleeping Merlin. How Morgan had got him inside, I would never understand. She must have spelled him into a great sleep and then forced him inside.

I warned Arthur against his plan to cut him from the tree, in case Morgan had some preventative measure in place. I tried to undo the spell, though I knew it would not work. Placing my hands upon the bark, I chanted every spell of unbinding, of reversal and uncrossing and loosing I could think of until my body threatened to rebel and I had to abandon my magic. Though I had not thought of her in years, I wished for Petronella. She would know how to free Merlin, and bring back the sister I loved.

Defeated, we returned to the presence-chamber to take a posset and spice wine, abandoning the thought of any sleep that night. Arthur looked severely abused, and would not see Guinevere, sending her away.

"I have sent word to Gore and to Cornwall," he began, his voice thin and weak with exhaustion. "But Morgan is unlikely to be there, she has no allies there. I have sent an emissary to the Orkneys to warn Lot not to shelter her, as my spies tell me he has before, but it could be a month before we hear from him."

I shook my head. "She will not have gone to the Orkneys, for she rode west as she fled, not east to the coasts to find a boat."

Arthur sighed. "She has gone to Avalon then?"

"Most likely."

He looked up at Nentres. "How soon can you muster troops from Garlot? And we will need boats also."

I interjected before my husband could answer. "Nimueh is the last Lady of the Lake. If she has vacated the island, the charms will bind themselves to Morgan. She, for obvious reasons, will not allow us to pass the wards."

"Blasted magic!" cried Arthur, banging the table with his fist. "It has been the bane of my rule!"

I drew back. I had not the patience for his rage, or the control of my own tongue that night. So, for fear of further harm to him, I let him rage against my kith and kin, of the very thing that I was, that I was proud to be.

When he had finished, he ordered Nimueh brought before him. Arthur, who had forgiven entire kingdoms for rebelling against him, seemed harsher and colder than ever before.

"You have committed treason, Nimueh," he intoned. "Do you know the punishment for a woman who commits treason? Or how about how the priests punish an evil witch?"

"Burning. Death by burning, I know."

"Do you wish me to burn you, Nimueh?"

She shook her head.

"Because you know that you would burn either way, whether I execute you for treason or hand you over to the priests?"

Still silent, she nodded.

"Or I could pardon you?"

She looked up at him, confused and hopeful.

"Pardons are not free, not at my court. You will have to work for it."

"I can tell you now, I can never free Merlin."

"You could try. Or I can burn you in the morning."

She sighed. "It won't do any good. The spell is too intricate and well crafted. And Morgan never let me know all of what she did."

"But Merlin still taught you the Druidic ways? The ways to see what is to come, to spy on our enemies from far away, enchantments of protection and victory in battle? And the old laws which still govern many of the kingdoms of Britain?"

"He did."

"And you can put this knowledge to use in my service?"

She nodded reluctantly. "I can."

"I will have an oath drawn up alongside your pardon. You will sign one and I the other, and your life will depend entirely on your adherence. You will spend some time here, in the dungeon, until we can be sure of your fealty. Then, I will put you in Merlin's tower, with his books and supplies, under guard of course. But, Nimueh, mark this. One single scent of anything untoward, and I will have Elaine cut off your head. No trial, no warning."

He gestured for her to kneel, and she did. Then he sent her away and commanded Sir Bedevere to work with the scribe to draw up the pardon. When we were alone again, I addressed him.

"That was cruel Arthur," I chided. "Perhaps from me, it would be expected, but from you? I am most surprised."

"One cruel turn deserves another," he replied. "She betrayed Merlin and me."

"Well, I will not be cutting off her head. I am your sister, and the Queen of Garlot, not your butcher."

Arthur shrugged. "It matters not to me, or Nimueh for that matter, who cuts off her head, only that they do when the time comes."

"Why ever would you install her in Merlin's position? Surely any magic you have need of, I can oblige?"

"Because Merlin taught her high magic, which you know nothing of, as you are so blastedly fond of reminding me, despite all these years you could have learnt."

"Merlin would not teach me, no matter how often I asked."

"Even Merlin was not above official decree. Anyway, I can kill Nimueh, I cannot kill you."

"What do you mean?"

"It is time that I finally take the decision my Lords have been petitioning me for so long. Tomorrow, unless by written decree of the king, the practice of magic is forbidden in the kingdom of Britain, punishable by death."

"Putting my personal feelings aside, you see that you will undo your work to bring peace to our two religions. Magic is a part of the old faith of Britain."

"Magic is the work of the Devil," he said.

"There is no such thing as the Devil."

"Really?" he replied. "Because I thought she was hiding on a buggered island in the Summer Country."

"Without magic, Arthur, you would not even have been born."

"Right now, I wish for nothing more."

With that he stalked off, leaving me speechless.

Chapter Thirteen

Reeling still from the loss of Merlin, Arthur grew sullen and uncommunicative, talking to no one but Guinevere, with the occasional kind word to Anna. He spent many days by the hawthorn tree, resting his head against it like a tender lover until Guinevere persuaded him to leave it be. So he ordered a stone tower be built around it, an exact replica of the one Merlin occupied in Camelot. All of Merlin's possessions were moved there, like for like, almost as though the magician had returned and cast a spell to transport his workroom from one place to another.

Nimueh was installed there, in all its sad beauty. Truly beautiful it was, with the hawthorn sprouting from the hall of the tower and up alongside the staircase. Its branches twisted here and there in intricate patterns, and it bloomed into pink-white flowers, though the odour was horrible in high temperature, like the breath of a poisoned dog.

I was with her for the first few weeks as her guard, working alongside her to understand Merlin's books and writings, to determine a way to break Morgan's spell. I was not patient or understanding with her and disposed to give her the occasional slap if she was particularly recalcitrant. That was until Nentres reminded me of a young woman once locked in a tower and made to do magic against her will.

I left Nimueh in the care of various knights and returned to the walls of Camelot. It was hopeless. Only Morgan could undo the spell. If she even knew how, of course. It would not be unlike my sister's pride to create a spell even she had no counter for. I shared my thoughts with Arthur. He ordered Nimueh to continue with her work, but even he could see the cause was lost.

He sent out trusted men to watch Avalon for any sign of movement from her, but to no avail. The only man to ever get close to her, he having the thought of trying to swim to Avalon, was returned with a great red mark upon his face, as though someone had pressed a hot cooking pot to his flesh and scalded him. Arthur put a price on her head and left it be.

I knew Morgan, though. She would be filled with courage from robbing Camelot of Merlin and would try another of her nefarious plots. I knew I must try to safeguard Camelot and its inhabitants where Arthur and Nimueh could not, so I sought out a weapon I knew could truly destroy Arthur.

My letter to Morgause was brief and vague.

Sister,

Morgan grows more impatient and more reckless. She has struck a blow to the very heart of Camelot, and now we are without Merlin. Victory will make her bold, and she will attack again. Send Mordred to court so he can be safe from her spells.

Your loving sister,
Elaine

I wanted to dream walk to see her, but Arthur's recent ban on the use of magic had me fearful my brother might turn against me, and I did not want to give him cause. Instead, I quietly spelled the letter so that it would reach its destination quickly and without interference, and paid the man to take it via boat from Londinium.

Her response came within the month to say she would send Mordred as soon as Gawain was due to return to court and a boat could be spared when the fishing season was over. She was quick to add that she knew nothing of Morgan's plan against Merlin, which was so overt in its denial that I suspected she knew quite a bit about it. Wine from the Orkneys. Had that come from her?

Knowing that Mordred would not be with us until the autumn, I returned to Caer Mor. Arthur's decree against witchcraft soon reached us in Garlot and we had no choice but to enforce it. Women began to come to me from all over our lands and begged me to intercede. Some remembered Roman times, the purges and the strict doctrines of Christianity which had seen many of their number hang, burn or be pressed to death.

I knew who these women were, for we know each other quickly enough by sight, and some had come before to invite me to join them, but a queen cannot easily join a coven where she must submit herself to its priestess. I had to turn them away with a warning. We would not punish any woman found to be practising, but Arthur may take it upon himself to send inquisitors among us, so the art must be kept for only a time of dire need.

I was back in Camelot after the first harvest festival of the year. Mordred then came to court not long before the autumn equinox, in the company of his older half-brother Gawain, who had been sent north some time ago to receive a report from his father on the state of the kingdoms of Lothian and Orkney.

Mordred was exceptionally beautiful for a boy-child. Arthur's fair hair and Morgause's flaming locks combined to create a gently curling tapestry of a colour, eerily like that of a sunset. His features were defined, proud jutting cheekbones showing our kinship, and green eyes like that of Anna spoke to a closer relationship than half-cousins.

But most of all, he was like Morgan. Not always in looks, though his mouth was slender and his nose sculpted in an undeniably Roman fashion, but in deeds, and how he carried himself. He was bossy and secretive, and, when he did not get his own way, quick to threaten the retribution of his fearsome parents, or that of his warrior brother Gawain.

No one could ever know the hand Morgan played in his birth, not even my beloved Nentres, who knew only that which he heard pass between Morgause, Lot and myself. Yet Morgan was clearly a force in the boy's life, manifest in his quiet but sharp-tongued demeanour.

Arthur took to him at once, gifting him a horse and fine robes, and always asking him to accompany him about Camelot. The boy went eagerly enough. I wondered if Mordred knew who his father was, and if Arthur had ever been informed by Morgause of the truth. Regardless, he was given anything he asked for.

With such power over Arthur and a son of Lot in his own right, the boy could be a force for good if given the proper guidance. Morgause and Lot were too covetous for such a task, and Gawain too busy as a knight, so I instructed Hoel and Anna to make their cousin welcome in Camelot and become his companions.

Since Mordred came to court, we did not often retire to Arthur's solar. Nentres found it not to his liking, having grown surprisingly curmudgeonly as he approached his fortieth year. He said it was too like a nursery, now that Mordred, Anna, and Hoel were all thought grown enough to join us. They sat in the corner and giggled about some silly story they had heard and, more often than not, Arthur joined them.

Arthur catered to Mordred's every whim. If the boy was too hot, the fire was extinguished. If he was hungry, fresh food was brought from the kitchens. If he was lacking in diversion, the whole of Camelot would grind to a halt as Arthur called a hunt and all of us would have to traipse the muddy countryside looking for deer, lest we were called boring and uncharitable by our High King.

Guinevere and Lancelot too were rarely to be seen in the solar. Lancelot's whereabouts were unknown. Guinevere was said to be praying, but rarely had I seen a light in the chapel window those past months.

This all irritated Nentres, and often I too, so instead we repaired to our chambers and caught up with the business of ruling a kingdom from afar. That night, though, Hoel was with us and sat by the fire. He had not spoken all evening. He just sat there, on his stool, tapping his dull practice blade against the hearthstone.

"Stop that," warned Nentres, looking up from a letter.

"Sorry, my Lord Father," our son replied.

He got up from the stool to stand behind me, watching me as I scribbled in the ledger, counting up the cost to Garlot of contributions to Arthur's campaigns.

"You have something to say to me, do you not?" I asked.

He scrunched up his nose, just like his father, and took a deep breath.

"Mother, I do not wish to be cousin Mordred's companion any longer," he said.

I turned to look him. "Why, whatever is the matter?"

"He is very strange."

"Because he is quiet? And does not enjoy roughhousing, or sneaking mead or harassing the kitchen girls like your other friends?"

"No...He likes to hunt."

"So do you," I replied, confused.

"But he really enjoys it. And he..."

"Spit it out, Hoel."

"When we fell something, like a boar or a deer, sometimes he likes to leave it to bleed to death, rather than finish it cleanly. And once, he said to me, he thought we should have hunting grounds filled with people. He said it would be more fun."

"He was just trying to scare you. And I will have Gawain speak to him about the hunting."

"No, Lady Mother, do not! He'll know I told on him."

"Then, what will you have me do? He is your cousin, and family is very important in this world. If he says anything that upsets you again, you must ignore him. He is only doing it because he can see how it distresses you."

He nodded and took himself off to bed. Nentres looked up at me.

"Are you sure that was the right way to handle that?"

I shrugged. "I am walking blind. It is what Bronwyn would have said to me. It is not as if Igraine has given me much to go on."

Hoel mentioned no more of that behaviour to me, and he, Anna and Mordred continued to be firm friends, inseparable. Still, as he grew older, I worried about Mordred. He did indeed have strange ways, and Arthur's dotage on him had emboldened him. He did not hold back suggestions

304

and had grown even to command those around him.

Above all, I did not like the way he stared at everything, as though he would take it. He stared at food, at gold, and as he got more bold, at women. Mordred stared at Nimueh, prancing about Camelot in only a simple white shift, and at Guinevere, who was still beautiful for a woman now in her thirties. But most of all, he stared at Anna, and it frightened me. At fourteen, they were nearing the age that betrothal and declarations can be taken seriously, and the world knew them to be half-cousins, not close enough for the prohibitions of kin.

The small council had been abolished with the demise of Merlin, and Arthur returned to the Round Table, though his idea for a Roman government had long since been abandoned. In truth, I was grateful for the end of the small council, or Mordred would surely have been appointed to it. He had a seat at the Round Table while I had to stand through lengthy meetings, or if I tired, sit upon a stool in the corner like an errant child. But at least in these great meetings, Mordred's childish voice was drowned out by a score of aging knights.

Our subject of that council meeting was the Roman Empire, the one we thought gone from Britain, and broken too at its heart, fleeing to the east into Byzantium. But no. We had held a feast when Arthur returned from a small battle against the rebels in the Summer Country. But there was a clamour at the gate, and some men demanding entrance. Arthur was never one for caution, so he demanded these men be brought before him, and they turned out to be twelve old men, bearing branches of olive trees.

They said they came as the ambassadors of Lucius, the Emperor of Rome. We laughed at them, but when we saw they were not mummers come to play the fool with the High King, we cleared the hall and listened to them. We had heard the rumours of its restoration many years ago, but when no more came of it, we dismissed it as sailor's stories.

The emissaries demanded tribute to Rome, gold, fabrics, grain, treasures we had not the wealth to give. We refused, and they threatened Rome's chastisement, polite double-speak for war. We were incensed by their audacity, and Mordred was most vocal in calling for their heads, a proposition I was not heartily opposed to. But Arthur found them good lodgings in town, forbidding violence against them until the council had met and given their decisions. Thus, we met to prepare our response, and for once we were in accordance.

"Send them away," said Lancelot. "And if they come back, we kill them."

"We owe no tribute to Rome," said Sir Bedevere. "The Romans are gone from Britain, and should be dead too. We will make Britain ready if they are brave enough to land on our shores."

Arthur smiled at his loyal knights and gestured for his priest-scribe to begin drafting a response.

"You know, uncle," began Mordred. "They might very well owe us tribute."

"How so?" asked Arthur.

"Well," he replied. "Was Emperor Constantine not out of Britain?"

"That he was."

"Well," smirked Mordred. "Does not that mean that the lineage of Constantine is British in its extraction? And thus, now that Lucius, who I am sure is no relative of Constantine, is Emperor, could the argument not be made that he is not the true Emperor? And that it is to Constantine's get that we should look for an Emperor. You are a relative of Constantine, are you not, Sire?"

"I am," agreed Arthur. "Through my uncle, Ambrosius Aurelianus. But surely you are not suggesting I become Emperor? That I depose this Lucius fellow?"

Mordred shrugged. "I am simply informing you of all the possibilities, uncle."

"Now, Sire," warned Lancelot. "We need not escalate things. Let them play at empires abroad, but we should not anger them further, and make threats we cannot commit."

"But, Lancelot," said Arthur. "Why should we not advance upon them, as they have done to us? Especially when the argument could be made that I am the rightful heir to the Empire?"

Lancelot stood up from the table, though he had not asked Arthur's leave, left the chamber and then returned moments later with a wild-eyed Guinevere.

"What is this nonsense about Rome?" she demanded.

"You enter council without my leave?" Arthur asked of her.

"I do, Sire," she replied. "When the news I am told worries me gravely."

"Sire, begging your leave," interjected Sir Bedevere. "But the queen is right to be worried. We do not know the strength Lucius has. He would not be victorious if he invaded Britain, where we have the advantage, but to traipse across to the continent? We might be outnumbered by whole countries."

"And," added Nentres. "We are not well liked, not by Gaul, or by the Franks. We have many enemies across the sea."

"Arthur!" pleaded Guinevere. "Listen to your council! We cannot commit to such a campaign. My father has not the gold, and you have not the men. And will the Saxons not strike while you are abroad?"

"Your wife gives wise council, Sire," I said.

Mordred scoffed, and I wished I could slap the boy, but Arthur would not have him disciplined so. "Will you listen to the crying of women, uncle?"

Arthur, emboldened, agreed with him. "No, nephew, I will not. Elaine, take your Queen and see that she lies down. She is clearly exhausted by her feminine humours. I want to hear battle plans from my knights, not their disagreement."

I opened my mouth to protest, but Arthur interrupted. "You have your King's command, sister."

I took Guinevere by the elbow and guided her away. She cast hurt looks over her shoulder while I resisted the urge to run back and strike Mordred in his grinning face, right between the eyes.

"This is all Morgan's fault!" exclaimed Guinevere, when we were back in her chamber. I had heard Morgan blamed for many different things over the years, but that was a new one.

"I hate her!" she cried. "I have been barren these past thirteen years because of her!"

"Come now, Guinevere," I replied. "We cannot be certain she cursed you. I have told you many times, Anna's birth was difficult. That is why you cannot conceive. Some women never fall pregnant, not for want of trying. Look at me."

Guinevere huffed, and worried her handkerchief between her hands.

"I am sure Arthur hates me. Look at what happened in council. He would have never disregard me so if I bore him a son."

She turned her fierce blue eyes upon me.

"His protégé, Mordred. His mother is Morgause?" asked Guinevere.

"Yes, Highness, you know this," I replied.

She pursed her lips.

"What troubles you?" I asked, regretting my question almost instantly.

She fixed me with a steely gaze, one I imagined sent many a maid fleeing for her life. "You would tell me, if it was otherwise?"

"What, that Morgause was not his mother? I am sure she is, she paid me a visit when she was pregnant, and months later he was born."

"And he is not, perhaps, her foster child?" she asked.

"How could he be? He is the very likeness of her, and of Arthur and myself."

"He is more like Arthur than any of you."

I tried to keep my voice level. "What are you suggesting? Speak plainly, my Lady."

"Is he, or is he not, Arthur's son?"

I summoned forth a guise of mirth. "How silly! What makes you say that?"

"They are too alike. And how he dotes on the boy! Never once has Arthur permitted me to sit in council with him, or hear petitions, but on his second day, Mordred sat at his feet. The boy has never fought a battle, but Arthur plans to bestow the title of Sir Mordred upon him."

"One can have a knighthood, without ever fighting. It is the least honour he is due, the son of a king."

"Yes, but the son of which king? He may make him his heir, so dear Lancelot tells me."

"Is Anna not his heir? I know a girl cannot rule in her own right, but will he not choose a husband for her, who will be our High King?"

Guinevere shrugged. "Matters of state are rarely discussed between us now. He talks only to Mordred, and those who sit at his Round Table. He would not be the first king to name an illegitimate child as his heir."

She stood up, and poured wine for us, sitting back down heavily.

"You would tell me, would you not? If Arthur had lain with some harlot before our marriage, and sent the whore's offspring to his sister in the Orkneys? I hear the rumours too, you know. I know that Lady Lisanor claims she has two bastards by him."

"You have thought too much on this. Anyway, pay it no heed. Lisanor's lips are looser than her corset stays."

"That is not an answer."

I gritted my teeth into a forced smile. "Morgause is most definitely Mordred's mother. That is not to say Arthur is not his father."

I may have said this with a smile, though deep down, my stomach was twisted in knots. Guinevere picked up her wine cup, scoffing. "Could you imagine, Arthur laying with his own sister? What man would ever do that?"

"Yes," I replied. "What man would ever do that?"

I did not deign to attend dinner in the hall and asked the servants to serve me in my chamber. Let Arthur send for me if he so desired my presence. One offense offered was enough for one day. Nentres returned straight after dinner, eschewing the drinking for my company.

"Well," I questioned. "Do we make war on Lucius?"

His grave reply was affirmative, although I knew the answer before I asked. I sank down onto the bed, and he sat beside me.

"I am worried Elaine. I do not know if we have enough men. The larger kingdoms have already pledged ridiculous amounts."

"Like what?" I asked.

"Well, your cousin Cador has offered thirty thousand from Cornwall. While Garlot cannot offer such troops, Arthur will expect us to match what we can. It will stretch us to our limit."

I sighed. "We have already raised a levy twice this year. The people will revolt. And that is before we even discuss feeding and arming them. As Guinevere says, even her father is running low on gold, and we cannot keep selling timber to Cradelmant to fund wars, or Garlot will be as bare as a monk's head."

"You and I must return to Garlot," said Nentres. "To soothe inflamed tempers, and most likely to barter with Meron. He will have my kingdom if we continue to run to him for men."

"Do we take Mordred?" I asked. "I fear Morgan constantly now, and what Mordred may say or do without us."

Her binding remained intact, even after all those years, so I could not tell Nentres exactly what threat he faced from her. It was only with a spell of my own devising that I was able to tell him that he could be Arthur's downfall in Morgan's hands, and my beloved husband had trusted my word.

Nentres shook his head. "He is safe here from your sister, Arthur is well guarded. My thoughts on the boy are this. Let him dig his own grave. He will

311

go too far with Arthur and have to learn a lesson in humility. We can leave Hoel too if you do not object. He is making good progress here in his lessons, with both sword and pen."

"That he is. I trust our son, and he will temper Mordred while we are gone. Has Arthur named a regent for while he is absent on campaign? I feared it would be Mordred."

"No, thankfully. It will be Guinevere, assisted by Sir Baudwin as governor and some of the lesser Knights of the Round Table will remain behind."

"But you must go?" I asked, with sadness.

He gave a grim nod. "He has named me one of four generals."

I reached for him, and he pressed his lips to mine. Already I could feel tears dampening my cheeks, and touching his. I missed those early days in Garlot, when Hoel was small enough to play in my bed, and Nentres and I had no concerns other than our provincial problems, and each other.

So we went back to Garlot and struck every bargain we could think of to render men in service to Arthur, though we still fell short of Arthur's demands for the levy. But I remembered too keenly a time when we had over-committed our resources and had no men to repel a Saxon invasion, and kept enough men back.

I heard nothing of Guinevere's capture until she was safely returned to us, we having been away in Garlot for some time. She had been riding with her ladies and a light guard, garbed in green to gather flowers, a bizarre amusement she had contrived. There, in a field not far from Camelot, she was set upon by a knight called Mellegranz, who had at least twenty men-at-arms and a similar number of archers, far outnumbering Guinevere's ten

knightly guards and her retinue of unarmed pages
and waiting-women. He captured her and took her
hostage in his castle.

Mellegranz fancied himself in love with her,
ever since he had been fostered for her early teen
years at her father's court. He had pressed suit on
her, but Merlin had convinced his father to withdraw his support for the match, in exchange for
gold from Leodegranz. He had never abandoned
his desire for her, and being the High Queen only
made her more alluring.

I went at once to Camelot upon hearing the rumours in Merriwyn, clad in armour and ready to
lead a war-band to rescue her.

"Peace, sister, she is returned to us safely," said
Arthur, as I entered the solar. "We have had her
back three days past, thanks to brave Sir Lancelot."

Guinevere was sat in the corner, Lancelot not
far from her. She looked well-rested but bore some
purplish marks about the face. She stretched out
her arms to me, and I pulled her into an embrace.
There were some days I despised her but never had
I wished harm upon her. I knew too what kidnap
did to a woman.

She had obviously been accosted for retellings
many times before, and launched into her tale
without being prompted, helped by Lancelot where
necessary. Having killed her guards, Mellegranz
took her to his castle, and Lancelot exhausted two
horses chasing after her. He then was forced to
take a ride in a cart driven by a dwarf and fought
a great battle against Mellegranz' men to get her
back. Guinevere herself made her own attempts to
escape, which were less successful, until she spied
Lancelot in the courtyard, and, to my astonish-
ment, turned her overdress into a rope with which

to lower herself from the window to the safety of Lancelot's cart.

"Morgan was there," she said. "I saw her only briefly, but from what I understood of her conversation with Mellegranz, she had procured the gold for his Gaulish mercenaries and given him the idea of capturing me."

"What purpose would that serve?" I asked.

Guinevere scowled with distaste. "She had convinced him that, if he married me and got me with child, he would, by the old laws, had the right to be High King."

"Only if he slew Arthur," I said.

"Hmm," responded Guinevere. "Morgan was dealing with the easy part of the plan first, it seems. But let us forget about it, and speak no more of it."

She claimed to be fine from then on, but something changed within Guinevere. Yes, she was more fearful, and eschewed leaving the safety of the solar, but that would pass in time. No, it was other aspects of her demeanour. She was less fond of prayer, or proselyting, and she was quicker to anger than before.

It was particularly noticeable with Lancelot. She was more affectionate with him, and he wore her colours in every tourney and sparring match, and if he was hurt she would run to him. So too, would he run to her, if she fell, or if she had need of a cup of beer. She was grateful, and he was protective, but I feared that rumours would again begin to fly in the hamlet-like Camelot, and threaten Arthur's rule.

I went to worship that full moon, to pray for my husband's safe return, and cast spells for Arthur's victory. I did not believe in his campaign, but I did not want my brother to die. All I could to do help, I would. He was still the king I believed in, even if I did not see it often enough.

In the stone circle, built by our ancestors not far from Camelot, there were other women there, dancing around the bonfire, or sat in quiet contemplation, one whom I recognised. Nimueh nodded to me, silent. There could be no enmity here, no words unless they were sacred.

Once the rites drew to a close, and the circle was broken, I began my quiet walk back to Camelot. There, in the courtyard, illuminated by the dying light of the full moon were two figures. One was tall and lean, clearly a man. The other, smaller and curved, was a woman. They were huddled close together. She turned her head, and he leaned down, and they kissed. A cloud passed from the moon's surface, illuminating them briefly. It was Lancelot and Guinevere. I turned my head away and wished I had not seen it.

I saw no more evidence of an affair, but knowing about it consumed me until I was sure I wore my knowledge of it upon my face. The political implications ate away at me, and the softer part of myself worried for Arthur's broken heart, and the anguish Lancelot and Guinevere must feel to hide how they felt. Obviously more had passed between them in her rescue than we knew.

The eve before Arthur was to march out for Rome, we held a great feast in the hall. Lancelot was absent, saying that he had gone to pray for the Christian God to look favourably upon the campaign, and Guinevere had begged off the festivities, claiming a headache. But I knew that they had probably gone to spend one last night together before the men marched.

I grew so fixed upon the idea that I had to seek solace alone, and went up the stairs to the solar, intending to sit in silence. As I reached the door, I stopped, my hand just above the intricate iron knocker. I could hear voices. Two voices I knew immediately. Guinevere and Lancelot. I knew I should barge in, put an end to whatever was going on behind closed doors. For Lancelot, to even desire her was treason. For her, to desire him in return meant death for both.

"I am sick for love of you, but I tire of these moments we steal," he said, his raw, hoarse voice struggling to whisper. If men believed they could cry, then Lancelot had been sobbing previously. "I am not a thief," he continued.

"You are. Every time we are together you steal from your King and your dearest friend." Her icy tone faded. "You have stolen my heart."

"Stop Guinevere! I am not a shepherdess with her swain. Poetry does not placate me. I want you, body and soul."

"Hush, you fool! Have you taken leave of your senses? Someone could be listening."

Pity you do not have the art, I thought. You would live in less danger, High Queen. He must have reached for her. I heard her tut in disapproval and then there were sounds of kissing. I should go, I thought, but better I hear than Arthur. He would not be long from the solar.

"You sin, Lancelot, and bring me in your handcart to hell," she said.

"I live each day in hell, every day without you," he replied. "Run away with me."

"Must we discuss this again? Where would we go where we do not bear the mark of our shame?"

"Ireland? Or further still? To the east, where the Christ lived, or the land of Qin where the Romans got their silk? We could live as husband and wife and none would know?"

316

"We are already married! Would you condemn me? No matter how we live, we sin. I will burn for my love of you, in this life or the next."

My senses, both innate and supernatural twitched. Arthur approached from the staircase, flushed ruddy with mead.

I rattled the door knocker.

"Arthur!" I exclaimed. "You are quite an unusual colour!"

"That would be the mead, I suppose. There was ale and wine too!"

I threw open the door, and Guinevere sat stitching by a dying candle while Lancelot perused her chapbook across the room.

"Then you must settle yourself," I continued. "Or you will disturb your humours and be mightily ill tomorrow."

He sauntered past me and sat beside Guinevere, throwing a casual arm around her shoulder. He smiled deeply at Lancelot and I swore I had never seen a happier man. I could be there not a moment longer and bowed my leave to my king and brother.

And so Arthur Pendragon went unto Rome and brought with him my husband as his general once more. He also brought Mordred, making him a knight, to my annoyance and Hoel's loud and constant vexation. They were gone a year, and I worked hard to keep Garlot under my control, even ordering Hoel to return and rule by my side, and silence the grumblings of the remaining vassals. Guinevere too had her struggles and we were in near constant contact.

But Arthur returned eventually and proclaimed himself the new Emperor of Rome. Nentres decried that it would not last, since he could not enforce this from Britain, but they had put paid to any designs on Britain for another generation.

There may have been peace without war, he grumbled, had Gawain not been so hot-headed. Apparently, at a parley between Lucius and Arthur, Gawain slew a Roman that offended him and a great battle erupted, with Arthur finally killing Lucius in single combat. Arthur then laid siege to any city loyal to the dead emperor he passed and made them subservient to Britain. My husband too had received great honour for felling Alifatima, King of Spain, and a strong supporter of Lucius.

But I did not care whether Arthur was now the ruler of the whole world. I was just glad to have my husband back, despite his new scars, and prayed there would be no more war for Britain.

Chapter Fourteen

It had been three years since Merlin was bound in sleep, and we were no closer to freeing him. Eventually, Nimueh admitted to me she had abandoned her attempts some time ago, and focused more on fulfilling her role as court Druidess, blocking Morgan's magic where she could.

Morgan had been quiet enough these few years, with only a few incidents to note. She had tried to kidnap Lancelot again, but he escaped well enough. She then sent a drinking horn to Guinevere as a gift, claiming to be the Queen of Nubia. But I recognised the neat hand upon the letter and brought it to Nimueh. Together we deduced there was some charm upon it to reveal a secret, her love for Lancelot no doubt, so we smashed it, and replaced the pieces in the presence-chamber, as though some careless servant had damaged it.

Guinevere was mightily upset and threatened half the servants with a beating. She then decided to send a pretty jewel to the Queen of Nubia in return. I told her I would arrange its delivery, and went to Londinium where I sold it to a travelling merchant and distributed the gold among the city's poorhouses. What Guinevere did not know, could not hurt her. We heard no more of Morgan, save a rumour she had travelled through Benwick en route to the Frankish king to persuade him to seek revenge on Arthur for his defeat sixteen years previous.

Our cousin Cador had died, and a crisis of succession had arisen within Tintagel. It was the thought of the Cornish nobility and headmen that Cador's son Sir Tristan was unsuitable as the next Duke and sought instead Sir Mark, the late duke's brother. In Camelot, we agreed, and Mark was proclaimed Duke of Cornwall. Arthur bestowed further honours on Sir Tristan, to sooth any pride of his that may have been hurt.

The matter was considered final, so when Arthur summoned me to Camelot to discuss matters of Cornish importance, I knew that something else had occurred.

"Elaine, I have something to ask of you," he began, as I settled down in a chair.

I was not supposed to sit at the Round Table, each knight having their own designated seat, and there being no place for a woman, but having ridden most of the day to be there, I was less inclined to keep to etiquette. Besides, I did not think Nentres would mind if I sat in his seat.

"You know Arthur, that I would do anything you asked of me," I replied.

"We have discussed often enough at council about our problems with the Irish, and how Cornwall and Northgales suffer the greatest with raids. We have shown force against them, but short of actually invading Ireland, I feel there is little we can do to put an end to their raids, until now."

"Something has given you hope?" I asked.

"A new chieftain has risen among those on the eastern coast, and it seems he cares little for raiding. I gather that the country is in turmoil enough of its own, and little is gained from these raids to justify the risk."

"A treaty then? At what cost to us?"

"Land, for one thing. This chieftain, Angwyssh, desires a new settlement for his people. And so I have decreed that this will be in Northgales, which has the most land to spare, much of it mountainous and barren."

"Does the King of Northgales agree?" I asked.

"He has little choice in the matter. He can rebel again if he so chooses, but I am in a far stronger position than when I was sixteen."

"What else does he desire?"

"Allies in Britain. He has already made a treaty with our cousin Mark, Duke of Cornwall, and I have given permission for it to be extended to all of Britain. It is to be sealed with a marriage."

"Ah, I see now where I am needed. I was hoping for a glorious battle."

"Alas, sister, there is no battle to be fought," he said. "Mark is to marry the daughter of this Angwyssh, and I would like to send a high-ranking lady to be her chaperone, but Guinevere will not go into Ireland. As my sister and the cousin of the Duke of Cornwall, you are the most obvious choice."

"And because I am not afraid of Ireland?"

"That too. I promised a host to ride behind her, but still she would not go."

I shrugged. "It will be an adventure. When do you need me to depart?"

"Before the new moon. If you can ride to Tintagel, Duke Mark will see you right. Hopefully, by the time you return, I will be at Tintagel to greet our new Duchess, and sign her father's treaty."

I went then, to Cornwall, with a few of my trusted men, and Portimus too, moaning about his sore buttocks the entire ride to Tintagel. I had not intended to bring him, but Nentres said he spoke some of the Irish language, and I thought he would be useful. He also suggested I bring a maidservant, but I had gotten so used to dressing myself in the mornings, now Mila suffered terribly with pains in her hands. Besides, a maidservant would be no use if we were attacked by the Irish, being already hindered by our fat scribe. However, Duke Mark would see to our protection. It was, after all, his future bride at stake.

The return to Tintagel was uneventful. I had imagined I would break down in tears, sobbing at my return to my childhood home after all these years, but I realised, dry-eyed, that I felt nothing. The shadow of my father's death and my mother's betrayal still hung over the place and, in the end, it was only a stone castle. Caer Mor was my home, and Camelot I held some affection for.

Still, it was invigorating to smell the salt of the sea air, and hear the crash of the waves against the shore. I could see it, still there after all those years, down on the shore, Petronella's little hut. By rights, it should have been demolished or given to another when she moved into the castle, but she kept it for when she needed peace from Igraine.

Cador told me, in his rare visits to Camelot, that after she died, he had intended to take it down, since she had never owned the land on which it was built, but the people prevented it, fearing it was cursed. Petronella would have laughed at that, and would have smirked at it still standing nearly fifty years from the day she bartered spells for the wood to build it.

Tintagel looked different to me as we approached. Perhaps, it had been changed over the years or, more likely, that my memories had faded, and that its spiking crenulations and stout walls were not as I once remembered.

Duke Mark stood at the gate as we rode across the drawbridge.

"My dear cousin!" he called, waving.

I rolled my eyes, then hoped we were too far for him to have seen me do so. Mark and I had met only twice in my life, yet he claimed close kinship with me more often than not. I dismounted in the yard and looked around. Not much had changed within the walls of Tintagel, and it disconcerted me more than it comforted me.

"You are most welcome," said Mark, inclining his head in greeting. "How does it feel to be home?"

I tried to smile. "Thank you, Duke Mark. I am sad to say that Tintagel has not been my home in some time. Is all ready for our crossing into Ireland?"

He looked uneasy. "I will not be going with you. There is too much to do here."

He was lying. His eyes gave him away, but I could understand. If you had spent your life killing Irishmen, would you want to travel to Ireland?

"But, Sir Tristan will go with you," he continued, and he beckoned the young man forward.

He could rival Lancelot for handsomeness, despite his uncanny resemblance to my father Gorlois. His hair was jet black and well-kept in the Roman style, his beard close-cropped too. His smile was wide and white, and, when he spoke, he turned his head and leaned it, as though everything that was said was of the greatest import. I could have sought a position at Camelot soothing the hearts his sea blue eyes had broken there.

"Sir Tristan," I said, presenting my hand. "Do you fare well since we last saw one another?"

"Yes, my Lady," he replied, as he took my hand. "It is good to see you again, cousin."

"Now," I began. "Tell me of the arrangements for our travel."

We stayed the night at Tintagel, and departed the next morning, in a large boat with a prow decorated like a serpent. It required most of our men to row it, and I was tempted to set Portimus to oar if he continued to complain about the journey.

The crossing into Ireland was uneventful, though I had only ever been on a sea-boat twice before, when I had invaded Gaul and my return. Ireland itself was different from how I imagined it. I had always thought it to be some barren, rocky wasteland, my explanation for why the Irish raided so much.

No, it was a green as any British hillside, if not more so. It reminded me more of Garlot, a place untouched by Romans. As we rode through their country, and I saw their round, thatched houses, built from wattle and daub, like those in Garlot's countryside, I felt more at home than any stranger should.

We were greeted by Angwyssh's men, who wore patterned leggings and rough tunics, covered by thick woollen cloaks richly died. Indeed, it was like being in Garlot, unlike Camelot where the Roman fashions of robes and mantles prevailed. They were accompanied by a priest who spoke Latin. Between his translation and Portimus' broken Irish, we were soon underway to Angwyssh's fort.

It looked how I envisioned Camelot to have once been. It was built on the top of a high hill, with part of it cut into the hill itself, jutting out like a brown window under the earth. We were brought into the hall, where Angwyssh sat in state, his daughter at his side.

My first observation was the strength of her beauty, like the day I had first seen Guinevere. There was not a hint of Roman stock within in her. Her nose was small, and her mouth too, set in a round face of skin like cream. Her hair was like burnished gold and curled delicately down her narrow shoulders. Somehow, Mark had got the better end of the deal.

I tried the words of greeting that Portimus had taught me. I hoped he had not tried to embarrass me by teaching me something foul, or I would finally get to the bottom of his mysterious past, so help me.

Isolde smiled at me with her pretty mouth. "Thank you, my Lady. But as you can hear, I speak Latin, my Lady, and I have been learning your language these past months."

"How impressive," I replied. I wondered if, I had known about my marriage, would I have learnt more about Garlot, or would I have conspired to escape?

"I am looking forward to seeing Cornwall," she said. "And I have heard Tintagel is a mighty castle."

"Near-impenetrable. It has only ever been won by guile."

"And tell me, is Duke Mark handsome?" she asked.

"He is pleasing to the eye," I replied, though what eye would be an issue of some deliberation.

The priest translated for me to King Angwyssh, and he told me he was pleased to have peace between our two nations, and honoured that Arthur's sister herself had come to escort his daughter to her wedding.

We stayed two days at Angwyssh's court. I spent most of that time with Isolde, learning more about the girl. She was as smart as she was pretty, and well-read for her eighteen years, knowing many tales from abroad. When I opened my pack to take out my embroidery, she caught sight of my scabbarded sword within.

"Oh!" she exclaimed. "There are two things I cannot do. Sew, and use a sword."

"Both are exceedingly useful, Isolde," I replied. "Perhaps you should."

"Perhaps I should," she agreed. "I can learn to sew from any lady, but who will teach me to fight? I have heard there is an island in the north, where there live only women, and they taught a great warrior of my people to fight. I should like to see it."

"Perhaps you will," I said and felt a tinge of sadness. Cornwall was more traditional than Garlot. Duke Mark would take her straight to his bed, and she would spend the rest of her days within the keep of Tintagel, bearing children and seeing to the running of the household. She would never see any of those places she had read about. I resolved I would visit her as often as I could so that she might have at least one friend by the sea.

She liked Tristan well enough, and he made every effort to sing the praises of his uncle to her. He danced with her at the feasting and helped her practice her speech in the language of the Britons. When we dined before we left, I sat down beside him, making sure to thank him for his efforts towards the alliance.

"It is my pleasure," he said. He raised his cup towards Isolde, who curtseyed in return. "She is truly beautiful."

"She is," I agreed, then I caught sight of how his eyes twinkled when he looked at her. "But she is not for you."

"She could have been, if I was the Duke of Cornwall. You sat in council, did you not, Lady Elaine, when that was decided?"

"I did, but it is no reflection on you. The lords of Cornwall wanted someone who was older, and more experienced. Remember, when Mark dies, he

326

may die with a young heir, like your father did. He is marrying late in life, like your father. Your chance to be Duke may come."

"Perhaps," he said. "Or I should look elsewhere for glory."

We set out the next day, but far later than we intended due to some delay with the horses. Isolde rode pillion behind me and had been silent nearly the entire journey. She was homesick already, and I understood that, so I let her keep her peace.

Tristan threw up a hand, and the caravan drew to a halt. We were not far from where the ship sat, but I could see why he had stopped us near this wood. It was high ground and the woods would be good cover if we were attacked, unlike the sparse beach which was flat and had no retreat but the sea.

"We will have to make camp here," said Tristan. "It is darkening, and it is best to sail out when the day is early and the light good."

"Very well," I agreed, though I had an uneasy feeling about the woods around us. I was certain we were being watched, and I hoped that it was simply my imagination run wild. I bid the men begin construction on the camp. They looked at me and Isolde expectantly when it came the customary time to eat, but I reminded them that just because we were women did not mean we were there to see to the cooking.

Isolde went to lie down while I helped gather firewood. As I returned, I noticed something strange. Ahead of me went a black shape, a crook-backed woman with a basket, a hood pulled over her head.

"Who was that?" I asked one of Tristan's men.

He shrugged. "A peddler woman. The Princess wanted to look at her wares."

"Fine. But make sure that no one else enters the camp. Her safety is paramount."

I put down my bundle and began to add it to the campfire. I took a seat, and helped myself to the rabbit from the spit, and the porridge made of the grain and leeks we had brought with us in our provisions.

The campfire was a quiet place to sit, bar the crackling of the fire. Tristan's men had little conversation for a lady of my rank, and even my own men were unaccustomed to spending such intimate time with their queen. Isolde's waiting woman spoke no Latin nor our language, but that did not stop the men casting her admiring glances. Tristan was nowhere to be found, and Isolde had not risen, having eaten in her tent. I was worried she was greatly upset, so I went to speak to her.

But when I got to her tent, her Irish guard would not let me past.

"My Lady," said the guard, in his best Latin. "The Lady Isolde is indisposed."

"Then she will want a woman with her," I replied.

He did not move.

"I am her chaperone," I continued. "You will let me pass, or feel the wrath of Duke Mark when we get to Tintagel."

His face tensed but fear won out. He stepped aside and I began to walk into the tent. Then I heard it. Low, breathy moans, and the rhythmic slapping of flesh on flesh. I burst into the tent, tearing the drapery aside. Inside, there lay Isolde and Tristan, naked and in the midst of what the Christians rightly called fornication.

328

"Cover yourself!" I cried, picking up her discarded shift and tossing it to her.

"Lady Elaine," she begged. "Please, do not..."

"Do not what? Tell your husband to be, the Duke of Cornwall, that you betrayed him with his nephew?"

"You do not understand!"

"I understand rightly. Get dressed. Tristan, get out!"

He went with some speed, trying to cover himself and pick up his clothing as he left. I was furious. Not only that our treaty was now in ruins, but that I had failed in my mission. I had failed Arthur, and I had failed Britain.

"Are you so stupid?" I cried. "Mark is a Christian. They value virginity above all else. You had one task - marry Mark. You could have had your sport with Tristan after you had married Mark and sealed the alliance with Ireland. Do you realise the position in which you have put me? If Mark finds out you are not a virgin, I will be blamed for not guarding you. If I do not tell him, and he later discovers what happened, he will accuse me of colluding against him!"

"It was not my fault," she replied.

"He forced himself on you? I will have the guards seize him at once..."

"No, it was a peddler woman. She sold me a tonic, told me that it would make me beautiful and that my worries about my marriage would fade away. But once I drank it, I fell in love with Tristan at once."

"A likely story. I supposed he was visited by her too."

"No, but he said that he knew the exact moment I drunk the tonic, for suddenly he could not bear to be away from me and rushed to my side."

"What have you two done? Cornwall could go to war with Ireland over this. Tristan and your father could well die to slake your lust!"

My stomach turned to lead as my mind caught up with my words. "This peddler? What did she look like?"

"She had dark hair, very dark. It was the darkest I had ever seen, but she was so very pale. I should have been suspicious right away, she looked so little like my people. Was she a faery?"

I thought about the hooded woman I had seen leaving the camp. It would be easy to fake a crookback, the appearance of an old woman, to fool me long enough to get away. That is, if you were as talented at glamour as Morgan.

"No, much worse," I said, my voice weary from this never-ending battle. "She is a sorceress, and Britain's greatest enemy."

"What cause what she have to wreak such mischief?" asked Isolde, distressed.

"Her plans never make such sense, but in her head she believes that her acts will win her the duchy of Cornwall, what she thinks is hers by right."

No matter her art and craft, no witch can create love, hate, life or death. These four are the true elements of the universe, more so than earth, air, fire, and water, for they drive our very existence. Even Morgan, who studied the most forbidden of magics in pursuit of vengeance cannot create love. She can incite lust, which many readily confuse for love, or simply reveal that which was already there. Whichever spell she had worked here, she had once again brought Britain and her peace to its knees.

I went from the tent, my stomach churning in anger. I walked straight into the woods, and

330

walked in circles for hours, but I knew that I would not find Morgan. As I left the woods, I found Tristan standing here, sheepish, waiting for me.

"Cousin..." he began.

"We are not family!" I spat. "Family would not betray each other the way you have betrayed your uncle, and your cousin, the High King."

"I love her," he said. "And there was a potion..."

"Oh, do not try that offal of an excuse on me! Isolde might well be spelled, but you were fine, and you had her anyway."

He could not meet my eye. "I will marry her, and the alliance will stand."

"The alliance will not stand, you stupid boy! She is promised to the Duke of Cornwall, not one of his warriors. And, if this is known, you will not be one of Mark's warriors for long. And you think Angwyssh will keep the peace when you dishonoured his daughter?"

He rubbed the back of his head, his glance still stuck on the ground. "What do we do then?"

My mind raced. Then I took a deep breath and settled on a plan. "We will continue our journey, it is either that or you and Isolde stay here, and the whole alliance will rot. We will go back to Tintagel, she will marry Mark and you will come to court to serve Arthur, and keep far away from her."

"But..."

"There is no but!" I exclaimed. "Now go and tell Isolde this, or I will strike you both like the stupid children you are."

By noon the next day, we had arrived back in Tintagel. I made Isolde and Tristan sit separately on the boat, watching them like a hawk for any sign of attempted escape. We made our way up the shore into the castle, and neither of them made a sound until we reached the great hall, and Isolde was presented to the Duke of Cornwall.

She smiled and accepted his kiss on his cheek. I pretended not to see the look of disgust that flashed across her face or the hurt in Tristan's eyes. As the Duke bid me take Isolde to my mother's old chamber, I caught Tristan by the elbow.

"I suggest you find somewhere else to be until the wedding," I said.

He gave a reluctant nod and then shrugged off my hand. I marched Isolde to my mother's old room, but she did not try to speak to me, and I thought my warning back in Ireland had been clear enough. Still, I made sure I walked her past her chamber every hour to make sure that she would not be so foolish to consort with Tristan within the walls of Tintagel.

The next day, preparations for the wedding were well underway, but Isolde had not surfaced to break her fast. I was stopped on my way to the great hall.

"Cousin!" called the familiar voice, and I tightened my mouth so I could not grimace.

"Duke Mark," I said, bowing.

"Might you be able to do something for me?" he asked.

I nodded. He leaned in to whisper.

"Please see to Isolde. The High King's outriders say he will be here soon, but my maidservant cannot gain access to fit Isolde for her dress."

"I will see what I can do."

I went to Isolde's chamber, but the door was bolted. I whispered a quick charm.

"Isolde, open this door."

I could hear the bolt being drawn back. I pushed myself inside, ignoring her confused glances, as she looked at her hands as if they had betrayed her. She was not wearing her wedding gown. Instead, she wore a rough tunic and cloak, and was now hastily throwing things into a saddle-bag.

"What are you doing?" I hissed, locking the door behind me.

She looked me straight in the eye. "I am leaving to be with Tristan," she replied.

"Oh, no you are not!"

I marched over and snatched the bag from her hand, tossing it roughly to the floor. "Put on your wedding gown."

"I shall not! I am leaving, and you cannot stop me."

I could not allow Morgan to win. Not like how she had conquered Merlin. So I steeled myself to do the things I would never forgive myself for, but that my country needed.

"He does not love you. You do not love him. It is Morgan's potion."

She shook her head. "I have consulted with wise-women hereabouts. They say you cannot make someone fall in love with you. Only bring forth hidden feelings. That is what Morgan has done. We must have loved each other all along."

"How can you love him? It has been a sennight since you met."

"You do not need time to know you love some-one, only feeling," she replied.

"Tristan has a score of women like you, all over Britain. Dishonoured and discarded. If you go to meet him, he will not be there."

"Really?" she asked, sitting down on the bed, deflated.

I sat down beside her and put my arm around her. "Things will not seem so bad later, when you are Duchess of Cornwall."

She was silent, and merely leant her head against my shoulder. Finally, she got up and put on her wedding dress, and to spare her any more pain, I adjusted it for her myself.

Arthur arrived later, with Mordred in tow, and my husband following. As soon the proper greetings had been observed, I contrived to be alone with Nentres, where I told him everything that had occurred.

"You were right to be silent," he agreed. "The alliance depends on it. It is black work, Elaine, but you did right."

"I hope so," I said, leaning my head against his chest. "I do not know how much longer I can stay here before I go mad."

But I did not go mad. I stood and smiled as the wedding took place. I bowed my head like a pious monk at the ceremony, ignoring the anguished look on Tristan's face as he watched. I rejoiced at the feast, even sharing my dish with Mordred. I danced with Arthur, and I clapped with everyone else as Mark led his smiling bride to his chamber under the garland of flowers.

"We leave tomorrow," I said to Nentres, as we left. "Pretend I have taken ill, I do not care. I want to go home."

The day following the wedding, I was shaken awake by Nentres.

"Get up," he said. "We are summoned to the great hall."

"What is it?" I asked, but I feared I already knew.

"Mark has called a court of justice. Isolde and Tristan are accused of some crime."

Hurriedly I dressed, sprinting towards the great hall. Inside was the Duke, sat at the great table, with Arthur and Mordred either side of him. Tristan and Isolde stood in the centre of the room, surrounded by a shocked assembly.

"Good you could join us, cousin," said Mark, his voice dripping with poison. "The Lady Isolde was just discussing how she and my nephew tried to abscond in the night. Our wedding night, no less."

"My Lord," argued Tristan. "I was merely taking the Lady Isolde riding. She wanted to make a pastime of it."

Mark scoffed. "Too long you have taken me for an idiot. Who goes riding with a purse of gold and a change of clothes? I might have believed you, were it not for this letter that came before you left."

He threw it down on the ground before Tristan. He picked it up and read it. I held out my hand, and he passed it to me. In the neat hand of my elder sister Morgan was written *Look to your wife, Mark, and watch your nephew.*

"It is true, my Lord," argued Isolde. "But I told you, I am the victim of magic. The enchantress Morgan of Gore has worked a curse on me. She disguised herself as a beggar woman, and made me drink a potion."

"See, we have a confession!" harked Mordred. "Though she continues to lie about the potion."

My heart raced and it was my selfish hope that she would not mention my role in deceiving Mark.

"For the crime of betraying your husband, and your new lord, you are sentenced to death, Isolde," pronounced Mark. "For your crimes, you will be fixed upon a pyre, and set aflame until death."

"Stop!" I urged. "This goes beyond the duchy of Cornwall. This jeopardises our alliance with Ireland. This is the decision of the High King."

I looked at Arthur, and he nodded. Together Arthur, Nentres and I went upstairs to the solar. To my consternation, Mordred followed us.

"Please, Arthur," I begged once inside. "Show her mercy."

"What would you have me do?" he asked. "She has broken the law. It is Tristan and Isolde who have tossed the alliance asunder."

"But surely she would not lie about Morgan? And this is exactly the sort of mischief she would work."

"Why are you so quick to defend her?" asked Mordred. "Do you have evidence of Morgan's plot?"

Arthur looked to me.

"Did you know about this?" asked Arthur.

I looked at Nentres. Imperceptibly, he shook his head.

"No, Sire," I lied. "But I believe her well enough about Morgan. This is exactly what she would do."

Mordred scoffed. "She is making it up. A witch made me do it, the oldest excuse in the book. And when someone told her about Morgan, she must have thought all her feast days had come at once. She could put a name to this sorceress that enchanted her."

He looked to Arthur. "Isolde is lying, and my aunt is helping her. That is what women do. Anyway, we must make a stand here. The Irish think they can worm their way into an alliance, and then make fools of us?"

"You are right, Mordred," agreed Arthur. "Her sentence stands. She married Mark, and that makes her a British subject, and therefore she must abide by my ruling. Mordred, take my command to Duke Mark."

My nephew bowed and went from the room.

"Arthur, no!" I screamed, but he ignored me, following Mordred from the room.

In that yard, I had once played with my sisters, had waited on my mother returning from Londinium, and had bowed before Uther that fateful day. Now it held a wooden stake driven into the ground, the pyre to which Isolde would be tied and burnt alive.

Arthur would not see me the next morning, and Mordred would not be reasoned with. Isolde was to burn, he said with delight.

They had to drag her the entire length of the yard, from castle door to pyre. She went screaming the entire way, mostly in her own language, then she turned to begging.

"Please! Please, stop! Tristan, help!" she cried. "Tristan!"

But he did not come for her. Mordred had doubled the guard on the room on which he had been held in. He could not escape in time, no matter how he tried.

They lashed her to the pyre, and then covered her feet in kindling. At Mark's nod, his second lit the torch and laid it at the foot of the pyre.

"Please, Mark!" she cried. "Forgive me! Relent!"

He turned away. She struggled against the ropes and cried out in pain as the first spark licked the bare flesh of her legs.

I tensed. Mordred, now at least a head taller than me, leaned into my ear and whispered. "Do nothing aunt, or I will see you burn too."

The fire took hold and crawled up her lower body. A grey smoke was billowing out, with the foul odour of over-cooked meat. It began to rise up the pyre, floating out over Tintagel's walls towards the crash of the waves, as if her spirit would escape back to Ireland. Slowly but surely it consumed her, until she was a vision in the flames, screaming until her lungs were too scarred by the smoke to continue.

I stood and I watched as her flesh turned red and then black. It sizzled and crackled, melted and bubbled. But I dared not close my eyes, or look away, lest Arthur see, then he would accuse me of rebelling against him. I stood and I watched and hated myself every moment that I did.

My hand itched and I tucked it beneath my cloak so it did not move of its own accord. I could save her, I thought, as she burnt. I could take Mordred's sword from its scabbard and cut her free. Nentres would have no choice but to defend me, and the two of us were the equal of any here in Tintagel, save Arthur. But, by the time I had resolved to free her, she was beyond saving, and I had to let her burn.

She stopped screaming after the first while, but it took hours for her to finally die. Mark had been cruel in his jealousy and betrayal and had her brought to the pyre in a wet gown so that the burning took longer. We stood for those hours, feet aching and hearts broken, until the smoke had faded and the fire burned out, leaving only the charred remains of Isolde, now nothing more than a burnt skeleton.

Chapter Fifteen

I did not sleep the night after the burning. Nentres and I lay awake together, holding each other, trying to banish those horrific images from our minds. Then, when morning came, we debated the issue, like the greatest of Roman senators.

"To a man like Mark," he replied, when I said again I could not understand why he executed her. "An affair is always a woman's fault, his faith tells him they are naturally sinful, deceptive. And he could not execute Tristan, in case he became a martyr to a rebellion."

"So, he walks away unscathed, but we had to watch a girl burn for his lust? In what Britain, especially Arthur's Britain, is that just?"

"He did not walk away unscathed. He was banished, his knighthood stripped. That is like a lingering death for a knight."

"Nentres, I love you more than life itself but, sometimes, you are the biggest idiot I have ever clapped eyes on! Would you burn me? If I took a lover, would you burn me?"

He raised a hopeless hand and then lowered it. "You would never do that."

I fixed him with a steely gaze. "But what if I did? What if I was Morgause, who takes her pleasure wherever she can find it?"

"I could never do you harm. But if such a thing was true, I would be forced to. It would make me weak in the eyes of my warriors, and my kingdom would be lost to a man like Meron. Surely, you have you learned after all this time, that what we do in public will always be different from what we feel in private."

He reached out to touch me, and I let him. We had been together too long let this come between us.

"This is why I fell in love with you. The woman who stands up for what is right."

"I failed, this time," I added.

I wrote to Morgan before we left Tintagel. I could have spelled a letter before, but I had naught to say to her then. I whispered the charms and then tied it securely to the leg of a magpie which had appeared at the window of my chamber, as though it had known it would be needed. It would not be able to land until it had delivered its message. There was only one line written on the parchment:

You did not need to do that.

There was no reply. I had not expected any, but a little part of me hoped Morgan would show some remorse. We went home, the alliance in Ireland in tatters. I raged and raged about Morgan, and about Mordred's cruel response to the situation.

Tristan's banishment was enforced by Arthur, and he was sent free from Tintagel, with not a scar but the shame he wore. I was so angry with Mordred, and with Arthur for giving in to him, that I went home to Garlot, and did not return to Camelot until I was summoned for the feast of Arthur's birth.

More and more was made of the celebration of his birth each year, until it became a grand spectacle, with mummers and jesters galore in Camelot. This particular feast, Arthur had gathered on the balcony above the yard to wave to those who had come.

They gave a great cheer, and I wanted to step back inside. Having seen battle, great numbers of people had the power to make me nervous. But Arthur always insisted that I come with him, and

340

usually his favourites too, so Bedevere and Mordred were there too. The Queen should have been there, and Lancelot too, but they were not.

Arthur waved again, and there was another cry of joy from the crowd. Suddenly, there was silence. They were captivated by something, and no longer paying any attention to the High King. All attention was on the great arch that gave entrance to Camelot.

A horse trotted slowly into the courtyard, before the assembled nobles. On its back was Tristan. He was bound with ropes that extended all over, keeping him upright on the saddle, and moving ever forward. His right hand, elaborately bound between saddle and breastplate into an elevated position, bore a plain white shield.

"That is odd," said Arthur. "That is not his heraldry."

I raised an eyebrow in disbelief. "Tristan is tied to a horse, forced to ride into Camelot, by the looks of it, and you think the shield is odd?"

"Something is written on it," he said squinting at the rider.

I too turned my gaze towards it. There, in Morgan's perfect hand, was written GUINEVERE IS LANCELOT'S HARLOT. Arthur's knuckles were white around the balustrade. All around us, gasps, whispers and giggles erupted. The crowd was beginning to read the shield.

"Sir Bedevere," I whispered. "Please go at once and get him down from there."

He nodded. Arthur turned to me, ashen in pallor. He opened his mouth, struggling for words. No sound came forth. He turned from me and moved to leave the balcony. I put my hand on his arm.

"Arthur, please, take a moment. How you behave now is crucial. If you become angry, you give truth to these rumours, or you will look weak, easily riled by words."

He shrugged my hand away, silent, and stomped from the balcony.

"Presence-chamber, now" he called over his shoulder, and none of us dared argue.

We gathered there, Mordred and I. Bedevere returned from untying Tristan, and had him thrown into the dungeons, for his banishment still stood regardless even if he was made to come into Camelot against his will. Gawain too was summoned, along with other Knights of the Round Table. None of us were permitted to speak.

"Is it true?" asked Arthur.

None of us would answer. To admit to knowing about it was to admit to knowing about treason against the king, and to knowingly conceal treason was in itself treasonous. However, I could be certain, after all those years, it was common knowledge among all there. But none of us wished to hurt the King, or Lancelot or Guinevere.

"It is, Sire," said Mordred. "It is known to almost everyone, but I had no evidence, or else I would have brought it to you."

I held my breath. Here Arthur's anger would begin.

"All of you knew?" exclaimed Arthur. "And you kept this from me?"

"Sir Gawain knew, most certainly," said Mordred. "He has known all along. Lancelot all but admitted it to him, and then he caught them together. Aggravaine and I tried to get him to bring this to you, but he would not."

"What!" cried Arthur, and I had to put my hand on him to stay him, or he would have strangled

Gawain there and then. Gawain could not answer, only hang his head in shame.

"Seize them. The Queen, and Sir Lancelot," ordered Arthur. "If they resist, slay them."

"Happily," said Sir Mordred. He had not even bothered to conceal his smirk.

The two of them were caught by the guards together in the rose garden, and that was evidence enough of an affair for Arthur. He had the two of them arrested and thrown in the dungeons until a trial could be held. Arthur would not speak to me, nor any other others. We had betrayed him by not telling him, he said.

The High Queen was marched before us in the great hall. She still wore her rich purple gown, now flecked with the dirt of whatever hole Arthur had ordered her slung into. At her side was a woman in a sober worsted smock, pulling Guinevere by her arm as though she were a slattern caught stealing, not the highest lady in the land. I had never seen this woman before, but I supposed we must have had jailers for our women criminals.

Guinevere kept her eyes firmly fixed upon the stone floor, her curls dripping over her face like honey. The High Queen was broken. She looked like a pauper dressed up for our entertainment.

Lancelot too was brought before us, escorted by the point of Sir Kay's sword. Arthur stood up to address the accused. He looked older, paler, and his blonde hair had lost some of its sheen, as though he had gone grey overnight.

"Guinevere ferch Leodegranz, you are found guilty of treason. I hereby strip you of your rank of High Queen and sentence you to death. You will be taken to a place of execution and fixed upon a pyre, in accordance with our customs."

Guinevere let out an unearthly cry, as though she had already died and her spirit returned to haunt us. She tried to protest, but the stern matron at her side clapped a hand across her mouth and held firm as Guinevere writhed in anguish.

"Lancelot du Lac, you too are found guilty of crimes against the King. I hereby strip you of your rank as Lord and Knight and sentence you to a punishment yet to be determined. Guards, take the prisoners back to the dungeons."

"Why does he not kill Lancelot?" I asked Nentres, whispering. "I thought surely he would have him executed."

"Arthur is indecisive. He knows he should execute Lancelot and silence rumours of weakness... he is angry enough to kill him...but he cannot risk rebellion in Lancelot's holdings until he has found a replacement."

"I am sick of this. I do not know if I can watch another burning."

"No, wife, I do not know if I can either."

We went back to our chamber and sat in silence, words escaping us entirely. There was the sound of running feet, and into our room burst Anna. At sixteen, she was the image of mother all those years ago. She ran to me at once, and I held her tightly, letting her cry.

"Aunt, is there nothing you can do for my mother?" she begged. "My father will not let me speak to him, but surely he will see you."

I shook my head. "No, dear Anna, there is not. The King will have me dragged from his presence if I mention Guinevere. We can only hope that he will cool his anger before the morning and pardon her. She will not be allowed to stay at court, and Arthur will probably ask his bishop to annul the marriage. She might be allowed to go into the nunnery at Glastonbury. Your mother would like that, would she not?"

"Yes, she would," she agreed. "She would like that very much. I will pray that my father will be filled with God's grace and see that he must forgive her sins, and render her unto the service of the Lord and its repentance. I will go to the chapel, I do not care if I have to kneel all night."

With that, she turned promptly on her heel and exited.

"You gave that girl false hope," said Nentres sternly.

"Better she spend the night on her knees," I replied. "Trying to save her mother with her prayers, than blaming herself and us when Guinevere dies tomorrow."

"The Elaine I know should be frantic in trying to save a woman from such a punishment. You are letting your enmity with Guinevere cloud your feelings."

"I am not," was my response. "True, I barely tolerate the pious, simpering ninny, but to burn for her love of Lancelot...you cannot deny that they love each other...it is horrific. But she betrayed Arthur, and we cannot interfere. My concern is Anna. I must remain calm if we are to save her."

Nentres shook his head. "Arthur would not declare her illegitimate, even if Guinevere's rank has been stripped. She will not go hungry at any rate."

"But her position is weaker, and that is worrisome. Perfect for an opportunist lord to swoop in and marry her, take away her mother's shame and inch himself closer to the throne. And Mordred? What if he sees a shift in her rank as the perfect time to press his suit? How can we explain why they cannot be together?"

"Arthur must know the truth. I know he has never mentioned it to us, but he must know, surely. Even if Lot never blackmailed him, can he not see the striking resemblance between himself and the boy? Even for a nephew it is too strong."

"This is Arthur, who he himself gave into lust for his sister, and cannot deny Mordred anything he wishes. Do not be so sure," I warned.

"What of Morgan?" he asked. "This was her doing, you were certain of it."

"Oh, most entirely. She grows more desperate, turned her attention from curses to sheer audacious plots. I...I provoked her, though, I am certain of it."

"You cannot take to blaming yourself for all she does. Few days do not go by where you do not mention how you wish you had prevented Uther sending her away, or that you had convinced her to abandon her path or the many times you believe you should have killed her."

"But this time, I think, it is my fault. I wrote to her, after Isolde's death."

"Why ever did you do that?" Nentres asked.

"I was angry. That is the short answer. I was angry, at her, at everyone's behaviour, at my own failings in preventing the collapse of the alliance. I damned her for her actions, and this was her retaliation."

"Hmm," said Nentres. "I do not think so. This was coming, Elaine. If Morgan did not expose them, they would be caught eventually. More than us had knowledge of this."

Nentres looked to me. "We can do nothing, Elaine."

"I know," I said. "This is Arthur's justice."

The word justice seemed to gag in my mouth.

We assembled the next day in the yard, the pyre constructed. This was the second burning I would be forced to attend, and I wondered if there was a supply of wooden stakes at every castle for such things, and Caer Mor was simply the exception. I did not want to go, but Arthur had made it clear that we had betrayed him in concealing the affair and anyone who did not attend was betraying him a second time.

Unlike Isolde, Guinevere was calm. Arthur spared her the horror of a wet shift and she walked as serene as if she was going to prayer. Did her faith give her that strength, I wondered? I would be fighting with every last ounce of my strength if it was me.

"Have you anything to say?" asked Arthur. "Any final words?"

"I love you," she replied.

He turned away from her and signalled the executioner to tie her to the stake.

There was a clamour of hoof beats, and a great warhorse road towards the pyre. People flung themselves to the ground to avoid being trampled underfoot. It was Lancelot, mounted upon his steed. How he had freed himself was a mystery.

He jumped down from the saddle. Arthur ran at him, but Lancelot struck him with his fist, and our High King tumbled to the ground, knocked unconscious. Lancelot drew his sword, and the executioner turned tail and fled.

"Lancelot is free!" cried Bedevere. "Knights, stop him!"

Aggravaine drew his sword and raced at Lancelot, meeting him with a great clash of steel on steel. But Lancelot would always be the greater swordsman, and with a riposte, disarmed him. Lancelot spun and sliced Aggravaine across his back.

Gawain bellowed, and launched himself at Lancelot, but his guard was too low. With a great stroke of his sword, he cut Gawain's throat, and my nephew fell flat upon the ground, blood spurting across Lancelot's tunic. I screamed. Nentres started towards him.

"No! Nentres do not!" I cried, throwing myself upon my husband. I struggled against him, trying to force his sword back into his scabbard. "No, you will be killed! You will kill Lancelot!"

"Leave off Elaine! I cannot stand by and let a criminal escape!"

Our eyes locked as he tried to wrest me from him. At once he relaxed, and though we were standing in a crowd of a hundred or more, it was as if we were alone in our bedchamber in Garlot.

"Hit me," he said, his voice low.

"What?"

"Arthur will punish me if I do not help prevent Lancelot's escape. Hit me!"

He was serious. I took a deep breath and swung out for him. My fist tapped his cheek lightly.

"It will do," he sneered, as he threw himself to the ground.

His hand flung out and caught me by the wrist, and together we rolled into the muck. I was so surprised by this that I needed to take no part in his spectacle and I struggled against him, thinking he had gone mad. By the time we had finished our roughhousing, the crowd was silent, staring at us. The gate to Camelot lay open, and Guinevere and Lancelot were gone.

After the bodies of Gawain and Aggravaine had been laid to rest, Nentres and I were called before Arthur and taken to task for our failure to prevent the escape of Guinevere and Lancelot.

348

"Nentres, why did you not come to the aid of our fallen brethren?" asked the High King.

Nentres stepped forward, and I thought that he should have been a mummer, not a king. His face was the perfect representation of an angered husband.

"My wife interfered, and by the time I subdued her, the traitor was gone."

"Elaine!" cried Arthur. "Why ever would you do that?"

I kneeled before my brother. "I feared for my husband, Sire. I feared that Lancelot would slay him too!"

"I am betrayed once again! You should have taken up your sword too!"

"I know, brother. I have failed you."

"You have," said Arthur, storming from the room. "You have all failed me."

Guinevere wrote to Arthur sometime later, and it was enough to send him storming from the presence-chamber. I picked up the letter to read it.

My dearest Arthur, it began.

I write to you from the abbey at Glastonbury, but I write not to beg forgiveness. I have sinned against you and must face my punishment, even if it is not the death you would have willed upon me. I have taken sanctuary here, and the only way to repent of my sin is to become a lay sister.

Instead, I write to beg you to look kindly upon Anna. I know that I will never see her again, for you will never permit her to visit me and I can never leave these abbey walls. You are within the law to disown her, but let not the sins of her mother be upon her. Find her a good marriage, and love her where I can no longer.

Lancelot is here too. I will not have you hear it from idle gossips. But he too has become a lay brother, and we see each other only at mass on feast days. He carries a great wound in his heart for slaying Aggravaine and Gawain, knowing that it was for the love of me, and of course feels he has committed a grievous sin in betraying you. That is why we have decided to remain apart and do penance for our sins.

I am sorry. I love you. Always and forever.

Putting down the letter, I went to find Arthur and heard him within his chamber. The room was in complete disarray. Furniture overturned, hangings torn from the walls. There, on the floor, were Guinevere's clothes, slashed roughly with a blade. Arthur himself was sat on the floor, curled up against a wall. There were tears staining his face.

"Arthur. Brother...I..."

He looked up at me, eyes red-rimmed and puffy. His pain was tangible, radiating out into the room like waves crashing against the shore.

"I am sorry," I said. "Though it means so little now."

"Make her come back to me again, make her love me. Do a spell, I command you as your King."

"I cannot," I said, answering honestly. "No spell can make someone love you. I could curse her with restless feet so that she cannot stop moving unless she returns to the castle, or strip her of her will, so that she can do only that which fulfils your every whim. But make her love you? Impossible."

"Then Lancelot. Curse him instead. Make his cock fall off, the bastard!"

"Well, I could do that easy enough. But, would that bring her back to you?"

350

I knelt down beside him. "Arthur, would harming Lancelot, your dearest friend, make you feel any better? Do you think unmanning him would turn her gaze from him?"

He shook his head, sullen like a boy. "I knew," he said. "I knew, deep down. But I thought nothing would ever come of it. I thought, let them be friends, let him take for her silly walks around the flower garden. Let him do the things I had no time for. But that she would share her bed with him? That she would give away her crown to live in shame with him?"

"There are women, Arthur," I said "who know their duty. They know that they must keep a home and bear children and make the best of it. And often they were raised by such a woman. But Guinevere had only her father, who no doubt filled her head full of tales where women marry for love."

"Are you making excuses for her?"

"No. She has done wrong, that much is true. And Lancelot too."

"And yet I can do nothing. She has claimed sanctuary, and he too. I would betray my God if I marched upon them. Mordred urges me to seize Cameliard and Joyous Gard, but I cannot. I am too weak for war."

"That is not a bad thing," I said.

The news reached us that Elaine, wife of Lancelot, had taken her own life, having heard of Lancelot's affair. Arthur was deeply grieved by this, so he had Galahad, Lancelot's son, sent to Camelot to be raised. I hoped that having the boy near would temper the anger and sadness he felt, and prayed that Arthur might recover from the betrayal of his wife and dearest friend.

Chapter Sixteen

Uriens finally died that year, the seventeenth of Arthur's reign and his son Yvain ascended to the throne of Gore. He proved himself loyal, writing to tell us that his former step-mother had made overtures to him to rebel against Arthur, but he had turned down her offer of gold and men. Finally, we had some good news.

But Arthur never recovered from the loss of his wife and his best friend. Still we were no closer to releasing Merlin, and that weighed on him yet. He was uncommunicative, rarely joyous, and spoke only in confidence to Mordred. Even I was the last to know of anything. But he depended on Nentres and me more and more for the ruling of Britain.

We were so often at Camelot that we were forced to give some of our crown lands to Lomar so that he did not chafe at the increasing number of duties we placed upon him. Arthur would not release Hoel from his knightly training either, so we could not even send our prince to rule in our stead.

I was now a permanent fixture on Arthur's council of justice. I heard the testimony of more criminals and victims than I ever had in Garlot. People came to us from across Britain when their lords had failed them, and it was in that role that I came to Camelot just after Easter to hear more petitions.

We gathered in the great hall. Arthur sat enthroned, with Mordred and I stood beside him. Nimueh remained too, still wearing very little. She had no official role in the hearing of petitions, but Arthur still allowed her there for an unknown reason. I often thought she reminded him of Merlin.

She certainly reminded me of him when she made a sneering remark.

Among the petitioners was a young woman. She was young and pretty, with her slender figure and fair features, set beneath her fair brown hair. But, with her rough spun dress, she was not a lady of wealth. But if you do not have gold, beauty will ensure that you are first among the petitioners when Mordred sits in council.

"Who is next?" asked Arthur.

Mordred gestured to the woman, and she came towards the dais. In her hands was a bundle, wrapped in furs and tied with a ribbon. She held it out towards the High King.

"What can the court of Camelot do for you?" asked Arthur.

"I come as a bearer of gifts, Sire."

She reached out and undid the ribbon. The furs parted, revealing the robes within. I could not see much of them, but it was clear they were of dazzling purple and made from the most exquisite fabric, which shone in the light of the great hall.

"Very impressive, mistress," said Arthur. "But, forgive me, I take it this is not a gift from you."

"You are correct, Sire," she replied. "I am a messenger for the Lady Morgan, formerly the Queen of Gore."

Arthur gasped, a noise of both shock and anger.

"I want nothing from my sister. I consider her dead to me."

"The Lady Morgan said she wishes only that she might live out her days in peace, and sends this gift as a symbol of truce."

"And where exactly does the Lady Morgan live?" asked Mordred. "Avalon?"

The woman shook her head. "She has not told me. She came to my steading and paid me handsomely to deliver this to you."

Arthur beckoned to her. "You may come forth."

The woman approached the dais, proffering the folded robes. Arthur stretched out his hand to feel them.

"Arthur, do not!" I said, before I knew what words I spoke. He drew back his hand.

"Why?" he asked. "Is something amiss?"

"I sense a malevolence here," I replied.

"Yes Sire," said Nimueh, chiming in. "It stinks of Morgan's magic."

I wondered if she would have kept her silence, had I said nothing.

"This woman? She is Morgan's assassin?" asked Arthur.

"Perhaps unwittingly," I replied. "I believe the robe is cursed."

The woman bowed her head. "Sire, the Lady Morgan said you would think this. There is no spell or poison upon the cloth."

"So she says," replied Arthur. "Morgan is not to be trusted."

Mordred stepped forward. "Good lady, you believe your employer to be true?"

She nodded. "Yes, milord, I do."

"Then this is all very simple. Put on the robe, and show your king that all is well."

The woman shook her head. "Milord, it is purple silk. It is a crime for someone of my rank to wear such a garment."

Mordred shrugged. "I doubt anyone would bring a case against you when you do so in the service of the king. And you are not really wearing it, are you? Testing it, perhaps?"

"Milord, please do not make me do this," she begged.

"Why not?" asked Mordred, smirking. "Clearly something must be amiss, or you would not be so reluctant. When would a peasant like you ever get to wear purple silk again?"

I looked to Arthur. His face bore no signs of any emotion. Mordred urged her to don the garment again, and again she said no.

"Put it on," said Arthur.

I could see she wanted to shake her head again, tears brimming to the surface of her eyes.

"Remember it is a crime to refuse your High King," added Mordred.

"Sire," I began.

"Silence!" hissed Mordred. "You do not command here, aunt."

I drew in a breath of rage, and prepared to rebuke my nephew, but Arthur held up his hand.

"Quiet, sister. If Morgan's intentions are true, then her servant will come to no harm."

"Sire," said Nimueh. "We do not know the nature of Morgan's spell..."

"Be quiet!" he warned. "Or I will make you wear it."

"Put it on," said Mordred to the woman. "Or I will have my guard put you in it...piece by piece."

I saw her eyes dart around the room, but there was no escape, none to come to her rescue. Taking a deep, fearful breath, the woman reached into the wrapping and pulled the robe free, letting the fur fall. Despite her shaking, she could not hide the admiring gaze she gave the fabric as she laid it across her arms to smooth it.

Then she pulled it over her head. It was a man's robe so it hung loosely on her body. The silk settled onto her frame with a flutter. We watched in horrified anticipation. But nothing happened.

The woman breathed a sigh of relief. And then she screamed. The robe had clung to her skin. It was as if it was melting, getting tighter and tighter.

"I can't breathe," she cried. "Help!"

I looked to Nimueh, but she shook her head, confirming what I already knew. There was nothing we could do.

The woman collapsed onto the floor, rolling from side to side as the robe grew tighter. She convulsed upon the floor, gasping for breath. Then it turned to purple liquid, soaking her from head to toe. I thought that was the end of it, but with a bloodcurdling scream, the liquid became flames.

"Help me!" she screamed.

It was too much like Isolde, too much for me to bear witness to again. I closed my eyes and held them shut as she screamed. She burned quicker than Isolde, growing quiet within in minutes. When I opened my eyes, all that remained was a charred corpse, smouldering gently upon the hall floor.

I could feel Arthur head turn, his eyes upon me. "And you would have had me suffer such a fate, sister, were it not for Mordred."

I looked away from her blackened body. I picked up my skirts and began to walk from the hall. There were more gasps of horror from the assembly. I was leaving Arthur's presence without being dismissed. Perhaps in the privacy of the solar, such a thing would be of no consequence. But here, in front of the people of Camelot and those from further afield, it was a great insult. Still, I strode on, my chin held high, my eyes fixed firmly upon the door from the hall.

I made my way to our quarters, though tears threatened to burn their way forth from behind my eyes. Nentres and Hoel were there, Nentres gesturing to the recent despatches from Garlot. They knew at once something was wrong.

"My Lady Mother?" asked Hoel. "Are you quite alright?"

"Yes, son," I replied, though I still placed my hand upon the back of his neck for comfort, and sighed with relief when Nentres took my other hand.

"What news from Garlot?" I asked.

Hoel launched into an explanation of recent events in our home, and I had to focus on each individual word, so that I did not lose my composure. He stopped, and I was about to reassure him I was listening, urge him to continue, when I realised why he had stopped.

Somebody else had entered our chamber. It was the High King.

"Leave us," commanded Arthur.

Hoel left at once, but Nentres merely withdrew into the corner of the room.

"How dare you leave my presence without being dismissed?" exclaimed Arthur.

"How dare you allow Mordred to speak to me so?" I cried back. "How dare you kill a woman in our hall?"

Arthur strode forward until he was mere inches from my face. "It is not your hall! It is mine! If I want to kill a hundred assassins in it, I shall!"

I was very conscious of the fact that this man no longer spoke with the tender tones of the brother who had wanted to meet his long lost sister. He spoke like a king. Not the king who had such a vision for a Britain of equals. He sounded like his father on his worst days. In fact, he sounded like Mordred.

I looked to Nentres, but he would not be able to save me. Insulting Arthur could have great ramifications politically. So I did the only thing I could think of. I swallowed my pride and my anger. I got down on my knees, and prostrated myself before him, my forehead touching the rushes scattered about the stone floor.

"Forgive me, my King," I urged. "Forgive me, brother."

There was no response from him. When I was brave enough to look up, he was gone. Nentres came to help me to my feet.

"What have you said?" he asked.

I told him the whole sorry story and tried not to cry as I did.

Arthur spoke little to me the rest of the sennight, though he seemed placated by my obsequiances. Mordred must have eventually heard that I got down on my knees before Arthur because he smirked continually throughout the passing days. Arthur did not permit me to hear any more petitions from then on. Mordred had eclipsed me as his chief advisor.

Chapter Seventeen

Lot shocked us all that cold winter. Nearly eighteen years from the day he had surrendered the rebellion he had orchestrated when Arthur first came to power, he took up arms against his brother-in-law once more. He came with the full force of the Orkneys and Lothian, as well as Gaulish mercenaries, Saxon hordes, and troops pledged by the Picts and the Scoti.

This became known as the Battle of Terrabil since that is where the majority of the conflict took place. Lot captured the Castle of Terrabil, a second castle formerly owned by my father Gorlois, deciding that Cornwall was a perfect staging area for an invasion of the southern countries. It worked well. Lot was able to take troops straight by ship, avoid being spotted marching overland, and bring the rebels in the Summer Country under his banner.

Lot brought many men to the field that day, and Arthur had only half the force of Lot. But Lot was not the greatest war leader in the field, and like my father all those years ago, was provoked into challenging the scout force outside Terrabil, instead of remaining ensconced within the walls. The scout force was not all of Arthur's men, and his hidden troops rode out from over the hill, laying waste to Lot's war-band.

In the fray, Arthur's close ally King Pellinore slew Lot. Better that, I thought, than the punishment Arthur surely had reserved for him if he captured him alive. When the destruction at Terrabil was done, Arthur summoned Morgause to discuss the future of Lot's kingdoms, of which she was regent.

I had seen Morgause only once since her flight from the Orkneys, at an assembly of kings and lords. Her island home was too far away to come over land, and many would balk if they knew she had once made the journey in a chariot while four months pregnant. Her husband could not spare the ships from Arthur's charge to defend the coast, so travelling by sea was not an option either. On reflection, I was so often at Camelot that her seeing Arthur would have been inevitable, and thus, for both their sakes, she was better at home.

Time had been kind to her, if not her craft. Still her hair shone with golden fire, and she wore it wild, loose and curled, not in our mother's style of tight, elaborate braids that Morgause once favoured. Her face was absent of all but a few lines, and curves which would have gone to fat in any other matron remained defined and supple, as though she was only on the cusp of womanhood. There were no widow's ashes for Morgause. She stood proudly in her sea green dress, fur trims and intricate necklace, her face rouged and eyes kohl'd. She bowed to our brother King.

"Sire, I come not as your sister, or as the wife of Lot," she began. "But as the Dowager Queen of the Orkneys, and the acting regent of Lothian. Our kingdoms cry out in shame for Lot's actions, and we capitulate to you, and await your punishment, begging on our hands and knees for your forgiveness. See, I have brought tribute to you, Lord, King, and Caesar - salted fish, expensive furs, and gold trinkets. The bounty of the north and its seas are your due."

It was an impressive speech. I almost wanted to clap. Morgause was right to speak first. I doubted the rowdy Gaheris or the timid Gareth could have carried the moment with such weight.

362

Morgause had missed her calling as a bard, and the flattery would balm Arthur's wounds quickly enough.

"Queen Morgause, we accept your tribute," replied Arthur, grim-faced. "We invite you to hear the terms of your capitulation."

A priest stepped forward, one of Arthur's scribes, and read a sober proclamation in Ecclesiastical Latin, so heavy and wordy that I had trouble following. From what I understood, it was a near-poetic retelling of Arthur's victory over Lot. When the scribe finished, Arthur addressed Morgause.

"So, Morgause, I propose this. That you are regent for your sons Gaheris and Gareth, until the times that I can spare them from their duties as my knights."

She bowed low. "You do me much honour Sire."

He stepped down from the dais and helped her to her feet. "My dear Morgause, who has always been my most loyal sister."

Nentres leaned in close and whispered, "Say nothing, Elaine. Ignore him."

Approaching from the crowd was Mordred, and her other sons Gaheris and Gareth. Mordred was still as handsome as ever but was the clear opposite of his brothers, who were both dark like their father. Gaheris was over six feet in height and towered above even Arthur, who was one of the tallest men I knew. Gareth was tall too but had taken to stooping and crouching as not to stand out so much.

I remember when Gareth came first to court, hot on the heels of his older brothers, though he was far too young at fourteen to be in Arthur's service. But still, he made the long journey from the islands to Camelot by himself and this so impressed Arthur he made him the youngest knight to ever serve at the Round Table.

"My Lady Mother," they said, greeting her in turn.

"I am overjoyed to see you," she said, and she drew them close to her one by one. "But I will speak with all of you later. Dine with me in my chamber."

She came towards me.

"Sister," she said, and clasped me to her. "Come, we must speak alone."

She took my hand, and I led her to her chamber.

"It was her, it was Morgan." she began, as soon as the door shut, not giving me time to speak. "She convinced him. She poured poison into his ears, said that Arthur had deliberately dishonoured him by laying with me all those years ago. Told him that Arthur was playing at being Mordred's father, when Lot was the one who raised him. And when she turned to the deaths of Gawain and Aggravaine."

She had to stop and bite her lip to hold back tears.

"Lot was always a prideful little bastard," she continued. "And she set him right off. They were all her ideas. It was her idea to launch the invasion from Terrabil, it was her that somehow got hold of the gold to pay for all those men, and she called in every favour she had to get him those troops from all across the world."

"I can see you are much troubled Morgause," I said.

She nodded and leant her head against my breast.

"I loved Lot, and he loved me. In our own way. It was perhaps not the marriage that I dreamed of as a young girl, but it was our way. I have lost so much Elaine. I have lost my husband, and my son, and Gawain was so very dear to me too. I am done with Morgan. If I ever see her again, I'll kill the bitch."

"How long will you stay?" I asked her, trying to turn her mind from her anger.

"A few weeks," she replied. "To settle everything with Arthur, and for his outriders to reach Lothian, so they know to expect my continuing role as regent. And, of course, to rest. It was a long journey, made in much haste."

Those few weeks were glorious. Together, at last, we had much to acquaint each other with. She told me about her life in the Orkneys and at the court of Lothian. Her new role as regent in these countries also worried her, and she had many questions for Arthur and me on ruling a kingdom.

But a shadow also loomed over Camelot. Sir Lamorak, the son of King Pellinore, came to court, having finished his time routing the remaining Picts and Scoti from Cornwall to their lands beyond the wall built by Emperor Hadrian. Gaheris had already challenged Pellinore to a duel, and Arthur intervened, forbidding it. But now he turned his attention to Lamorak, who was brash and loud, and had many admirers at court for his role in the battle that killed Lot. Lamorak would not consent to a duel, and Gaheris often extorted Gareth and Mordred to join him in avenging the death of their father.

Mordred said he would have no part in any illicit violence, but Morgause confided in me that he had already asked her for permission to raise a levy in Lothian and lay siege to Pellinore's kingdom. She had denied such a request in obvious sense, but she did not know how long she could prevent any action on his part.

But what worried me as much as any rebellious violence Gaheris had planned was the behaviour of my siblings.

"Arthur has been acting secretive," I said to Nentres. "Disappearing off alone after dinner. I think he has a lover at court, and Morgause has been acting suspiciously too."

"You fear they have resumed their love affair?" asked Nentres

I nodded. "Arthur's marriage no longer holds, and Lot is dead. Apart from their relation, which did not stop them before, there is no impediment."

"I have heard nothing," shrugged Nentres. "Arthur has every right to take a lover, to remarry even. And Morgause will be Morgause, as you yourself have said often enough. Do they do wrong now, if they are careful?"

"Perhaps not," I conceded. "If it makes them happy. But it could still cost them both their crowns and their lives."

That night at dinner, the storm cloud brewed thicker and threatened to burst. Now that Arthur's kin at court was so numerous, we had our own table, and I sat down beside my nephew Gaheris, noticing his thunderous expression.

"What has you so ill-grieved?" I asked Gaheris.

I winced at my choice of words, his father, and brothers not long dead. But he did not take any offence, too focused on his observations to recognise what I had said.

"My mother," he replied. "She is talking to Lamorak."

I looked to where he had gestured with the lip of his wine cup. She was indeed conversing with the son of Pellinore. She saw us looking and inclined her head to him, excusing herself.

"What business have you with our father's killer?" demanded Gaheris as she passed to her seat.

Morgause gave him a withering look.

"Pellinore killed your father," she replied. "And justly too, because he rebelled against our High King without cause. I have dealings with the son of a king because I am Queen of Lothian, and of Orkney."

Gaheris opened his mouth to speak, but she leaned in close to him. "There is a reason you are not now king in Lothian, and that has nothing to do with Arthur needing you here at court. It is because you are unfit to rule, with your temper and your manners. So do not speak to me like that again, boy."

He huffed out an angry sigh and stood up, knocking the tableware askance. He stormed off from the hall while Morgause merely shrugged.

"He is a surly boy," she said, by way of explanation. "And needs a strong hand to keep him in line. Lot would want me to."

Gareth sat down, and Mordred too. Dinner was always a quiet affair, as I had little to say to Mordred. I had faced him down in the council chamber too often for us to be easy friends, and Nentres could only talk with him about swords for so long. When Arthur finally declared dinner at an end, all of us were relieved to get up.

I noticed our brother had approached, and thought he would invite us to the solar for a game of chess.

"Will you come to the solar, sister?" I asked Morgause.

Her eyes twinkled. "I have a prior engagement."

I looked to our brother. He shook his head.

"I too am otherwise occupied. You must be hostess tonight."

Morgause held out her hand for Arthur to take. "Will you escort me?"

"Happily," he replied, and the two went from my presence.

The solar was cold and lonely, so I retired to my chamber to await Nentres' return from the hall. There was a knock at the door, and when I got up to open it, it was a page boy, panting and with an ill colour.

"The High King bids you come, milady," said the page.

I followed the page from the room and across the castle to the chambers of residence. He hurried ahead of me, and I raced to keep up with him. But when we reached the corridor, he would not go any further, pointing at a chamber and saying that the High King was inside.

I did not know who had taken this chamber as theirs. Running the castle of Camelot was now the responsibility of Anna's ladies-in-waiting, I had no time for those things anymore.

Mordred sat outside the door, slumped against the wall. I asked him what the matter was but he did not answer. His face was white, frozen in some unknown expression. He could only wave me away, so I went on, into the chamber.

There was blood everywhere. The room was painted with it. A great streak was splashed against the wall behind the bed, flecked out over the wall coverings, the hangings of the bed, the wood of

368

the side table. In the centre of the bed was a great puddle of blood. The very room itself was stained with it.

The source of the wave of blood also lay upon the bed. It was the naked body of a woman, save for her head, which had been hewn from the neck in a rough, ragged cut. The head was nowhere to be seen, and I presumed it was on the other side of the bed.

A younger Elaine would have felt sick, and probably gone to vomit in the privy. But that past decade upon battlefields had made my stomach stronger than that of the average woman.

Across the room, Gareth had Gaheris pinned against the wall, using all of his body to keep him at bay. Gaheris looked like a berserker, lost in the rage. His face was red, his veins bulging and his mouth frothing.

"What has occurred here? Who has been slain?" I asked.

"It is..." began Arthur, but the words died in his throat, and I could see tears cloud his eyes.

Then I looked down and saw the crown upon the table. That dress of near-purple upon the floor.

"No," I said. "That is not Morgause. There has been a mistake."

"It is her," said Arthur, choking through sobs.

"But...? Who would...?" I asked, struggling to find the words.

"Gaheris," he said, and I felt my legs tremble beneath me.

"I will kill him!" I shrieked. "I will kill the little bastard!"

Arthur was faster than me, and caught me by the elbow before I could launch myself at him. He pulled me close, and I could feel tears burning their way from my eyes and into his tunic.

My sister was gone. There could be nothing left of Morgause in that broken shell. How could there be? How could her bright smile, her teasing eyes and her fiery temper remain when her body was battered and torn?

My memories of that night remain distorted with pain and disgust. I remember Sir Kay entering the room, demanding to know what had caused all commotion among the servants. It was some time before we could speak again.

"Why was this done?" asked Sir Kay.

Gaheris had calmed enough to speak, but still he had to be held by Gareth.

"She has shamed our kingdoms with her adultery."

Arthur opened his mouth to protest, no doubt to say that she was free to do as she pleased as a widow, but Kay gently shushed him, with what little privilege he had as his foster brother.

Then I realised that it was not Arthur she had been with as I had supposed. He was fully clothed and had no blood upon him, save a smear of red on his forearm where he had brushed against the sheets.

"Who was she with?" I asked, biting down to keep from screaming.

"She was fornicating with Lamorak," spat Gaheris. "She betrayed our father with his sworn enemy."

I wonder if he knew how unlikely it was that Lot was indeed his father.

"Where is Sir Lamorak now?" demanded Kay.

"He escaped," replied Gaheris. "Ran like a girl with only a sheet to cover himself."

"Don't you dare take that tone with me, you little shit," said Kay. "I'm not the one who killed his mother. I'll see you hang for this."

Kay marched across the room and took Gareth's ear in his big hands, tugging it. "What role had you in all this, virgin?"

Gareth let out a painful squeal. "None," he protested, though he still tried to hold back Gaheris, who now looked like he would take after Sir Kay.

"Gaheris said our mother had been behaving suspiciously, and he asked Mordred and me to come and surprise her. It turned out to be Lamorak, and that would be grounds for a duel, but Gaheris just lost it and drew his sword."

"All three of you will be sent to the dungeons," pronounced Kay.

"I did nothing wrong!" cried Gaheris. "She was the whore!"

"I have to leave," I said. "I have to leave."

I remember little else, walking from that room. Nentres holding me while I cried. Hoel and Anna, white-faced at the death of their aunt. Being alone with Arthur while he sobbed.

We laid Morgause to rest not far from the castle. I tried to help with the last offices, as was my duty as her sister, but I could not. Each time I saw what remained of her, I could only shake and shiver, heaving my empty stomach. In the end, women specialising in such things had to be brought from the town.

Gareth and Gaheris were forbidden from the ceremony, and Mordred had declined to attend. Arthur did not want the pomp and circumstance of a state funeral. It was only our closest friends. We carried her bier ourselves, helped the servants fill in the grave, piled up the rocks over the freshly turned earth with our own hands.

And one by one the funeral goers went from that place, until it was only I, staring at the pile of rocks, a jewel hidden among them as a grave offering. Alone, I called on all the forces who owed me allegiance as one of the Wise to bring her back to me, but none answered. There was only silence.

But as dusk drew closer, I knew I was not alone. There was the sound of footsteps on the dewy grass. Approaching from the north, ever-clad in her black robes was Morgan. Her pale skin was haggard and her eyes red-rimmed with grief, but even in her saddest moments did she not look any older than thirty. She could have said she had returned from an eternity dancing at a faery ring and rightly I would have believed her.

I drew my little knife that I wore on my belt. It was dull from daily use, cutting meat at table or other household tasks, and did not look very threatening.

"Back, sister, or I will use this!" I called, anger giving life to my voice which had been little used in the past days.

She raised her hand, as if to spell the knife from my grasp, but aborted her movements, shaking her head.

"Morgause would not want us to fight," she said, her voice flat and dull.

"What would you know of Morgause's wishes? You never cared for them before," I retorted.

"Can there not be peace between us, at least this one night?"

"There can never be peace between us," I spat. "Are you happy Morgan? Have enough died for you?"

"I did not strike off her head!"

"You might as well have! It was you who made her a widow!"

372

"Lot did as he pleased. I had only ideas for him, he acted upon them. And she would have hopped onto Lamorak's thighs regardless, husband or no."

"Morgan! You should not speak of her so."

"Why? She cares not where she is."

I looked at the grave, the stones piled on top of the fresh turned earth. "She is with our mother now, and our grandmother, wherever that may be."

"That is the best place for her now," said Morgan. "She and Igraine were so alike. She was always her favourite. I was too smart for her to love, and you were too plain."

"This is not about our mother," I replied.

"Everything is about our mother," she responded. "All of us live out her legacy."

"If she had loved you, Morgan, would that have made a difference?"

She shook her head. "If she had loved our father, perhaps. If she was content with her duchess' coronet, and did not seek the crown."

I rounded on her. "You match our mother for ambition. You would happily take Arthur's crown!"

"I only ever wanted Cornwall!" she screamed. "That is all I ever wanted!"

"You were never going to get Cornwall! Never! Britain is not for women to rule, not in their own right."

"It was once, and will be again. For my actions? Blame Uther Pendragon, who murdered my father and stole my rightful inheritance. Blame Merlin, who conspired against me and sent me to live as an old man's plaything. Blame Arthur, who could not free himself of either's influence or do what was right. But, mark me, sister, do not blame me. If a man had done what I did, if a man had set out to avenge his father and reclaim his ancestral lands, they would be singing songs for him up and down the length of Britain."

I was stunned into silence and could think of no response. Morgan slumped her shoulders beneath her robes. She appeared only a fraction of her height.

"I am tired," she said, almost inaudible. "Tired of killing and lying and scheming. For what? A castle at the ends of the earth? No more."

She turned her back on the grave and on me, her shoulders slumped. Morgan pulled up her hood and strode off into the night. "I am done," she called over her shoulder. "Arthur has won. Let him have Tintagel and may he be happier for it."

I let her go. Truly she was beaten and I did not feel any joy from it. I was relieved that I would not have to kill my sister, as I vowed that day by the hawthorn tree, but it hurt me, to see her so broken. All she had was her revenge. What was she to become without her quest to avenge our father?

I walked in hush back to Camelot and sought out comfort in Nentres' arms.

"I saw Morgan, at the grave," I told him.

He asked what had passed between us, and I recounted our conversation.

"Where will she go?" he asked.

"Back to Avalon, perhaps?" I suggested. "Or further north, to the wild parts of the country, where her magics can scare the simple people into making her their queen."

"Will she come against us once more?"

I shook my head. "I do not think so. She told me she was done with all her plans, and for some unknown reason, I believe her."

"Then put her from your mind, Elaine. Think of her no more."

374

"We will meet again," I replied. "I can see it there, in the fire." I gestured towards the hearth. "I see myself, asking something of her."

"Let us hope that day will never come."

"Yes, let us," I said, resting my head against his shoulder.

Arthur called me to the presence-chamber. Still we grieved for the loss of Morgause, but a kingdom could not be ruled in grief. I knew he wanted to discuss the sons of Lot, who had been languishing in the dungeons since that night. I hoped he would put at least Gaheris to a swift death, and we could begin to heal.

"When do you execute him?" I asked him.

He looked away. "I cannot," he replied.

My anger flared. "He cut off Morgause's head!"

"By the laws of Britain, he did no wrong."

"She was Queen of Lothian and the Orkneys. It is treason to kill a queen."

Arthur drew a sharp, haggard breath. "I have consulted the men of law. The law of family is greater than the law of regency, according to them. She had not remarried, and thus had committed adultery, with the son of her husband's killer no less. Beheading was a swifter death than they would have pronounced upon her."

"Those men are wrong," I responded. "Those men have always been wrong, putting women at fault for everything."

"Do you not think I would do something if I could?" he asked. "I am the King, and it is my duty to uphold the law, change it only if it is necessary."

"It is necessary! You loved her, Arthur. You loved her more than any of us. It was a different kind of love, but it was the strongest."

"And do you not think I want to punish him? Do you not think I want to tear him limb from limb..."

With that, he burst into great, heaving tears. I pulled him to me and held him as he sobbed, like he was a young Hoel in a tantrum. Tears pricked at my eyes too, and I closed my eyes, imagining that there was a place somewhere where all of us lived together in peace, free from the concerns of kingship. A happy world in which we had all just been the children of a sheep farmers a steading somewhere.

We were forced to let Gaheris go free, but he was banished from court, sent to do the knightly duties that in truth should have been beneath him as the future ruler of Lothian, patrolling contentious lands, dealing with poachers. Mordred and Gareth faced no punishment, and Mordred, once he had recovered, was insufferable as ever. For no one could say anything to him, now that he had lost his mother.

Then word came that Gaheris had found Lamorak upon the road, staying at a hostelry, and slew him unarmed, completing his revenge. But the killing of an unarmed knight was a crime in Arthur's Britain, no matter what wrong you felt he had done, and Arthur stripped him of his rank, sending him to wander the roads. I was certain Mordred had been there too. Even Arthur could see the grey dust of the road on Mordred's cloak, when he said that he had been riding out in the grass fields. But Arthur could never bring himself to punish his beloved Mordred.

That year was a difficult one for me, grieving for Morgause and worrying about Mordred who now had no impediments to the thrones of Lothian and Orkney. But the worst was yet to come.

Chapter Eighteen

The following year, I turned forty and felt older than I should have. Hoel was nearing twenty, and those happy times in which I had birthed him seemed so long ago. Camelot was much changed from the days of Uther Pendragon, and the early days of Arthur's reign seemed so long ago, like a memory of a dream.

Mordred was now Chancellor, Lord of Coin, Lord of Justice, and many other titles that had never existed in the history of Britain. Many of our knights were released from the Round Table, except for loyal Sir Bedevere and Sir Kay. The rest all went back to their lands because they could not take orders from Mordred, and the chamber in which the Round Table sat became dusty and unused.

Nimueh went from court, married to Sir Pelleas. Though I was shocked to say it, I was sad to see her go. She no longer idolised Morgan, and could be trusted entirely. She was one of the few dissenting voices against Mordred, but we could not keep her from her happiness, and she and Pelleas were truly in love.

I was forced to make permanent residence in Camelot, and Garlot did not see me for near a year. I saw Nentres perhaps twice that year. But Arthur had none other to speak against Mordred's aggressive stance on all from farming to the safety of our people. War was his solution to all problems while Arthur's answers grew more hare-brained.

He became obsessed with something he called the Thirteen Treasures of Britain, ordinary objects that supposedly possessed great magical powers. He withdrew into Merlin's tower to study the old enchanter's books and parted with a great deal of gold for more information about their whereabouts. They would help him restore order, he said, in the face of growing dissension. A cloak of invisibility or a plate that could make food, I could understand, but a chess board that could play itself? What good that do? And why could he not understand it was Mordred that caused so many to leave his court, disagree with his rulings?

In the middle of this fit of madness, he called Mordred and me to the presence-chamber. Upon the table was a large piece of parchment with a map of Britain drawn upon it. There were also several points marked with a cross.

"Forget the Thirteen Treasures," said Arthur. "I have found something worth pursuing. The Holy Grail, the cup from which the Christ drank at the Last Supper and later caught his blood at the Crucifixion. The monks tell me it was once at Glastonbury, but was lost. But I have studied the books, and it may be nearby, perhaps in the kingdom of Pellam."

"Powerful indeed, Sire," said Mordred with his perpetual smirk.

"If I had that, none would argue with me, is that not correct, Mordred? Call all the Knights of the Round Table to me, they must begin a quest at once."

"The Grail is a myth," I said, exasperation creeping into my voice. "The Christ never visited Britain, nor did Joseph of Arimathea. They brought no magical cup here! It is something the monks have made up to bring pilgrims to their abbey."

"My aunt lies," said Mordred. "Like all the Wise, they want all the power for themselves."

"You snide little bastard," I said. "You are lucky your mother did not live to see this. I have held my tongue for too long. You want this quest to go ahead, so you can send all those knights scurrying at your bidding, and leave Britain in your control. Arthur, your victory at the battle of Badon Hill will not keep the Saxons from our door forever."

"You are too unfair to Lord Mordred," said Arthur.

"Lord Mordred?" I scoffed. "He has no right to such a title."

"He has every right. He has been a dear friend to me these past years, and he supports me where others do not. Unlike my own sister, who dissents here in the very heart of Camelot? Mordred, call for the knights."

"I forbid it!" I cried. "I forbid you from ordering these men into foolishness when they are needed in their lands."

"Know your place, sister!" cried Arthur in return.

"Am I not your devoted counsellor?" I asked. "Have I not stood by your side for over twenty years?"

"Too long if you ask me!" he replied.

I drew back, stung. I stormed from the room, ignoring Arthur's cries to return to the presence-chamber and ask his leave. I returned to my own rooms, where the visiting Nentres was playing a game of chess against himself.

"I am done," I said, with an air of finality that astonished me.

Nentres looked up at me in surprise, at once the bewildered young man who approached me in the kitchen courtyard of Camelot.

"You are done?" he asked. "With what?"

"With Camelot. With the affairs of Britain. With Arthur."

"You do not mean that, Elaine."

He got up to take me in his arms and asked after what had happened in the presence-chamber.

"You are tired and angry," he continued. "Things will seem better in the morning."

"No. I promised Uther and my mother that I would support his ascension to the throne, help in his early days. Those days are long past, and he cares now only for the counsel of his ill-begotten son."

He stroked my arm soothingly. "You are sure? You know that I will go wherever you go. And it has been many years since you and I were both in Garlot at the same time."

I nodded. "We will leave in the morning whether the King permits it or naught."

"Remember the last time a great lord left court without the King's permission?" he chided.

"The King cannot declare his two most ardent supporters enemies of Britain. The vassals will seize upon his disloyalty as an excuse to rise up. Let him risk another rebellion if he chooses, it will not matter to us in Garlot."

He kissed the top of my head. "As always, you will get your way. I will tell the servants to prepare for our departure. Hoel will want to stay, of course."

"Hoel is almost twenty. If he wants to stay, he can. I cannot conduct his affairs for him his entire life."

Arthur sulked the next morning like he was sixteen again and hurt by every perceived slight. He did not come out to say goodbye. Mordred bowed low to my husband and me, smirking the entire time. In the end, Hoel did stay, shaking his father's hand and kissing me lightly on the cheek, with a flimsy promise to write often. I warned him to be

382

wary of Mordred, and reminded him that Garlot would be his kingdom to rule someday, so he should not be a stranger to it.

We departed that castle, the place that was our second home, in a carriage fitted with plush furs, our old bones too weary to ride. I would never set foot in Camelot again, I could see it in the clouds, but I thought no ill of that. Arthur was my brother, and still I loved him dearly, but no more was I to be a voice in his ear. I must look to my own kingdom, and pray that Britain could tend to herself.

I folded myself back into the quiet life at Caer Mor. With Mila gone, I saw to more of the household duties that I ever had cause to. There were lands to patrol, villagers to feed and I thought I might bring life to my old plans and send for the daughters of the local steadings to educated by me and find good marriages.

Tales of Mordred's barbarism reached our ears many times, of women burned for immodest dress and men flayed for stealing a loaf of bread. Each time, we would rise to our feet, call for horses and supplies, we were for Camelot at once, to show the High King the error of his ways and expose his wretched protégé. And then, we would feel our bones creak, and our spirits grow heavy with thoughts of another battle. We would sit back down and carry on regardless.

I blamed myself that Mordred could wreak himself on Britain; that I could not stay Morgan's hand or dissuade Morgause from carrying the pregnancy to term. Was it his parentage that led to his cruelty, some defect of birth? Or was it how he was brought up, the cuckoo in Lot's nest? Or are some men simply evil, without cause or reason, and it our great misfortune that he be born the son of the High King? But my guilt was not so strong to overcome my comfortable life in Garlot, and three years we stayed at home, ignoring every invitation to come to court until eventually they stopped, and we were forgotten.

Until we were remembered again. A messenger came riding into the courtyard, bearing the seal of Mordred. A despatch, I thought, or orders for gold or men. We would do what we could, and disobey where we could, like in all the times before. But when Nentres came up the stairs to me chamber, his face white and hands trembling, I knew it was more than Mordred's demands.

"What is it?" I asked.

"A letter from Mordred. Arthur is dead, and he is demanding we come to Camelot to swear loyalty to him as King."

I was speechless. The room was closing in on me.

"It is not true," I said. "It cannot be."

"You think Mordred lies?" he asked.

"No!" I spat. "He may well tell the truth, but Arthur was a healthy man. He would not even be forty yet. If he is dead, Mordred must have murdered him."

I was panting with anger and grief. My chest was tight like it had been struck. I wanted to scream and cry. I wanted the power to fly to Camelot and tear Mordred limb from limb.

"This cannot stand," I said. "I will never swear loyalty to Mordred."

"It is not unlikely that Arthur made him his heir," replied Nentres.

"I do not care," I said.

"What do you propose we do, Elaine? We are two old warriors."

"As long there is breath in my body, I will fight this."

384

"As well you say that, any action may very well cost you your life."

"So be it," I said.

He drew in a breath and then smiled at me.

"I cannot let you do this alone. Garlot will stand behind its queen, as it has these past twenty years."

In my head I was already weighing up possibilities, thinking of strategic positions, the cost of feeding and arming a host of men, who I might turn to for aid. Better that, than accept Arthur was dead and weep myself into bed.

"You must muster as many men as Garlot can field," I said.

"We will not have enough, not unless I ask Meron," he said.

"Ask him then," I replied. "If he refuses, strip him of his steading and bequeath it to Forwin. I will not pander to that man any longer."

I went to the foot of the bed, at the chest that had once held my wedding items. Now it held my armour. I opened it and hefted out my leathers, my breastplate and bracers, and my short sword.

Nentres looked at my armour. "Promise me you will not take to the field, not under any circumstance."

"Why ever not? I am your warrior queen."

He smiled fondly but was once again serious. "Hoel cannot lose both his parents. Not when the kingdom lies in ruins and our future is so uncertain."

"I want Hoel to see that there is a time when you must fight for what you believe in. Speaking of which, do you think you can get to him?"

"I will try with all my might. But if he is truly our son, he will have fled Camelot at the first mention of this. I will ride out to look for him. But you do not want to come?"

"I have other business elsewhere," I said.

"Where are you for?"

"For Glastonbury. We need old allies."

Chapter Nineteen

It was a hard ride to Glastonbury, with only Anwyl keeping pace behind me. We rode through the night, which is never safe, even in Arthur's Britain. But let the bandits come, I thought. It would give my sword some practice before I turned it on Mordred.

I reached the gate and swung down from my horse, tossing the reins to Anwyl. Hammering on the gate, a little panel slid away to reveal the porter.

"Open this door," I demanded. "I am the Queen of Garlot."

He stared blankly at me and went to slide the panel closed. I reached down to draw my sword and, before he could shut the panel, I had it through the gap and against his throat. He gulped, and swung back the door. I withdrew my sword, scabbarded it and passed through.

"Where will I find Sir Lancelot?" I asked.

He pointed towards the brother's house. I took off in a sprint and stopped the first monk I could find within, demanding he found Lancelot and woke him. He showed me to an unused cell and bid me wait as he did as I asked. Within moments, Lancelot was standing at the door.

His hair was grey and cut short to the scalp, including the bare tonsure at the back of his head. He wore a brown robe of rough fabric and was much thinner than I had ever known him to be. I knew he had taken the robes of a lay brother in exchange for his sanctuary, but I did not know he would embrace the lifestyle so wholeheartedly.

"No," he began. "I had the same thought as soon as the Abbot read the letter at dinner, and I have resigned myself to it. He is dead, and there is nothing we can do about that."

"Mordred as our new King?" I replied. "Not while I live and breathe. But I cannot do it alone. Be the hero Britain needs, Lancelot."

Lancelot looked incredulously at me. "Why do you fight so hard in Arthur's name?"

"Why should we not?" I responded. "After all, he has done? People do not starve anymore, not in Arthur's Britain. Apart from Lot's rebellion, we have not had a single quarrel among the vassal kings. We have freed the people of Gaul from the tyranny of Frollo and put paid to Lucius. Were it not for Morgan, he could have done so much more."

"And that is where you are to blame," he said. "None of us had the power to stop her save you, and yet you shied away. And you have the gall to preach about duty to me. "

"And that is the burden I will bear to the end of my days, Lancelot. When my end is upon me, I will see her face and hope that we will be reunited in the Otherworld so that I might put paid to her once and for all."

Lancelot's response died in his throat, and I followed his eyes. Guinevere stood in the door. She wore a plain grey robe, a nun but not quite. Her hair was not braided, nor styled, nor did it bear any of her fine accoutrements I was used to seeing. It was tied back with a length of spare linen.

"I heard you were here, Elaine," she began. "Have you come about Arthur?"

"I have," I replied. "But not as you think. I mean to rise against Mordred. Surely you agree that he has murdered Arthur and seized the throne."

"Undoubtedly," responded Guinevere. Her face was tear-stained. "We cannot let this continue. I do not do this for Anna, I do not care who comes after Arthur, but it cannot be Mordred. I will write to my cousin Guiomar, who is steward in my lands, and tell him to muster all the men of Cameliard."

"You must do the same," she said, addressing Lancelot. "Go at once to Joyous Gard, and round up your men. Now Arthur is dead, the sanctuary does not matter anyway. Rebellion is a greater crime."

I wondered how often they had the chance to see each other in Glastonbury, as two lay members of the order, and felt sorry for them that this was how they may have been reunited. He looked at her, and I could still see the same love and anguish that he had looked at her with all those years in Camelot. And I could still see the power she had over him.

"I will do it," he said. "For the love of Arthur and for you, not for Britain. I will go as soon as I can. If can muster them, where are we for?"

"We will make our stand at the hill fort of Camlann," I replied. I had decided it would be so on the road. "If its keepers are with us, we have a good strategic place to hold. If not, the hill itself will still give us a good advantage. But we cannot do this alone, not even with Garlot, Joyous Gard, and Cameliard all together. We need the Round Table."

"I will write to them, and you two can sign the letters also," said Lancelot. I could see the old fire return to him, and he was already more lively. "Our three names. That will surely bring out everyone from the old days."

"We do not have time for you to deliver them," I argued. "You need to go to Joyous Gard at once."

"You are right," he agreed. "I will get my brother monks to deliver them. They can travel unnoticed."

He looked briefly to Guinevere and then held out his hand for me to clasp as if we were not a former lord and lady, but two warriors after a tourney. He went from the room, leaving Guinevere to stare after him.

"I have something to ask of you, sister Elaine," she said.

"Anything. Anything I can do for you, I will."

"Please, bring her to me," she begged. "Anna was still at court. God knows what designs Mordred has on my daughter. She has a good claim to the throne in her own right."

"I will, Guinevere. The very second Mordred is defeated, I will march on Camelot. My own son may be there too."

She reached out and hugged me, and I could feel the trembling frame beneath my arms. She drew back.

"Had I a sword Elaine," she said. "I would ride out with you."

"I can get you one easily enough," I said, laughing.

She smiled at me, but I could see the determination in her eyes. What a queen Guinevere could have been, if she had been allowed to rule, not simply adorn Arthur's hall and fill his treasury.

"I have no place on a battlefield," she said. "I will stay here, and call in what little loyalty is owed to me. There must be some of my father's gold left. If there is, I will buy men where none will come."

I bowed my head and took my leave. It was not a time for words, but action.

390

I rode back to Garlot, nearly tiring my horse, but I would have run the whole way, such was my determination to see this through. Once back, I oversaw the rest of the muster. Nentres returned with Hoel in tow, my clever son having fled Camelot at the first sign of trouble. As we prepared to move to Camlann, more and more letters of support flew in from across Britain. Gore, Cornwall, Rheged, Northgales and much more were all with us. But reports told us Mordred too had a vast army. It was not made of up any one nation. From all over Britain, men who wanted to betray their lords for the promise of power and gold in Mordred's new kingdom flocked to his banner.

By the end of the sennight, we were in the hill-fort at Camlann. I did not know which way the keepers of Camlann would turn and breathed a sigh of relief when they threw open their gates and declared themselves for Arthur. More and more familiar faces arrived – Yvain, Bedevere, Kay – all of them came, and brought men. Guiomar came, and finally Lancelot. We had near fifty thousand men now, and if we could keep them fed and armed until Mordred came, we would surely be victorious.

"Old friends. You are most welcome," I said, as all of us gathered in the hall of Camlann.

"There is no place we would rather be," said Bedevere. His moustached face was creased and red. He, like all of us, had been crying. He was always one of Arthur's most loyal knights.

"For Arthur!" I cried, and it echoed around the room.

We sat at Camlann and plotted. On maps we marked out the routes Mordred would take, places we could ambush him, or lay a reserve force. Our supply lines too were marked, for we knew we must protect them. On the fourth day, there was a rumbling of men on horseback, and we knew that our sojourn at Camlann would not have gone unanswered.

"My Lords!" said the man-at-arms, entering the council chamber. "And my Lady, forgive me. But there is a host approaching."

I looked at Lancelot. "We must take arms."

"No, my Lady," the man interrupted. "The host, it bears the banner of the Pendragon."

"It could be a trick," said Yvain.

"Or Mordred," said Lancelot. "He probably thinks himself worthy of the Pendragon banner."

"Go," I bid Sir Bedevere. "Take post at the gate. You will surely recognise anyone leading such a host. Determine if they are friend or foe."

He returned some time later, and I heard the gates opening. I hoped that he had not been fooled by a false friend. My hand lingered on the hilt of the knife in my boot. I would not let our mission fail, even if I had to fight tooth and nail for it.

"Who comes?" I asked Bedevere, as he entered. He was smiling from ear to ear. A friend then, or so it appeared. He shook his head, declining to answer.

"Who else, but I?" said a man's voice, more than a little familiar.

There, in the doorway was a face I knew well, but one I was not sure I would ever see again. His blonde hair had gone to grey, but he was still broad and well-muscled. Those green eyes shone brighter than ever before. The room erupted into a cheer. Arthur Pendragon was not dead.

I ran and clasped him to me. "I knew you could not be dead."

"Oh, my dear sister," he said. "I have been cruel to you."

"Shh," I whispered. "Now is not the time. We will have many years for apologies. We must deal with our present troubles."

"He tricked me, Elaine. He said the Grail could be found in the Frankish kingdom. I went forth, with trusted men. They tried to slay me, Elaine, while I was sleeping. I kept the last the one alive, and he told me Mordred had paid them to assassinate me."

Tears swam across his eyes. "I loved him. He was my son. My son with Morgause."

"I know," I whispered. "I know."

"This is my sin," he said. "My sin for laying with my sister. I have offended the Gods, the old and the new, and this is their punishment."

"Do not blame yourself," I said. "There were forces plotting against you since before you were born."

He shook his head, blinking away the tears. "I will not let them win. I bring what loyal troops remained in the Frankish kingdom and Gaul."

"He will not win," I vowed. "He will not destroy what you have built."

"What we have built," he replied. "He will not destroy what we have built."

He gestured to the knights assembled around us. "What we all have built."

They cheered again, and swarmed towards us, enveloping our High King.

Mordred's forces were spotted beyond the ridge within a day of Arthur's return. The scout said that he must have had forces to rival our own. Arthur was not prepared for a siege. He would ride out and fight him, and we agreed that was the best plan of action.

"I will be in the second charge," he said, laying out his plan. "Lancelot, you will lead the mounted cavalry in the first charge. Nentres, you will direct the archers, and then take them on foot to join the third wave."

"And what of I?" I asked Arthur. "This is no time for chivalry. You need everyone to fight."

"I have agreed on this with Nentres," he replied, and I rolled my eyes. "You will lead one of the reserve forces."

I said nothing. It was better than being locked in the grain store for the duration of the battle.

"For Britain!" he cried.

"For Britain!" I cried along with the others, banging our fists on the table.

"I love you," I said to Nentres, as he tightened the last strap on my breastplate.

"And I love you," he replied.

I looked him in the eyes, and saw the fear there, as well as the love. But I had nothing I could add, except the fear and love in my own eyes.

"What more can we say to each other?"

He shook his head. "There is not much more we can say, that has not already been said. That does not need to be said."

I leaned against him, and we took silent comfort in each other.

I opened my mouth, and Nentres held up a finger. "I know what you will say, but Hoel must take to the field. You cannot insist upon your going, and say that the Prince of Garlot cannot. Do not worry Elaine, I will have him with me at all times."

It was a cold day upon the battlefield, as we rode out to face Mordred's oncoming force. But our armour warmed us, and a fair few had taken to drink too beforehand. I stood upon the prow of the hill with Yvain, the men of the two reserves behind us, ready for a signal from Arthur, watching to see if the battle had turned against us.

First, the archers let fly, and I saw the arrows fly down to strike the first wave of Mordred's onslaught. From what I could see, Mordred had not led them himself. Lancelot's cavalry surged forward, meeting Mordred's in a great cloud of dust and the thunder of hoof beats. Arrows let fly again, to strike down any who breached the line, and then I saw Nentres draw his sword. The archers cast down their bows and raced to follow Arthur onto the field.

Then I spotted it. A small war-band, bearing the standard of Mordred, heraldry Arthur granted him when he had the right to none. They had broken off from where the main armies were engaged and were approaching our hill. I drew my sword.

"Knights!" I called. "With me! Mordred is here!"

Yvain appeared by my side. "Stay back, my Lady," he warned. "Mordred is formidable."

"Do not argue with me," I said. "I am a woman with a sword, and I am not giving up my chance to kill that little bastard."

"Then forward!" he cried, and the two of us ran at them, the men following behind.

At the sight of our rally, Mordred drew back behind his guard, who rushed out to meet us. Our two forces clashed in a great heave. I swung out with both shield and sword, knocking men down, and slicing at them to get to Mordred. Yvain and I were like two vicious wolves as we battled our way towards him.

Our way was blocked by a large, bearded man dressed in rough furs. A Saxon, probably procured from among the treaty-men with Mordred's gold.

"Go!" I urged Yvain. "Get to Mordred."

I barrelled straight into the Saxon with my shoulder and winded him. He tried to bring his seax knife down onto my back, but I brought up my shield to deflect his blow. With the edge of the shield, I struck his throat. As he gasped for breath, I leant in close and impaled him upon my sword.

By the time I had freed my sword from his bulk, Mordred and Yvain were locked in a duel. They carried no shield, and Mordred had removed his helm, discarded among the grass. Yvain appeared to have the upper hand, scything his sword through the air from left side to right side, giving Mordred no time to respond, save only to block what he could.

But Yvain tired, and his last few strikes were slower than they should have been. Seeing his chance, Mordred swung a heavy blow and Yvain spun away, exposing his back to Mordred. With a mighty stroke, Mordred cleaved Yvain's skull in two. The son of Uriens and the King of Gore fell down dead, blood and brain leaking from the wound at the back of his head.

"Ah!" I screamed and flew at him.

He was not prepared for my assault. Our blades met with a clang. I thought I had the advantage, carrying both shield and sword, but without a shield, Mordred was able to move faster and turned away from my blows. With his last strike, he was able to force my guard low.

He brought down the sword hard against the blade of my own, and my hand jarred, causing the sword to drop to the ground. I ducked and spun away to avoid his second swing. Loosening the leather strap of my shield, I let it fly towards him. It struck his side and he dropped to the ground.

I rushed towards him. I stomped down on his hand and heard his fingers crunch and break under my boot. He released his grip on the sword. I drew my knife from my boot, and pulling him by the hair, I held it to his throat.

"By the law of Britain," I said. "You are defeated, Sir Mordred, and I take you prisoner in the name of Camelot and King Arthur."

"You fight like a girl, aunt," he said, flinging out his elbow. It made contact with my nose, and I could feel blood drip from my nostrils. I tried to cut his throat with what little reach I had left, but he pulled the knife down and away from him, tossing me over his shoulder.

I hit the grass with a thump and felt the breath go out of me. He bashed my hand against his knee, and I was forced to let the knife fall into the grass. He bent down to pick it up. I drew in a sharp breath and tried to pull myself to my feet, but he was already approaching me.

I swung out, trying to use the weight of my bracers instead of my fist, but he batted it away, as though I were a troublesome fly. He straddled me, blocking the kick that I was preparing for him. I tried to buck him off, but the weight of his armour was too much for me.

All I could see was his horrible smile above me, and the glint of my own knife in the sun, my own knife being used against me. I threw up my wrists to push against his forearms. He drove the knife downwards, and I could feel the tip inch closer to my armour. I pushed and pushed with my wrists, but his weight was greater.

397

"Goodbye, aunt," he sneered. "I shall not miss you."

Mordred let out a great oof, and tumbled from me, rolling across the grass. I closed my eyes and turned my head in case his knife fell against me. When I opened my eyes again, he was lying in a heap and Arthur was holding out his hand to me.

"Up, sister!" he commanded, a touch of humour in his voice. "The Queen of Garlot cannot lie in the grass during the Battle of Camlann."

"I am not lying in the grass," I hissed through my teeth, and took his hand to pull myself to my feet. He helped me up and guided me to Sir Bedevere, who let me support myself against him.

Arthur turned then to face Mordred, who had pulled himself to his feet and taken up his sword once more. Arthur ran to meet him. I strode forward too, but Sir Bedevere put out his gauntleted hand to stop me.

"Forgive me, my Lady," he said. "But this is about Arthur's honour. If he must be saved by his sister, he may as well lose the battle, for he will have lost the respect of all his followers."

They took up their stances, as though they were in the practice yard and not the battlefield. They circled each other, looking for their opening, seeing who would move first. Mordred's impatience won out, and he ran at Arthur.

Arthur's great speed belied his age. He was gone from the line of Mordred's attack within a second and was behind him. Mordred turned to strike, but Arthur brought his sword down, hammering blow after blow onto Mordred's blade until it was forced too low to be of any use.

With a great flourish and twist, Arthur disarmed him and sent his sword spinning away. Mordred was exposed. Arthur sidestepped and thrust

398

out, and the sword cleanly pierced Mordred's side, up into his armpit where his armour left a gap.

"Yah!" cried Arthur, and pulled back to free Excalibur from his son's dying body. But it did not give, such the power of his strike, and Mordred gave a great twist of his body. Arthur stumbled and together they fell.

In that briefest moment, where Arthur had no grip on Excalibur and his hands were free, Mordred struck. With the last vestiges of his strength, Mordred pulled his dagger from his belt and drove it up, into the belly of the falling Arthur.

"No!" I screamed, and Bedevere let out a horrible groan, as if he too had been stabbed. I raced forward, letting propriety be damned. I crossed the small distance between us in only a few seconds, but it felt like I had been running for centuries.

Arthur had freed himself from Mordred's knife and flopped to the grass. Blood flowed freely from the wound. He was shrieking, and desperately stuffing the edges of his armour and tunic into the wound to stem the flow of blood.

"Easy, Sire, easy!" urged Bedevere, and he sunk to his knees beside the king. Tearing a strip from his surcoat hem, he began to bandage the wound.

"This will hurt, my king," he said, and with that, he pulled the linen tight around Arthur's midriff. The king gave another blood-curdling scream.

"Brother!" I cried, and dropped to my knees beside him. I tried to take his hand in my own, wiping tears from my eyes with the other. But I could not catch even one of his hands as he flailed about wildly in pain.

"Elaine," begged Bedevere. "Long have we pretended we do not know, but now is not the time for modesty! If your witchcraft can save him, do it, and let the consequences be damned."

399

"I know of no spell that can save him," I said weakly, yet still I reached out my hand and cast a charm. Arthur grew silent and was soon asleep.

"To give him some respite from the pain," I added to the mystified Bedevere.

"What about...?" he asked, pointing at Mordred's corpse. Indeed, a corpse he was. He lay on his side, at a most unnatural angle, and Excalibur protruded from beneath his arm, jutting proudly as though it had been the one to kill Mordred unwielded.

"Let the crows feast on the traitor," I said and stepped over to him. Planting my foot on his shoulder, I tugged with all my might and Excalibur came free. I let the blood run down the fuller onto the ground, before wiping it on his leggings. I held it out to Bedevere.

"Take this, Bedevere, and dispose of it. Let no man here forth have its power, for no man was as deserving of it as Arthur."

I felt sick to my stomach, acting as though Arthur was already dead, but too much danger came from having such a thing as Excalibur in the world, and should Arthur live to once more hold the sword, it would forever be tainted with the blood of his son.

"We should return it to the Lady of the Lake, that was Arthur's command should anything happen to him," said Bedevere.

"The Lady of the Lake is long dead. She cares not for swords where she is."

Bedevere looked unsure. "Still, I will find a body of water in which to return it. Meaning no offense, but she was a Druidess, and I fear a curse could be placed upon it."

I shrugged. "Do what you must. What of the King?"

"I will summon some stout men to carry him. The abbey of Glastonbury is not far in haste, and one of the monks there is well travelled, with much knowledge of medicine. He has helped the king before, and perhaps can do so again."

Hope kindled in my chest, but I did not let it overwhelm me. I could not hope. It was a belly wound and I had felled men with a lesser cut than that inflicted on Arthur. I struggled to hold back the tears, as the men came to lift Arthur.

Chapter Twenty

The battle raged on under Bedevere's command, but I cared not for news from the field. Mordred was dead, and those who supported him would soon vanish like wraiths, leaving only the fools to fall upon their own swords. We loaded Arthur into the back of a cart bought from a nearby farmer with an extortionate amount of gold and trundled towards Glastonbury. Kneeling beside him, his fingers interlocked with mine, I did not know whether I was casting a spell or praying, such were my racing thoughts and desperate hopes.

We arrived at Glastonbury, and I remembered that, apart from my call-to-arms for Lancelot, I had only visited this place once before, when my mother had been on her deathbed. I hoped that I would not have to lay my brother to rest beside her. Guinevere ran out to meet us, her face puffy and red. Word travelled fast despite it being a nunnery.

Arthur was taken from the cart, not gently enough for my liking, and delivered into the care of an elderly monk, the abbey's infirmarian, and his apprentices. His age concerned me. Even at my own age I was prone to forgetfulness, confusion and to be slow of hand, but this man looked as though he remembered the days of Vortigern. He could as easily kill Arthur as save him.

They carried the High King into a cellar used for such purposes. I moved to follow, but the infirmarian barred my way.

"This is no place for a woman."

Had I not been relying upon him for Arthur's survival, I would have struck him hard, fuelled by my anger and unspent aggression. Instead, I sat with Guinevere, and we held each other as though we had been dear friends our whole lives, taking turns to comfort one another through the sobbing. Lancelot had come thundering into Glastonbury upon hearing the news and joined us in our vigil. He cared not for the talk of others, and merely sat beside Guinevere, holding her hand tightly.

Many hours had passed, and I went in search of some food for us, and perhaps a change of clothes, my leathers causing me to sweat deeply despite the chill of the old abbey. When I returned, Guinevere and Lancelot were gone. I stopped a novice, and he told me that they had gone inside to see Arthur. I bid him fetch his master. The aged monk emerged from the chamber.

"What news?" I asked.

"We cannot save him, my Lady," said the infirmarian, his voice measured and practiced in such things. "He has time yet, but he will die within the week."

"You can do nothing for him?"

"It is a belly wound, and the blade touched much of his insides..."

I held up a hand to silence him, my knees quivering at the thought of such a horrific injury. I imagined Nentres and Hoel, lying in these vaulted places of death, cold and trembling from the pain.

"I did not come just for your medicine. The Christ, he can do nothing for one that laboured so long in his name?"

"God has a plan for all of us..."

"Blast his plan!" I exclaimed.

The monk crossed himself.

"My Lady, you should not blaspheme so!"

I clenched my fists. Arthur could not be allowed to die, not when the kingdom needed him most. The once and future king could not meet his end here.

404

"If you cannot help me, I must seek other counsel."

"Perhaps you might change..."

He looked down at the leather plating, the breeches and the sword in its scabbard.

I smiled involuntarily. "I will need armour where I am going."

The borrowed barge sailed quickly to my destination. I did not truly know where I was heading, but I let fate guide me. I rowed myself, but the current moved with me. She was already standing on the beach, awaiting me.

"Do not step upon the shore sister, do not tarry," said Morgan, her hair as dark as the day I last saw her, though mine had greyed in places. "Time works differently here, and I sense that you do not wish to be delayed."

I rowed as close as I could without running the boat aground. It was as it had been described. An island in the Summer Country, almost totally surrounded by trees, apart from one little beach, and appearing so tiny, it could almost have been a boulder in the lake.

"You know why I have come?" I asked her.

"I cannot save him," she replied.

I felt my knees give away underneath me and I sunk to the floor of the barge in an ungainly heap. "But the land is tied to its king. Without him, without a true heir, Britain will die."

"He had a son and a daughter. Both could have been true heir."

"One born of incest, and the other no doubt cursed like her mother? You have scarred them both Morgan. Neither is fit for such purposes. Besides, Mordred died last night upon the field."

Morgan's face saddened.

405

"You care so deeply for our nephew?" I asked. "I confess, I could not love him, not after all he has done these past years."

"I...I came to think of him as my own son, for it was my plots and spells that begot him."

She looked away, blinking cold tears from her eyes. "What do you ask from me?"

"Can we do the binding? Move the kingship to another?"

Morgan shook her head. "Do you have a suitable heir?"

"I would not wish that upon any man. But yet no one comes to mind. Regardless, who am I to crown a king? You are certain you cannot save Arthur's life?"

"Through dark and twisted means, as you would say. Yes, if you permitted me to do my very worst, then yes I could. But he would scorn you for it. He would hate what he would become, and you would hate yourself for what you had done to make him that way."

I shook my head in despair. "Then Arthur will die this evening."

I brushed my hand along the smooth wood of the barge. Silence had settled across the mouth of Avalon. No night animals made their sounds, the water did not ripple around me. Already the land was mourning for its King. Then I stood, my mind alert with ideas.

"You owe Arthur a debt, Morgan," I said. "Unless you wish to pay it in the next life?"

She shook her head. "I will not tip the scales against me more. I sense I will have much to repent in my next existence. Whatever help I can give, I will give it freely."

"Can you keep him alive, until I can bring him here and the plan is done? The journey will not kill him?"

She nodded. "Blood magic, I think. Though something will have to die in his place. A rabbit perhaps."

"Spare me the details."

"But that is not all you ask of me?"

"No sister, it is not," I said.

I told her my plan, in the cold moonlight. She gasped and refused, but then her mind began to trundle with possibilities and she agreed. Morgan could never resist a challenge, nor an opportunity to show how skilled she was with magic. After making the necessary preparations, she stepped aboard my barge and we returned to Glastonbury.

We were an impressive sight that day, the two sister queens united as one at the head of the barge, cleaving through the mists. The monks crossed themselves and threw themselves to the ground begging for God's grace to save them from the devils. In later years, the tale became much conflated, about how three faery queens came from Avalon to carry Arthur away. Perhaps they could see what we felt. We were the only two in the barge, but behind us, we could feel the spirit of Morgause standing behind us.

Arthur was awake when we arrived. He was shirtless, a great bandage wound around his stomach. Despite the insipid chill of the room, he was sweating profusely. He rocked from side to side, groaning ever so slightly. Guinevere sat on one side and Lancelot the other, each of Arthur's hands in theirs.

They caught sight of Morgan and leapt to their feet at once. Lancelot reached for a sword he was not wearing, and Guinevere surprised me with her ferocity. I thought she would surely fly at Morgan.

"Peace," I said, holding up my hands. "She has come to help."

"We want none of her witchcraft!" cried Guinevere. "Let my husband die in peace."

Morgan snorted. "My husband, is it? And you do not want my help? Keen for him to pass on so you can marry Lancelot without shame?"

"How dare you!"

"Enough!" I commanded. "Time moves fast, and we have naught to lose to petty words!"

Guinevere opened her mouth to speak, and then closed it as a weak voice fought its way to our ears.

"Who is there?" called Arthur, his speech a struggle. "Who has come?"

"I have returned, Arthur," I called. "And I have brought Morgan."

At that, he struggled to sit up. It failed him, so he beckoned with his hand. We approached the bed, my hand on Morgan's back to keep her true.

"I thought you dead, sister," he said, his voice a mere rasp. "When you had been so quiet, I thought you had died in Avalon."

"I am sorry, Arthur," she replied, surprising us all. "For the things I did. For blaming you for Uther's mistakes."

"I am sorry too, Morgan. I am sorry I did not divorce you from Uriens. I am sorry I did not even give you the castle of Tintagel."

"None of that matters now. We must save you."

"If I thought you could, Morgan, I would bid you do so. But I know that you cannot. I may not be one of the Wise, but I can foresee my own death. Call for a priest, let all my sins towards you be shriven and let me die in peace. I know not what

408

God I will meet in the next world, but it is best I go free of my earthly burdens."

Her voice was so tender. It reminded me of rare moments in Tintagel, in Camelot, when she was done rebelling, and would stroke my hair and tell me stories.

"You know the story of the Fisher King?" she asked Arthur.

"Yes, Merlin told it to me, in my lessons in kingship."

"And you know that if the true king dies, Britain dies too? That is how we fell to the Romans, we did not have a true king. The once and future king you might say."

"Merlin kept much from me, but I know the significance of my crowning. You fear the same will be true?"

"If you die, Britain will go hungry, our rivers will run dry and Saxons will overrun us."

"So what must we do? My stomach worsens. The pain, Morgan, do something for the pain."

She beckoned to the lurking novice and made a list of herbs he could fetch her, along with a pewter goblet. He was to make no protests about the use of such tableware, it was the High King's orders, she warned. When he had brought what she requested, she mashed them in the goblet and lifted it high like the chalice at the Christian mass, speaking in a language unknown even to me. The contents smoked like a little fire had been set and Guinevere crossed herself, but she did not intervene as Morgan poured it down Arthur's unresisting throat.

"I feel much better Morgan," he said, his words slurring together.

"You will soon fall asleep Arthur, but first, you must give me your consent. Elaine has a plan to save you. I am sure it will work, but I will not do it without your consent."

"I consent, sister," he said and fell so soundly asleep I feared he had died there and then.

"What do you propose?" asked Lancelot.

Morgan and I looked at each other, willing the other to speak first. Finally, she gave in and explained.

"I can put Arthur in an enchanted sleep."

"Like you did with Merlin?" asked Lancelot.

"Exactly so. He will not age, nor decay, nor starve. He will be exactly as he is, until such times as he will awake."

"What of his wound?"

"It will not worsen, but it will not heal either. We hope that he will awake, when Britain needs him again, and their healing arts will be great enough to save him where ours cannot."

Lancelot looked horrified. "You cannot take that risk, or subject him to such sorcery."

"He will die if we do not," I said. "We must bring him to Avalon, where he will be safe, and cast this spell."

"All men must die," was Lancelot's response.

"Few men's deaths will have such consequence as that of Arthur Pendragon's," I replied.

Lancelot looked ready to challenge me, with a sword if need be, but Guinevere spoke.

"Do it," she said. Her word was law in that moment, and Lancelot was silenced.

Together, with the aid of the fearful novice, we dressed Arthur and laid him upon a stretcher, carrying him to the shore. We placed him in the barge and draped a heavy blanket over him to keep out the chill of the dusk.

410

"Tell none what you have heard," said Morgan to the novice. "For I know you have heard much, listening at doors."

He ran from the shore as fast as his sandaled feet would carry him. I looked at Morgan for an answer.

"I was in his position once. It will be around the abbey by noon tomorrow, and across the kingdom by the end of the sennight. Let it become legend, and feed my spell."

We stepped into the barge and went to take up the oars.

"You will need help," said Lancelot. "The two of you alone cannot manage him. I will go with you."

"To the isle of Avalon?" asked Guinevere, with shock in her voice.

"I lived there as a boy, it is not so fearsome," he replied. "And what if they drop him? You must come too."

She hesitated.

"You must come now," warned Morgan. "The wards will only allow you to pass if you are with me."

Lancelot held out his hand to Guinevere and together they stepped aboard the barge. I set to rowing, hoping to make good time.

Arthur did not wake again. We laid him on an old style bed found within the stone structures of the island, accessed by an ornately carved wall hidden against a hill.

I was anxious to begin, but Morgan said that we had time yet, that all the energies must be in alignment, and that no one did good work on an empty stomach. We dined in a chamber with a great table, strangely unharmed from its long days of being unused, eating a simple meal of Morgan's foraging in the groves of holly and mistletoe.

"Where will we do it?" I asked.

"There is a chamber, deep in the bowels of Avalon, with biers upon which you can lie," she replied. "I have pondered much on its existence, it seems to serve no purpose, but it is one of the oldest structures on the island. Some long-dead mystic must have foreseen this day."

"Good, then we know our plan will succeed."

"Perhaps, but all we truly know is that we are destined to do this."

Guinevere and Lancelot excused themselves to another room. Morgan jeered after them, making lewd comments about their quest for solitude, forgetting that they had probably not been alone with one another since he rescued her from Arthur's pyre. I shushed her.

"It is time," intoned Morgan, her head cocked like a hunting dog listening for deer.

I called for Guinevere and Lancelot, and at Morgan's direction, the four of us lifted Arthur onto the stretcher again, carrying him down a sloping corridor. It was unpaved, more like a tunnel than a passageway, ending in a dark chamber, hollowed out from the island itself, but unfinished, unlike the rest of the structures.

There were four stone biers in the room, evenly spaced. They were unlike the bare room, with intricate knotwork designs carved across them, like Petronella remembered from her youth. We laid Arthur gently upon one, careful not to tear open where his wound had been sewn shut.

"Lancelot and I have been thinking," said Guinevere.

"You do not have to do this," he began. "I will…"

412

She interrupted him. "We do not know when Arthur will be awake. It could be many years into the future, when his name is forgotten and this place turned to dust. He should not be alone."

"I can sleep alongside him. You can return to Glastonbury," said Lancelot.

"No," she replied. "My daughter is grown into a beautiful woman and no longer needs her mother. The two most important people to me are in this room, and I cannot be from their side."

"Just as I cannot be from yours. Wherever you go, Guinevere, so will I."

"Can you do it?" she asked Morgan.

Morgan nodded. "It is no different than putting Arthur to sleep. When he wakes, so shall you."

Guinevere nodded and led Lancelot to the corner of the room. Morgan sneered in distaste, while I turned my back, as they had begun to embrace. When they had finished, they went readily to the biers and lay upon them. I opened my mouth to speak, but she held up a hand.

"No, Elaine, speak not, or I shall not go," she said.

She closed her eyes, and silence filled the room. Morgan looked to me.

"Take my hand sister. I will need your power for this spell."

We clasped our hands together, and the ritual began. Morgan began to sing, a high chant, again in that unknown language. I closed my eyes and focused entirely on her, opening my core and letting my power flow through her. Our hands grew hot, like a poker fresh from the fire, and a wind whipped around us, despite us being so far underground. I struggled with the sheer power of the spell. This must be how Morgan feels all the time, I thought.

"Stay strong," I heard her say, though I was certain she had not stopped singing.

I held fast, pouring in my love for Arthur, my hopes for Britain and my promises to Uther and Igraine into the ritual. The final wave of heat rolled over us, and together we said "Bind the spell, and it is done. As we will, so mote it be." We raised up our hands and made the sign to close the working.

It was done. The three slept, like people carved from stone, like the statues of saints that adorned the walls of Glastonbury. Their stomachs did not rise and fall, and no breath hissed from their noses, but I could sense they were still alive. We extinguished the torches and left them in the dark chamber.

Morgan showed me to the hut in which she lived. We both needed to rest, seeking the basic comfort of Morgan's straw bedding. It was a far cry from the grandeur of Tintagel, Camelot and the castles of Gore, with its simple furniture and circular walls of woven branches, but she swelled with pride when she told me she had built it herself.

Seeking to distract myself, I asked about her life on the island, and of the mysteries of the place she now called home. To my great surprise, she started to cry. Tears rolled down her cheeks, and I could not recall when I had last seen her cry.

"I wish Morgause was here," she said. "And Igraine. And Petronella. By the Gods, I even wish Uther Pendragon was with me on this forsaken island. I felt them in the barge, but no more. I am haunted, Elaine, by the whispers. You asked why I do not reside in the halls. Because down there, I hear them. Our ancestors, who tell me I have

414

shamed the Wise. Gorlois asks why I do not avenge
him. And all the people who have died for my revenge? Accolon and Lot battle over whose turn it
is to torment me. But the night, it is the worst."

"How so?"

"I hear her screams."

"Whose?"

"Isolde. I hear her flesh crackling and I hear
her beg Mark for his forgiveness. It curdles my
blood Elaine. You know, I have not eaten meat in
some years, for I will not light a fire to cook it. I
shiver and starve rather than be reminded of what
I have done."

"Come back with me," I offered, though I knew
my words were mere placation. "When this is done,
come back with me and live with me in Garlot."

"You know that cannot be. Many times I have
thought of asking your forgiveness, so that I might
have my sister back. But I am wanted by the sons
of Lot for my part in their father's death, and Gore
and Cornwall both cry out for my blood. Elaine, I
have committed high treason, I have conspired to
murder a king many times over. There is nowhere
in Britain that is safe for me, save the Isle of Avalon."

She was quiet for some time, her tears now dry
upon her face, and then spoke.

"I have been thinking Elaine. About the fourth
bier."

"Yes?"

"Someone else must sleep alongside Arthur.
When he rouses, he will not have long to seek help.
You must sleep alongside him, so that your magic
can preserve him until he can be healed."

"I? If he needs a healer, it must be you."

"I cannot. The spell of sleep is beyond you to
cast. I felt that earlier."

"But what will you do? You will be alone again."

"I am resolved. I will stay here, to care for you and the island, so long as I live. I will find an apprentice to take over, when my time comes. Perhaps Nimueh might come to me and take up her birthright once more."

I tried to argue, tried to find a reason that this should not happen. But I knew it when Morgan spoke. She was not my sister in that moment, nor even the great sorceress who scourged the land of Britain. She spoke with the authority of the Gods themselves in that moment.

In fact, I knew the moment I spied the fourth bier that my destiny was as fixed as that of Arthur himself. Whoever had foreseen us here on the Isle of Avalon, fighting to keep the once and future king alive, had seen me too on that stone slab. Some moments are indeed written in the stars.

Morgan fetched the oil and the herbs for me, helped me to draw the circle and anoint myself, my hands shaking too much to do so for my own self. She took a seat and I lay down to begin the dreamwalk.

I was standing at the foot of the hill, ready to ascend to the Temple. But I did not walk that path. Instead, I turned into the forest and walked. I did not know where I was going, but I followed my heart. Then I came upon a clearing.

Stood in the centre was Nentres. He was at once the man I saw a week ago and the boy I married twenty-five years ago. Time was immaterial in this place.

"This cannot be real?" asked Nentres. "Am I dreaming?"

"Yes, you are dreaming," I replied. "But why should it be any less real?"

416

He crossed the span of the clearing in a few steps and pulled me close. We kissed, then I drew back and folded my hands into his.

"First, my love, what of the kingdom?" I asked.

"Mordred's rebellion has been quashed, but the nobles are sure Arthur is dead from his wound. Hoel is to marry Anna, and they will rule together."

"Our son is to be High King?" It was not the time to share my doubts, or lament my son's fate. At least with Arthur slumbering, Hoel will not be bound to Britain's burden. "He will be a wonderful king, with his father at his side."

"I know you, Elaine," he said. "You would not bring me to this place merely to ask after our son. It has been many days since you took Arthur to Glastonbury, and I have heard all sorts of strange tales about faery queens. You will not return to me, I know it."

Tears moistened my eyes. "How did you know?"

"My heart has never hurt so much in all my life. I feel as if it has stopped beating."

He reached out and brushed away my tears with his thumb, still as gentle as when he first touched me.

"You are right, Nentres," I said. "Arthur is on the verge of death, and we cannot save him."

"Let him die then, and come back to our son. Come back to me."

"I cannot. He is the once and future king, the true king of Britain. The land will die without a true heir, Anna is not that, and neither is our son. You know that their union will not be fruitful?"

"I suspected as much. Morgan's hate would have it no other way."

"She has repented, and we have found a way to save Arthur. The sleeping curse, under which she placed Merlin. It will keep him alive until Britain needs him once more, and hopefully, their healing arts will be greater than ours."

"All magic comes at a cost. You taught me that. This magic sounds powerful. And expensive."

I nodded. "I see now its price. I too must sleep, or else Arthur would not live to be saved. To save Britain, I must give up my husband, my son, my very life as I know it."

"Please do not. I will beg if that is what you want."

I clasped his hands tightly. "You and I will be together again, Nentres. We have lived a thousand lifetimes as husband and wife and we will live a thousand more. No matter where you are or who you may be, I will find you."

I swallowed my tears and leaned into his arms, echoing his words from all those years ago. "I will always find you."

"May the Gods reward your sacrifice, Elaine of Garlot. And may they be merciful and bring us together once more."

I reached up and kissed him. There was a surge of white light and I was once more lying upon the straw in Morgan's hut. Morgan sat in a chair, beside the darkened and dusty fire-pit.

"You have said your farewells?"

"I wanted to speak to Hoel and Anna, but I think it would not be permitted."

Morgan nodded, wearing her best attempt at a comforting smile upon her face. "It is not much of a price if you are able to make your peace with it."

She poured a cup of water for me and I took it gratefully. Silence had descended upon the hut. I lay down and tried to sleep but it failed to come.

Perhaps the Gods knew if I could dream, I would surely return to my son and husband and never come back to Avalon. Morgan joined me on the straw mat and held me, like we were children again.

I sobbed into her shoulder and my whole body shook with great spasms until I could cry no more. I raged that night, like never before. I called Morgan every name I could think of, I cursed her plans for revenge. I shouted and raved, and damned Mordred's twisted birthing, Morgause's depraved desires, Uther's lust, Igraine's ambition, Gorlois' weaknesses and even poor Petronella for coming south to Cornwall and taking residence in that hut by the sea. Morgan stayed quiet and patted me gently until my tears ran dry and my mouth had no more words. Silence reigned once more in the hut.

We woke at dawn and made our way from the hut to the mouth of the rocky doorway. Descending the roughly hewn steps, we travelled down into the very heart of Avalon. Morgan carried with her a great iron torch, which she lit, my shaking hands unable to strike the flint even now. Her other hand was entwined with mine. We were not alone, though. Just as in the barge, we were accompanied by the spirits of those gone before, and it gave me as little comfort as it could.

Lancelot, Guinevere, and Arthur lay upon the biers, as still and as white as the day we bound them in slumber. Morgan released my hand and moved around the chamber, lighting the torches in their wall brackets. As I made my way past the sleepers, I patted their hands for good luck, too afraid of disturbing the spell for much else.

Morgan had lent me an old gown of Niniane's, found in her chamber when Morgan had first arrived here. It was pure silk, and must have taken

419

her some time to make. But then, what other occupation had she upon the island? My armour, leather plating, and short sword lay folded upon the end of the bier.

"In case you have need of them," said Morgan, finishing arranging them.

When the time came, Morgan had to help me onto the stone slab. She adjusted my robe so I was comfortable.

"You are like my little doll," she said, unwinding my hair from its braid and smoothing it out against the cold stone.

I could feel the chill of the bier radiate up into my back and legs. I shivered and tensed my knees, so I could not jump up and run. Lancelot and Guinevere were brave, and I must be brave too.

"What will happen?" I asked.

"I do not know truly," replied Morgan. "But you will experience most of it. Some will be a dream and others will be visions of the world around you. I would imagine, wherever you are, Arthur, Guinevere, and Lancelot will be there too. Merlin also, perhaps. You will not be alone."

My voice was low and scared, barely a whisper. "What if we do not wake?"

"The Gods will see you right. If Britain will never need Arthur again, I believe you will pass from this world, and be reunited with your husband and son in the Otherworld, or perhaps in a new life."

"I am frightened, sister. I know my duty, but I am frightened."

She smiled. "You will come to no harm. I am a great mistress of magic, remember?"

"The very greatest," I replied.

She leaned down and kissed my forehead. It was time to close my eyes. She began to sing the spell. I could feel it whip around me like a wind. I grew tired, and the world shifted behind my eyelids. My spirit soared like an eagle and I knew at once I had left my body.

I flew higher and higher, into that unknown realm. It was indescribable, like both a dream and the most real thing I had ever experienced, both lonely and never alone, both blind and all bared to my eyes. On and on I spiralled, as Britain shaped and changed above me, the very mountains rising and falling like a great breath exhaled across the land.

And so still I lie here, in the contradiction of wakeful slumber, knowing that one day, Britain will need Arthur once more, and hoping that it needs me too.

ABOUT THE AUTHOR

Kieran Higgins is a Belfast-born author. He wrote his first novel at age 5 — he also received his first rejection letter at this age. He has been writing ever since and has produced his debut novel The Forgotten Sister.

Inspired by JK Rowling, Garth Nix and Mary Stewart, Kieran writes the type of stories he wants to read — exciting tales full of compelling characters with believable motivations, captivating locations, strong females and, most importantly, magic.

Kieran is currently undertaking a PhD in environmental economics at Queen's University Belfast. He hopes to use his love of writing to help preserve the environment, and currently blogs about environmental news and eco-friendly living.

Find out more about Kieran at his website www.kieranhiggins.eu. Subscribe to his mailing list for original flash fiction delivered straight to your inbox every Friday, and follow him on Facebook, Twitter, Instagram, Pinterest, and Tumblr.

Made in the USA
San Bernardino, CA
05 April 2018